CRITICAL PRAISE FOR *THE BROTHERS' LOT*
BY KEVIN HOLOHAN

"A witty, brilliant, devastating expression of outrage . . . this novel is so
subtly imagined, so elegantly structured, written in such hilarious prose but
with such horrifying details, that what it offers is an overpowering, vision-
ary judgement on a society."   —*Times Literary Supplement*

"The mix of dire experiences that goes into the education dished out at
the Brothers of Godly Coercion School for Young Boys of Meager Means
adds up to a mordantly funny debut from Dublin native Holohan."
                                                      —*Publishers Weekly*

"Kevin Holohan takes us to a harrowing place. This vivid book aims to
break your heart while it makes you catch your breath. It is powerful and is
not afraid of the dark."
                          —Luis Alberto Urrea, author of *Good Night, Irene*

"Taking dead aim at the hypocrisy of the Catholic Church and the atmosphere of repression that allowed abuse to flourish, this first novel uses
satire to stinging effect . . . Terribly bleak and terribly funny, this skillful
debut pays tribute to the irrepressible spirit of all the rebellious young boys
who would not give in to authoritarian rule."   —*Booklist*

"[Holohan] possesses his own distinct voice. Especially useful as therapy for
recovering Catholics or to tweak apologists of the church, this impressive
debut is highly recommended."   —*Library Journal*, starred review

"Holohan's ability to write the kind of free-flowing naturalistic dialogue
that so potently conveys the anarchic spirit of schoolboy warfare . . . is
grounded by a shadow play of macabre references to horrors that ghost
around the edges of the narrative, many eerily similar to some of the more
infamous real life reports that have emerged in recent years."
                                                      —*Irish Times*

"The book is funny, fast-paced with one crisis after another, but always
pulls at the heartstrings."   —*Brooklyn Rail*

"*The Brothers' Lot* takes on serious subject matter—the grim aftermath
of World War II, the abuse of childr   at
lends comic relief to an otherwise da   st

T0285631

"Upon this ethical foundation for an entertaining tale, Holohan follows a satirical tradition which questions authority, undermines cliché, and upends the social order. Reading *The Brothers' Lot*, I thought not only of Flann O'Brien and Kafka but of another Dubliner, Jonathan Swift."

—*PopMatters*

"Kevin Holohan's strange yet disconcertingly recognizable world has echoes of Flann O'Brien's and Monty Python's, but there is rage as well as absurdist comedy. *The Brothers' Lot* is a memorable, skillfully wrought, and evocative satire of an Ireland that has collapsed under the weight of its contradictions."   —Joseph O'Connor, author of *Star of the Sea*

"Kevin Holohan's wickedly funny debut novel, set in a rundown Dublin religious school where the spirits are low but the Gaelic pride runs high, will make you laugh almost as much as it makes you weep, for beyond their almost comical incompetence and a thin veneer of piety the Brothers who run the place are sad, flawed men, whose weaknesses range from sadism to depravity. They educate by cudgel and dole out discipline with a leather strap, while protagonist Finbar Sullivan and the other long-suffering students bear it all with the kind of wise-cracking cynicism, irreverence, and pranks that one would expect at that age."

—Preston L. Allen, author of *Jesus Boy*

"*The Brothers' Lot* is a screamingly funny indictment of the culture of repression and abuse that has plagued Ireland for generations, but it is much more than that. It is a brilliantly told tale, compassionate and brutal. Most important, it celebrates the spirit of reckless bravery and rebellion, the spirit that draws back the curtain on iconic institutions to reveal the frailty of an ecclesiastical house of cards."

—Tim McLoughlin, author of *Alcohol, Tobacco, and Firearms*

So You Wanna Run a Country?

KEVIN HOLOHAN

BROOKLYN, NEW YORK

Published by Akashic Books
All rights reserved
©2024 Kevin Holohan

ISBN: 978-1-63614-160-2
Library of Congress Control Number: 2023946111
First printing

Cover art: Smartphone, Artos/Shutterstock.com; Background, Marco Bicci/Shutterstock.com; General on Horse, Roman Starkov/Dreamstime.com

Akashic Books
Instagram, X, Facebook: AkashicBooks
info@akashicbooks.com
www.akashicbooks.com

To the cherished memory of Frank Spain and Ed Kadysewski,
beloved old friends, trusted readers, listeners, and sounding boards.
Gone too soon, sorely missed.

Here is what helming is, and trust:
We rest or we take the watch, we do what we must.
—Theo Dorgan, *Watchkeeping*

MINUS ONE

ASSEMBLY

I

t was the best of times, it was the worst of times, it was the age of wisdom, it was the age of foolishness, it was the epoch of belief, it was the epoch of incredulity, it was the season of Light, it was the season of Darkness . . . Skid flicked to the last page. "Four hundred and eighty pages of that tiny print? Can't even decide what it's all about to start with? No fucking way I'm reading that!"

Skid put the dog-eared book back on the end table. He arched upward and pulled from under him the magazines he'd fallen asleep on. His mother still liked her words on paper.

The leathereen couch squeaked and farted under him. Otherwise the house was quiet. His mother was still out. That was good. They needed a break from each other. For two months now he had been staying with his ma "for a few days to get me head together," ever since his now-ex, Cloda, had kicked him out of her flat: "Get the fuck out and don't come back, you freeloading, lying bastard. Get a job!" He still had no job.

He turned on the ¡box. The sleek wall screen, which his ma had set to sleep as a giant print of the little girl with the huge tearful eyes, immediately powered up to where his mother had last been. The external audio was off, so Skid let an Xtreme Grand Prix race unfold in silence. There was something quite soothing about watching the fortified supercars speed through the almost deserted streets of this week's rundown NoGo city without all the overexcited commentary.

Skid hefted his new ¡think 9.7 in his hand. The resolution on the smaller screen was not as good as the in-head optics. It was far worse than the 9.6, probably to drive people in-head. Skid had been using in-head since the shaky 9.4 with the convulsions waiver you had to sign. It was like having two sets of eyes and he had to learn to focus his attention on the ether stream and stop seeing with his real eyes. It made him nauseous for weeks until he got used to it.

The granite casing he had chosen felt cool to the touch. It was smaller and thicker than the earlier 9s and sat in his palm like a big worry stone. He was not ready for the 10 series with the contactless implants. He had heard horror stories of people blinded and deafened and only able to experience the world indirectly through the ¡think. Some people might be ready for that, but Skid was not.

Sooner than he expected, the lead race car slowed into a sharp bend and was rammed off the road by a huge log on wheels. Locals, whose primary source of income was ransoming race drivers, swarmed and dragged their victim off into the surrounding streets. The remaining cars sped past, eager to collect their survivor premiums. Running these races through the world's most dangerous NoGo slums and putting a bounty on the drivers was a recent development and had hugely revived the slumping ¡ball capture for car races.

Skid, however, was already tired of it. He slid the thin discs from his ¡think case and placed them against his temples to jack in. He felt the comforting downward pull and surge of the ¡think in his head. He relished the reassuring shudder of full jack-in. Then the calendar kicked in. "Mag, don't forget: Wednesday, half eight, ski-jumping in Clontarf with Tracy and Marie," said the smoky hoarse voice of a young woman sounding a bit like his ma. "I must tell Clare Grogan about that bingo app. Don't forget to look for the back door key before Friday—"

This was interrupted by a bass male voice that purred at you like you had just taken his eager hand and put it down the front of your knickers: "DON'T LET CHRONIC FLATULENCE RUIN

YOUR LOVE LIFE! TAKE TWO SUAVITOL JUST BEFORE INTIMACY AND—"

What the fuck? Skid did a hard unjack from what was obviously his mother's ¡think. It was as if he had just shoved someone else's toothbrush into his brain. When the fuck had she upgraded to a 9.7? Her last one was an 8.4 that didn't even do in-head. Why did she have no security on it? Anyone could jack into it the way she had it set up. Skid tried furiously to blot out any suggestion of what "intimacy" might be saying in the context of his ma.

"I must tell Clare Grogan about that bingo app"? Wow. So that voice was how his ma thought she sounded: Inchicore's answer to Marilyn Monroe. Skid was glad she didn't have the ads in her own voice; that would have been just too creepy. He too had tried a custom ¡nnervoice but then hated the weird adenoidal Dubliner from outer space it had produced. Instead, his ¡think used the threatening mumble of Beast, the drummer with the metametal band Mörön.

Skid retrieved his own ¡think from the floor where it had fallen while he slept. He jacked in and synced the in-head audio with the optics of the end of the race. The sound was pristine and all-enveloping, so much more convincing than real-ear sound.

What a cruel and depressing show. Skid flicked away to pan pipes and bells over some cliffside meditation scene, then turned off the ¡box and abruptly unjacked from his ¡think, unsure how much of that *cruel and depressing show* thought had actually been his own. Usually he knew when he was doing his own thinking because it felt pallid and flat, but this was uncertain and unsettling.

Ten more minutes and he could head to band practice. Skid was the drummer—partly because he could borrow his cousin's van. He wasn't an awful drummer, but he was not good either. They had a gig at the Jockey's Bollocks in two days. They badly needed to practice.

Confronted with ten minutes to kill, he reflexively jacked in again. *In-pulse New Game. Vixen Jungle Warrior,* he thought to his ¡think, and flopped back into the soft embrace of the couch and the tantalizing hypersexualized jungle gamescape that flowed into his head. He would order a new ¡think shell and some socks at the first level-up.

II

"What do you mean you're not quite sure where it is?" The Utter-minster's tone was the point of a very sharp blade.

"Apparently, one of our Newer York embassy employees dis-appeared with it some years ago, when we still had an embassy, Utterminster. In the haste to abandon the premises, no one missed it until it was too late."

"*Some years?* More precision."

"Well, about five years after you sent it there for safekeeping. So, about forty-five years ago."

"NOW you tell me this?"

"I didn't think we would ever need it," replied the Archixprest.

"Well, we do now! I do not like the restlessness among the pubble."

"Couldn't we just make another one?"

"Are you that stupid? No one can cast trepanium like that anymore! A copy wouldn't work. We must find it!"

"I will have the Clarion requisition a fresh consignment of seeing herb from the Sisterhood."

"Good! Inform me as soon as it arrives and we are ready to talk to the horse."

"Very well, Utterminster. Azhuur be served!"

"Azhuur be served!"

⚭

I am General Gaspar D'Izmaïe, Utter Potentate of Inner Azhuur, Salvation of the Fatherland, Marshal of the Quartel, Commander of the Phalanx of Mög. I now subsist in the afterdark of memory, on the far edge of my own death.

Eighty years ago, I won the war against the secessionist dogs of Outer Azhuur. I remade and ruled over Inner Azhuur for thirty years with unflinching authority and unwavering devotion to the teachings of Mög. This returned our fallen, softened people to a simpler, purer way of being, gave them order and structure and strength. Of course, I made some enemies. I took precautions. I removed enemies. I did not remove enough. Some pestilential insurrectionists survived.

I remember the last day. Fifty years ago, a cadre of treasonous pubble placed crude explosives in a ditch and blew up my carriage while I was blessing their hovels. On my standing orders in the event of my untimely demise, every prole within a mile of the assassination site was marched to the Vale of Victory and drowned in the lake.

⚘

The Azhuurse embassy employee who knew the statue was solid trepanium and was on his way to sell it heard echoes of this D'Izmaïe voice in his head, just before he fell down the subway stairs to his death. This sent the statue of General D'Izmaïe on an unplanned trip to the bowels of the Megalopolitan Newer York Locomotion Authority's lost and found.

For a whole year, the three-foot-tall brassy statue of a short, tubby, self-important-looking, uniformed guy squatting like he was on a horse held its ceremonial sword aloft among the umbrellas, water bottles, dead ¡thinks, skis, backpacks, potted plants, wicker armchair, flat-earther model of the world, and the other miscellaneous detritus of careless commuters' forgetfulness. Then he was auctioned off with all the other unclaimed objects at a warehouse in Queens.

That was where Cyndi bought him for an embarrassing pittance. She thought he was marvelously kitschy. She gave him to her boyfriend Malice, who had just opened a rockabilly bar in one of the archways under the Manhattan approach to the Brooklyn Bridge.

Following five years of relative stability high up on a shelf in Malice's Rockabilly Roadhouse surrounded by 1950s paraphernalia, peculiar prints of colorful anime ponies, and curiously reworked images of Che Guevara driving old Chevrolet automobiles, it all came to an abrupt and unforeseen end. After half a decade of acrimonious break-ups and passionate reconciliations, Cyndi and Malice finally married in a small ceremony in the bar. During the wedding after-party, a hasty pinball wager between Malice and Colum, one of the regulars, resulted in General D'Izmaïe becoming Colum's.

This led to ten long years of gathering dust in a corner of Colum's filthy walk-up apartment just above the waterline on Avenue B. Colum only ever left his apartment to go to the Rockabilly Roadhouse and survived on deliveries and an inheritance that replenished his ¡ching at the beginning of every month. This sedate existence was punctuated by Colum's rare and usually disastrous romantic entanglements, the most successful being an intensely physical dalliance with Cyndi during a time when Malice was involved in an onanistic doomsday cult. When that affair ended badly, it was several months before Colum dared visit the Rockabilly Roadhouse again.

One Tuesday night, Colum came home from the Roadhouse, fell asleep on his couch, and never woke up. Three weeks later, hazmat-suited operatives broke down the apartment door. They removed what was left of the late Colum in an opaque bag and then emptied the contents of his apartment onto the street, snapping the blade off General D'Izmaïe's ceremonial sword in the process.

Meggin, the young woman who lived in the basement apartment of Colum's building, grabbed the statue from the debris of Colum's life just as the garbage truck approached. She carried the surprisingly light D'Izmaïe four blocks to Irffone's Antiques and Curios on 3rd Street, where she sold him for twenty ¡ching. Irffone placed his new acquisition just inside the door with a price tag of fifty ¡ching. If either of them had realized the statue was made of solid trepanium, these prices would have been astronomically higher.

The Slatricks came the following day, bargained Irffone down to forty-five ¡ching, and for the next five years the figure of D'Izmaïe sat on a yellow plaster giraffe on their front lawn in Perth Amboy, New Jersey, among the garden gnomes and lawn jockeys of varying size and scale that were either guardians or devotees of the derelict chiminea.

Enter the first Thoroughfarian, the one before Mooney. Umlaut experienced an irresistible attraction to the shiny statue upon first sight in the Slatricks's garden and stole it. His preaching and evangelizing on behalf of the statue brought in a steady trickle of small change, until one day Umlaut stole a rather busty statue of the muse Erato from a garden center in Chelsea as his new deity, discarding D'Izmaïe outside the nearby Food Drome. That was where Mooney came along.

Umlaut's enduring contribution to the vagaries of the statue's existence was adding the skateboard. Mooney had simply assumed the board was an integral part of the whole. The squatting horse-riding position resembled a surfer, so it made sense to Mooney, who figured it was the Patron Saint of Skateboarders or something. And so he named the general Captain Dude.

III

Oh crap! Damn! Fuck! Shit!

Wendy managed to pirouette away from the heavy chef's knife that fell off the countertop and plunged into the floor where her foot had been just seconds before. She grabbed a smaller paring knife, wrapped it in a dish towel, and stuffed it into the bottom of her bag. Then she grabbed three packs of peanuts and, from the very back of the cupboard, a roll of trepanium filament vacuum-sealed in plastic and a hefty roll of antique gold coins bound together with gaffer tape. She stuffed these into her bag as well. The black-market trepanium had cost an arm and a leg, but it was good for barter almost anywhere. By now, all the ¡ching in her account would be poisoned and useless and all her subscriptions, log-ins, and travel dox would be screaming, *TOXIC! WANTED! CRIMINAL!*

In the living room she quickly scanned her stylishly over-priced stuff for anything she either needed or needed to ensure no one else ever found. She grabbed her ¡think and stuffed it into her bag, making sure the battery and trepanium pack were disconnected. She kicked off her heels and stepped into a pair of work boots. There was no time to change out of the dress. The ¡box on the wall was still on: "¡ching values diminished by 7 percent today after the monthly casting of yarrow sticks at the Monetary Monastery on Mt. Rainier. This, after three consecutive months of increase, brought some welcome stability to the markets—"

She froze when the ¡box interrupted itself and announced: "Further details on today's black hole. Executives at Hedgeer Hemlein Jai-Alai here in Newer York have expressed outrage that their latest ultra-high-yield investment derivative, the In-Croesus 300 Mutual Future Default Swap, has shown an acute recursive return arc, or, in other words, appears to be a derivative with no possible upside. Investors have discovered that this instrument consumed and eradicated not just their holdings in this instrument, but *all* of their wealth. Sources close to the firm's senior management say their forensic econometricists are urgently seeking clarification from the investment algorithmist responsible. The algorithmist has not yet been named. Reclusive CEO Knut Ho was unavailable for comment."

Fuck! Fuck! Shit! How did they trace it so soon? She had known full well they would figure it out eventually, but the algorithm had imploded much faster and left more traces than she had anticipated. At least they hadn't shown her picture.

From the back of the silverware drawer, she retrieved a home-made-looking ¡think peripheral and stuffed it into her bag. Her fingers brushed the heavy revolver. She hesitated a moment before it, too, went into the bag. Sweat ran into her eyes in stinging little droplets of pure fear. No one crossed Knut Ho like this. She ran to the bathroom and grabbed the used hair dye bottle from the bin. Why had she got herself into this mess? Because she could? Could she get out of it? Too late now. Far too many angry, newly impoverished, and publicly outed and humiliated people now baying for her blood. First out of the apartment, then work on getting away from Newer York alive.

She pressed her ear against her apartment door and heard the elevator down the hall ping open, followed by the preposterous sound of dangerous, heavy people trying to run stealthily on plush carpet. There was an unnatural crackling and sizzling, the unmistakable sound of a high-voltage stun instrument getting fired up. She took one last look around the living room, grabbed her combat jacket from behind the couch, and left through the window onto the balcony and the adjoining fire escape just as her doorbell rang.

"Delivery!" called a wholly unconvincing voice to the now-empty apartment.

ONE

ENCOUNTERS. DEPARTURES.

I

"**O**h, for Mög's sake! Just light it with an ordinary flame!"
"I am told that is very dangerous, Your Utterness," said
the Clarion.

For five agonizing minutes, the Clarion and the Archixprest
had taken turns trying to get the herb engine to catch. The
Utterminster stood furiously chewing on the mouthpiece. The
Clarion made one last attempt with the tiny tesla coil that was
supposed to send a spark across the herb in the bowl. This time
it sparked and the Utterminster started sucking furiously on the
mouthpiece. He watched the dried herb smolder and then glow.
The smoke snaked its way through the herb engine's glass en-
trails, spiraled through the cooling retort, and finally entered
the Utterminster's impatient mouth. With dutiful misgivings,
the Utterminster inhaled deeply and the herb smoke flooded his
lungs. This was the Sisterhood's best seeing herb, grown in the
most trepanium-rich soil in all of Inner Azhuur.

The first effect of the seeing herb was that the Utterminster's eyes stopped working. Then his legs got wobbly and his face
started to go numb. The mouthpiece fell from his lips. "Get me
to the horse!" he shouted while he still had use of his mouth. He
could not imagine how anyone could possibly want to feel like
this for recreation.

The Clarion and the Archixprest led the Utterminster into
the center of the Hall of Whispers where the statue of General
D'Izmaïe's horse stood on a low table. The trepanium statue, the
seeing herb, and the trepanium-lined Hall of Whispers—this was
their best bet. There was enough trepanium in the vicinity to

run a hundred billion ¡thinks. The Utterminster reached blindly for the statue. He got his left arm around its belly, grasped the phallus-like pommel that protruded from the saddle with his right hand, and leaned his head against its neck, a peculiar and almost pathetic posture.

Despite ¡thinks being officially banned in Inner Azhuur, the Utterminster secretly used one and was familiar with the sinking sensation of jacking in. This did nothing to prepare him for being able to think and see directly into the ether. He was catapulted into an everything that was, and at the same time a boundless nothingness. He was in the ether. He was *of* the ether. There was no up or down. There was no distance. Through the nothingness between matter, the trepanium connected him to every ethereal device on the planet.

How was he supposed to find Newer York in this endless nowhere? He pictured the mounted statue of D'Izmaïe as he remembered it. For an instant he glimpsed it, and then it was gone. "Don't reach. Wait. Think connections and let them find you," said the Sistermost's written instructions. At the time it seemed utter nonsense, but now, as he and the ether were hurtling through each other, her words made more sense.

He thought stillness. He thought horses. He thought of absence. His sense of self wavered and disappeared and he *was* the horse and then the mounted statue of D'Izmaïe. He saw Mooney. He saw him sleeping in a round tunnel. He felt Mooney's dreams slide around him. He became Mooney's dreaming. It took a huge effort to stay quietly in Mooney's dream. "When you are fully part of it, you will feel at ease." He felt it in a jolt, a symbiotic dance of dreamer, dream, and his ether self. He poured his will into Mooney's dream. He gave Mooney the vision of it all and poured it into his tomorrow. He knew when Mooney understood. It was done.

Now he could do anything he wanted to: be anywhere, anyone, anytime. He could be Ferdinand Maximilian, doomed emperor of Mexico. He could be Cleopatra. He could be a seagull. The ether roiled and surged within him and he was inside whole other lives, eons flashing before him in an eternal instant. *What is the largest prime number?* he wondered. Then he felt the husk of his body drawing him back and down from the light and there was dark, the nothingness of complete, empty dark.

A million miles away he could hear voices: "The herb has left him. He is not waking. Call the Spinster Uilkitz, tell her to get the medics." A cold slab of total silence fell over the Utterminster's absolute dark.

II

For the first time in years, Mooney woke with a definite plan for the day. More than a plan, perhaps more accurately, a mission. It was not a *vision* as such, more like a shopping list that had been drilled into his dreaming: Take Captain Dude to the tip-top of the Chrysler Building; retrieve the letter; show the letter at the Mohawk Hotel reception. The rest would be taken care of. And put money on a horse called Outlying Hermitage at Belmont. That last part seemed odd and he would probably ignore it, but the rest was compellingly clear.

From the point of view of the productive citizenry, Mooney was barely visible, just another of the unjacked, the Great Unwired, the Thoroughfarians, their homelessness eliminated by rebranding it a lifestyle choice. He hid in plain sight. He was almost all the way out of the game. He had his clothes, his makeshift ¡think that he never fully jacked into and used solely for credit, and his tiny inflatable sleeping pad which he had legitimately purchased at the Retail Reformatorium or ReRe on 23rd Street with the proceeds from some poetry he had recited on the F train until people paid him to stop.

His only other possession was Captain Dude, more a Thor-

oughfarian prop than a possession; it was good to have a gim-
mick. It struck him as a sad little figure. He had no idea who it
was supposed to be. The tubby little man's right arm was raised
defiantly, brandishing the empty hilt of a broken sword. The uniform, for all its stiff collar, medals, braid, and buttons, somehow
managed to be too tight and showed the flabby rolls of stomach
fat. Mooney understood it was supposed to be a flattering statue,
but somehow it managed to convey a pudgy, bad-tempered, ferret-
faced, insecure man playing military-hero dress-up. He could almost feel the little man seethe with shame and resentment.

The skateboard the statue was bolted to just added insult to
injury. The wheels were cheap black rubber and the front trucks
were so damaged that, when in free motion, the board veered
wildly to the right. To correct this, Mooney had added a piece
of nylon rope, with which he pulled Captain Dude along behind
him, one more little float of oddness in the parade of off-kilter
that, for tourism reasons, Newer York still tolerated on its streets.

Mooney was forty but carried himself like a much younger
man. His shock of light-brown hair was cropped into an unflat-
tering pudding bowl. His eyes were of a deep brown color and appeared focused on some faraway source of perpetual puzzlement.
His slightly crooked nose provided a prominent and unwavering
contrast to the not-quite-thereness of his eyes. The combined
effect of these features was neither conclusively attractive nor
repellent. He was one of those people who you would have to
try quite hard to even notice, but then, once noticed, could not
really take your eyes off.

The yellow dungarees and the blousy brown linen shirt he
wore were faded and worn but not dirty, thanks to his first Thoroughfarian elder guide who had taught him how to dangle his
clothes in the steam escapes from the server farm housed in the
granite fortress of the former Federal Reserve. In the intervening
five years, he had always managed to keep himself and his clothes

clean by assiduous use of this steam. This was something he felt was important.

Mooney stretched and turned over on his hands and knees to exit the length of concrete pipe where he had been sleeping for the last two months without disturbance. It was important not to be on the streets at night. The Burn Boys had been very active recently. Bored, bitter scions of the well-to-do, they trawled the city streets at night looking for vulnerable Thoroughfarians to douse in the expensive aviation fuel from their parents' helicopters and set alight. LawnOrder seemed unable or unwilling to do anything about them.

The Burn Boys would never venture into a place like this, where they could not easily drive in and out. This waste ground would remain unoccupied and the rubble unmoved while the massive lawsuit over the foundationless Hudson Ho Downs luxury condo buildings dragged on. The last quake had reduced them to rubble the day before their grand opening. The pipes had been brutalist art pieces in the condos' cathedral-like lobbies and many had survived the recent quake and collapse in a way the buildings themselves had spectacularly failed to do.

It was still quite mild for April. It hadn't broken a hundred yet. Brimming with purpose for the day, Mooney did not at first notice the throttled whisper-shouting. He moved toward the sound. He saw a figure in another pipe with its back to him, hunched over and rocking back and forth while it berated itself. Mooney made a large arc to approach the figure from the front.

"See what you've done? Did you really think you could get away with it? How could you BE so fucking stupid? Blame it on Dender? Just because she mistook you for a protégé and took you as her guest to Life4z? And you found yourself in a bathtub filled with drugged kittens supposedly absorbing their life force as they died? All you had to do was listen to her dumb career advice, let her get off on her *sisters together* mentor trip, and say thank you.

She didn't even pressure you to go to the Fuckotel to try out her new favorite cunnilinguist. You could have just gone home, had a long hot shower, and put the whole thing behind you. But no, you had to go and burn the whole joint to the ground to prove your principles. Principles! Ha, look at the fucking result! Hiding out in a pipe with a life expectancy of about twenty-four hours. Well done, Wendy. Epic job! Fuck! Fuck! Fuck!" A guttural, grinding keening, somewhere between choking and weeping, replaced the words.

The figure snapped its head up and Mooney found himself staring at a very unexpected sight: a woman in a combat jacket with badly dyed black hair and electric-green eyes pointing the business end of a .38 revolver at him.

"Who the fuck are you? Stay the fuck away from me or I will blow your face off!"

Mooney put his hands and the skateboard above his head: "Hey! No harm. Just thought you were in trouble."

"What the fuck is that?" Wendy pointed to the figure on the skateboard.

"Captain Dude."

"What?"

"That's what I call him: Captain Dude. Look, I'm going to kneel very slowly and put the skateboard down, okay? Then we can listen to your story. You tell as much as you want and I'll listen as much as you need me to. Sound okay?"

Wendy nodded and aimed the gun at his chest instead of his face.

Mooney squatted down and put Captain Dude on the ground in front of him, then held up his empty hands. He noticed the red evening gown under the combat jacket, but had the wit to say nothing. You didn't ask questions about stuff like that if you wanted to be friends. Despite the combat jacket, she looked stylish. Her blue leather shoulder bag looked expensive too. She did not smell of street. She smelled recent. Fresh traces of indoors. Hints of jasmine.

"I'm Mooney."

"Wendy," she replied.

"Wendy?"

"It's the only thing my mother ever gave me, so I kept it. Yeah, my parents were apparently hoping for some girly-doll-beauty-pageant-type kid, but they got me instead." She scrunched her stubby nose and Mooney caught the spark of smiling eyes that had not smiled in a while. Then she stared beyond Mooney into the sky and shrugged. "I tell you my first name, you tell me your last. It seems a fair exchange."

They sat in silence for what felt like a long time. Wendy pointed the gun at a spot on the ground between them. "Power off your ¡think."

"It's in this little bag here, okay? I am going to take it out really slowly."

Wendy nodded and pointed the gun at his chest again. "Oh my god! Are you fucking kidding me? What even is that? A 6?" She laughed. "How unjacked are you?" She rested the gun in her lap.

"Pretty far. I only ever use it for ¡ching. I do poetry on the subways until people pay me to stop. Still gotta eat, right?"

"So you have no clue what's going on in the world?"

"Nope! The world has no clue what's going on with me either. Seems fair."

Wendy cracked an actual smile and nodded again.

Mooney spoke softly and quietly: "It's okay. I get it. You don't have to tell me anything. I can see you're afraid. I don't need to know why. You need to stay here and stay out of sight? This is a good spot. I've been safe here. Not many COPters fly over, but there are some. So you need to stay in the pipe. You unjacked?"

"Yeah. I pulled out the battery and the trepanium pack."

"Good. I see you're new to the streets. You have to be careful.

I'm out here five years. Got sick. Got creditwhacked for the bills. Lost everything. I was lucky. I met decent people and learned street sense. I am still careful every day."

"You think I'm not being careful? You think I'm not afraid enough? You have no fucking idea what I'm dealing with here!"

"You're right. I don't. And that's okay. I trust you. I can tell you're not LawnOrder. They are clueless when they do undercover."

"You have no friends? You're not part of a Thoroughfarian sect or gang or something?"

"We don't really do that. That's fear-porn news. I know others but we don't band together. There's danger in numbers. Makes you easier to find. LawnOrder looking for someone to blame. Burn Boys. Stuff like that."

"So you just hide here all the time?"

"No. I do stuff. Like today I have a thing to do crosstown. I'll bring back food."

"*Thing to do crosstown?* Do you think I'm stupid? You're going to rat me out! Big reward!" Wendy pointed the revolver at him again.

"No, no. Look, I have no idea who you are or what you did or who's looking for you, and I really don't care. I have a thing. It's a thing I dreamed. Very detailed. Very real. I have to do it to see the *why* of the dream. It's hard to explain."

"No shit! Am I crazy? Why do I believe you?"

"I'm not going to rat you out. I don't know who you are or who to tell. We might want to stick together. Two is a safe number. That is worth more than any reward. And anyway: I found you, so I have to teach you safe. That IS something we do: Thoroughfarian code: finders keepers."

Exhausted, Wendy again lowered the revolver.

Mooney retrieved his sleeping mat from his pipe: "Here, you will be more comfortable with this. It's clean. I steamed it in the vents on Monday. I'll be back in a few hours."

"I am so fucked!"

"Shhhh. This is the now you have. It will be okay. You are safe here."

"Yeah? And then? Things look really promising for me right now, don't they?"

Mooney ignored this remark. "I'll be back. Stay out of sight."

"I have these." She held up a headscarf and big sunglasses.

"Well THEY don't look suspicious!" Mooney couldn't help but laugh.

"I know, I know. I grabbed what I could."

"Just stay out of sight. Do you have water?"

"Yes."

"Okay. I dug a latrine between those two green pipes. There's paper too. Soft kind. Hotel quality."

"Right. Listen, thanks."

"It'll be okay. Just promise me you'll stay put until I get back."

"Okay, okay, I get it."

Two COPters passed low overhead, but their algorithms were evidently targeting more important prey than a Thoroughfarian kneeling in front of a pipe. They kept heading north without stopping. Wendy flinched as they passed and put her headscarf and sunglasses on. A sudden gust blew a fine dust around them that smelled like cinnamon and bleach before it settled back on the nearby hillocks of broken concrete and twisted girders.

⁖

As soon as Mooney was out of sight, Wendy took out her ¡think and, before powering it up, slotted the small, homemade ¡dentity mask into one of the ports. She replaced the battery and the trepanium pack. The ¡dentity mask looked like a circuit board assembled by some awkward toddler: it dangled awkwardly off the side of her sleek sea-stone ¡think 9.9. She could not do in-head while the mask was engaged but could at least scan for mention of herself.

She hastily reviewed some newsfeeds on screen, then did a

dark search for herself and abruptly powered down. She removed the battery and trepanium pack and threw the ¡think back in her bag like it had just bitten her. LawnOrder and Knut Ho's private hit squads were all looking hard for her. They knew she was still in Newer York. She sat in the end of the pipe clutching her knees, thinking in ever smaller, ever darker, ever more terrified circles.

III

Mooney pulled Captain Dude toward the Chrysler Building. The czars of enterprise and economy were far too smart to start interfering with the names of landmarks. Doing away with any meaningful right to vote by turning it into a pay-per-play ¡think app was safe enough, but changing the name of the Chrysler Building was the sort of thing that could have toppled them.

Entering the busy lobby, Mooney tried desperately to make Captain Dude look like an apparatus for performing some useful service, and, even more hopelessly, to portray himself as the qualified operator of such an apparatus. No one even noticed him.

On the top floor, Mooney found the service door unlocked as promised. The spiral staircase wound up and up, occasionally giving him a beautiful view of the city below through the turret-like windows. He came onto a tiny landing and opened the small door in front of him. There it was, the mystery room at the very top of the Chrysler Building's shining spire: a toilet. It was a beautiful little room, immaculately clean and smelling of the fresh lavender in the slim vase on the tiny windowsill. The toilet clearly dated from the building's original construction. The bowl was high and elegantly proportioned and surmounted by a beautiful rosewood seat. The toilet paper holder was set into the wall and had a canopy of beaten pewter shaped into two leaping swordfish. The cistern was high on the wall above it and the pull chain was made of a series of interlocking griffins or lizards, ending in a teardrop ebony handle.

Mooney closed the seat and stood on it to reach behind the high cistern. He pulled out a large manila envelope.

He read the letter three times, luxuriating in the pleasure of an uninterrupted indoor shit. It did not make a whole lot of sense to him. He yanked the pull chain and listened to the satisfying flushing and gurgling with the deep appreciation of indoor plumbing shared by all Thoroughfarians.

From the Chrysler Building he walked toward Grander Central Station. He passed the vendors who sold *BREATHE! DON'T BREATHE!* air-quality alarm shirts that changed color with ambient toxicity and other souvenirs of the city.

Mooney let an uptown 4 train go when he saw a familiar-looking cop board it. Mooney knew the cop's spiel by heart and had been shaken down by him before: "Ladies and gentlemen, I am sorry to interrupt your day. The shutdown this ¡nterruptor caused to your ¡thinks is temporary. I thank you for your attentiveness. As you can see, I am a Newer York City LawnOrder officer. As you can also clearly see, I am heavily armed. What you may not be able to see is that I am in desperate need of money. I know you don't have a lot of wealth because otherwise you would be traveling in a Safe Car, but every little contribution will help. So, between the armed thing and the LawnOrder-officer thing and being-permitted-to-shoot thing and in-need-of-cash thing, you may already see where this is going. These are desperate times. I do not wish to hurt anyone, so as soon as your ¡thinks come back up, I would suggest you ¡ching me as much as you can, keeping in mind I am also very sensitive and volatile."

Two white Retail Reformatorium trains festooned with black arrows sped through on the express line without stopping, packed with prisoners on their way to or from the indentured retail jobs by which they worked off their sentences. Then another ReRe train stopped in the station waiting for the signal. *EACH SALE BRINGS THEM ONE STEP CLOSER TO RE-BECOMING A*

CITIZEN! announced the display in the barred window. Then it flashed *RE RE* in huge letters and began to cycle through the mission statement, the *RE*s staying in place like two broken slot machine wheels while the rest cycled through:

REforms	*REprobates*
REadjusts	*REbels*
REconfigures	*REcalcitrants*
REconditions	*REcidivists*

The train pulled away and disappeared down the tunnel. Mooney had once sat opposite the Bryant Park ReRe and watched the whole thing until it began to repeat itself. It took about ten minutes and he had to say some of them, like *REstores REs Publica*, were a bit of a stretch.

As long as he could concentrate on the trains themselves and keep the tunnels out of his mind, he could handle the subway. It was a delicate operation and he worked hard to keep stable. On the next civilian uptown train, Mooney shallow–jacked in to his ¡think, just enough to receive ¡ching, and began reciting the poetry that was making itself in his head:

"*Who am I?*
Who are you?
We are to others the stories of us
That we will tell out loud
We are fully to ourselves
The unutterable stories no one knows."

He stopped in front of a young man dressed down in an expensive way who was busily playing *Vixen Jungle Warrior* on his ¡think. The young man glanced up at Mooney, upped the audio flow, and shook his head disdainfully. Mooney sensed Cap-

tain Dude tightening around the poem. He turned on the illegal
¡ntrude app that suddenly converted every device in the subway
car into a loudspeaker for his poem:

"The dark of us only we know
Letting Amber Howe be expelled
For your silence on a window you smashed."

Mooney now had the young man's full, undivided, horrified
attention.

"The shame that creeps
Up your back
Every time you remember
That New Year's Eve . . ."

The young man shot his hand up and ¡chinged at Mooney's
¡think. Mooney smiled pleasantly: "Thank you, young man. That
was very generous of you. I think my poem is over now. Enjoy the
rest of your game."

The young man's face was a pale, sweaty mask of relief. He
bolted toward the doors and leaned his forehead against the glass,
itchily waiting for them to open at 68th Street. The woman now
closest to Mooney, who looked familiar, preemptively ¡chinged
him and moved to the other end of the car. Mooney vaguely remembered a poem a few months before on the A train about her
leaving the scene of a traffic accident.

He wasn't sure where the poems came from. Sometimes it felt
like they dropped straight into his head from the ether. He rode
the rest of the way in silence to 86th Street.

IV

The Mohawk Hotel house manager showed no surprise when

Mooney approached the front desk carrying Captain Dude. He read Mooney's letter, nodded, smiled, and immediately came from behind the desk and personally escorted Mooney to his destination with much fawning and ceremony.

A tidy woman in her twenties was waiting at the door of suite 8407. She smiled delightedly at Mooney and Captain Dude. "So wonderful to see you! I'm Tanya! With a T! Thank you SO much for coming! Come in!"

She showed them into the spacious drawing room where there were already four people waiting. Mooney noted without comment that there were ¡see cameras everywhere in the room. No one looked up at the new arrival.

Even to Mooney's untrained eye, the other occupants of the room looked like an unsavory bunch. In a wingback armchair near the window sat some general type. The braid and medals on his dark-gray uniform blindingly reflected the sunlight. In the opposite corner sat a woman in flowing black silk robes emblazoned with rubies. She held something that was a cross between a scepter and a disemboweling tool. On the divan beside her was a tall, intellectual-looking man wearing half-moon glasses and an impractically warm tweed suit. He looked like someone Mooney had once seen in a movie about the lord high lieutenant protector of some colony who had spent the country's GDP buying extravagantly overpriced antique Victorian sex toys at auctions. He could not remember the name of the movie. One other individual sat in a corner in a straight-backed dining chair. He was in his fifties, jittery and unshaven. He wore a once-white linen suit now generously covered in sweat and vomit stains. He fidgeted with a bottle of very cheap whiskey that made no effort to fit discreetly into his jacket pocket. He kept touching his face like it was unfamiliar to him and mumbling to himself.

Mooney sat on the edge of the chaise longue opposite the silk-robed lady and tweed-suited man and gratefully accepted a coffee and yet another beaming smile from Tanya with a T. Just then the ornate double doors to the rest of the suite opened and a stick-thin woman in her thirties wearing riding clothes and a triple-tiered tiara stormed out, shouting: "Preposterous! I will not stoop to this!"

&

"Where did they get these ludicrous hams? Who did the casting for this? It's not like this was cheap. Make sure they never work again! Did I ask for a cheap stereotype convention?" The Utterminster sat propped up in his convalescent bed watching the live feed from the Mohawk Hotel.

The Archixprest stood nervously at his bedside. "Utterminster, please calm yourself. You are still not fully recovered from your herb journey into the ether. The Sisterhood warned you it was dangerous. You must rest."

"Rest? Calm? How am I supposed to stay calm with this cartoonish shambles going on? He'll smell a rat and make a run for it. Then we'll have to kidnap him or something clumsy. He needs to believe this and go along with it. I need him to return the statue, at least for the moment."

"Let us see how this unfolds, Utterminster. I am hopeful of a favorable outcome. My informants assure me the producers will favor our candidate. We have done everything we can to orchestrate the desired result. Azhuur be served!"

The Utterminster scowled at the Archixprest and returned his attention to the feed from suite 8407.

&

Tanya with a T nodded to the lady in the black silk robes who strode into the inner room, pulling the double doors closed behind her with an impressive regal flourish. Five minutes later, a much chastened, far less regal lady exited the interview room and left the suite without raising her eyes from the floor.

The man in the linen suit went in next. He was inside for almost fifteen minutes and the general was showing signs of impatience. Mooney caught his eye and smiled understandingly. The general scowled back contemptuously. Mooney shrugged and spun the front wheel of his skateboard.

When the man in the linen suit eventually emerged, he looked a little dejected but now carried a full bottle of very expensive single malt. The general straightened his tunic and marched toward the inner room.

"Thank you! Goodbye!" said a loud clear voice inside the room before the general had fully entered.

The general stood dazed for a moment, then, mustering all his considerable haughtiness, clicked his heels and marched from the suite muttering ominous-sounding maledictions under his breath. The tweed suit stood up uncertainly and went to the double doors. He peered blinkingly into the inner room only to provoke a howling chorus of derisive laughter. He shuffled from foot to foot and the laughter grew louder. He shambled confusedly out the door and it was suddenly Mooney's turn. He had hoped for more time to figure out what was going on.

Mooney entered the sumptuous inner room cradling Captain Dude in his arms. He was greeted by the shine of a huge mahogany table and two welcoming faces and one blank one that sat behind it. These faces belonged to two immaculate business suits and one callow-looking thirtysomething manboy in a pre-torn Jimi Hendrix T-shirt who eyed Captain Dude's skateboard appraisingly. He did not seem to notice Mooney. The suits' eyes were still filled with the laughter of their encounter with the tweed suit. The woman suit to Mooney's left introduced herself as Edwina Carnage, senior vice president of Human Capital, a cheerful fortysomething who had the air of someone who might have been a poet or a painter had it not been for the financial lure of Human Capital. The man suit on the right was Lœhængen Winwin, senior VP for Traction and Metrics, a grave close-on-thirty who exuded a precocious air of deriving inordinate pleasure from white pocket handkerchiefs and being extremely clean-shaven. The callow youth in the T-shirt was Brad Just-Brad. He slouched in his chair at the right end of the table, like a victim of Bring-Your-Insouciant-Child-to-Work Day.

Winwin motioned Mooney to sit down. Mooney sat and placed Captain Dude on the chair beside his.

Edwina began: "Great! You okay with the ¡sees? We want to capture every moment of this for the behind-the-scenes and the making-of offshoots. Just ignore them. Let me fill you in. We are recruiting for a new show called *So You Wanna Run a Country?* You've probably seen our product—we take people who seem to be completely unqualified for a job, put them into that job, and see how they go. This time it's a whole country, and we need a regent. We are extremely excited about this. Does it sound like something you might be interested in?"

"Uhm. I guess," Mooney heard himself say. His mind was trying desperately to absorb what was being hurled at him.

"Great! Now, which one of you is Mr. Mooney?"

Mooney had not anticipated this. He hesitated for a moment. "Well, mostly me, but this, uhm, is Captain Dude, my, ah, adviser."

Winwin beamed. "Ah, right! Fantastic! Great! Wonderful! We have no objection to advisers. In fact, we encourage them. The stranger the better!" He and Edwina smiled reassuringly at Mooney and nodded deferentially to Captain Dude with an almost robotic synchronicity. They had done stranger things in their careers than nod deferentially at odd statues. Brad took his ¡think from an imitation BOAC bag at his feet, jacked in, and started poking at the screen.

Edwina continued: "Mr. Mooney, have you ever held a falcon?"

"Just Mooney. No Mr. To be truthful, no, I haven't, no. Not familiar with birds that way."

"Not to worry. It would be a nice touch. Perhaps you will take it up." She sat back and made some notes.

Winwin cleared his throat and with a look of gravitas asked: "Have you ever seen *Lawrence of Arabia*, Mr. uhm, I mean, Mooney?"

"So many times! On the ¡gantics. It's one of my favorites."

"Marvelous! Yes, ¡thinks are pitifully inadequate for the purpose; one really must see it on an ¡gantic."

"So true! Gotta see it on film. Analog. Seventy mil. Only way!" said Brad without looking up from his ¡think.

"Have you ever or would you ever consider taking bribes?" asked Edwina.

"Is this a trick question?" Mooney responded. "I don't know. Am I supposed to?"

"Drugs? Alcohol?" the suits asked in perfect unison.

"Yeah, sure, if they are there. But it's not like I have to," Mooney replied.

Edwina straightened her sheaf of papers and smiled at him.

Brad snapped his head up. "I knew it!" He held up his ¡think. On the screen, a man in his twenties wearing bright-orange dungarees, a blue wig, and a red clown nose was dancing with two companions wearing soft felt costumes of a purple giraffe with yellow spots and a bright red whale.

"That's you, right? You were Haydon Happyhouse!" declared Brad, now bristling with manic energy.

"No. But you are not the first person to say that," said Mooney, mildly amused.

"Okay. Whatever. Those could be the same Fungarees you're wearing. Just all faded. Doesn't matter. We can still rumor it up big. I think with that and the crazy statue adviser and the Thoroughfarian thing, we have plenty to work with. This is all good." Then Brad abruptly left the room: "Gotta talk to my people, private like."

"So, as Edwina said earlier, the falconry would be nice but no pressure. I'm sure you'll find other hobbies," blathered Winwin to fill the silence that followed Brad's departure.

"I have one final question," Edwina said. "It's one we have to ask: have you ever run a small- or middle-sized state in a phase of upheaval and transition before?"

"Honestly, since I lost my job holding a sign for Stavitz the tailor on Coney Island Boulevard and got sick and got credit-whacked and ended up on the streets because I couldn't pay the bills, I haven't really had any kind of job. I do poetry on the subway sometimes."

Brad stuck his head back into the room, grinned at Mooney, and announced: "Rock and roll, kids! This is ¡gasm. This is going to be spectacular and ¡ballacious. Mooney, Captain Dude, you're in!" He smiled wildly at the suits. "Guys, make it happen. He's the one. I mean, *they're* the one. Whatever. You know what I mean. ¡ball magic! Make it work. Gotta go. I'll be in touch." He nodded conspiratorially to Mooney and was gone again.

Edwina smiled and nodded at Winwin, who smiled and nodded back at her and then at Mooney, who smiled and nodded back at both of them.

"Mr. Mooney," Edwina said, "we have other candidates scheduled, but that is merely a formality now, as I think our executive producer, Brad, has already made quite clear." Here she looked to Winwin, who nodded his enthusiastic support. "We are in a position to offer you the role. We will arrange a suite here at the Mohawk for you while we finalize the arrangements and lock down the terms of your engagement. We will have your accommodations readied immediately and arrange to move your things. You say you live on the street? Do you have any possessions you would like to retrieve?"

Mooney's head was doing somersaults trying to think this

through. "Just a sleeping pad, but I do, uhm, have a girlfriend—well, not girlfriend but—"

"Oh, that's perfect!" responded Edwina. "I do hope she will join us! We can send a car for her right now. I don't think you'll be needing the sleeping pad." She turned and spoke directly to one of the ¡sees: "We can cut that last bit from the feed and roll it back into the making-of segments, right?" She turned back to Mooney: "So, where shall we pick up your friend?"

"It's best if I go and direct you. It's a little complicated. It's not like it has an address or anything. One other thing: let me go alone and talk to Wendy first. This is going to be a bit of a shock for her."

"Not a problem at all. Understand completely."

V

The Mohawk Hotel staff treated Mooney and his party with all the ceremony usually afforded figureheads of state. When he, Wendy, and Captain Dude arrived, they were ushered to their suite by a phalanx of bellhops and floor managers. Their suite was larger than any single indoor space Mooney had ever had to himself.

Wendy was still reeling from the last thirty minutes that had taken her already-weird new world, turned it inside out and upside down, and shaken everything out of its pockets. She had been alarmed when Mooney told her they were moving and panic-stricken when she found out that meant indoors to a hotel. When she saw the sleek black car waiting for them, she nearly bolted, and only the most plaintive overtures from Mooney could stop her. She double-checked that her ¡think battery was out and her mask in place before getting into the car.

There, things had gotten worse: "What the fuck are you talking about? Regent? Where? How are you getting there? What do you mean *regent*? You? I can't get on a plane. I really can't. They'd make me . . ."

Her brief, masked ¡think session rerouted through a hospital in Iceland had shown her that they were looking very hard for her. If she could get out of the city and to the other side of the world, she might be safe, but she couldn't go through an airport.

"It'll be a private plane," called Edwina from the front seat. "We won't have to go through migration control or anything. It will all be taken care of. We will be very cautious."

Wendy's mind flashed through her recent sightings of what might have been Knut Ho's goons: the guys lurking at the Brooklyn Bridge walkway entrance, all the people who had suddenly started inspecting subway exits, the sightseeing boats that passed up the river with the same few passengers scanning the edges of the island—all of it hummed itself into one compelling thought: *YOU MUST GET THE FUCK OUT OF NEWER YORK NOW!* Her head sifted through her quickly diminishing options and came to the only possible conclusion: "Okay. I'll come. I just don't like planes."

∞

Their belongings, which now consisted of Captain Dude and Wendy's bag, sat almost invisible on the expanse of lush carpet. Mooney was struggling with the voice-controlled faucets in the bathroom when a young woman from the show arrived. She had with her the usual crew of camera operators, or ¡seers, and an interviewer from the trade journal *Governing Today* and another man whom she introduced as Nikolian: "Ex–secret service. Trustworthy. He'll be your, uhm, field producer, chaperon, minder, whatever. You get the picture."

Nikolian bowed reverently to them and said nothing. His big square face looked like it had been carved from stone, his half-closed yet attentive eyes making him look like a particularly relaxed Easter Island statue. He was a man of few unnecessary words and relied for his livelihood on being smart, discreet, strong, and deadly fast when needed. They would be safe in his hands.

"*Nikolian?*" said Wendy.

"Yes. Typo on my ¡think when I was born. My mother wanted to call me Nikola. After Nikola Tesla. What can you do? I'm used to it now."

His smile was brief yet warm. Wendy recognized the dangerous efficiency of Nikolian's presence and was very happy to be on the protected side of it and not the business end. The crew seemed to intuitively understand something profound about Nikolian that made them go to great lengths to keep him out of their shots.

Wendy ran and hid in the bedroom the instant she saw the ¡sees getting ready.

"The Consort to the Regent will not be joining us," Nikolian told the man from *Governing Today* in a tone that invited no further questions. He followed Wendy into the bedroom. "Everything okay?"

"Rather not be seen."

"I understand."

"Do you? Really? What exactly IS your job?"

"Like the young lady said: field producer."

"What the fuck is that?"

"I make sure that things happen as planned and nothing unplanned or bad happens to you or Mooney."

"So you're a bodyguard."

"If you like to think of it that way, certainly."

"Yeah. Right now I would really like to think of it that way."

"I quite understand. Knut Ho is an unsavory, dangerous, and vengeful character." Before Wendy could react, Nikolian tapped the side of his nose to convey that this was their little secret. "While we are on this sensitive topic, I believe the weapons you're hiding are more of a danger to you than a defense. You are not the kind of person who would ever use them on the kind of someone who would be too happy to use them on *you*. Would you like me to dispose of them?"

Wendy pulled the revolver and knife from her bag and handed them to him with obvious relief. "I'm not even going to ask how you knew about that."

"It's my job. You can keep the trepanium and the gold coins, though I doubt you will find any use for them in Azhuur." He smiled amicably and secreted the gun and knife in his inside pocket.

⅘

During the brief interview, Mooney was unable to answer any of the questions he was asked. Not that he couldn't come up with anything to say, he just didn't get the chance—the young woman from the show smoothly interrupted and answered for him each time.

The young woman from the show seemed to really enjoy this bit of her job. At one point in the interview, she turned to Mooney looking puzzled and asked him to consult with Captain Dude. All of this added greater mystique to Mooney's cachet as Regent.

⅘

That evening, Mooney and Wendy were taken on a private after-hours shopping trip to enhance their wardrobes. Mooney was stunned to see they were bypassing the Bryant Park ReRe and going to a FreeRe, a retail store where nonprisoner, paid workers sold a much superior class of prison-manufactured goods. Mooney had never been in a FreeRe and was used to shopping in the LetOut OutLets, the retail villages annexed directly to the prisons in the urbs, or to the ReRes in the city.

Wendy flinched as they passed the ReRe. If LawnOrder caught her, the best she could hope for was doing nails in a ReRe, though even that was unlikely. Her crime was way too large. She would be lucky if she ever got out of horizontal solitary: life in a lightless filing drawer with intravenous fluids and a catheter, with no possibility of parole, or perhaps having her sentence commuted to death. If Knut Ho got her first, she couldn't begin to imagine what would happen.

". . . So, Mr. Mooney, we also need to get you some codpieces. I have some options for you. I have models from Totum Scrotum on West Broadway, Balzac's of Paris, and Genital Confections of London."

Mooney stared at AnQony the coutureista and shook his head: "No codpieces."

"Okay, you let it hang whatever way you like, my friend. Let's look at some pants then."

"No pants. Five shirts, dungarees, T-shirts, shorts, and pairs of yellow socks. Cheapest you got. No more suggestions, please."

"Found it in alley," Wendy said abruptly when she saw one of the assistants taking note of her Flavio Berghentini evening gown and desperately hoped none of the staff would recognize her as the once-free-spending financial algorithmist from Hedgeer Hemlein Jai-Alai so recently outed on the infotainments and currently on trial in absentia live on Justice5. Wendy busied herself stocking up on overpriced yet beautiful headscarves and sunglasses. She also got some silk parachute pants and a selection of saffron-colored linen blouses. Mooney bought a pair of prescuffed work boots to complete his ensemble.

⚮

The following morning, they were four hours late to the airport because Mooney jumped out of their vehicle when he saw they were taking the tunnel out of the city. Wendy chased him down and calmed him, but it was clear they would have to find another way to the airport.

"Can't go in if I can't see out! Can't go in if I can't see out!" Mooney chanted.

Traffic over the bridges was impossible, so Nikolian organized a helicopter, which, although terrifying in its own way, scared Mooney much less than the prospect of the tunnel.

As promised, they bypassed migration control and boarded the *So You Wanna* private jet bound for Paris, the first leg of their journey to Azhuur.

TWO

VECTOR

I

"**A**nalog! All on paper! You have to love it, eh?" remarked the cheerful young man whose Celtic brooch announced him as Clerk Michael. He tucked Skid's forms into a bright plaid folder. "That's about the closest I can find for a family tartan for Skid. It's the McSkitridge tartan. Right then, Skid. You're in. You are now officially welcome to the Glasgow Experience Experience! You're on Thoroughfare Ambiance. Corner of Union and Gordon streets. Ask for Clark. You'll spot him easy enough. Six foot five. Yellow mohawk crest. Just pop up to the third floor to Costumier Sally. She'll help get you kitted out."

"*Thoroughfare Ambiance?* Am I some kind of human air freshener?"

"Nah! More like a fake street yob. I think you'll get the hang of it."

⚉

Skid winced yet again at what Costumier Sally pulled off the rails. "Are ye off yer head?" he said, already starting to affect the local accent.

"No, no," Sally responded. "This one will really suit you. I promise. I'm good at this. I used to design costumes for the theater. This is your look, Skid."

"Does it come with blue suede shoes?"

"Indeed, it does! Wouldn't be complete without them. Go on, try it on. I know it's a look you never would have thought of for yourself, but it'll work, believe me. It's going to be fabulous!"

Ten minutes later, Sally was fussing around a thoroughly transformed Skid. She produced a tub of hair oil and worked it into his hair. She combed it back into a DA and, with a deft twirl of the comb, pulled one tiny oiled curl down into the center of his forehead. "Perfect!" She clapped her hands and handed Skid the comb. "It's steel; if you want to go for real authenticity, I know a bloke will sharpen half the back of it like a razor."

Skid finally reemerged onto the street. He had to admit Sally was good at her job. He felt nine feet tall. He stood proudly and almost preened in his sky-blue teddy boy outfit. He felt good in these clothes. The three-quarter-length drape jacket was trimmed on the collar, pockets, and cuffs with rich navy-blue velvet. The neon-yellow socks Sally had insisted he take screamed out at the world from the three-inch gap between his dark-blue suede crepes and his narrow drainpipe pants. The crimson-and-gold silk paisley vest, the watch fob, and the shoelace tie completed the look. Sally was right; he looked sartorially ahistorical in a cool, slightly dangerous way.

Dublin could have done with a scam like this: a whole city turned into a cheery terminal-unemployment Themetown, and he was its newest teddy boy. He liked Glasgow so far. The low granite buildings that squatted among the empty, formerly cocky glass towers resembled stout, disapproving grandmothers standing in doorways sucking hard on their false teeth. Skid liked them for that.

⚜

Skid easily found the corner of Union and Gordon streets, where a menacing-looking group of three skinheads and a yellow mohawk were standing. They greeted him with:

"What time machine shat you out?"

"Who cut yer hair? We'll get a gang after them for ye!"

"Does yer mammy know yer out dressed like that?"

"Have ye got a match?"

"Yeah, your face and my arse," Skid cut in.

"You must be the new guy. Wow! That's some outfit! I'm Clark."

"How's it goin'? I'm Skid," he said from behind his mirrored sunglasses, the one anachronism Sally had agreed to.

"Good. We're doing great," said Clark. "This is Tommy, Rachel, and Framji. This is *our* corner."

"I kinda guessed that."

"Good thing your name's already Skid, cos that's what I would've called you cos of the hair oil," said Rachel.

Skid ignored her: "Do I have to get me hair hacked off?"

"No, but it might help us as a team, you know?" said Clark.

"Right. Well, I don't think that's going to happen, so I suppose we have ourselves a bit of a skinhead/mohawk/ted alliance going on then, right? So, what exactly are we supposed to do? Find goths, mods, and hippies and beat the shit out of them?"

"No, no, there's none of that. Officially at least," explained Tommy. "They have their own corners. We hang around and take the piss out of the tourists."

"They like that?"

"Oh yeah," said Framji. "Makes them feel like they're in a real city but without all the muggings, kidnappings, organ harvesting, and all that. Bit of a NoGo urban risk experience, you know, but safe."

"Sounds all right, but is that it?"

"Yep. You get to look menacing," said Clark. "There's no real fighting and only mild piss-taking and no bad language."

"What? You're fucking joking."

"During the day. Family-friendly. Until nine p.m. Look on it as a challenge to your inventiveness. If you want to swear, you can do a night shift."

Skid shook his head. "But isn't it supposed to feel dangerous? You think the streeties in NoGo are watching their fucking language?"

"No, I don't, but this is not NoGo and them is the rules and we follow them, or we end up back where we came from," said

Clark. "This is the first thing that remotely looks like a job I have had in eight years. I can't go back to live with my parents. Honestly, I know I couldn't survive twenty minutes if I ended up among real streeties, so this is what I have. This is our team. We all need this. You can't fuck it up for us. Are you in or do we have to send you back?" Clark looked around to the others, who nodded in agreement.

"We are just one more attraction in Themetown," added Rachel. "This is not Downtown Real. Get with it or get the fuck out. Make your peace with it and try to have some fun. Otherwise you're just pissing in our cornflakes."

"Here, let me try standing like this and frowning. That should really work," mocked Skid as he leaned back against the wall and lit a cigarette.

"Look out! Yer shadow's catchin' up with ye!" shouted Framji at a passing couple.

The couple looked back at the gang and giggled excitedly. What a wonderful vacation! Wait until they tell Hilk and Dromda at home about the street thugs they escaped from in Glasgow!

Skid stayed against the wall and stared up at the sky. He would probably get the hang of this. He was certainly not going back to Dublin with his tail between his legs to tell everyone he had been kicked out of the band right after they got a deal. THAT was just not going to happen.

∞

Their last gig in Dublin had gone great, and they'd been approached by some overgrown teen representing Tractatus Entertainment who wanted to sign them on the spot and get them to London "instanter, visas not a problem—all sorted." Skid had the added bonus that night of being approached by an attractive young woman. Their romance had been short-lived and ended with her pouring a pint over his head and threatening to feed him his balls. Not the first time.

Signing them was possibly the record company's desperate experiment in "cassette tape only" backlash, but who cared? The lads' world was going to change from In Dublin to Outta Dublin and someone else was paying for it? No problem!

Afterward, they had gone to Regan's for "a couple of pints" to celebrate. This resulted in an inebriated three a.m. scavenger hunt around the city. They had decided to build themselves a saint out of all the relics they could *borrow* from the churches in town. They didn't get very far. Skid nicked the index finger of the Venerable Saorseach O'Rahilly, the founder of some long-defunct teaching order; Ronan got the gold nose of Blessed Dominick Dunne; and Johnner got the ear of St. Dearbhla of Dunmoice. At the fourth church, they thought better of it all and left the relics in a box on the doorstep of the Fitzgibbon Street cop station with an apologetic note.

For a week it went well in London, until: "I'm afraid to say, despite being a very spirited young man, my people tell me you are simply too market-unwieldy, young Skid. Desperately sorry, old chap, but you're off the ticket."

Skid had not hung around. He grabbed the first train out of London, which happened to be going to Glasgow. At least they had kicked out that sap Ronan too. "Irredeemably nondescript," Makeshift-Gimlet's people had called him. He tried to wish Johnner and Colin well, but he knew deep down he hoped the whole thing would fall apart.

They had paid him off, so he wasn't too short of money. Now he was in Glasgow and determined not to go back to Dublin; he would try to knock some fun out of Thoroughfare Ambiance.

II

When Skid got downstairs, Fygor was in the kitchen pouring nutty, insecty, wholesome things into a bowl, so he could cover it all with goat milk and moss and call the resulting mess breakfast. He carried this out with the same excess of enthusiasm that he put into everything he did. Skid was used to this by now and could live with it. As lottery-appointed flatmates went, he was fine.

"What are you up for today, Skid?" munched Fygor.

"Same as last week and the week before that and the week before that: Thoroughfare Ambiance. Jaysus, it's such shite! I mean, one of them's an MA from Princeton who thinks saying 'Excuse me?' really loud is terrifying, and the others don't even know how to spit right. It's a mess. I've already been cautioned twice for 'overmenacing deportment.'"

"It'll get better. You'll get used to it."

"Costumier Sally got me into evening walking tours, though. I tell stories about famous razor fights."

"You know about famous razor fights?"

"No. I make it all up and do it in this stupid fake Glasgow accent: 'This is the corner where Brodie McTavish slit off Jamie Bruce's ear over a salacious comment about Maggie Corewyn's lovely ankles. This altercation eventually led to the Great Battle of Murray Street in which Tovvy McDougal lost his nose. He and Maggie Corewyn later married and moved to Cumbernauld, where they now live with their three children: Bovver, Tosser, and Cack.' Then I sell them all sharpened steel combs as souvenirs. They think it's great."

"That is highly hilarious, I surmise," said Fygor. "I must go now and defecate before my performance. I'm in the Godspell flash mob on Queen Street at ten. Please excuse me. Enjoy your day!"

Skid left the house and the front door clunked shut behind him. Halfway down the street, he decided to take the day off. He collected his meager three daily inebriation vouchers—trollied tickets, as they were known in the vernacular. Instead of going to the team corner, he made for the Pickled Goat, a nearby failed gastropub, now frequented solely by locals. He couldn't face another day of Thoroughfare Ambiance. The tours in the evenings helped, but not enough to lift his mood out of the mental quag created by three straight days of relentless rain.

III

Skid woke the following morning with an unruly coalition of somethings with badly trimmed claws tearing painful strips from the inside of his skull. He rolled over and something prickled against his face. He drew back and slowly focused his eyes:

That was fun. Surprisingly good for a young fella pissed out of his head. Let's do lots more of that. See ye later.
XXX-ratedly,
Kate

The note was pinned to a very skimpy lace thong.

Kate? Who the fuck is Kate? Skid checked his ¡think quickly, at first disappointed but then strangely relieved he had not recorded any of the night.

Gradually, things slunk back to him. He'd skipped work and gone to the Pickled Goat. In the bathroom, a tubby, sweaty little "corrupt official" had sold him a wad of trollied tickets for the day. Then he began chatting with people and buying rounds with his contraband. A group of "local color" on their day off: the bloke who stands at bus stops with a goldfish in a bowl singing "Scotland the Brave" to it; the Alaskan woman who used to work on an oil rig but now gets a stipend for giving erroneous directions to tourists in an outlandish fake Scots accent; the bloke who kept ranting about soccer: "They're all owned by the same shagging bastards anyway, so it's no surprise they put them all on Majorca and run it like a fucking giant TV studio, eh?"

These were all well and good, but still no *Kate*.

Then he rememberheard her laugh: one of those sexy, smoky, hoarse laughs that bypassed his ears and ran its eager fingers along the inside of his thigh. Slowly she came back to him: Maybe forty. Not beautiful in any obvious way, but there was something in the way she moved and held herself that announced she was utterly comfortable in her skin; she knew and liked her body and knew how to pleasure it. She dressed young and tight on her full figure, though she could have worn mechanic's overalls and the effect would have been the same: she was just one of those distractingly sexual people.

Flash! They had taken passport photos in the booth in that weird night club! Skid leaped out of bed, resolved not to make any more sudden movements, and eventually found his pants on the landing. In the back pocket he found the strip of four photos. He sat on the bed and stared at them. In the first, they were both laughing: Her long red hair reminded him of someone famous. In the second, Skid was looking at her cleavage and she was faking disapproval, but her mostly knowing and sensual smile again gave him a ravenous ache in the pit of his stomach. In the third, the surprise on Skid's face indicated that Kate had just slipped her hand down the front of his pants. In the last, they were kissing, open-mouthed and hungry. Despite his tired and hungover state, he stiffened.

Downstairs he heard Fygor stomping around the kitchen preparing breakfast. Skid groaned, flopped back onto the bed, and pulled the pillow over his head to revel in the afterglow of Kate.

He was just drifting back to sleep when his radio app barked out with knuckle-tightening cheeriness: *"It's nine thirty-five, so if you're not out of bed yet, here's some help from Gestalt Face to get you up and running! So cutting edge, it is only available on cassette tape!"*

Music from his ¡think drifted into the space behind Skid's eyelids where he was searching for sleep. Five seconds later he was very awake.

"The bastards! The shitty, poxy, fucking bastards!" he snarled at the morning. Gestalt Face were not new to Skid, nor was their new release. It had only been five weeks since he'd fled London for Glasgow and already his old band Master Plans had become Gestalt Face and had their first release. The drummer was good, he had to admit, but the songs? They sounded like deodorant ads! They'd turned them into supermarket music.

Well, out of that! Glad not to be caught up in all that branding optimization, positioning, market-penetration nonsense. Who needed success if that was what you had to go through to get it? And London was too big and record companies were assholes and he never really liked being in the band and . . . and . . . "Stupid bastards," he growled once more, and hurled his ¡think across the narrow width of his room.

For someone who REALLY didn't care about not being part of Gestalt Face, Skid was suddenly plunged into a very, very bad mood.

Skid hoped ¡thinks were designed to withstand being thrown at bedroom walls like that. He now found he could not get back to sleep. He was hungry but could hear Fygor still pottering about downstairs. He was in no mood for Fygor's buoyancy. He resolved to stay in bed all day. What was Thoroughfare Ambiance going to do to him? Fire him? Fuck that. Let them! What did he care?

As soon as Fygor went out, he would go to the kitchen and stock up on provisions for the day that would minimize the amount of times he would have to get out of bed. But, fuck it— he had no cigarettes and no tobacco vouchers left. That's what long nights of drinking do to your cigarette allowance: it quickly becomes very inadequate.

IV

Skid shuffled down the street to Thaddeus McMack's General

Provisions. McMack was one of the few native Glaswegians who had refused to give up work. The locals voted him eccentric enough to pass for a tourist attraction and he was left alone to run his little corner shop in its time-honored way.

The shop was newly de-furbished, courtesy of Themetown Interiorization. It exuded an irredeemable brownness and smelled of old floorboards, peat smoke, and wet dogs. There was no sign of McMack and the only sound was the faint babble of the radio from the back room.

Skid knew better than to disturb McMack's "stock-taking" in the back and perused the battered cork bulletin board where locals posted notices and announcements.

Kind, honest, nonsmoking, and reliable dog lover available to walk your dog and/or old person.

Pencil pleat curtains for sale. Lovely color. Lightly soiled.

Child's tricycle for sale. Perfect working order. Used only twice.

Dairy farmhand required, Dumfries. Experience working in herringbone and rotary milking parlors a must. Familiarity with mastitis a plus.

Exotic dancer available for parties and events.

Adjutant urgently required for Regent of isolated statelet. Immediate start. Relocation required. Auditions today, corner of Clyde and Gorbals streets. 10 till 8.

Experienced carpenter available. No job too big or small.

McMack emerged from the back room with the faint aroma of hashish about him: "Ah, good morning, ehm, eh, Skid." He remembered everyone's name but had real problems with Skid's. He liked Skid, but his mind simply refused to process *Skid* as a name. He had no problem with Fygor or any of the other exiles with odd names who had settled in Glasgow. It was only *Skid* that refused to gel in his mind as something state or parent would ever decide to call a child.

"Morning, ehm, eh, Mr. McMack," chided Skid. "Listen, I'm a bit stuck. Will you give me some smokes for these pet food vouchers? I never use them, but they keep giving them to me."

"Ach, ehm, Skid, you know I'd love to help you out, but if I was caught, I'd be out on the streets in a ridiculous kilt scraping bird shite off bus stops. Would you consider trying to smoke some cat food? Or maybe some birdseed? I imagine there might be a wee bit of a hit off that."

Just then, Mrs. Argyle from number forty-three came into the shop. "Good morning, Skid. Taking the day off, are we? Mr. McMack, I really cannot put up with this anymore. I have filled out the forms you gave me three times now and they are still sending me cigarette vouchers for Flossy. Whatever am I to do? Surely they don't expect me to start the poor wee creature smoking. Though god knows, it might help her to get over the hunger pangs. The poor mite has been crying all morning and not even a tiny liver biscuit to give her."

Two minutes later, Mrs. Argyle was in possession of a large box of Kitty-Yum-Yum Fish Head Snack Bikkies, Skid was making use of Flossy's cigarette vouchers, and Mr. McMack was happy to see their problems solved without being directly implicated in any irregularities concerning the misuse or bartering of vouchers. He had gone to the back of the shop for another quick plausible-deniability consultation with his morning-time bong while Skid and Mrs. Argyle transacted their business.

Skid walked back along the street with Mrs. Argyle, buoyed by a sudden nicotine-induced rush of bonhomie. He listened attentively while she prattled on about her only daughter, who was away in the Middle East "doing very well for herself—something to do with exporting snow options . . . Och, Skid, it's terrible sad. All these people living for nothing and just collecting their dole—that's what I call it, it's still dole, even if you have to make a fool of yourself for the tourists for it. I mean, it's all right for the likes of me with one foot in the grave; it makes no difference. But there are young people here frittering their time away living fake lives for tourists. Isn't that terrible sad? They should get out and see the world."

"You're dead right, Mrs. Argyle. Well, here's me. Bye now. Let me know next time you want to trade in your smoke vouchers. It'll be our little secret."

"Take care now, Skid. Mind how you go."

"Will do."

Skid turned onto his street. Knocking on the front door of his house was a hulking shape trying to look like a casual caller. His too-young clothes hung awkwardly off him in a way that announced, *Undercover Dublin cop!* Skid backed carefully around the corner and ran back to McMack's shop. He jotted down the address from the bulletin board: *corner of Clyde and Gorbals streets.*

V

Beside the bridge, Skid came to a disused lot maybe intended for a wider road that never happened and was now where people fished in the Clyde, a real sporting challenge requiring a deep spiritual commitment to the act itself, as the chances of catching anything living were remote. In the lot, there were about forty people milling around a small wrestling ring.

The team had done a lot of careful thinking about how to recruit an adjutant for their next season. They didn't want a career-track power-monger from some high-powered business school, so they had placed their ads among others for unskilled manual workers, community bake sale announcements, and the like.

Despite the *So You Wanna Run a Country?* team's caution in placing the ad, the job had attracted several unsuitable career technocrats and a few more ambitious individuals who were clearly hoping to use this post as a stepping stone to becoming a ruler in their own right. Even Skid could detect the aroma of transnational management school emanating from some of the crowd.

"Hi, I'm Mindy! With an M! Thank you so much for coming! Why don't you sign in right here and we'll get you auditioned shortly," Mindy enthused at Skid when he approached her small table. "Oh! Skid! What a fun name!"

Skid, emboldened by his recent encounter with Kate, looked her straight in her large hazel eyes. *Any chance we could slip off somewhere quiet?* his eyes asked hers.

Not a snowball's; this is my work cheeriness. I wouldn't touch you with a forty-foot barge pole, ye septic little prick! hers replied, still smilingly.

Skid finished signing in and waited with a pantheon of evil-seeming individuals. They looked like people who would sell their own mothers. In a couple of cases they already had.

The nearby ¡gantic sprang to life: "Welcome to auditions for *So You Wanna Run a Country?* You'll remember last season when our team of know-nothings took the principality of Treblik and cut its GDP in half in just four months. Who can forget the clearing of all those miles of forests to spell Prince Kremore's name large enough to be seen from the moon? This year's secret location will be bigger, crazier, and the most spectacular ever! Do you wanna be part of it? Do you have what it takes to be the next ¡think sensation? Then let's do it! Let's find our adjutant!"

The small crowd of candidates cheered, whooped, and

punched the air. Skid did his best to seem similarly enthusiastic. Two by two, Mindy selected names and candidates entered the ring.

Skid had three quick and successful head-to-heads. He was very comfortable once he understood that he was in a big slagging match. In a strange way, his hangover really helped. All he had to do was mock and denigrate his opponent.

Skid's final bout was a little more challenging. Iñaki really wanted the job, and all six foot six and 280 pounds of him bellowed about how pitifully unsuitable Skid was, while shoving Skid in the chest. "I have a master's in recursive econometrics! When I was eight, I sold my brother's dog to vivisectionists. This pile of shit is weak. Weak!" shouted Iñaki, and pushed Skid to the floor.

Skid easily avoided the clumsy kick Iñaki aimed at him and stood up. "This is total crap. I'm only in here killing time. If this tool wants to work himself up into a heart attack, fine! I don't need to spend my time in here with this big, stupid bollocks shouting at me!" He kneed Iñaki hard in the nuts and stepped out of the ring.

"Congratulations, Skid! That was perfect. Let me get a contract and we can settle everything," cheered Mindy over the sound of Iñaki throwing up.

"As long as I don't have to go near London."

"No problem! The planes are all canceled because of all the volcanic ash again, but you can take the nonstop ThroughTrain from New Hadrian's Wall straight to Paris and connect there if you leave tonight."

"So where is this place?"

"I suppose I can tell you now. It is a little country called Inner Azhuur. It's been closed off from the rest of the world for the last eighty years. We don't know much about it. I'd never heard of it until last week. Out of nowhere they suddenly wanted to host the show. It is all very mysterious and exciting! Apparently there are no train lines inside the country, but someone will meet you at the border. So you're all set. I'll put all the dox straight onto your ¡think."

"Eh, okay, I suppose. I'm game. Let's do it!"

"Welcome aboard, Skid!" Preemptively, Mindy's eyes added: *And no, being in the show does not change anything, I would not sleep with you in a fit.*

VI

Back home, Skid flopped down on the bed. He picked up his ¡think, put it down again, paced around the room, started to pack, then came back and picked up the ¡think again. His ma refused to communicate with real people by ¡think. She paid an inordinate fee to maintain a hardwired landline. Few civilians had one anymore. The phrase "when the whole thing goes to shit again" was relentlessly invoked to defend this decision. Skid put his ma's number into the Olde Time Landline app and waited while the rotary dial graphic went through its slow, agonizing mockery.

"Yeah, Ma, it's me."

"Ah, Skid love, how are ye?"

"Grand. Things are good. How are you?"

"Ah, ye know, not bad. Listen, I heard about the band thing. Johnner's ma came around the other day. Don't worry about it. Better off without all that. Where are ye anyway? Are ye all right for money?"

"Yeah, I'm grand. No problem. They paid me off to get rid of me. I'm in Glasgow but I'm heading off tomorrow for Paris and then a place called Inner Azhuur."

"Oh, Paris! Me and Peggy were there last weekend for the greyhound racing. Fiona Crotty's niece was there for two months, ye know, au-pairing like, she loved it. I wonder, did the French invent au-pairing? It sounds French."

"Yeah, right, but I'll only be there a couple of hours before my train to this Azhuur place. Planes are all canceled again."

"I know! The smoke is terrible. Listen, thanks a million for ringing. I have to run. Clare Grogan is driving me down to the wrestling. Listen, look after yourself, right? By the way, there were two fellas here looking for you. Looked like the law. They were asking about a saint's finger. I told them I knew nothing about it and you had nothing to do with other people's fingers. You'd think they would have better things to be doing with their time! They said they would get in touch with you. Anyway, give us a ring when you get a chance again and we'll have a chat. Bye, love."

"Yeah, Ma, bye, take care." But she was already gone. He could picture her hanging up the awful yellow phone in the hall and running around the house picking her coat off one chair, her scarf off another, and her bag off the kitchen windowsill beside the ever-dying, never-dying geranium where she always kept it. He closed his eyes to drive out the picture of his mother in her chaotic little house. Whatever he had wanted to say, whatever had prompted him to phone, whatever he had hoped she would say, was all still inside him hanging like a bag of wet sand from his lungs. He had to dispel the feeling that was dangerously close to wanting to be back in that little house, lying on the sofa watching *Football Island* while the tempest of his ma organizing herself to go out casually raged around him.

The finger thing was not good. That explained the cop earlier. How had they connected him to it? That cowardly prick Ronan again? How had they tracked him to Glasgow?

He hastily packed his things. He held his drumsticks in his hand for a few moments, hesitating before finally dropping them into the bin. He wrote a quick note and put it in an envelope on the kitchen table. On the outside he wrote: *Fygor. Have to leave. Key under mat. If a woman called Kate comes looking for me, please give her this note. Sorry, Skid.*

Mrs. Argyle had a point. He was tired of being a disaffected clown on display to give the tourists fake scares. He was tired of making up razor fights that had never happened to titillate well-heeled voyeurs. And now the law from Dublin were looking for him? He had to go. He locked the front door, put the key under the doormat, and hurried down the street. The new gig couldn't be any worse. At least it would be a change of scenery.

He barely made his connection for the overnight train at New Hadrian's Wall. He tried to sleep while it zigzagged its way south-ish through the countryside as if searching out every lonely station with a light on and a package to send. Hopefully it would get to Paris faster once it had collected these items.

THREE

CONFLUENCES

I

"Wait here," said Nikolian, and headed toward the cluster of low buildings at the ramshackle General Gaspar D'Izmaïe Airfield some ten miles from Azhuur Kapital. The place was completely deserted. The flat sunbaked panorama reminded Wendy uncomfortably of the arid horizonless plains on which she had grown up. She could almost smell her leaky plastic paddling pool baking in the sun.

Nikolian returned accompanied by two uniformed men pulling a small handcart who reverently took Captain Dude from Mooney and trundled it away. Nikolian led Mooney and Wendy across the runway toward a decrepit-looking hangar where they were greeted by a whole team of dressers and beauticians. Nikolian left them there and sat outside in the shade to smoke his pipe.

An hour later, Mooney and Wendy emerged from the hangar wearing identical purple sashes covered in militaristic medals and ribbons. Wendy insisted on still wearing her sunglasses and headscarf. Nikolian assured the consternated dressers that this was good for the show and he accepted full responsibility.

"That took an hour?" said Nikolian, pointing at the sashes.

"Nope. Most of the time was spent convincing them we did not want strips shaved across our heads," said Mooney.

"Ah, right. Those would be the Tonsures of Mög."

They walked toward the horse-drawn carriage that was waiting for them, a giant Fabergé egg on wheels. A freshly polished Captain Dude had been mounted on the carriage's roof.

"Trick or treat," whispered Wendy to Mooney.

"Your job here is to get to the carriage and ignore the ¡sees, okay?" Nikolian said.

"No problem there, right, Mooney?" Wendy responded.

It was relatively easy to ignore the ¡sees, but impossible not to spot them: through some production miscommunication about how to blend in, all the ¡seers were costumed in clownish Elizabethan garb like ghastly Renaissance fair extras. Mooney and Wendy climbed into the carriage and Nikolian sat opposite them with his back to the horses.

The carriage and its cavalry escort moved through the airfield and onto the road in a tiny procession. Despite the heat in the carriage, they closed the windows to keep out the dust. The scenery along the way was, at best, unprepossessing. The predominantly flat earth was a reddish-brown color and what wasn't reddish-brown was mostly stones. The distant hills shimmered in the heat. The soil looked more suitable for making pots and plates than for growing things. There were a lot of small fields delineated by low walls of the rocks cleared to make them. These were dotted with livestock and little whitewashed adobe houses. Stubborn crops grew in the fields under the wrathful eye of the Azhuurse sun.

"What about our stuff?" asked Wendy suddenly.

"All taken care of," said Nikolian. "It will be waiting for you in your rooms. We were lucky. We were the last flight before the ash clouds grounded everything."

"Do we need to learn Azhuurse?" asked Mooney.

"No. I imagine you were able to make yourselves understood with the dressers? Many people speak Yute, the international English of late Internet, popular here before Azhuur cut itself off: 'Hi, guys, what's up? Sverk here! Today I will be totally showing you how to sidestack your VPN without breakback throttling.' You know the kind of thing? They are officially not supposed to speak anything but Azhuurse, but they do. And then the gentry here speak a version of English called Frockshow, learned from old TV costume dramas. You'll know it when you hear it."

"What the hell is that? It must be twenty feet wide!" shouted Mooney. "And there's another one. And another way over there. They're all over the place." He pointed to a huge glass sphere mounted on a glass pedestal that towered over them at the roadside.

"Those, I am told, are opticons," said Nikolian. "They are some form of public address and broadcast system. They are all over Inner Azhuur. We have absolutely no idea how they work."

Mooney and Wendy stared at Nikolian with incredulity.

He shrugged helplessly. "Really! That's all I know."

At intervals along the route, they saw carefully marshaled knots of rustics who waved and cheered, and flapped little purple flags in their left hands while holding their noses with their right. Mooney lifted his hand to wave back and found a firm restraining grip on his wrist.

"Not done," said Nikolian with an apologetic smile.

"Are those Azhuurse flags?" asked Wendy.

"I believe so, Mistress Consort."

"You need to call me Wendy. The *Mistress Consort* thing is messing with my head. And the nose thing? Does it stink where they're standing, or what?"

"That is the traditional Azhuurse show of deference. I believe it stems from an ancient practice of nose-cutting as punishment. It is the reverential Azhuurse greeting, 'I give you one thousand of my noses.'" Nikolian demonstrated by making a loose fist with his right hand and then holding his nose in the circular space made by his thumb and forefinger and twisting his hand counter-clockwise until his wrist could bend no farther. "You are not to use this greeting. I understand your correct response to this is a tilt of the head as if to look down your own nose at the subject."

"Are there a lot of rules?" asked Mooney without taking his eyes off the landscape.

"There are. You may ask me any questions you wish, but there is a lot of protocol and I think it will be best if I advise you as things arise."

The procession trundled on toward Azhuur Kapital. Wendy had a sinking feeling in her gut and held out little hope for the city. In her mind's eye, an agglomeration of dirt streets and shanties bobbed in time with the slow rocking of the carriage and the clip of the horses' hooves on the incongruously well-surfaced roadway.

As they got closer to Azhuur Kapital, the crowds along the roadway were bigger, louder, and better dressed. Mooney started to get very nervous as it dawned on him that he might have to speechify at even larger groups of people when they got to Azhuur Kapital. That, in his mind, was what regents did: orate in front of stadiums packed with excitable followers.

"What on earth is that?" he asked, pointing at a huge expanse of postindustrial wasteland to their left.

"An old oil refinery," Nikolian replied.

"An oil refinery?" said Wendy. "Is there oil in Azhuur?"

"No, there isn't," answered Nikolian softly.

"So where's the nearest port?"

"Four hundred and eighty miles directly south of here, and it's the only port not in the hands of neighboring Outer Azhuur . . ."

Wendy and Mooney stared eagerly at Nikolian. He shrugged, produced his pipe, and raised his eyebrows. They both signaled their permission for him to go ahead.

Nikolian lit his pipe, took a few puffs, and continued in a soothing bass voice that was quite at odds with the content of his discourse: "Azhuur has long been a closed, inward place, and many records were destroyed and all information and images were purged from the ether. What is known with some degree of certainty is that eighty years ago, this place was a thriving little nation—until the split with Outer Azhuur. Then it was taken over by an, uhm, strict, uhm, tyrant type by the name of General Gaspar D'Izmaïe."

"The guy they named the airfield after?" asked Mooney.

"The same. D'Izmaïe was a disagreeable man with few friends even among tyrants, though at the time there was a small but significant lithium-mining operation that kept his enemies nice, until it was exhausted. Anyway, near the peak of his paranoia, before the real darkness came down, he built this oil refinery as far as possible from any foreign state or the sea to prevent attack.

"He ordered the excavation of an enormous pipeline to connect the refinery to the sea. He was consumed by the idea of going down in history as the man who built a 480-mile pipeline large enough to accommodate a double-decker London bus. A few engineers dared to point out that the pipeline should not be so wide. When they disappeared, word quickly spread through the engineering community that criticizing the pipeline dimensions was a very, very bad idea.

"After four years of feverish construction, which brought all other activity in the state to a complete standstill, the pipeline was inaugurated with a big ceremony. General D'Izmaïe had a double-decker bus specially shipped from London and he and his cabinet and some invited dignitaries drove the whole length of the pipeline from the coast to emerge at this end to the choreographed celebration of the inhabitants of Azhuur Kapital.

"As you can imagine, this was a very costly undertaking, particularly when you have started to cut off contact with the outside world. So D'Izmaïe came up with his Great Leap Backward. He exhorted the citizens to live off acorns and dance their hunger away in traditional performances at crossroads. In the following five years, he turned Azhuur into a near feudal society. Every year he held his 'free and fair elections.' Gentry, functionaries, pubble: everyone got a vote. In fact, everyone HAD to vote. Ballots had each voter's name on top and only one name to choose from, which came prechecked. Everyone got to participate by putting their vote for D'Izmaïe in the ballot boxes.

"It was during the last stages of the pipeline excavation that they discovered a rich vein of trepanium ore. In no time, the refinery was almost forgotten, which was good because the pipeline was so wide it could not function and crude had to be transported in trucks along its length and this kept hidden from D'Izmaïe. Within weeks, there were two hundred thousand people working the largest open-cast trepanium mine in the world and the wealth was flowing in, mostly to D'Izmaïe's pocket. However, economics is a funny thing and it became apparent to certain interested parties that it was more profitable for them to pay Inner Azhuur NOT to mine trepanium. So it stopped.

"Three years later, D'Izmaïe was a very wealthy corpse, ripped from his armored carriage by nearly half a ton of manure-based explosive. There were many suspects, but when the cartel behind the not-mining subsidies made it clear to D'Izmaïe's successors, the Utterminster and the Archixprest, that the roundups and show trials could not continue, the matter was dropped.

"After the general's death, the Utterminster and Archixprest, two D'Izmaïe loyalists, took over. They are still alive. Apparently, both are over a hundred years old and still going strong. Something about the trepanium deposits makes the gentry here very long-lived. For the last fifty years, they have continued the Great Leap Backward with the help of Outer Azhuurse mercenaries, the muscle paid for by the trepanium subsidies.

"So that is Inner Azhuur: locked in the Middle Ages, isolated from the world, surrounded on three sides by its mortal enemy, Outer Azhuur, and on the other by a sea basin so thoroughly mined and poisoned by General D'Izmaïe that only unmanned cargo Ro-Boats can enter it. No one can survive passing through it. That's how imports get here, in case you were wondering: in vacuum-sealed, lead-lined containers, and then hauled by cart through the pipeline to Azhuur Kapital.

"A few months ago, for reasons no one quite understands, they suddenly made contact with the outside world and applied to host this season's *So You Wanna Run a Country?* That's where you and I come into the story. You did not, of course, hear any of this from me and will please be seen to believe whatever version of history your hosts choose to serve up to you."

"Ohmyfuckingod, what have we got ourselves into?" said Wendy. "How come no one ever invaded or intervened to stop any of this crazy shit?"

"In layman's terms: the trepanium stockpile. They could flood the market and prices would plummet." Nikolian took a long draw on his pipe, bringing the tobacco in the bowl to a hot, whitish orange.

"That's everything you know?" asked Wendy.

"I think that is probably enough for the time being. Absorb that first and let us see how your *roles* evolve."

"Gotcha . . . I think."

"We will inevitably discuss these matters again."

Shortly after the refinery, the dwellings began to appear. To Wendy's relief, they were not lean-tos scattered along dirt streets. The road had become a highway-wide boulevard, and to each side of it stretched cobbled streets of modest adobe houses. In preparation for the Regent's arrival, the dwellings lining the road had been painted in festive colors—if *painted* is the correct term for low-flying airships strafing habitations with paint.

"Did the houses just get bigger?" asked Mooney.

"Apparently, the city is made of concentric residential rings. The higher one's status, the closer to the center one lives and the bigger one's house."

"So that's what the shaved stripes across their heads are about," said Wendy, indicating a flag-waving cluster of citizens at a corner.

"Exactly—they get wider as you get more important," said Nikolian.

Wendy continued to stare out the window. "What, there are still no cars?"

"None since D'Izmaïe shut things down."

"So, this horse-and-carriage thing is not just for show? This is transport here?"

"Yes."

"Radical! It's like the land that time forgot, found again, and threw back."

"One of the production advisers in Newer York suggested you think of this entire journey as a visit to the thirteenth century with very limited access to the ether, if that helps to calibrate your expectations of this experience," said Nikolian.

Wendy shuddered at the mix of relief and panic inside her. "No ether?"

"I am told it is very strictly limited and controlled."

"Limited? Controlled? But ether is everywhere. It just IS. It's how all the bits of trepanium talk to each other. It's like everything is stored in the quantum nothing between things."

"I understand your perplexity, Wendy, but that is what I have been told, and until proven otherwise, I assume what I have been told to be fact given that my own ¡think has been dead since we landed."

"What about falcons?" said Mooney. "They said there would be falcons."

"That was just a standard interview question. Don't worry, there are no falcons."

II

"That's it?" Wendy pointed to their left at a wall of tall trees on the far side of some water, behind which they could glimpse the tops of high stone walls, towers, and fortifications.

"I believe we are about to cross the bridge to the precincts of the Quartel," answered Nikolian.

They passed between two huge sandstone obelisks covered with intricate runes. There was now water on both sides of them and they could see the waterfront homes stretching away behind them in both directions. The few better-dressed citizens who had earlier been allowed to wave their obeisance from the side of the road had now disappeared altogether.

"Where the hell did all this water come from?" asked Wendy. "The rest of the place is parched."

"Underground aquifers. The place is apparently littered with them," said Nikolian.

The other end of the bridge was marked by two identical obelisks. There were now dense woods to their left and more waterfront Azhuur Kapital to their right. They were approaching the Quartel—the citadel of General D'Izmaïe, Azhuur's political center of gravity, the seat of power and organization.

After about a quarter of a mile, the trees on their left gave way to an ornamental park and then the roadway made a sharp left turn away from the water.

"Hey, look at the crazy statues." Mooney pointed to the huge statues that now lined the wide driveway. Tall, muscular, handsome reimaginings of General D'Izmaïe fighting Alexander the Great, D'Izmaïe slaying a dragon, D'Izmaïe designing the pyramids of Egypt, D'Izmaïe straddling two volcanoes in full eruption, and other assorted pieces of delusory self-aggrandizement. It would have taken great acuity to see even the tiniest resemblance between these heroic sculptures and the tubby, angry Captain Dude.

Elaborate fountains made intricate geometric patterns in the air, creating a welcome coolness. The horses walked cautiously on the smooth paving underfoot and the carriage entered a wide semicircular patio that gave a partial view of the Quartel. Mooney was impressed: it reminded him of the kind of museum you had to pay to enter, even on Tuesdays. In reality, it was an impregnable granite fortress built over centuries with little concern for architectural harmony. It had two jobs: to keep people out and to announce its own importance. It did both in a hysterical clamor of turrets, crenellated walls, moats, palaces, machicolations, ramparts, redoubts, towers, lookouts, battlements, and barbicans that covered almost three square miles.

The carriage stopped opposite huge wooden doors set into the walls. Mooney and Wendy made to get out. Nikolian shook his head gently and motioned them to stay put. They waited for a few moments until two attendants took Captain Dude off the roof and placed him on a small altar halfway between the carriage and the Quartel. They then opened the carriage door and put steps in place.

Nikolian ushered Mooney and Wendy out. "I am afraid I have not been briefed on this next part. All I was told was there would be a welcoming ceremony. I assume you will be prompted, so do nothing unless you get direction."

"My aunt May always joked I would end up in some kind of circus," muttered Wendy as she stepped out.

Mooney stood beside her, blinking at the cacophonous blur of newness, unable to find any one part of it where he could safely park his senses. Mercifully, the Quartel's massive doors swung open to reveal an entrance hall the size of a train station, filled with silent dignitaries eager to pay their respects. This gave Mooney somewhere to focus his gaze. He gripped Wendy's hand and squeezed it tight. He so wanted to be back in the concrete pipe with her. There things made a little more sense.

The attendants invited Mooney to come and take Captain Dude. He stepped toward the small altar and the silence in the inner hall palpably intensified. Mooney hesitated for an instant and then trundled Captain Dude off the altar down the little ramp provided. The dignitaries inside exploded into a long, sustained whoop and twisted their noses repeatedly.

From the center of the crowd, a tall, heavy-set man in a purple hat and matching tunic that stretched to his ankles shuffled forward. He looked like a giant suede cone. "I am the Utterminster of Azhuur, Neck of State, General's Remembrancer, and it is my honor to be the first and the last to greet you." His tone struggled to sound friendly but could not help sounding like a furtive shape in a dark alleyway sharpening a long knife. He stood stiffly before Mooney, Captain Dude, and Wendy, and bowed deeply. He then took his right hand from the copious left sleeve of his tunic where it had been resting and struck himself three solemn strokes on the forehead with a large dead fish. "Behold the Carp of Acquaintanceship!" he bellowed. "Be we now acquainted! Azhuur be served!" More whooping followed this.

Mooney and Wendy looked respectfully down their noses at him. The Utterminster, still not quite recovered from the exertions of his ether excursion, struggled back to the entrance hall to pass the carp to another greeter.

The next to come forward was a corpulent red-faced man in an orange tunic. He had a lateral tonsure, a four-inch sweaty line shaved across his head from ear to ear through his luxuriant hair. "I am the Archixprest of Azhuur, the Pinnacle of the Phalanx of Mög, Arbiter of the Bloodied Moonaxe of Mög's Forgiveness, and Spiritual Guardian of this Fatherland. Be we now acquainted! Azhuur be served!" He made sure the ¡sees were recording him and then he too hit himself on the forehead with the Carp of Acquaintanceship.

$$\infty$$

An hour later, Mooney and Wendy were still peering respectfully down their noses at the last few personages who came forward to hit themselves on the forehead with the now-quite-worse-for-wear carp. Mooney and Wendy suffered the whole procedure with good grace and quiet resignation.

"Do you think they're being especially weird for the ¡sees?" asked Wendy under her breath.

"I wouldn't bet on it," whispered Mooney.

Finally, with the last dying thud of carp on reverential forehead, the Utterminster returned, regreeted them, and the crowd in the hallway parted and Mooney and Wendy were motioned to enter.

The Utterminster turned to them at the threshold: "As I said at our first meeting, I am the Utterminster of Azhuur. Every wish and need of yours is my most pleasured duty to see fulfilled. If you will permit, I will make some introductions."

The coolness of the big stone hall was a welcome relief. The Utterminster reintroduced them to some of the more prominent dignitaries they had already ceremonially met. This time there was no dead fish involved, just the bowing to Captain Dude and the customary nose-twisting.

The Archixprest gave them a deep-voiced cheerful hello, flashed his ready smile: "You must both be tired from your journey, but they say traveling to a new place always sharpens the appetite for knowing and, I suppose it must be said, for food."

"You could say that," replied Wendy warily, "but right now I would kill just for a drink of water."

The Archixprest made a gesture in the air and immediately water was brought for Wendy and Mooney.

"How thoughtless of me! You will forgive me. I won't detain you any longer. You have more people to meet. It has been wonderful to have this opportunity for this brief chat and I trust and hope we will have many more of them." The Archixprest then bowed, twisted his nose solicitously, and backed away into the throng.

A small ancient-looking woman with raven-black hair stepped forward.

"This is the Spinster Uilkitz, Keeper of the Keys," said the Utterminster.

"It is a most longed-for and whelming honor to make your acquaintance," intoned the Spinster Uilkitz with great reverence and seriousness. "I will make myself available at your convenience to help you familiarize yourselves with your domain and acquaint yourselves with its facilities and chambers." She twisted her nose to Mooney, Wendy, and Captain Dude in turn, and then glided away into the crowd with an ease and grace that belied her ancient appearance.

"They all talk like old vampire movies," whispered Wendy.

"I guess that's the Frockshow that Nikolian mentioned."

Mooney and Wendy met the Clarion of the Quartel, the Invigilator of Internality, the Monger of External Affairs, and a host of others whose names and functions blurred into an overwhelming stream of functionaries, flunkies, courtesans, henchpersons, sycophants, and advisers. All of them had strips of differing widths shaved into their hair, some from ear to ear and some from one ear to the crown. Just when Wendy thought she could take no more and was frantically looking around for Nikolian to save them, the banquet horn sounded, assaulting the air like two crowded school buses colliding at high speed and sandwiching an unfortunate bronchitic cow.

The Clarion of the Quartel came and stood between Mooney and Wendy, taking each of them gently by the elbow. Then, in his loud, clear, and melodious voice inherited from a long line of ancestors who were Clarion before him, he bid the guests enter the banquet hall. Mooney was ambushed by a sudden sense of discomfort and glanced around again for Nikolian. There was no sign of him.

"Please do not be troubled, my liege. Nikolian has business to attend to. Everything is in order. I have assured him I will see to your every need."

Wendy turned to look at the Clarion and found herself immediately and oddly at ease. The old man's calm self-possession was contagious, and he somehow made her believe, for the first time since they arrived, that all the proceedings were truly in her honor. The Clarion guided them into a small antechamber, where they and Captain Dude were to prepare for their ceremonial entrances.

III

The cavernous circular banquet hall shimmered in the golden light of the myriad tallow candles set in its walls and reflected in the polished domed ceiling. After some frantic last-minute negotiations between Nikolian, Brad, and the Utterminster, ¡sees were allowed into the banquet hall.

The air was hot and thick with body heat, smoke, and expectation. The dignitaries all sat at the outside of a marble table that encircled the chamber. In the center of this ring was a raised dais on which sat a small table and two dining chairs.

The general hubbub in the room died down organically. Mooney and Wendy emerged from a trapdoor in the floor and seated themselves at the small table. They wore identical linen tunics.

The Clarion nodded to Mooney, who stepped off the dais and walked onto a section of floor that had already started to slowly rotate. He faced the diners who encircled him and took a long scroll from inside his tunic. He scanned the contents of the scroll as he had rehearsed with the Clarion and then draped it over his right arm and extended his left. The Clarion stepped onto the rotating ring of floor beside Mooney. He took Mooney's left hand in his right and then, as mouthpiece for He Who Is Too Mighty to Sully Himself with Public Speech, one of the many titles and sobriquets of the Regent of Azhuur, he cleared his throat and began to declaim Mooney's speech into the expectant silence around them. Out of deference to the Regent and the *So You Wanna* contract, he spoke each sentence first in Frockshow and then in Azhuurse.

"Luminaries, citizens of Azhuur, subjects, I stand before you on this auspicious day. Not an auspicious day solely because I am now your new Regent. No! There is a greater and more important augury that shines on this day."

Can an augury shine? Who wrote this crap? thought Wendy. As if to rebuke her for such disrespectful musing, the dais she was on jolted and began to inch to the left. The Clarion had not mentioned this. She sat rigid and ready to jump off if the thing picked up speed.

"The light that shines on us today is not a new light. It is not the light of so-called progress. It is not the searing blinding light of acquisitiveness and selfishness and convenience. It is a softer, more benign light. It is a light of tranquility. It is a light that comes from the simple tools of the decent craftsmen among us as we build our bridge back to the golden age of Mög, a time of unparalleled contentment in this land, as you all know from the annals."

Wendy was getting too distracted following the movement of the dais to pay attention to or critique the rhetoric. The dais came to rest and the spot where it had been originally began to open, sections of it soundlessly retracting like the blades of an old camera shutter, to reveal a perfect open circle.

"As I stand here, I can see before us a dangerous gulf we must ford, and we must make this bridge strong and true if it is to take us across the dark, swirling waters of outside influence and the showy lures of the venal world. But it is a glorious and wondrous future that awaits us across that bridge to the past. On the other side, I can see the soft comforting light so beloved of Azhuur. It is the gentle soothing light of the welcome dawn of a gentler age for you and your descendants."

A new section of floor rose to fill the open hole in the center of the room. On it sat a simple green marble altar the size of a pool table bearing a metal horse about three feet tall.

"But we do not need to cross the bridge alone," continued the Clarion. "We need not be afraid. For there has come to us a symbol so potent, a talisman so powerful: a standard around which to rally that will make us one united and strong nation of Azhuur. And let it ring clearly to the world—we do not recognize the treasonous artificial state of so-called Outer Azhuur. There is only one true Azhuur."

A dramatic low bass thrumming filled the room. Mooney and the Clarion turned to face the altar.

The Clarion raised his left hand toward the dome. The thrumming swelled as the figure of Captain Dude glided down into the chamber. About ten feet above the horse, it slowed its rate of descent. Mooney could not take his eyes off the figure. The skateboard had been removed, but it was not only that; this figure, so long familiar, now looked almost unrecognizable to him. The music intensified and a mix of fright and wonder rippled through the guests. The Clarion and Mooney turned again to face the crowd at the encircling table.

"Let our enemies tremble, let them reckon hard the cost of our enmity!" exclaimed the Clarion, his voice reaching a crescendo. "Let them reckon it in blood and treasure, for one long lost to us has now returned. The riderless horse of state shall know again a firm hand on the reins. From his long exile I have brought back the unseated rider. I have returned the great General Gaspar D'Izmaïe to his rightful place among his people."

At this moment, the figure of D'Izmaïe slotted onto the pommel protruding from the horse's saddle and the guests dutifully let out a sigh of admiration and relief. Here the Utterminster had wanted a team of servants to rush out and weld the figure back onto the horse while the speech detailed D'Izmaïe's return for good and how this rider would never again be unseated. The Clarion and the Archixprest had eventually convinced him that the sight of arc welders being applied to the general's crotch could not possibly be an uplifting sight. The Clarion wisely resisted the temptation to point out how the visual of the pommel sliding into D'Izmaïe's butt was already distracting enough.

"With General D'Izmaïe to guide us, we will cross this bridge to the past with caution. We will choose our allies carefully. We do not want fair-weather allies who will be swayed by the petty requirements of politics or economics. We will seek loyal allies who believe in an Azhuur triumphant, an Azhuur united, committed to and inspired by our greatest leader. If we find not such allies, we will travel this course alone as we have done before, but with a renewed commitment. The ship of state is rudderless no more! The steed of state is riderless no more and we follow its charge into a new age of time-honored, traditional Azhuurse values and rules. We will stand united and defend our ways against perfidious Outlander influences and interferences. We are announcing to the world that Azhuur is reawakened. We smell your plots and scheming against us. We will no longer live in fear that the Outlander conspiracy will stop bribing us not to mine trepanium. We will not be bullied. We will not be cowed. We will resist all Outlander plots to the last drop of our pure Azhuurse blood. General D'Izmaïe has returned and, united behind him, we will show the world the real power of Azhuur. Azhuur be served!" The Clarion bowed his head.

"Azhuur be served!" chorused the guests.

Mooney released the Clarion's hand and both gestured dramatically toward the statue. There was enthusiastic whooping and nose-twisting among the assembled, and then the Quartel chorus struck up in great voice and sang the "Anthem of the New Age of Azhuur." It was an ugly and tuneless reiteration of what the Clarion had just said on behalf of Mooney, sung in the stylized hacking and retching of Old High Azhuurse, a ceremonial language spoken by almost nobody and read by only a dozen scholars like the Clarion. It was such an unwieldy language that the anthem took another fifteen long, hoarse minutes.

Finally, the anthem hawked up its last phlegmy leitmotif and spat out its final bars. The Clarion twisted his nose to Mooney and moved to the marble altar. D'Izmaïe and horse rose back up toward the dome, the Clarion and the altar slid back into the floor, and the dais where Wendy was still sitting slid back into the center of the room. Mooney rejoined her and a series of flagstones in the banquet hall floor slid noiselessly open, and liveried scullions stepped up from the warren of kitchens and cellars below.

Six scullions in all attended Mooney and Wendy's table, way more attention than they wanted. Mooney kept glancing at the hulk of metal suspended thirty feet above his head. He had never felt entirely comfortable with Captain Dude, and the revelation that it was in fact General D'Izmaïe, from what Mooney already knew about him, confirmed that feeling. He felt dirty, used, and confused. Wendy sat beside him, very troubled by the speech he had just been the ceremonial mouthpiece for.

The scullions brought out plate after plate of local delicacies to the accompaniment of a twelve-piece orchestra. Ten of the instruments were rudimentary accordions and the other two were tight-skinned drums with rounded poles which were pulled through a small hole in the skin. They made a rhythmic sound somewhere between a drone and a deep low buzz.

Amid this constant discord, the guests heaped their plates with finch hearts on beds of oysters, braised larks' tongues, sparrows' livers tossed with asparagus, warbler egg omelets, grilled whole wren, robin gizzards in a red wine syrup, braised blackbird thighs, pan-seared swallows' legs, solomillo of swift, and thrush breasts lightly sautéed with artichoke hearts.

"I think I'm going to be sick," said Wendy, who was a vegetarian.

"Don't say it too loud or they'll bring out an ivory sick bucket and have a three-hour ceremony before they let you throw up," replied Mooney, hoping to distract her.

She smiled wanly at his joke and somehow the renewed awareness of the absurdity of her surroundings actually made her nausea subside. Nonetheless, there was still the question of hunger. No need could drive Wendy to eat songbirds, no matter how delicately prepared, marinated, or seasoned, yet there was no escaping the fact that she hadn't eaten a proper meal since they left Paris.

She caught the eye of one of the scullions who was trying very hard not to stare at her. She motioned to him as discreetly as she could, but he made no sign of coming near. Wendy was so intent on getting him to approach her that she failed to notice how the general buzz of eating, music, and conversation had become a breathless headache of rapt silence.

Through the silence came the soft sound of the Clarion hurrying toward her. He conferred with her briefly, signaled the orchestra to resume, and then sent the scullions away in search of fresh vegetables and fruit. What Wendy got out of this was a bizarre salad of apples, turnips, tomatoes, oranges, pine cones, onions, cabbage, lettuce, strawberries, some avocado-like fruit, and blackberries. She thanked the Clarion profusely and then spent the rest of the meal eating around the turnips and pine cones.

Dessert consisted of a simple mint ice cream served without any fuss. People began to get up and leave as soon as they had their fill. The Utterminster and the Archixprest were among the first to leave. There was no nose-twisting or bowing; people stood up and left as if they had just realized they were late for another appointment. After a whole day of pomp, this disorganized breaking up of the evening soon left Mooney and Wendy alone in the huge room feeling somehow slighted.

"Did we do something wrong?" Wendy asked Mooney. Her voice echoed around the huge emptiness of the banquet hall.

"Not at all," replied the Clarion's warm voice. He emerged out of an alcove from which he had observed Mooney and Wendy's perplexity. "I am sure you must find our ways very strange. You have done well. You navigated the Passing of the Carp of Acquaintanceship and this evening's festivities with great poise and dignity. Please do not take anything amiss in the way the banquet concluded. That is our way. It is a species of unclosed circle. You have obviously noticed our penchant for elaborate ceremony. However, we do not like to mark the finishing of things. We are uncomfortable with signs of finality. The guests departed as they did to avoid taking their leave. No offense was intended. The Spinster Uilkitz will conduct you to your chambers. In the morning we can discuss the choosing of your attendant courtiers."

Mooney started to speak but hesitated.

"Is there something else?" asked the Clarion.

Mooney pointed upward toward Captain Dude, who was still suspended above them.

"The figure of General D'Izmaïe will stay there for the night. It will be perfectly safe."

"And the skateboard?"

"In the furnaces."

Mooney winced: Captain Dude was no longer Captain Dude and was not his anymore. It felt like a relief and a hurt at the same time.

Wendy jumped into the awkward silence: "So? Seriously? What's with these Tonsures of Mög?"

"Ah, you noticed those," said the Clarion.

"Hard to miss really. They tried to give us some when we arrived."

"Quite. They are based on the alleged width of Mög's bloodied handprint, now lost. As one's importance increases, the width increases. The lowliest of the gentry have a little finger's width from left ear to crown; the most important have a full hand's width from ear to ear. Within each width, full ear to ear outranks right ear to crown, which outranks left ear to crown, and so on.

I believe you are both entitled to the full hand ear to ear, which only the Utterminster and Archixprest may wear. You will observe I myself wear a full hand from the right ear to crown, the second-highest tonsure of honor."

"I think we'll pass on the tonsures for now, thanks," said Wendy.

"As you wish, my lieges."

Out of nowhere, the Spinster Uilkitz was suddenly beside the Clarion, curtseying and twisting her nose. She too had the full-hand tonsure from right ear to crown.

"I don't want to be rude, but how old are you two?" blurted Wendy.

"It is not rude at all, Mistress Consort. We are both one hundred and fourteen," said the Clarion. "It is not uncommon for gentry of the Quartel to live to one hundred and fifty."

"Wow, you are in great shape for your age," said Mooney.

"Thank you, Regent, but we can take no credit for what is an accident of birth and rank. I will bid you both good night now." The Clarion twisted his nose and left.

Leaving the ¡sees behind, the Spinster Uilkitz led Wendy and Mooney through a labyrinth of dark marble corridors to the entrance to their chambers. She opened the door and ushered them into a tennis court–sized room lined with polished wooden benches. In the center was a small ornamental fountain.

"This is the courtiers' anteroom." The Spinster Uilkitz extinguished the candle which had been their only light through the corridors.

On the wall behind the fountain was an enormous mural. It looked like someone had hastily organized an orgy in the middle of a medieval battle scene. Armored warriors hacked, stabbed, and kicked at each other, seemingly unaware of the arrestingly beautiful voluptuaries in their midst who coupled and cavorted in every conceivable combination and configuration. The voluptuaries, in turn, seemed unperturbed by the chaos and slaughter around them.

"You are staring at the wall. It is of the Synergetic school: war is sex, sex is war. Both are power. Very popular among the elite here. Personally, I'd take the sex over the warring anytime, although I do like a man in uniform."

Each side of the mural depicted identical fortresses. The Spinster Uilkitz led them to the right side and they saw that the fortress gate coincided with a real door. "These are the Mistress Consort's chambers." She pushed the door inward to reveal extensive apartments decorated in an odd homely monastic style. "Tradition and protocol dictate you maintain separate chambers. It is the way. Good night, Mistress Consort. We will dispense with the courtier undressers for tonight, as you have not yet chosen them. I will now conduct the Regent to his accommodations. You will easily find the connecting door, should you have need of it."

The Spinster Uilkitz led Mooney to the other end of the mural and opened his door onto an identical set of chambers. She twisted her nose and bowed and then made her way across the courtiers' anteroom and out again into the impenetrable darkness, not once hesitating or faltering.

⚯

"Can I come in?" Wendy stood in the open connecting door. She stretched her hands high above her head to unkink her back. "Excellent chance to get a look at my tits, if you are interested. Well?" She peered down at her cleavage and then back at him.

Mooney obediently glanced at her breasts and sputtered: "Uhm, yes, you have very nice, uhm, breasts."

Wendy lowered her arms. "Hey, I'm sorry. I was just messing with you."

"Yes. No. It's okay. You are very confident. You are comfortable with you. That's good. It is nice to see."

Wendy ran toward the huge oval bed and then dove onto it, scattering decorative cushions everywhere, a childlike release after the long, strange day.

"Alone, finally. You're safe here," Mooney sighed, and sat on the edge of the bed.

"Safe? Not so sure about that."

"Feels weird not to have Captain Dude, though."

"D'Izmaïe, you mean. Creeps me out."

"It's only a statue."

"Yeah? You heard what the Clarion read out for you?"

"I heard some of it. Honestly, I found it hard to concentrate. The Azhuurse translation drove it out of my head."

"That was some weird jingoistic shit." Wendy took Mooney's hand in hers. "Hey, thanks for, you know, getting me out of Newer York. You're right—I am safer here." She suddenly pulled him toward her and kissed him. Their kissing quickly became hungered, became embracing, became nakedness, became de-vouring, became fucking, became abandon, became holding and entwining again.

"I guess that orgy mural got me a little horny," said Wendy. "That was kinda fun."

"Was it?" said Mooney.

"What sort of shitty, messed-up, mind-game thing is that to say? Is that your thing? That is so fucked up!"

"Oh no, I mean, it's just, I never, you know, I never did it be-fore," stuttered Mooney. "But I really enjoyed it. You are so lovely to hold. Soft and smooth and warm. Will we do more of it?"

"Really? Never? Wow. I don't know, Mooney. Let's say that got the tension out of the air. Tomorrow we can start over and see where we go, okay?"

Mooney nodded and beamed at her. Wendy put her arms around him. It wasn't the worst sex she'd ever had. There was something desperately tender on Mooney's side of it, and since she appeared to have totally sabotaged her life, right now there was a reciprocal tender loneliness on her side too. She felt immersed inside this simple moment, temporarily just a little less hunted and less alone. She was fairly sure they would never have sex again but was quietly glad they had.

IV

As soon as the *So You Wanna* technicians finished installing the ¡box, the Utterminster expelled them from his office. He did not approve of all this shiny technology—it marred the stone wall of his office, making a mockery of its ancient grandeur. "Well? Make it work then!" he snapped at the Clarion.

The Clarion consulted the instructions the technicians had left and then faced the ¡box. "Intimeet, runacountry 103," he told it.

The screen flashed to life to reveal two business-suited youths and Brad, the producer, sitting around what appeared to be Brad's desk, if the superhero action figures on it were any indication.

"Yo! Archie! Udder! How are tricks? Good afternoon, Clarion. Have you met my suits? Vincent and Flower. Great people. The best. Team players. To the nth degree and beyond!"

Vincent and Flower waved politely.

The Clarion struggled not to smile at the obvious discomfort being addressed as *Udder* and *Archie* caused his superiors. He would share this later with the Spinster Uilkitz; he was sure she would derive great amusement from it.

"Okay. Enough of the formalities. Everything going okay? Saw the Carp of Acquaintanceship stuff—niiiice! Very ritual. Old style. Big hit. The marks loved it. ¡balls very high. Numbers very healthy."

"The Regent's arrival and welcome went according to plan, as you saw," said the Utterminster stiffly.

"Great! Listen, guys, we are getting a lot of poor-quality ether response out there. Feed from the banquet was barely usable.

What's the story? It's not our equipment, and our technicians think there is some type of blockage. I didn't know it was possible to block the ether. How do you guys do that?"

"That is our prerogative and our knowledge alone," answered the Utterminster. "I thought we had opened sufficient resonance in our ether. We will have our technical people investigate."

"You have *technical* people? Can we hook them up with our techies and speed this up?"

"Yes, we have technical people, and no, you cannot *hook* yours to them. Do not presume to patronize us, Braid. We will open some more dedicated resonances for you, Braid. The Clarion will see to it and make the necessary communications."

"That's *Brad*."

"Indeed. I have a question then, Brad. Will your ¡seers continue to be dressed as cartoonish Elizabethan nobility in their pathetic attempts to blend in, or can we hope to see an end to this buffoonery?"

"We'll figure out something on the costumes. Dial your blood pressure down a notch there, Udder. You'll live longer that way."

"My longevity does not fall within the remit of your entertainment product. On another topic, for your information we will be installing General D'Izmaïe between the obelisks on the Kapital side of the bridge, so the pubble can adore him. We will have a dedication ceremony or investiture to confirm him as patron of Azhuur and . . ."

"Great, great, we like the investiture thing—keep the crazy ritual stuff coming. We have enough for this week's episode. As we agreed, we will do a special live episode for all the big ceremonies. What else? The Frockshow-then-Azhuurse thing is working well. There are a few stray bits of Azhuurse, but we can translate and dub those, though we can't find anyone who can translate that Old High Azhuurse stuff."

"That is unsurprising," said the Utterminster. "The

Archixprest will see to it that you receive a translation of any Old High Azhuurse that will be used."

"Okay, great! So, here's what we are seeing from the game side of things . . ." said Brad.

"I beg your pardon? The what?" interjected the Archixprest.

"The game side." Brad gestured to Flower, who took over: "On parallel track with the CRUD, or Consumer-Responsive Unscripted Drama, or show, as you might know it, we have a CREALITY, or Consumer Reactive Endproduct App for Low-Impact Test Yarns, interface. I know, I know! Obviously, we started with the acronym and worked our way backward. Anyway, we have set up a parallel game where followers can log on and play from the POV of one of the characters and make decisions independent of whatever is actually happening. It's very basic beta 2.8.6 stuff right now. We only have thirty programmers working it, but we're liking the traction. Promising ¡ball uptake and retention."

Brad jumped in: "You should check it out. You could play as each other, ha!"

Flower resumed smoothly: "Anyhow, from the gaming trends, we can assess preferences of our core demographic and, using these feedback loops, determine the trajectory for the reality we wish to portray. In essence, we gain an idea of what people would like to see happen in Azhuur, and we can weigh that against our dramaturgical objectives. So, we'll be in touch with what we need to happen."

The Utterminster and the Archixprest nodded dumbly.

"Anything else, guys?" Brad gestured to his suits.

Vincent cleared his throat and then seemed to gaze at the ceiling of the Utterminster's office. "We appreciate the additional ether resonances, but you still need to grant more access to the ¡seers. We need more feed. No feed, no ¡balls. No ¡balls, no show. No show . . . well, I don't need to spell it out—you get it."

"Like he says: please make the ether okay and let the ¡seers in more places," said Brad. "Great meeting, everyone, gotta run!"

The ¡box went dark. The Utterminster and the Archixprest fumed in silence.

"Do you . . ." began the Clarion.

"Speak to the Sisterhood about letting those people into more of the ether. Now leave us," said the Utterminster between clenched teeth.

The Clarion ran down the corridor to find the Spinster Uil-kitz. As soon as he had told her about the Intimeet with *Udder* and *Archie*, he would contact the Sistermost.

V

While Mooney and Wendy slept late, the lumpenprole—the pubble of Azhuur, those outside the Quartel's bureaucratic and sycophantic circus—were busy pursuing their normal day of toil somewhere on the edge of the thirteenth century. Those who could remember when things were not like this did their best to keep those thoughts to themselves, because worse than their current surroundings were the memories of how the country ended up like this: the vile civil war and, for most, the horrors of the Generalitate that followed. The women and men who were bodily able worked on the roads or labored in the fields. Those who were less able tended livestock, wove, or worked as serving staff in the Quartel.

"What the fuck is that?" Wendy sat up so suddenly that she banged her chin on Mooney's arm, which had been lying across her.

"What?"

"That!" Wendy replied as the foghorn of a small but very loud ship sounded again. "It's coming from the desk."

Mooney cautiously approached the desk and waited. When the sound happened again, he noticed the stoppered pipe beside the desk. He removed the elaborate closure and the noise ceased.

"Regent, I am most sorry to intrude, but it is already past

eleven and the aspiring courtiers have been assembled for over two hours," announced the Clarion's voice through the pipe. "May I suggest now as a time to rise?"

"Okay, give us five minutes."

Wendy grabbed her clothes and hustled out through the connecting door. It closed with a soft airless rush behind her. Mooney lay back down among the last traces of her body's warmth.

⚭

When the bell tinkled, Mooney called "Come!" the way he had seen in ¡gantic movies about olden times.

Simultaneously, the Clarion and the Spinster Uilkitz entered Mooney's and Wendy's respective chambers, bearing to Wendy's great relief breakfast trays of coffee, tea, juice, baked goods, and fruit. Not a delicately cooked songbird in sight.

"When you have finished breakfast, please join me in the courtiers' antechamber and let us choose your favored courtiers."

⚭

"Thank you all. We have concluded the choosing for now," the Clarion informed the perplexed courtiers who packed the antechamber. "Please clear the room."

"Nikolian, can you help with this crap?" pleaded Wendy as the room emptied.

"Clarion, I think we have to reach some compromise on this. It is clear the Regent and Mistress Consort cannot tolerate all this constant attention."

"But the dictates of etiquette—"

Nikolian continued: "Listen, Clarion, I understand the needs of etiquette, but you and I know this is just a way to keep courtiers so busy vying for position and keeping up with the latest court fads that they don't have time to breathe, let alone plot a revolution. Do you actually think revolution is a real fear anymore, particularly with these two and Azhuur being center stage for *So You Wanna Run a Country?*"

"It is not for me to say. Ultimately, I have to answer to the Utterminster and the Archixprest."

"I don't envy you there. Okay, how about we put it like this? The Regent and Mistress Consort are at this moment being extremely judicious in the granting of favors to encourage the courtiers of Azhuur to show their very best. For the moment they will be choosing only the following, one each—you getting this, Clarion?—a boiled egg topper and a napkin unfurler. They have determined that you, Clarion, and the Spinster Uilkitz will serve as secretary and valet of the bedchamber to the Regent and Mistress Consort respectively. More appointments may be made in the future, but this exhausts the roll of favors for the moment."

"No toilet seat warmer?"

"Not on your life!" yelled Wendy.

"I am honored to serve as valet and secretary. I will convey these decisions to the Archixprest and Utterminster when next I confer with them."

"I, too, accept this honor with great gratitude, Mistress Consort," said the Spinster.

"Great! So, are we finished for the day then?" asked Mooney.

"I am afraid not, my liege," the Spinster replied. "You will be so kind as to accompany me to the Map Room?"

Mooney and Wendy shrugged a *Why not?* at the suggestion.

The Spinster turned to the ¡seer: "You cannot accompany us to this destination. Please wait here. I understand your superiors have been requesting wider access for you, but this is not a place you will ever see nor know the location of. You will be sent for in due course."

Tej the ¡seer shrugged and sat down against the wall. He was on overseas allowance and per diem, so he didn't care, and so far, other than the really uncomfortable doublet and hose he had to wear, this was way better than *Shrikey Dween on Tour: All Her,*

All Day, All Night, All Access. He took off his ruff and opened his leather jerkin with great relief.

∞

The Map Room was somewhere inside the Quartel. That was as much as Mooney and Wendy could say after following the Spinster through the maze of corridors and stairs that would have been the envy of any unhinged pyramid builder. The only clear impression either of them had on entering the room was standing on the floor of a bright, windowless silo of a room perhaps a hundred feet tall and thirty feet in diameter. The interior walls were covered in abstract murals resembling Venetian plastering that seemed to illuminate themselves and the chamber itself with something close to the look of natural winter sunlight. In the exact center of the room, a pointed spike of dull white metal tapered upward from its foot-wide base to a needlelike point fifteen feet above their heads.

"What is that thing for?" said Wendy. "Please don't tell me there are impalings in here."

"No, no. Please, nothing of the sort. That is the Point, the center of Inner Azhuur, the point from which all distances in the country are calculated."

"So everywhere is measured by how far from this pole it is?" said Mooney.

"Exactly. All roads begin here. And all roads must pass through here."

"Wait! What? *All* roads? But no one even knows where this thing is! How do you guys measure the distance between two places that are both a hundred miles from here?"

"We simply add their respective distances from the Point; they are two hundred miles apart."

"Even if they are beside each other?" said Wendy.

"They are still two hundred miles apart," replied the Spinster

"That's what I thought you were saying."

"Is that how people have to travel?" asked Mooney.

"No, no, my liege, not at all. They are free to travel by the most direct route, but they must never refer to the actual distance between the two points and must always cite the distance involved in first passing through the Point."

"That is nuts!" said Wendy.

"It is custom, my liege, and one important to observe. It is considered treasonous to ignore passing through the Point when discussing the distance between any two points in Azhuur."

"How do you enforce that?"

"We don't have to; it is a symbolic law to remind everyone of the importance of the Quartel in all things. Knowing the law exists is more important than actually obeying it."

"Yeah, but what's the point?" said Mooney.

Wendy giggled: "Yeah, it seems pointless."

"As you wish, Mistress. Now, if you will accompany me, we will inspect the maps."

"Point the way," grinned Mooney.

Still exchanging more excruciating point puns, they followed the Spinster up the narrow stairs that lined the walls from gallery to gallery. You could tell from the tension in her shoulders that she was trying very hard not to turn into some impatient schoolteacher.

Two galleries from the top, the Spinster pointed across at a panel of beige swirls on the far side. "That," she proclaimed with much pride and solemnity, "is Azhuur. You will need to use these for the image to resolve."

From a compartment in the wall, she produced two small pairs of opera glasses. Mooney and Wendy looked through them at the map on the opposite side. What had looked like gestalt daubs on the wall now resolved into maps of minute crystalline detail.

"Wow, almost completely surrounded by Outer Azhuur. A tiny slice of coastline and one lake in the whole place?"

"Yes. That is the, ahem, Vale of Victory. We are fortunate that there are many underground aquifers."

"Really? One lake in the entire place and you go and name it after some, *ahem*, stupid bit of bloodshed? Come on. Seriously? *Freedom Dales, site of the first-ever automated laser massacre of peaceful protesters!*"

"I will be pleased to tutor Mistress Consort in the recent history of Azhuur at some later time. You will please note that all the maps here in the Map Room were hand-painted by specialized artisans skilled in the oddities of azimuthal projection for concave surfaces, which gives the maps both their beauty and their extreme accuracy. They were executed to complement the special lenses in the opera glasses you hold. If you adjust the focus, you can see down to the tiniest detail. You can read the runes on the obelisks guarding the bridge, should you care to zoom in. All of this was based on arcane and immensely complex calculations and techniques known only to a handful of people."

"I know you are fobbing me off, but I love that stuff," said Wendy. "Can I go see how they do it?"

"Ah, I am afraid the Sisterhood exists in seclusion."

"Sisterhood?"

"Yes, they live in the Outlying Hermitage several miles east of here. You will see it on the map. They are, as I say, a closed order. They produce the most skilled work to be seen in all of Azhuur. They perform many indispensable services to the Father . . . uhm, nation."

"Can I join? Like a temporary member? I AM the Mistress Consort to the Regent."

"No one can join. Sisters reveal themselves and new ones are divined by the Sistermost, the most senior sister, when one passes. There are always 360. There has not been a new sister in several years."

"So you have all these women cooped up together? What do they do for fun? Are they all lesbians?"

"No, not all of them. They are free to consort with their lovers. They choose to live apart. That is the purpose of the Sisterhood. It is not some institution where women are *sent*, it provides a refuge for women who are more comfortable out of the maelstrom of this world. There are always such people. We can discuss the Sisterhood at length another time." The Spinster pointed upward toward the last line of maps before the mirrored ceiling: "There is the one and only existing map of the Quartel. Very few are ever allowed to glance at it. Your noble selves may of course come here at will to familiarize yourselves with it."

"No one can see the map of the Quartel? That's absurd," said Wendy.

"Rest assured, Mistress, everyone knows no more than is good or safe for them to know, least of all the location of the Map Room itself, the most guarded secret of all. You will note that it is not marked on the Quartel map."

"Even better," said Wendy, "a map no one can see stored in a room no one can locate."

"And now, with your permission, we should repair to the Cypress Gardens, where the Archixprest and the Utterminster await you."

They followed the Spinster along more corridors, up and down flights of disorienting stairs, through several concealed doors, and into two odd elevators that did not so much move as snap from one place to another and finally back into a more peopled part of the Quartel. Mooney and Wendy flinched as everyone dropped into a crouch when they passed.

"My lieges must get used to the crouching. No one can ever be taller than you. I count myself fortunate to be short enough of stature to be safely in your presence without having to bow or crouch down. Even when you are without headgear. No disrespect intended."

"None taken," said Wendy.

The Spinster led them through a small hedge maze and out into the Cypress Gardens, where the Archixprest and the Utterminster were taking tea at a wrought-iron table on the terrace. "I shall return presently," she announced, then saluted and left.

After the usual outbreak of nose-twisting, everyone sat. The Utterminster poured tea for Mooney and Wendy, careful to keep his eye level just below theirs. After a preliminary silence punctuated by the fussy tinkling of spoons on thin china, the Archixprest cleared his throat and then from it issued such a long stream of preemptive comments, preambles, euphemisms, flattery, and circumlocution that, by the time he got to the real purpose of his speech, Mooney and Wendy were so relieved to have something meaningful to listen to that they gave him their undivided attention.

"We have installed General D'Izmaïe in between the obelisks where he can be seen for miles. The pubble are pleased by this. Already there is a healthy cluster of artisans selling small carved replicas, and there are makeshift shrines and altars appearing among the pubble's dwellings," explained the Archixprest, knowing full well that the carvers and shrine makers were mostly Quartel agents and that few proles would find anything to celebrate in a revival of the cult of D'Izmaïe.

"We will have a competition for the best carved replica and present the winning prole with a prize of some sort," said the Utterminster.

"Oh, that would be nice. Maybe like a new house or something," said Wendy.

The Utterminster smiled patronizingly. "You spoil them. I had been thinking more along the lines of a half-dozen turnips and a brightly colored ribbon."

Further tea-drinking silence followed.

"Well, this has been a lovely interlude, but you must excuse us now," said the Utterminster as he crouched and backed away. The Archixprest waddled off behind him.

"What are we supposed to do now?" called Wendy after them, but they didn't respond.

As soon as they were out of sight, the Clarion appeared as if by magic. "I have been instructed to take you to review the carved replicas the artisans have been making and to choose a winner."

"But how? When? I mean, they just decided that and they left before you arrived," stammered Mooney. "How did you even know?"

The Clarion smiled. "It is my job to know these things as soon as, and sometimes before, they do. I am more than just a loud voice."

VI

Skid's waking was filled with the frantic staccato rhythm of his heart coming to terms with too much cheap cognac. He had struggled to find the edges of Dream-Skid so he could yank them hard and dislodge himself. He reminded himself to breathe and Dream-Skid was replaced by a leaden awareness of being asleep but being unable to move or even sigh. He couldn't make the slightest sound and felt his limbs sink deeper and deeper into the substance of the berth with sudden, sickening drops. One final drop took his breath away and he hit. Dazed, emerging into the light, his mind struggled to catch up with his eyes and identify the dizzying carnival of lights and colors that assaulted him.

The scene rolled, blurred, and wavered until it arranged itself into a configuration Skid's mind finally recognized as the train compartment. His whole body was screaming out for water. He still had some in a bottle in his backpack.

With the minimum of possible movement, he turned in his narrow berth and reached under it for his backpack. Failing to find it this way, he resigned himself to sitting up and looking properly. He took a deep breath and then launched his heaviness into a sitting position and swung his legs out and let them flop to the floor. All the blood rushed from his head while his brain continued upward for three miles along the trajectory started by sitting up. He waited nervously for it to return.

When it did come back down, it brought with it nausea, breathlessness, and some minor heart palpitations that Skid could have really done without. He closed his eyes and held his breath while uttering a silent prayer of *Neveragain*. When the nausea and the prickling sweat on his forehead subsided, he risked re-opening his eyes. The focus of everything was too sharp, almost jagged. The train clack-acked along at speed and swayed in a way that might have been soothing to anyone who did not have a crushing hangover. Skid, however, was painfully aware instead of the diesel engine's low thrumming.

He gingerly put his head between his knees to look under his seat. No backpack. Maybe he had put it on the luggage rack last night? But wait! No shoes either. He had definitely not put them on the luggage rack. Then he noticed he was still wearing them. The relief was short-lived as it slowly dawned on him that the only things he now owned were the clothes he had slept in.

⅚

The conductor listened to Skid's tale with the tired, sincere sympathy of one who had gone through this exact conversation far too many times. He poured a more than generous shot of cognac into the coffee and handed it to the reluctant Skid, whose stomach heaved at the smell of the liquor.

"It helps clear the gas haze."

"Gas?"

"Oh yes. You thought you were hungover from the cognacs you had with the cooks after dinner? No, no, you were gassed and robbed. It is not uncommon on these overnight trains."

Skid closed his eyes and braced himself against the shock of the evil-smelling black liquid. After the initial jolt of taste, the warmth and sweetness spread through him and it did, much to his surprise, have a very soothing and calming effect.

"Finish your coffee. I will inform the train captain. You wait here please," said the conductor, and left the dining car.

Skid realized the man was simply going through the motions. They both knew Skid's things were already far away, making the rounds of the back streets of some port where a new ¡think 9.7 with travel dox would fetch a good price.

The conductor soon returned with his supervisor. "Sir," said the train captain, "as I am sure you now know, this is not an entirely uncommon occurrence on these trains. It is regrettable and we do take all the steps we can to minimize it, but I am sure you will agree it is a daunting task. Particularly if our passengers forget to lock their doors, as sometimes happens."

Skid shrugged helplessly, unable to confirm or deny this.

"Normally," the man continued, "these things are solely an annoyance and a monetary loss. Unfortunately, Outer Azhuur is more stringent than most places. We will arrive at the Outer Azhuurse frontier in under an hour. I am, of course, working on the assumption that your ¡think was taken too."

Skid felt his scalp prickle with sweat again. He nodded and looked at the floor.

"All I can do when we reach the frontier is tell them you showed me your identity in a misunderstanding over compartment reservations. Please write out your full name, date and place of birth, and your ¡dentity number so we can all be in concord on the facts when questioned by the military."

VII

"¡thinks! ¡thinks! Set to ¡dentity! Travel dox! Frontier Control!" called the youth with the heavy machine gun as he made his way through the train. He awkwardly scrutinized each passenger's ¡think using the two mounted mirrors on his helmet, in observance of a recent Outer Azhuurse diktat against looking directly at the screen, intended to protect the nation's soul from corrupting Outlander influences.

Skid sat in the dining car with the train captain and listened to the dreaded voice coming closer, door slam by door slam. Skid forced a grin. "Sounds like someone who enjoys his work."

The train captain tried to smile reassuringly.

Skid had that childhood you're-in-for-it-now knot in his gut. It made his limbs heavy and slowed time down into a molasses-like sewer of pure dread. His breathing was loud in his ears and his palms felt too big for his hands.

Boy Soldier slammed the dining car's sliding door shut behind him and did his best to act like the shattering of its glass was intentional. He was a slight youth who had been given a grown man's uniform and equipment. He was grievously overarmed for the task of checking travel papers on a train. He was barely old enough to shave but had clearly tried to grow a mustache from a few feeble sproutings that disfigured his upper lip. Skid could not look at him without wanting to scream: *For fuck sake, just shave off that horrible mess and start again!* Recognizing the prevailing imbalance of power and weaponry, he refrained.

"¡thinks! ¡thinks! Show ¡dentity! Travel dox! Frontier Control!" Boy Soldier squinted at Skid with his small, mirthless eyes. Skid did his best not to stare at the clumsy mirrors swinging from his helmet.

Skid retold his story with help from the train captain.

Boy Soldier nodded and rubbed his chin. "No way undocumented Outlanders cross our frontier," he said in Yute, the English vernacular he had learned from shooting games before the recent ban on ether-based devices. "Let's go, dude."

"What? Where?" asked Skid. He looked to the train captain

to intervene. The captain shrugged helplessly. "How long will this take? What about my train?"

"No idea, dude. Maybe you make this train before the transfers are done. Vamoose!" Boy Soldier snapped.

"Transfers?" said Skid.

The train captain nodded. "Yes, we still have some time. The track gauges are different in Azhuur. We must change trains. We could be another hour maybe."

"But they're waiting for me at the other border. I have to—"

Boy Soldier jerked his machine gun toward the door. "Zip it! Lessgo, Outlander!"

Skid looked around for his stuff, remembered with a jolt that he no longer had any, and left the train car feeling the muzzle of Boy Soldier's machine gun uncomfortably close to his spine.

⚭

Colonel Prager gave the undocumented Outlander a once-over and then motioned him to sit down on what had once been the backseat of a school bus. No connoisseur of fashion, even Colonel Prager could not help but be struck by the historical and sartorial incongruity of this somewhat disheveled teddy boy now in his custody.

"You will complete these papers," he said, his clipped, formal diction in stark contrast to Boy Soldier's.

Boy Soldier took two thick printed forms from a drawer and handed them to Skid.

"You will need this," added the colonel, and handed him a pen. It was engraved with, *Colonel E. Prager, Commander, Frontier Post 17,* and a tiny crest depicting a griffin carrying a small dog in its claws. The colonel was inordinately proud of these pens. He had sent a courier forty miles over mountains to deliver two dozen to his illiterate mother.

"Nice pen," said Skid, self-preservation allowing his instinct to flatter to win out over his aversion to being civil to anything in a uniform.

109

"You will proceed," said the colonel.

Skid plowed his way through the questions on the forms. He didn't have the energy to object to the absurdity of telling this man his mother's birthday, at what age he left school, whether he had ever taken part in any international terrorist activities, if he planned to do so while passing through or remaining in the territory of Outer Azhuur, date and place of birth, etc., etc.

The colonel took the completed forms and clicked his tongue pensively. He picked up his radio and made a series of unintelligible rasping sounds into it, nodded, and switched it off again. "We will have to await confirmation from the nearest ¡think hub to your point of embarkation."

"How long will that take?" asked Skid.

"Difficult to predict. A week, perhaps two."

"What?"

"Calm yourself. Vociferating will achieve nothing. It will not move Paris any closer to us and it will certainly not make your stay here any more pleasant."

"You mean you have to talk to ¡think Paris?"

"No, no, no, that would not work at all. We do not talk to the Out There. We must write to them, on paper, like civilized people, send them a copy of your details, and then wait for them to make some investigations, reissue your ¡think, and then contract a diplomatic technician to make a formal identification and provide you with temporary transit authorization to continue your journey. We cannot give you a visitor's permit to remain here, nor an exit permit to leave, as we have no proof of who you are. We are willing to overlook that irregularity for the moment. In the meantime, you will remain here in confinement."

"But I have to be in Inner Azhuur—they're expecting me!"

Colonel Prager arched his eyebrows theatrically. "You do, do you? They are, are they? And why is that?"

"I am the Adjutant. In the show. *So You Wanna Run a Country?* or whatever."

"You? Adjutant? In that ridiculous outfit? Ha ha ha. Take him away!"

"Lessgo, Outlander, confinement time!" Boy Soldier snarled, and motioned Skid out of the colonel's office with his machine gun. He smiled as the train Skid should be on shuddered into motion and creaked away from the border post toward Spizt, the capital, and then on to its terminus at the border with Inner Azhuur.

VIII

"Patron D'Izmaïe, Regent, Consort, eminences, peers, pubble of Azhuur, I have grave news to impart to you," began the Utterminster, nodding toward the statue of D'Izmaïe on the bridge. From the Balcony of Pronouncements, he spoke into the open mouth of a small porcelain carp about six inches long. His voice came from the opticons everywhere in Azhuur with unnatural clarity. It was accompanied by an overhead view of the gentry assembled in front of the Quartel. The Regent, Consort, eminences, peers, and pubble all listened intently; the pubble stopped wherever they were by the announcement, fearing this was all just a pretext for another bread cut; the peers and eminences assembled in front of the Quartel half expecting another purge. Mooney and Wendy were wondering what on earth was happening now as they sat beside the Archixprest on the balcony.

The ¡seers struggled to keep the sound feed clean as they scrambled to capture this unscheduled announcement. However these opticons worked, they played havoc with the ether for the ¡sees. This sort of shit was so totally NOT supposed to happen. Nikolian, in his capacity as field producer, frantically nudged Brad on his ¡think to get instructions.

The Utterminster continued, greatly enjoying the obvious

consternation of the ¡seers at this unscripted announcement: "Our Monger of External Affairs has learned that the forces of traitorous Outer Azhuur"—here he paused for the loud hissing and vomiting sounds from the crowd—"have detained He Who Was Chosen to Be Adjutant to Our Regent."

Here, all twisted their noses to Mooney and simultaneously gave vent to their relief that the grave news did not concern them, and to their disgust at the unspeakable effrontery of the traitorous Outer Azhuurse. It was a strange and unrepeatable sound.

Brad nudged Nikolian back: "Go with it. This looks like good stuff. Get more reaction shots—it's real. No one was expecting this. We're doing a live special. ¡balls on fire. They smell war. Gaming ¡farm is all lit up!"

The Utterminster pressed on: "Instead of the small welcoming party that was planned to retrieve the Adjutant at the border, we have determined, in the spirit of magnanimous and peaceable dealing with our *neighbors*, to send the full complement of the Quartel's elite under the aegis of General D'Izmaïe to deal with the traitorous Outer Azhuurse on this matter." There was some confused hissing, scattered whooping, and a few bits of reverential nose-twisting. "Fear not! We will return triumphant with a right-hand man: an aide, auxiliary, and adviser for our most illustrious Regent Mooney."

Lots more whooping followed, some chanting, "*Azhuur will Prevail! Azhuur will Prevail!*"

"And so, to give good fortune to our venture and to impress upon the people of traitorous Outer Azhuur the importance to us of our citizens and rulers, I, on behalf of the whole council, humbly entreat our great Exalted Regent to accompany us in processional mode as we, a panoply of personages, leave other important business aside to take this matter of principle in hand and give it the utmost importance."

The crowd hesitated, not knowing if the speech was over, and then, concluding it was, whooped politely, and chanted a little more, uncertain what exactly was being announced to them. The Utterminster had been extremely tired by the time he got around to drafting the final paragraph, and it wasn't up to his usual rabble-rousing standard.

IX

Skid woke alone in Colonel Prager's office. He stood up and stretched away the aches of sleeping on the sofa. He was glad to be free of the hot, cramped shed he'd shared with the ailing diesel generator.

Prager had moved Skid to his office in the middle of the night, following his urgent radio call from General Bastrik. There were two people in the world the colonel feared: Boy Soldier's mother, whom he'd had the misfortune to meet one day when she came to bring freshly knit underwear to her darling son, and General Bastrik.

The general had conducted a long midnight radio conversation with the Utterminster of Azhuur. Their friendship predated the animosity between the two states. The Utterminster had forewarned the general that he was going to make a big production of the Adjutant's abduction. The general took the news in the sporting vein in which it was offered.

After his conversation with the Utterminster, General Bastrik had radioed Colonel Prager and conveyed his displeasure about this cock-up with terrifying clarity. The colonel could vent his spleen on Boy Soldier, but ultimately the blame would be laid on him and he would be lucky to find himself supervising sheep at a mountain pass as reward.

So, it was a much-altered Colonel Prager who opened the locked door of his office to bid his captive good morning. He carried a breakfast tray laden with goodies from his own black-market hoard—a stark contrast to the pineapple-and-on-ion-flavored gruel and the cloudy water that burned his nostrils which Boy Soldier had previously given Skid.

Skid sensed things had greatly changed overnight. The harder Prager worked to dismiss what had happened, the more it became obvious that he had screwed up monumentally and was now very, very worried about it. Skid stared blankly at him while drinking his fine coffee and eating his toasted muffins slathered with real apple blossom honey.

Finally, Prager gave in to his lowest, most desperate urgings: "Look, please don't tell them about the generator room. It has taken me ten years to get to here. I can't bear to be sent to the mountains again. It's horrible. They eat their dead up there. Please. Help me."

"Yeah, sure, whatever," Skid said after an excruciatingly long pause, and then stood up and walked out onto the porch of Prager's tin hut to smoke one of the colonel's imported cigarettes. He squinted into the already-hot, exceedingly bright air. He peered at the rickety buildings and the arid landscape with its few unusual-looking hardy plants and wondered how he had ended up in such a place. It had all seemed so predictable and dreamy once the band went to London: a few years on the road, gigs, groupies, drugs, drink, the occasional outrageous inter-view, and a lot of pricking around in the studio. Then, more or less forgotten, he would have retired to the south of France with his former-publicist bride and raced motorbikes or collected old planes or something. That was how it was supposed to go.

That the daydream version had not worked out was no big surprise, but he still could not quite get his head around how one little thing after another had happened and now here he was in the middle of some loony revolution in a place he had never heard of, smoking with a colonel straight out of one of those war comics he used to read when he was a kid. The thought of it jolted him and he felt very small, very lost, and very far from anything he understood. He watched the incongruous high-tech windmills that lined the horizon.

"Billions in cohesion funding for those. There are thousands of them. General Bastrik's brother-in-law built most of them and is now a very wealthy man. Most of the time they aren't on. There is currently very little demand, if you will pardon the pun."

Skid looked once at Prager and then back at the windmills. He waited in thickening silence.

"Uhm, well then, I'll leave you to your, uhm, sightseeing, shall I?" said Prager.

"Yeah, you do that," answered Skid without taking his eyes off the horizon.

X

"Udder, I got your nudge. What's up?"

"I am here with the Archixprest and your operative Nikolian."

"I know that. I can see you. That's why we use the ¡box, but if we're going the way of formalities, you can see I am here with no one. I want to get my head around this before I get any of the suits in on it. So, share."

"You are apprised of what has befallen our Adjutant en route to us?"

"Yeah. No ¡think. No travel dox. Detained by your bat-shit-crazy neighbors at the frontier. We got good ¡balls on your speech. Limped a bit toward the end, but pretty good. Now what?"

"My Monger of External Affairs has opened diplomatic back channels with the Outer Azhuurse high command."

"Nikolian, do we have this?"

"No, I have a re-cre team on it right now. We will double it up as a teaser for the game platform."

"Great. You got scripting working on this development?"

"Yes, we have some possible arcs in the works. Possible wizard motif for the gaming platform. We'll decide once Profiles get a good sense of him."

"Great. Sorry, Udder. Please continue."

"We have reached an accord with the traitorous Outer Azhuurse. They will drive the Adjutant to our side of the inner border and make a peaceable surrender. To enforce the importance of this event, and to crown our new Adjutant's arrival with a suitably impressive display, we will deploy the Tower of Thrones."

"The what of what? Nikolian, what is this?"

"Ah yes, I think this is a visual," said Nikolian. "I have a secure ¡seer at the hangar now, if you would like to see it."

"Hangar? Wow, sure, bring it on."

"One second while I add the feed . . ."

"Okay, I see it. But what on earth am I looking at? How big is that thing? Can someone go and stand beside it? Is it coming out of the side of a mountain?"

"I defer to the Archixprest on this."

"Okay, Archie. Share!"

The Archixprest leaned in: "Good morning, Producer Brad. The Tower of Thrones you see before you is an ancient Inner Azhuurse artifact. It consists of two master thrones for the Regent and Mistress Consort which sit on a slightly larger throne, which sits on another larger throne, which sits in its turn on another slightly larger throne, and so on through descending importance of the permitted occupants until we reach the lowermost throne, the dimensions of which dictate, a fortiori, the overall dimensions of the Tower itself, to wit, the overall height is approximately seven hundred feet and the sides are each three hundred feet. The legs of the lowermost throne are twenty feet by twenty feet. When in ceremonial use, the dignitaries sit on their assigned tier on replicas of the Regent's throne which are adorned with carvings of the Tower of Thrones itself, complete with the miniature thrones on each tier. It is a recursive infinitude of ever more intricate furniture making: Inner Azhuur's feudal pyramid rendered in wood, if you will."

"Astro-fucking-nomical! ¡balls and gamers are going to love this! But how do you get that thing all the way to the border?"

"Set into the base of each of the bottommost legs is a polished marble sphere some twelve feet in diameter. The structure is drawn along on a set of hardwood tracks congruent to the dimensions of these spheres. There are four 150-foot tracks for each side. If you watch carefully, you will see the Tower begin its move out of its anchorage. It is drawn by a team of three thousand hauliers—the position, like many others, is hereditary."

The ¡seer zoomed out to let Brad see the hauliers.

"Cleo-fucking-patra, this is wild!"

"When the Tower passes off a piece of track, the track sappers will move that piece to the front to receive it, and so on."

"How do you turn it then?"

"If needed, there are retracting trundles on the underside of the tracks."

Brad gaped as the Tower ground along the tracks. "So how do people get up onto it?"

"There is a service tower of two elevators at the back."

"What about uphill? Worse, downhill?"

"No concern. There is nothing but flatness between here and the border. Shall I outline the route?"

"No, no need. Can we get an ¡seer up top there?"

"No! No devices on the Tower. Only anointed dignitaries."

"No worries. Nikolian, you can use a couple of ¡flys."

"I have three ¡flys on standby and six ¡seers to travel with the procession," said Nikolian.

"You are the best, Nikolian. Coordinate with Flower to get the game people up on this Tower shit immediately. Intrinsicate this to the game platforms in time for the rescue. This is ¡balla-cious. Okay, everyone, great Intimeet. Let's roll!"

XI

"I have to be up there for three days? How do I eat, shit, sleep?" protested Mooney.

"My liege, you can descend for sleeping and meals and other necessities," said the Clarion.

"But why do I have to travel alone on that stupid thing at all?"

"It is important that the pubble see you. It is vital that the traitorous Outer Azhuurse are appropriately shunned."

"Okay. But do I have to be up there every minute in case someone wanders along to see me? Can't you organize them to gather every five miles or so? That would give me plenty of time to not be up there. I promise, when we get close to the border, I will stay up there."

"I will see what can be arranged, my liege."

"Thank you, Clarion."

⚭

"Everyone ready?" called Nikolian.

"¡seer one, go."

"¡seer two, rolling."

"¡flys on the wing."

Brad broke in: "Okay, I'm seeing full feed from all ¡seers. We're good to go. In three, two, one . . . game face everyone!"

TOM

Welcome to this live special of *So You Wanna Run a Country?* Last episode you saw how Regent Mooney received the distressing news that Adjutant Skid had been abducted by the Outer

Azhuurse. Well, that's not going to fly! Sandra, take us through what we are looking at here.

SANDRA

Thanks, Tom. What we are seeing here is the assembly of the expedition to the border to retrieve the Adjutant. In front you see the massive hulk of the Tower of Thrones.

TOM

Almost seven hundred feet tall, three hundred feet wide, twenty thousand tons of solid wood. Three thousand hauliers, four hundred track layers, or sappers as they are called. This amazing structure, according to what I am told, took eight hundred artisans over five years to build almost eleven hundred years ago. Real history, people. Right there. In the flesh!

SANDRA

So much history! So many numbers! Amazing! On top we see Mooney, the Regent, with the figure of General D'Izmaïe. Tom, any intel on where the Mistress Consort is?

TOM

Sandra, she is traveling in the carriage directly behind the Tower of Thrones. Apparently, it is unacceptable for the Outer Azhuurse to lay eyes on her, a tradition of suspicion dating back many centuries.

SANDRA

So much rich history right here in front of us. Tom, I notice the Tower appears to be traveling backward. Is that a technical thing, or what?

TOM

Great question. This is a very significant gesture in the complex language of diplomatic (and sometimes not-so-diplomatic) relations between the two Azhuurs. By approaching the Outer Azhuurse with his back to them, the Regent is conveying his official displeasure. This, I am told by the Archixprest, has not been seen since the early 1200s.

SANDRA

Amazing! We are so fortunate to witness this. I see behind the Mistress Consort's carriage the Utterminster's stunning emerald-encrusted carriage, and behind that, the Archixprest's wheeled barge, and as far back as I can see, one carriage after another.

TOM

Yes, Sandra. All in order of importance on the Roll of Heraldic Favor. You'll notice how the carriages
diminish in elaborateness from six-
horse teams to four and then to two
and then to pubble power: ten-prole,
eight-prole teams and so on, down to
single-prole rickshaws.

SANDRA

And behind them that dense block of
foot soldiers. Four thousand of the
Inner Azhuurse Utterforz in full battle gear.

TOM

The Utterminster's Praetorian Guard,
as it were. They are loosely called
"Inner Azhuurse," but quite a few are
mercenaries from Outer Azhuur and
beyond.

SANDRA

I wouldn't want to get on the wrong
side of them. Ha ha. Still, what a
truly awesome sight. And behind them
almost on the horizon?

CUT TO ¡fly2 panning back along the parade and showing hundreds of provision
carts.

>   TOM
> Those are the provisions and caterers
> for this six-day round trip.

>   SANDRA
> I think I can safely say we have
> never had anything like this before
> on any of our *So You Wanna* shows.

>   TOM
> I think you're right, Sandra. This
> blows the final episode of *So You
> Wanna Be Buried in a Pyramid?* right
> out of the water.

Mooney sat on top of the ghastly Tower of Thrones, alone except for the D'Izmaïe statue on the floor beside his throne. For such a long journey, it was not practical to have each throne level loaded with its full complement of courtiers. The Clarion was greatly relieved not to have to revise the purge and honors lists for the seating protocols. The haulier teams were similarly relieved to be spared all the extra weight on such a long journey.

For reasons not entirely clear, tradition dictated this enormous structure still needed to give warning of its proximity. To this end, the Tower herald, another of Inner Azhuur's hereditary and utterly useless offices for the gentry, walked five hundred yards ahead of the tracks waving a small red flag on a long whalebone stick to warn anyone who might otherwise fail to notice the approach of tracks, sappers, three thousand hauliers, and the grotesque hulk of the Tower of Thrones.

The state circus, as some of the more irreverent and daring referred to it in undertones, moved out of Azhuur Kapital and into what appeared to be a dried river bed. The pubble had been marshaled and were out in force to cheer their new regent on his first foreign mission. They did not know what had hit them. They had not seen so much spectacle since the death of General D'Izmaïe and many initially feared they were already seeing the fallout from Mooney's assassination and the prelude to some new power struggle.

Mooney looked over his shoulder at the long lines of sweating and straining figures inching the Tower along its tracks. He repeated to himself the strict instructions not to wave at the multitudes.

Wendy sat in her jeweled carriage and glowered at the tray of pastries the Spinster Uilkitz offered her. "Why can't I go back to the Quartel and ride out the day after tomorrow and catch up with you all? This. Is. So. Fucking. SLOW."

"I am afraid not, madam. This caravan is an official public spectacle, and your presence is essential."

"Why? So the Outer Azhuurse can't look at me? They could still *not* look at me if I stayed at home. Oh god, this is awful. I could walk faster!"

"Madam, I understand your frustration. But if we make gestures of disdain to the Outer Azhuurse, they must not be empty gestures. That would be spiritually corrosive."

"What about the corrosion on my ass sitting here like this for the next three days?"

"Try one of the pastries. My sister baked them. They are her *special* recipe. I do believe they will help pass the time."

Wendy arched her eyebrows: "Special? Are you having one?"

"I had two of the little filled croissants before we set out. I highly recommend them. Now, when I look out the window, I see a beautiful alpine landscape hurtling past. It's quite wonderful. Particularly all the lithe, naked, and oiled shepherds. I imagine the tiny scones are quite entertaining too."

XII

Skid stood on the shaded porch of Colonel Prager's shed watching the landscape buckle and shimmer under the midday sun. He noticed the growing dust cloud on the horizon and from it heard the approaching drone of engines.

Colonel Prager ran out of his shed and started barking orders at his troops, one of whom climbed up onto the roof to beat some of the dust off the three-headed wolf flag that sagged in the dull, still heat. Skid used his hands to shade against the sun's glare and saw a huge convoy of jeeps and trucks emerge from its own dust storm.

Colonel Prager shifted his weight from one foot to the other. He frowned, searching desperately for more orders he could bark at someone, but for once his troops were carrying out his orders to the letter and were busy assembling themselves into a creditable guard of honor. Boy Soldier was particularly eager to make sure everything was perfect.

The convoy drew up with a growling of engines desperately in need of a good tuning. Prager bounded forward to greet General Bastrik, who leaped out of his jeep before any of his flunkies could open the door for him. Prager drew himself to attention and saluted stiffly.

"Inside now, dogbrain!" General Bastrik snapped at Prager without returning his salute, and stormed toward the shed. On the porch, he acknowledged Skid with the slightest nod before striding inside.

Colonel Prager stood gaping around him for a few moments before he collected himself enough to stab his finger at Boy Soldier and gesture toward the shed. The colonel passed Skid without meeting his eyes and Boy Soldier scuttled along behind him looking like the unfortunate kid who has already shat himself in the first ten minutes of the day-long school trip.

Moments later, Boy Soldier appeared on the porch. "Please

go inside," he shout-whispered, gesturing hopelessly toward the door.

"Me? Really? Oh gosh." Skid beamed like some ecstatic pageant winner.

General Bastrik sat behind Prager's desk with his feet on the table. He twirled a length of electrical cord between his fingers and stared nonchalantly out the small window. Prager and Boy Soldier trembled at attention in the corner.

The general strode from behind the desk to shake Skid's hand: "I am General Bastrik. Delighted to make your acquaintance. I would hate to think these unfortunate bungled circumstances might sour the beginnings of a cordial acquaintance. Please, my friend, sit." He ushered Skid to the sofa, then sat back behind Prager's desk. He paused. He sighed. He picked up a photograph. "Your family?" he asked Prager with unmistakable menace in his voice.

"Yes, My General. My father is deceased but my mother—"

"Is still living on your family's remote and poorly fortified wheat plot in the foothills," concluded Bastrik darkly. "I know. I have been fully briefed."

The colonel got the message loud and clear. He stood stockstill and began to sweat slowly and steadily under his arms and in the crook of his elbows. There was no photograph of Boy Soldier's family, but he was already experienced enough to know what was being insinuated: formidable as his mother might be, she would be no match for one of General Bastrik's squads. Boy Soldier also knew howling for leniency now would be the worst possible thing he could do.

Bastrik meticulously tied a scaffold knot in the electrical cord and pulled the noose tight with agonizing slowness. "Now, there seems to have been some manner of grave misunderstanding here. My task is to get the facts, assign culpability, which there must be in a case like this so shot through with patent idiocy, and then decide on disciplinary action. Our honored guest from the Outlands is here to help us establish the pertinent facts, and it is to him I will direct myself. You two undisciplined yahoos will remain silent unless I address you. Understood?"

"Yes, My General!" bellowed Colonel Prager and Boy Soldier.

"Now, my friend, please tell me, in your own words and in as much detail as you can remember, how you came to be detained here by Colonel Prager and his, ahem, *men*."

Ten minutes later, General Bastrik had established the facts of Skid's arrival at the frontier without travel documents. "Were you in any way mistreated while in detention here?" he demanded.

The silence in the room crackled and buzzed.

Skid cleared his throat. Out of the corner of his eye, he watched Boy Soldier and Colonel Prager. For a moment, he was dizzy with the realization the next words out of his mouth could be a matter of life or death for both of them. It was exhilarating, heady, utterly sickening. It made the inside of his mouth tingle. He knew what he had to do. "I would have to say I was not mistreated in any major way, and the whole thing was a stupid mistake and we should all just forget it."

General Bastrik took a moment to compose himself before turning on Prager and Boy Soldier. "You two, out of my sight! Be thankful that this well-meaning, simple young man has seen fit not to lodge a formal allegation of mistreatment. Be very careful, both of you, because I will be watching. You won't see me, but I will be there. Out! Your detachment will ride in the trucks with the conscripts. Count yourselves lucky I don't tie you to my jeep and drag you all the way to the border."

Prager and Boy Soldier saluted stiffly and backed out the door, craven and chastised.

"I hope your forgiving nature serves you well in your silly Inner Azhuurse role-play game," the general said. "You may use this hut if it is to your liking while we make preparations for departure, or you may join me in the command jeep. We will be leaving for the border with Inner Azhuur as soon as the convoy has refueled."

Skid shrugged. "I think I'll just wait here, if it's all the same to you."

"Very well. I will send for you when we are ready." General Bastrik saluted coldly and left the room.

XIII

Skid woke again, this time stiff and badly rested in the back of General Bastrik's jeep. It had grown dark shortly after they left Colonel Prager's shed, so he had not seen a lot of Outer Azhuur. What little he had was surprisingly pleasant. Once they went down the mountain from the border, the land had grown lush and easy on the eye, rolling green hills and small towns along the way. Now it seemed they had climbed again and were on another high plateau where the landscape was back to being dry and stony.

He watched a slowly growing dust cloud on the southern horizon. All the Outer Azhuurse troops who had been lounging around smoking and scuffling started dashing about trying to follow General Bastrik's orders. When Skid got out of the jeep, he noticed it: stretching as far as he could see to left and right, they were separated from whatever was approaching by an expanse of bright red ash.

"What the fuck . . . ?"

"Our inner border," answered Bastrik. "It runs the entire perimeter of Inner Azhuur and is three miles wide."

"For fuck sake, I know borders are red lines on maps, but you lunatics had to go and burn an actual red line into the ground? What is wrong with you?"

"I am assured it can be seen from space. If it had been possible to chisel off Inner Azhuur and float it away into the seas, we would have. This is the best we have: a toxic red line in the sand.

Believe me, the feeling is mutual, as you will no doubt find out when you get to the other side.

"You can see by the dust cloud on the other side that our neighbors have arrived. It falls to us, as the transgressors, to make the journey to the other side of the borderline. I strongly suggest you use this if you ever plan on having children or have any wish to continue seeing or tasting food. The ash is very fine and full of large, complex, unstable molecules." The general held out an antiquated gas mask. "Don't worry, it is fully functional and will provide adequate protection for the short crossing. Private Prager will not be needing it."

"*Private?* That was fast. He is staying on this side?"

"Oh, no, I changed my mind. He and his young soldier are already on their new assignment high in the mountains. There is a goat pen of great strategic importance that requires the kind of security that only highly trained soldiers like them can provide." Bastrik's slight smile quickly died. "One of them informed the Inner Azhuurse of your presence. I am uncertain which, and while I could easily force either of them to confess to it, both will be punished."

Before Skid could respond, something strange appeared over the horizon. The hulking shape of the Tower of Thrones sent a fearful murmur through the Outer Azhuurse troops that gave Bastrik a new opportunity to shout at them.

⚬⚬

Keeping the train tracks to their left, the Outer Azhuurse contingent moved steadily across the scorched red earth of the borderline.

Although he traveled in the front jeep where the dust was minimal, Skid was glad to have the gas mask. "Ah, now, lads, what the fuck is that thing?" he shouted when they drew closer to the other side of the border and the full extent of the Tower of Thrones became visible.

When the ropes and the proles hauling it could be distinguished through the dust, Skid got an uneasy sensation in the pit of his stomach. He then looked behind him at the rest of the Outer Azhuurse convoy and the cloud of unnatural red dust it was sending up in its wake.

⁞

The Outer Azhuurse stopped on the toxic red dirt of the borderline where the train tracks ended, and General Bastrik walked with Skid to the edge into the shadow of the Tower of Thrones. There was some scuffling as Bastrik's escort made it painfully clear to the encroaching ¡seer that the capturing of images of Outer Azhuurse would not be tolerated.

The Utterminster's carriage advanced from behind the Tower of Thrones. The Monger of External Affairs ran behind it to open the door when it stopped. The Utterminster stepped down and walked to the border's edge. He stood facing Bastrik and ceremonially slapped him on the cheek.

"You, General Bastrik, will not foul the soil of Inner Azhuur with your presence. Although you cannot see it, know this: Our Regent is at this moment pointing the icon of General D'Izmaïe at you in admonishment, a sight you are not worthy to behold but one that should give you great shame. You will wait until we are out of sight before you recross the border. We will not be sullied by the dust of your departure."

The Utterminster then slapped Bastrik again and walked Skid back to the caravan, to the accompaniment of much whooping and nose-twisting from the exhausted Inner Azhuurse.

Skid was formally introduced to the Archixprest, the Utterminster, and Wendy before the Archixprest ushered him into the elevator to be hoisted up to join Mooney on top of the Tower of Thrones.

⁞

"Howya, nice throne! I'm Skid, your new Adjutant or whatever."

"Nice to meet you, Skid. I'm Mooney."

"That your real name?"

"That yours?"

"Yep."

"That your statue?"

"The rider used to be. I used to call him Captain Dude. Turns out he was General D'Izmaïe all along, just needed to get home to his horse. You always dress like that?"

"Yeah. It started as a costume. I was a street-theater ted in Glasgow. But I kind of like it now."

"Yeah. It's cool. It works for you. You should probably sit down, Skid. It's going to be a long, slow journey."

Skid flopped into the throne beside Mooney's and put his feet on the rump of D'Izmaïe's horse like an ottoman.

"Not sure I would do that," said Mooney, "some of them around here are very devoted to that thing."

"Fair enough. Respect that." Skid took his feet down. "Miserable, angry-looking little fucker, though, isn't he?"

"I never noticed it so much until they put him on the horse, but yeah, he is. I used to have him on a skateboard. He looked less angry."

"Makes sense. Oh, by the way, the little old lady in the carriage with your girlfriend sent these." From his pocket, Skid produced a selection of special pastries wrapped in a silk handkerchief. "She said they would help with the journey." He popped a mini scone in his mouth and then passed the selection to Mooney.

Mooney took two fruit tartlets and munched them hungrily. "You should have another, Skid. We might as well enjoy ourselves while we're stuck up here."

The mini scone was already kicking in as Skid took a raspberry tartlet. "Oh wow, I see what you mean. Fucking brilliant!"

Fortunately, the effects of the Relict Uilkitz's special pastries had more or less worn off when the Tower of Thrones was maneuvered into place in front of the Quartel. As soon as the gentry had parked their carriages and were arranged around its base according to rank, Wendy, the Utterminster, the Archixprest, and the Clarion boarded the elevator to the top tier.

"Wait for it," whispered Mooney to Skid as waited for the elevator to arrive. "There's probably going to be some business with people hitting themselves on the head with a fish. Just go with it."

"That's my job? Just go with it?"

"As far as I can make out, yeah."

The opticons snapped back to life and the ¡sees started streaming their images.

> TOM
>
> Hi, everyone. Welcome to this special livecast of *So You Wanna Run a Country?* What are we looking at here, Sandra?

> SANDRA
>
> Tom, to be honest, I'm just guessing here, but I suspect it may be some kind of welcoming ceremony for the Adjutant?

The Utterminster made sure he was featured on all the opticons before he nodded to the Clarion, who then spoke into the porcelain carp: "Honorable Regent, Mistress Consort, peers, dignitaries, citizens of Azhuur, interloping Outlanders, pubble of Azhuur, I give you His Utterness, the Utterminster of Azhuur!"

The Utterminster took the porcelain carp from the Clarion and quelled the carefully choreographed cheering of the gentry:

"We are returned triumphant, having humiliated the perfidious Outer Azhuurse and retrieved from their clutches the Adjutant to our Regent."

Skid appeared briefly on the opticons and waved awkwardly.

The Utterminster continued: "I will be the first and the last to welcome our new Adjutant." He took the fresh carp the Archixprest had been carrying and struck himself on the forehead. "Behold the Carp of Acquaintanceship! Be we now acquainted! Azhuur be served!"

Skid stood patiently staring into space while the carp was passed to Mooney, then to Wendy and to the Archixprest and the Clarion, before going back to the Utterminster, who repeated the greeting.

"Eh, thanks very much?" said Skid.

The Utterminster ignored this and spoke once more into the porcelain carp: "Be it now known that the Adjutant, among his other duties, will serve as Keeper of the Regent's Lions and Overseer of the Consort's Portraitist. Azhuur be served!"

The opticons went dark.

"We finished? I'm bursting for a piss," announced Skid.

Wendy would probably have contained her laughter had it not been for the look of horror and furious disdain that the Utterminster so spectacularly failed to disguise.

"We will reconvene this evening for your welcoming banquet, Adjutant," said the Clarion preempting any explosion from the Utterminster. "The Spinster Uilkitz will show you to your chambers when we get to the ground."

"Honestly, I just need the jakes before I piss meself."

The Utterminster snorted loudly and strode toward the elevator, followed closely by the Archixprest, who was now apparently in charge of disposing of the Carp of Acquaintanceship.

"We should probably let them take the elevator by themselves," said Wendy.

"I concur, Mistress Consort," said the Clarion, a barely detectable sparkle of laughter in his eyes.

XIV

"What the fuck? After all that mad rigmarole, everyone wanders off like they just remembered they needed to buy milk?" Skid's voice echoed around the now empty banquet hall.

"Yeah. They did one for us when we arrived. Ended the same way," said Mooney.

"But ours was really nuts," said Wendy. "Our little table kept moving around and there was the whole floor show of putting D'Izmaïe back on his horse. Remember that, Mooney?"

Mooney could barely speak through his laughter: "They lowered the statue down out of the roof and dropped it onto the horse. And there was a little pole in the saddle of the horse, so it looked like it was going into General D'Izmaïe's ass."

"Which it was," added Wendy.

"And the revolving floor? What's the deal with all that? I was already dizzy from the wine," said Skid.

"Oh, there was a lot more business with that for our banquet. That was soooo stupid!" shouted Wendy.

"So, in the morning, Mooney, am I supposed to feed your lions?" asked Skid.

"I have no lions. It's a symbolic office."

"Symbollix, all right. So I suppose you don't have a portrait painter who needs watching either?"

"Correct," smiled Wendy.

"Right. This place is fucking mad!" shouted Skid.

Mooney laughed loudly and then, as if suddenly aware of the Spinster Uilkitz waiting in her alcove to escort them all to their chambers and how his laughter echoed so hollowly around the banquet hall, stopped abruptly. With the dying echoes of his laugh, the mood seemed to shift gears.

"What the fuck am I doing here?" said Wendy in an undertone.

"Hiding out?" suggested Mooney. "What are *you* doing here, Skid?"

"Dunno? Running away? Not from anything in particular, just killing time, maybe? This gig just came along at the right time and I hopped on. You?"

"Not sure. Woke up with a dream inside my head and when I followed it, it led here."

Wendy shrugged. "Mooney brought me here. I needed to get out of Newer York."

"So we all just kinda ended up here?"

"I guess so," said Wendy. "Runaways. Fugitives."

"Oh, I like that. Los Fugitivos," said Skid. He refilled their wineglasses and raised his: "To the Regent, Consort, and Adjutant of Azhuur. To Los Fugitivos!"

"Los Fugitivos!" echoed Mooney and Wendy, and they all clinked their glasses.

From the half light of the hall around them came the soft sound of the Spinster Uilkitz chuckling softly to herself.

FOUR

DELVINGS

I

Alva finally reached the top of the ramp and rolled onto the ground and away from the slow pulse of bodies dragging themselves up behind her. Her legs spasmed and twitched with exhaustion. Every week the climb got a little longer. This afternoon's collapse of part of the ramp really didn't help. If what people had been saying was true, the pit was going to go a lot deeper, and once the climb in and out each day became too long, they would stop coming back to the surface at all. The back of her neck itched with sweat at the thought of eventually having to live under a tarp on a stony shelf near the bottom of the pit. Still, she reflected, it was better than being one of those who hauled the dirt from the excavation to the border with Outer Azhuur to build a decorative rampart.

She sat up and checked the inside pocket of her smock. The strip of leathery smoked meat was still there. She stared across the pit and could make out the night shift snaking its way down the ramp half a mile away on the opposite side. This gouging of the earth was unceasing. She pulled her gaze away from the tiny shapes of the night shift and looked at the others around her who were also waiting for the strength to come back into their legs before the walk back to the shelters.

As if in answer to some unheard command, the group around Alva got up and began the walk back to the camp, just in time to make room for the next exhausted wave to lie down and catch their breath and let their legs recover. Alva shuffled along, glad of the press of tired bodies around her to make and keep pace. Otherwise, she feared, she would just lie down on the path and sleep.

Beside her, a girl who couldn't have been more than fifteen stumbled and her legs buckled under her. Alva grabbed her elbow and kept her upright. The girl stared blankly into Alva's eyes and then plodded along after the barest nod of thanks.

Alva's preoccupations lurched jaggedly along in time with her footfalls. How much longer would her grandmother languish? Why her grandmother and not her? Why her grandmother at all? Wasn't this sorry excuse for a life already hard enough?

Her grandmother had been among the first affected by the visions, assaulted night after night with hideous dreams of being buried alive. They had been on a recobbling road gang and at first Alva thought it had something to do with whatever liquid they were using to shine the cobblestones. After a couple of weeks, her grandmother said she had dreamed she was the statue of General D'Izmaïe being buried alive. Each night the dreams grew more powerful and racking, and each night there were more dreamers: in the fields, in the mines, on the road gangs, among the servants in the Quartel. When the nightly visions became common knowledge in the Quartel, the Archixprest had gathered all the dreamers, exactly four hundred of them, into the Great Entrance Hall and interviewed them and made his dream interpretation according to what the Utterminster had already told him.

The Utterminster was very proud of the pharaonic scale of what was being proposed. He was also still numb from the waist down after using the statue and the Sisterhood's herb to push this idea repeatedly out into the ether and into the proles' dreams. The Archixprest pronounced launching D'Izmaïe into orbit from the bottom of a deep lake a richly spiritual gesture. This was a plan they could really mobilize around. Recobbling recently asphalted roads paled to frivolousness beside this new, grander, nation-building endeavor.

The dreams stopped the day the Archixprest turned his inaugural shovelful of dirt to reopen the old trepanium mine and the gentry decamped from the Quartel to be near the site—but the dreamers were left frightened, spent, and traumatized by the weeks of debilitating dreams. What if her grandmother started dreaming again and never got better? Alva pushed the thought from her for now.

She peeled away from the flow of bodies and down a rough path between two rows of makeshift shelters and crouched down to enter the shanty where she and her grandmother slept. The space was more crowded than usual, as the inhabitants of the lean-to next door had moved in after they all agreed to use its wood to give a decent cremation to the young man who had collapsed and died the day before. The man's mother sat forlornly in the corner fingering the family rune etched into the lid of the traditional heart pot that had settled over the ashes around her child's heart during the cremation. Next week they would scrounge up some flour to make dough, mix some of the ashes into it, and leave it out for the birds, sending him back into the circle of life.

Alva skirted the communal eating area in the middle and found her grandmother in the back corner where she had left her that morning, still on her back with her hands clutched together under her chin, staring up at the rough roof of branches and rags. Alva helped her grandmother to sit up and discreetly handed her the strip of smoked meat. "I got two of these by accident," she whispered.

"Oh, you are very lucky," her grandmother said unconvincingly.

Alva flinched. "I think the provisioner's boy may like me," she offered by way of further explanation.

"Be careful. I know the boy has no fuckrights, but don't draw the provisioner's attention. The provisioner has fuckrights. More of D'Izmaïe and Mög's poisonous *tradition*. Here." Alva's grandmother tore the strip of meat in two, a task made much more difficult by her missing thumbs. She handed half to Alva. "Take it. I don't have much appetite."

Every time Alva arrived back from the dig with an extra ration "found" or "left over," they went through the same ritual:
Alva pretending it was not her own meager midday ration; her
grandmother pretending to believe her and then pretending not
to be hungry enough to eat it all so Alva would have some. Yet
somehow it was working. With each day, her grandmother was
coming slowly back to herself and shaking off the sickly lassitude
the dreams had left behind. That was what mattered to Alva.
She could survive a few more weeks on half rations as long as her
grandmother kept getting better.

II

"Add more pubble!" shouted the Utterminster.

Brad looked up and waved angrily from the ¡box. "But
you've already got too many people down there all trying to do
the same thing. They are falling over each other. THAT'S the
problem."

Mooney and Skid burst giddily through the doors of the
council chamber.

"Sorry we're late," said Skid. "Mooney was trying to teach
me how to fence and we got into a whole thing with some fops
fighting each other to be our seconds."

"While it is fitting that the Regent pursue fencing," snarled
the Utterminster, "and that you accompany him as Adjutant, it
behooves both of you to conduct yourselves in a manner more
befitting of your station and less like overexcited schoolchildren."

While Mooney and Skid took their seats, Nikolian interjected a mollifying note: "To return to the subject at hand, there
is some disorganization and there are some issues with the dirt
quota. We have seen work teams dedicate themselves to stealing
dirt from other teams instead of digging it themselves. This is not
productive."

"And how are we supposed to motivate them without quotas?" scoffed the Utterminster. "Rely on their innate goodwill and patriotism?"

"The dirt quota caused this delay. Look at the footage," countered Brad. "That work team undermined the ramp because the dirt was easier and softer than anything nearby. That's why the ramp collapsed."

"But they should have known better!" retorted the Utterminster.

"Well, they didn't," said Wendy. "You unleashed a whole mess of people into an abandoned open-cast trepanium mine and told them to make it deeper, or else. No plan. Are you really surprised there are accidents?"

"With all due respect, Mistress Consort, you are a mathematician of sorts, an algorithmist, a wanted financial trickster. You thought I did not know about that? Ha! Anyway, you may make numbers dance and wealth evaporate, but you are no engineer."

Skid was suddenly paying closer attention. "Wait! What? That was you, Wendy? You did the Hedgeer Hemlein thing? That was so fucking brilliant. All those smug fuckers outed and broke. Wandering around shell-shocked, trying to figure out how to be Thoroughfarians, when they had never even had to open a door for themselves or wipe their own arses before. That was really fucking spectacular. Fair play!" He beamed broadly at Wendy, who grinned briefly before turning her attention back to the Utterminster.

"Correct, Utterminster, I am no engineer, but then you don't seem to have any engineers anywhere, do you? Did you have them all shot into a ditch as a sacrifice to your Mög?"

While Brad could see this sparring might be good for the ¡balls, they needed a solution fast. A massive hole in the ground *not* being dug by a disorganized peasant workforce wasn't going to work for him ¡ballwise for much longer. "Can we leave the bickering to one side?" he pleaded.

"I hear no constructive suggestions to better the current operations," responded the Utterminster.

"Oh, for fuck sake," said Wendy, "you have people counting dirt on the way out and recording it separately for each work team. You call that an operation?"

The Utterminster glowered at her. "I beg your pardon, Mistress Consort. Did you have something constructive to say here or are you merely venting? Would you care to share your wisdom on this topic in more detail so we may all bask in the reflected glory of your insight?"

"You are making dirt a commodity. You want dirt out of the pit as fast as possible. You don't want people wasting their time squabbling over it because it is how they get rewarded. One team, one objective. Everyone gets rewarded equally based on the daily tally. Saves on all the different counting. I know you guys love creating work, but if you want to speed it up, there's got to be a better way."

"I believe I may have a solution," said the Clarion in an operatic whisper, so quiet yet authoritative that it caused the hubbub of acrimony in the room to instantly die. All eyes and ¡sees on him, the Clarion continued: "We need to get the help of the Sisterhood."

The Archixprest smiled. Wendy's face lit up. Mooney and Skid looked around, trying to gauge the significance of what was being discussed.

The Utterminster ventured: "That is a fascinating proposition."

"We can enlist the Sisterhood to draw up work plans for the excavation," said the Clarion. "I am sure we can find a protocol that will work. I am, after all, the official conduit to the Sisterhood, and they used to oversee the trepanium mine."

"That sounds like a good idea," said Wendy.

"Well, if the Mistress Consort is so sure of herself," said the Utterminster, "perhaps she will help the Clarion in this endeavor.

It will provide something more than a mere ceremonial role, and I imagine it would bring Brad some ¡balls."

"I . . . I . . . I . . . uhm . . . okay . . . sure," managed Wendy. "While we are on the subject, what is the plan for filling the thing with water?"

There was a brief, uncomfortable silence.

"Moving on!" chirped the Archixprest. "The Sisterhood's charter actually encourages the use of their skills for the greater good, provided there is no direct contact with the outside world."

"Then we will leave it to you, Clarion and Mistress Consort," announced the Utterminster. "We look forward to a prompt increase in productivity. Azhuur be served!"

"Excellent idea, Your Utterness. Azhuur be served!" chorused the Clarion, eager to have the Utterminster feel ownership of this idea.

"But how are you going to fill it with water?" pressed Wendy.

"Yes, very good question, certainly worthy of further discussion," said the Archixprest.

Brad looked up from his ¡think. "Wendy, glad you are on the team."

"Well, that is enough for today, I think," said the Archixprest. The ¡box abruptly went dark.

III

The sun was not yet up and the grounds around the Quartel were still ankle-deep in mist when Wendy set out. It had been refreshing to spend the night at the Quartel away from the encampment's enervating crowdedness. As soon the dig began in earnest, the gentry had set up camp on the upwind side of the pubble's shanties to be near the action, leaving Azhuur Kapital and the Quartel mostly deserted.

Wendy hurried across the bridge and through the streets toward the rocky ridge the Spinster Uilkitz had pointed out. Once clear of the streets, she turned and waved back at the ¡seer who was trying to follow her at a discreet distance. "Good morning, Tej, you're up early." She hoped ruining the vérité look of his feed would deter him from following her. It did not.

It took her half an hour to reach the bottom of the ridge. The path was easy to find: it was marked by two glass pillars. Wendy started up the sandy switchback trail.

Tej called out to her: "Hey, Wendy, you're on your own. My ¡see is all messed up. It refuses to register that crazy cliff; it just shows empty space, and when I get on that path the whole thing dies. BIG resonance interference in the ether. I have never seen anything like it in my life. Total feed fry. I'm not going anywhere near that thing. ¡see you later."

Wendy climbed up the steep path. The exertion felt good. She stopped for breath at each switchback. Sweating despite the chill morning air and puffing for breath, she paused a moment before cresting the ridge.

The Outlying Hermitage could not have looked more unlike what Wendy's imagination had conjured. She had pictured either some fairy-tale castle, all turrets and arched windows and maybe a drawbridge, or a humble cliff-dwelling type thing filled with ascetics in caves or mud huts. Nothing could have prepared her for the reality of what she saw.

She was standing on the ridge above a crater that she judged to be about a mile in diameter. Below her, in the center of it, stood the Outlying Hermitage: three squat, sand-colored, identical cylindrical buildings, each one about three hundred feet high and twice as wide. It looked like someone had shoved three stubby, sandy pillar candles as close to each other as possible. The flat roofs seemed to be covered in vegetation and small structures Wendy could not identify from this distance. Rising up from the center where the three cylinders met was a three-sided spire with concave faces that gradually tapered to a point two hundred feet above the Hermitage.

She started on the downward path, continually glancing away from the Hermitage as the first rays of sunlight found it. The scale of it and its ratio of height to width were so perfectly disturbing to any sense of symmetry or proportion that it made Wendy queasy to look straight at it for any length of time.

On the crater floor, the air was noticeably cooler. She walked straight toward the cluster of towers. As she got closer, any sense of the building's overall shape was lost and she found herself moving toward a windowless, featureless sandy wall that gradually filled her entire field of vision in a most disconcerting way.

When she reached the wall, she hesitated before running her hand over its surface. It looked like adobe but so clearly wasn't. It felt cool and smooth like polished plaster. There were no joints or stones visible. She opened the Spinster Uilkitz's note and then walked to her right as instructed, keeping the wall close on her left, barely discerning its curvature.

Gradually she became more aware of the adjacent tower. She was now walking into the V where two of the towers touched. As the space between the two towers narrowed, Wendy peered up at the triangle of sky framed by the hulking structures that now closed in on either side of her.

Protruding from the alcove where the two towers met, Wendy saw the spindle window the Spinster Uilkitz had described: a small wooden revolving door set at chest level into the wall. She took out the note she had labored over with the Clarion's translation help and placed it in the little tray. She pulled the sash that hung from the top of the compartment.

The resultant sound could not really be described as a ringing, it was more like the silence suddenly buckled inward into the throbbing aftermath of a huge bell toll without all the acoustic fuss of it actually ringing. Wendy shuddered at the peculiarity of this pulsing nonsound and fought hard against a powerful impulse to run away.

Almost immediately there was the sound of quick, paper-light footsteps behind the wall and the spindle turned sharply through a hundred and twenty degrees, whisking Wendy's letter off to the other side of the wall to reveal another identical but empty compartment with no bell rope. There was a brief pause and the spindle turned again. This third compartment contained a small, flat, rectangular piece of marzipan.

Wendy carefully took the marzipan, and the spindle again turned to reveal the first compartment now empty. In the tiniest exquisite lettering, the icing on the marzipan read: *Very slowly, eat half of this. Please wait.* How had they made something so delicate so quickly? she wondered. She hesitated to eat something so extraordinarily beautiful, but then shrugged and bit off a small corner. It tasted of warm honey and roses. She let it melt on her tongue. She took another bite.

When the spindle window turned again, Wendy could not be sure if five minutes or five months had passed. Her mind was racing, yet glacier slow. She took the scroll that appeared and read the attached note: *Return to the Quartel and then eat the remaining marzipan and read the enclosed.* It took a moment to register that the note was written in Azhuurse and that she had effortlessly understood it.

The walk back to the crater wall and climb back up its side felt effortless. A heightened lucidity hummed through Wendy's mind, stopping her in her tracks when she reached the top of the crater. She turned and looked back at the Hermitage. It was beautiful to her now: its dimensions perfectly resonant with its place in the universe. Although she could not say why, she understood now that a giant trefoil was the only shape the Outlying Hermitage could possibly be and still stay in harmony with itself. She hummed her small part of a huge song that rose into her from the ground and thrilled through her into the newly apparent harmony of light that was both wave and particle, yet neither, and danced on the leaves and the leaves understood.

⚭

Seated at the window of her Quartel chambers, Wendy ate the other half of the marzipan and spread the scroll out on the table in front of her. She looked at the drawings and equations it contained, her mind uncomprehending yet marveling at the beauty and precision of the penmanship. At first, she saw only unfamiliar shapes and symbols, and then some she recognized but meant nothing to her in this context. Nonetheless, the beauty of the work held her gaze and gradually she felt the marzipan light up inside her again and she began to understand what was in front of her.

Her strange new lucidity told her these specifications were the most efficient and stable way to continue the excavation of the lake. At the bottom of the page were some more calculations accompanied by sketches and diagrams. Wendy immediately recognized the new ramps and new workflow specifications, optimizing the numbers engaged in digging and hauling dirt at any one time and showing new lines of people passing baskets of dirt and rock to the top instead of the current system of runners from each work team running relays up and down the miles of ramp to get to their team's tally point. It was not rocket science but was all the more convincing given the unadorned way the Sisterhood presented it. Evidently, the Sisterhood understood far more than the complexities of cartography and glass-making, though Wendy had a strong sense that these plans had barely taxed their abilities at all.

She spent the rest of the day alone in the Quartel, pacing around her room and jotting down hundreds of short notes to herself. Her mind rang to the tune of previously ungraspable bits of Gödel and quantum mechanics now slotting singingly into place in her understanding. She was stunned by the parts of her mind revealing themselves to her for the first time, thanks, it could only be concluded, to the Sisterhood's marzipan.

By midafternoon the marzipan quieted then faded, and Wendy slumped back into her old, familiar mind. She reread her notes while she could still recapture some of the fire in them, then ate some fruit and fell fast asleep in an armchair, dreaming of impossible towers that curled and thrust and soared into clouds that chimed with the silver-star songs of the perfection and chaos of all creation.

The following morning she had little trouble explaining the Sisterhood's recommendations to the council and the excavation workmasters. Her new lucidity helped her make such a convincing case that even skeptics like the Utterminster had to concede it all made compelling sense.

IV

Skid pushed his breakfast things to one side and unwrapped his newly arrived replacement ¡think. Nikolian had explained where the pockets of ether access were. He had sorely missed it. He had been jumpy and itchy. Despite being in a new place, the unmediated world around him looked too lo-def and inexact, its colors poorly saturated and its singularity of narrative line plain boring. He barely took a moment to register the sleek new fauxrcelain shell. He jacked in, eager for the sensual jolt of the soothing, sucking, sinking feeling of it surging into his head, that comforting feeling of—

Wait a fucking second! What is this shit? His inner eye watered as it struggled to accept the images thrown at it as any part of his life. His memory fumbled with the prompts being fired at it. *Fucker has someone else's head-dump inside!*

Skid had heard about this: ¡thinks getting restored from the ether and ending up with someone else's life-dump mixed in; it messed with your head in a very disorienting way. He unjacked and held the ¡think suspiciously at arm's length. He turned voice on: "Hello? Technical services."

"Hi there, this is ¡Ken!" answered a perky voice. "How may I be of assistance and encouragement with your ¡think challenge?"

"¡Ken, are you another fucking ¡think?"

"No, I am a real person."

"Yeah, right. And I am a banjo-playing meerkat with a doctorate in physics. Get the fuck out of here!"

"But I am the perfect synthesis of person nodes. I can show empathy in concert with my fucking clients to calibrate the exchange and enhance rapport. See what I did there? Are you not fucking assured? Do you not feel me feeling your fucking pain?"

"That's lovely, ¡Ken. Very impressive altogether. Now, just fuck off there and get me a real person, like a good little bot."

You could almost hear ¡Ken's language nodes frying in the struggle to interpret Skid's request. "If you insist. I will locate a Humanaide. Please stand by."

The resulting hold music was quickly interrupted by a "Hi there, this is Alex, how may I be of assistance and encouragement with your ¡think challenge?" so dreary and despairing that it left no doubt as to the speaker's personhood—no one would have created real-person nodes to sound so miserably redolent of lost chances, wasted potential, poor career choices, and an angry little kitchenette with crooked drawers and a broken fridge.

"Howya, Alex. Listen, I got a replacement ¡think and it's got someone else's head-dump in it. I mean it's lovely and all, much nicer than mine, flashy childhood, but they're not *my* memories—makes me dizzy and want to puke . . . What node? . . . Okay, here it is, 7992-452-75353-33RF12 . . . That's just stupid. Why can't you help me? . . . What? . . . SOUP-ER-VIS-OR, PLEASE! SOUP-ER-VIS-OR NOW!"

After another ten minutes of unrelenting muzak, Skid

abruptly powered off, stuffed the ¡think into the hip pocket of his drape coat, and contemplated his surroundings with a new distaste before heading outside to his bike.

&

"Good morning, Adjutant!"

"Oh, hi, Luod. How's it going?"

"It is going, thank you. How are you?"

"You know how it is: another etherless day, another pointless public event."

"Ha ha ha, very funny! I am almost finished."

Skid stood and watched Luod polish the chrome mudguard on the old Triumph motorbike the Clarion had found for him. So it went, almost every morning after breakfast Luod turned up at the refectory tent to perform some small service for Skid, wanted or not.

Skid had no official attendant courtiers and Luod seemed to have appointed himself to the job. This morning he had evidently decided to polish Skid's bike with the sleeve of his white jacket.

"You sure you don't want a cloth or something?" asked Skid.

"Oh no, this dirt I will wear with honor. It will bring distinction to my family."

"Jesus, man."

"Adjutant, you can see I have only the lowliest of tonsures. We live on the very outer rim of the city, one mistake away from being relegated again to pubble in the fields. You may think it ridiculous, but these signs of your favor are very important. They help my family."

"Okay, okay, I get it. It's just weird having people do stuff for me."

"I understand. I do have a special favor to ask you, though."

"Oh yeah?"

"I am about to ask Meha's parents for permission to marry."

"Congratulations, I think. You have to ask them? And?"

"Meha's parents, they look down on me. Could I stand behind the bike when you start up and maybe get spattered with oil from the exhaust or dirt from the back wheel?"

"Seriously?"

"It would be a big help. Believe me."

Skid stared at Luod, not much older than he, a little taller and more heavily built, but something about him was utterly familiar, something gave off that wrong-side-of-the-tracks air that Skid so recognized. "Okay. If you are sure it'll help."

Luod beamed at him, twisted his nose, and nodded.

Skid mounted the bike and rolled it off its kickstand. Luod stood behind it, lining his white pants up with the exhaust pipe and back wheel as best he could.

"Get ready, Luod. I'm going to rev the shit out of this and take off fast."

"Understood."

Skid kicked the bike to life and revved the engine to an eager whine. He put it in gear and released the clutch. The back wheel spun and burned and then the bike pounced forward and down the roadway between the tents, leaving Luod covered in a generous coating of dirt, oil droplets, and exhaust fumes.

Skid knew he was going too fast. He could feel his drape jacket fluttering behind him. He was already at the T junction and had to turn sharply one way or the other. He took the left too hard and slid out of the turn into the side of one of the pantry tents.

Miraculously unhurt, Skid found himself sprawled among crates of vegetables and fruit, and in front of him, tied to one of the main supports of the tent, was the very naked (apart from the high-heeled shoes he was wearing) Utterminster, evidently in the middle of a good spanking at the hands of one of the more fulsome kitchen maids, who wore nothing except for a rhinestoned eye mask. The Utterminster of Azhuur was also undeniably in the middle of fucking a sheep suspended in front of him in an elaborate harness.

"Hey, whatever lights your candle," said Skid. "No skin off my nose. Sorry for the intrusion." He picked up the bike and wheeled it back outside through the hole in the tent's side.

The kitchen maid stood dumbfounded with her riding crop in midair. The Utterminster glared darkly at the departing Skid. "Untie me this instant, you stupid slattern. If you breathe a word of this, I will feed you your children raw."

V

"You got good news for me?" Brad asked Vincent and Flower, his coproducers.

Flower jacked in and powered up the ¡box. "We're already seeing some patterns in the inputs from the gaming environments."

"Useful patterns," added Vincent brightly.

"Like what? A lot of these morons just plug in crazy shit to see what will happen to their game Azhuur and then screw it all up and have to reset it to Current Creality Playstate."

"Yeah, we're seeing a lot of that," said Flower, "but also a lot of pubble revolutions, some wacky sexual stuff with the Archixprest and the Utterminster and goats, but we know that won't fly ¡cast-¡ball-¡chingwise. A lot of people trying to role-play the statue, but the crazy big spike we're seeing lately is what the market refraction people are calling a 'royal wedding fantasy.'"

"Royal wedding? Are you shitting me?" said Brad.

Vincent jumped in: "It is a big hotspot. We see a big, warm receptivity node for some type of engagement/royal wedding-y thing for Mooney and Wendy. It seems to have sizzling pretraction, so we might want to get on that. Not right away, but top of the ideation pile."

Flower impelled a barrage of charts and metagrams from her ¡think onto the ¡box.

Brad watched carefully, his eyes darting all over the screen. "Wow, those are some hot data there. The gamers are eating this ceremonial shit up!"

"And Wendy headscarf sales are up 48 percent over last week. We have excellent penetration," said Flower. "But skateboard sales have plummeted. We expected the skateboard would stay in the picture longer. Also Skid merch is way down. He hardly figures at all. We have a big inventory of teddy boy regalia we need to move."

Brad considered this. "Ours is not to reason why. The ¡think community wants, and we provide. We aren't some prescriptive eat-your-leafy-greens deal, all full of interesting facts about gibbons and Manueline architecture. We make CRUD: Consumer-Responsive Unscripted Drama, right? *The CONtent that conTENTS*—like that? It's new. We'll be testing it next week. Anyway, if someone wants to inpulse Azhuur and play a S¡milireality game with it, we are not the ones to tell them how. Skateboards are dead. We will move the teddy boy merch—I will work on bigging the Skid profile. Take programmers off the *Sewers of Rome* game for the royal wedding scenarios. This is greenlit all the way up the wazoo and back again. It is beyond GO. We reparamaterize and run with it—I will tell Udder Man and Archie Boy later tonight that they need to get working on this: Mooney and Wendy are getting married!"

⚭

As soon as Vincent and Flower left, Brad noticed the cartoonish ¡ncrypt alert on his ¡think. He tapped *Receive* and a door in an alleyway opened and a hand waved a sheet of paper, a little cartoon spy in a fedora and a long trench coat ran to the door, grabbed the paper, hurried toward the foreground, and slapped the paper onto the inside of his screen:

You have probably noticed it on the ¡see captures, and this may not be of any importance, but the routine at the dig has changed. The images may not fully do it justice, but the atmosphere is different. At the beginning of each shift, the statue is now taken down from the Tower of Thrones and paraded around the rim of the dig while the pubble are encouraged to pay it homage and condemn the filthy mongrel Outlander conspiracy that is allegedly making the earth hard and slowing down the dig. Then the statue is returned to the top of the Tower of Thrones to supervise the work. It's hard to establish who resurrected this old D'Izmaïe conspiracy slogan, but I think we can guess.

Brad typed into the ¡ncrypt window:

Nikolian, thanks for the observations. This does not seem strategically significant. For the moment it is good ¡ball fodder. If the rabble-rousing starts to feel more like war-mongering, advise immediately. We don't need that. That would get messy. Stay observant.

He activated *Send* and his message crumpled up and was grabbed by the little cartoon spy in the long trench coat who ran into the distance and furtively knocked on the door in the alleyway. The door opened a crack and the little spy put the piece of paper into the hand that extended out. The door snapped shut and the little figure scurried off into the shadows trailing a speech bubble: *Message Delivered.*

There was a pause, then the door in the alleyway opened again and a hand gave a thumbs-up. Brad exited ¡ncrypt with a tired sigh. He did not dislike the ¡ncrypt technology per se; he just hated the cutesy infantilizing iconography of it.

VI

"Skid, thank you for making time. I see you've met ¡seer Val. Thanks, Val, for setting this up. Skid, this is just between us. No one else needs to know about this—do you get where I'm going with this?"

"I kinda got that from us doing this on some jury-rigged ¡think in the back of an equipment shed. Can you get to the point, Brad? It stinks in here."

"Sure, thanks, Skid. Point is, we see a lot more potential for you. We think you are not getting enough ¡ball time. I love the whole teddy boy thing and the old motorbike, but this hole in the ground is where it's at right now and you're not part of that. You're becoming a sideshow. You don't really seem to have a role."

"Suits me. They leave me alone."

"That's what worries me, Skid. That's what worries me." Brad paused. "Have you picked up on, what should we call it, a kinda ruthless vibe from our friends Udder and Archie? A kind of sell-your-own-mother thing?"

"Yeah. A bit."

"I know about the embarrassing bike accident and you dropping in on Udder like that. I doubt he was too happy about it. Powerful men often go in for that kind of kinky stuff, but I'm sure he would like it to remain a secret. I'm starting to believe the best way to keep you safe from him is to have you so much in the public eye that he won't dare do anything to you. Right now, just hanging out with Mooney and waving at the pubble from your bike, you are not very visible and that might make you vulnerable." Brad paused again to let it all sink in. "Of course, you are wondering why I would help you. What's in it for me? And you are right to wonder. You'd be stupid not to."

"Right?" said Skid, eager to have some part in this conversation.

"I want something we have never had before on any of the *So*

You Wanna shows. I want undercover footage. I want you to embed with the pubble on the dig. Classic prince-and-pauper stuff."

Skid had been nodding but now stared blankly at Brad.

"*The Prince and the Pauper? Trading Places?* Where the rich guy goes and pretends to be the poor guy? You, the Adjutant, go undercover to get a real idea of what's going on. It's a whole new angle. It will get you out of sight for the next few days, and then when we start to feed the footage in, you will be too much in the spotlight for the Udder to do anything to you. You get it?"

"I get it. But they'll all be talking Azhuurse. They'll spot us immediately."

"Don't worry, Skid. Val here has enough Azhuurse to pass as a native speaker."

Skid looked at Val.

"My grandmother," she said. "She was a refugee. She escaped to Newer York. I learned it from her."

"All right! Good! Val, you two should go into the pit first thing tomorrow morning. I'll send you the details. Skid, Val will pick you up six thirty sharp. Get a good night's rest and be sure to look under the bed before you do, eh?"

"Won't people notice I'm missing?"

"We'll hide your bike and say you went on an impetuous road trip cos you are exactly that kind of irresponsible Adjutant."

"Okay. What if we're discovered?"

"Then you're the Adjutant. Who's going to mess with the Adjutant?"

VII

"Keep a good hold on that rope. I like a girl with strong fingers," called Bagwipe the quarrymaster to Alva, who was working near Skid and Val. Then he grabbed his crotch and cackled drunkenly through his broken teeth. He took another mouthful of his alcohol-soaked dough and bellowed: "What are you looking at, dogshit?" He was addressing a young man who stood there staring at him.

"Tel!" Alva made a helpless, high-pitched sound of alarm in the back of her throat. But it was too late.

Bagwipe gestured angrily to his two henchmen to help him out of his armchair. He lumbered over to the young man. "Do you have something to say, dogshit?"

The rest of the work group pretended not to pay any attention to what was going on.

"Well, dogshit?"

Tel drew back to hit Bagwipe, but the henchmen were too fast. Tel found himself on the flat of his back as Bagwipe delivered a vicious kick to his ribs.

"All right, no lunch for you, dogshit, you work," said Bagwipe. "The rest of you, ten minutes!"

One of the henchmen searched Tel and snatched his bread from him, while the other helped Bagwipe back to his armchair.

The work party dropped their tools, sat down where they were, and took their bread rations from their pockets or the little bags they wore around their necks.

"What a bastard," whispered Skid.

"Shuddup. Just eat. Look at the ground. *Eat*," hissed Alva. "Be carefula Bagwipe. Girl, boy, dog, sleeping, dead, alive, he fuck anything. All same."

Skid turned to look at the slight but athletic woman sitting beside him. Despite the several lifetimes that seemed etched into her face, it was somehow obvious that she wasn't much over twenty-five.

"I am Alva," the woman said softly.

"You don't speak Azhuurse?" whispered Skid.

Val leaned across and said something to Alva in Azhuurse, then turned to Skid: "Stop drawing attention to us. She could get beaten just for speaking Yute."

Skid kept his head down and ate, occasionally stealing a sideways glance at Alva. She was watching Tel, who struggled to haul a large stone, obviously feeling the pain of Bagwipe's kick.

Bagwipe had moved from his armchair with surprising stealth and now stood right behind Alva. Through the vile fug of his body odor, they could still smell the crude alcohol. "I think it's time we gave you something more interesting to do with your pretty little mouth than chew on dry bread, eh?" He leered down at Alva and began to unbutton his pants.

Alva, trembling, kept looking at the ground.

In a flash, Skid was on his feet in front of the quarrymaster. "Leave her alone, you disgusting shit. Go fuck yourself."

Bagwipe shoved him effortlessly to the ground. The two henchmen laughed hoarsely at Skid's strange-sounding words and feeble intervention. Bagwipe took Alva by the hair and was just reaching inside his pants when Skid lunged at him. Before anyone could react, Skid stuck an index finger in each of Bagwipe's eyes and kneed him in the balls. Even the henchmen winced as the quarrymaster crumpled to the ground in agony.

"Take him away!" Bagwipe managed to croak, just before he threw up in the dust.

VIII

The Utterminster sat behind his gold-and-obsidian desk and studied his fingernails carefully. The carriage clock on the desk chimed midnight. He frowned at it, annoyed it had spoiled his dramatic breaking of the ominous silence that had presided since the prisoner had been brought in. He curled the fingers he had been inspecting into a fist and then laid both his hands flat on the green blotter in the center of his desk.

Skid glared at him. He had already been through this with five sets of increasingly higher-ranking officials since being dragged from the pit at midday. Functionary after functionary had taken advantage of the labyrinth of administrative protocol to pass this tricky matter on up the chain of command. Skid now found himself standing in stocks before the Utterminster's desk.

The Utterminster sighed resignedly before speaking: "So? You say you are the Adjutant, also known as Skid? A nod will suffice. I assume you find it difficult to speak after the silencing gas. Don't worry, the effects are temporary, but I prefer not to have you shouting and using foul language here in my chambers this late at night. A little decorum goes a long way, does it not?"

The Utterminster leafed through the documents in front of him. "This is all very interesting. This is a grave matter. You have failed to understand a customary practice among workmasters, and in so doing, you have committed a serious assault. I am sure you believed you were doing the right thing, but that is in your world, not in ours. I must give this case detailed consideration. In the meantime, you will be our guest here at the Quartel.

"Take him to the Deeps! Discreetly!" the Utterminster barked at his unseen minions. He returned his attention to the ends of his stubby fingers as figures appeared out from the shadows to take Skid away. "And bring me Adra. I will have a shave."

∞

The Utterminster sat himself in the erstwhile electric chair he liked to use for tonsorial activities. Adra wore the French maid costume stipulated by the Utterminster for these encounters. She set to lathering the shaven band that stretched from ear to ear across the Utterminster's bulbous head. He sat back and closed his eyes while she shaved the palm-wide tonsure across his skull. He let this pubble woman take a blade near him, instead of the more customary courtesan, happy in the knowledge that if she should so much as nick his scalp, her entire clan would immediately be rounded up by his Utterforz.

While he found this power dynamic arousing, he was not

fully focused on his lust. He limited himself to reaching out and groping her thighs under her short skirt each time she cleaned the razor. He loved the feeling of her contempt, anger, and powerlessness struggling with each other.

He luxuriated in Adra's palpable fear and hatred. He pondered until an idea came to him: all he had to do was make Skid's crime more serious, and the way would be clear.

"That was an acceptable shave," he said to Adra. "Another day we will reward you by engendering a soldier son for Fatherland Azhuur in you. Our seed will do well in you, you have the hips for it." He stared at her breasts.

Adra remained expressionless and tried to shrink her body away from him without actually moving.

"Unfortunately, I have affairs of state to attend to and do not have time to favor you with my pleasuring. But we will see each other again soon, when I am more disposed toward fornication. You may go now."

After she hurried out, he went to his desk and wrote a short note, then sealed it in a blue tube. He summoned his Invigilator of Internality.

"Deliver this immediately."

The Invigilator rushed out and returned fifteen minutes later with a ferret-like man in a gray smock.

"You may leave us, Invigilator. Azhuur thanks you for your service." The Utterminster eyed his new visitor. "Sit down, Kanker. How is the rope dispatch duty suiting you?"

"Very well, Your Utterness, thank you, honored to be an instrument of Azhuur's will."

"Good, good. Capital! You see how I reward my friends. But I am certain you would not be averse to becoming, let us say, Provisions Overseer Grade II now, would you?"

Greed widened Kanker's eyes ever so slightly, but he had dealt with the Utterminster before and had the good sense to say nothing.

"Of course, that would be an extraordinary promotion for anyone to receive, and I think it would not be unusual for such an event to be preceded by certain other extraordinary happenings."

Kanker processed the Utterminster's tortured circumlocution and nodded slowly. He knew the drill.

"So, if I were to suggest to you that if the quarrymaster Bagwipe and his extended family were to all somehow become tragically deceased tonight by, say, food poisoning that could not be attributed to any particular source, and the second extraordinary event of your promotion would swiftly follow, that would not seem unreasonable to you, would it?"

Kanker nodded his head in tentative agreement with this tormented statement.

"Splendid! I see we understand each other. Well, it has been most enjoyable chatting with you, but I must prepare for dinner. Goodbye and good luck in your new career. Azhuur be served!"

"Thank you, Your Utterness. Azhuur be served!" Kanker stood, twisted his rodent nose, and was gone.

The Utterminster took out his private journal and made a note: *See to Kanker. Rockfall? Crossbow accident? Have Kitxchenn fix him?* He clapped his hands together in great satisfaction, then opened his door. "Get me Adra again immediately!" he shouted to his attendants. "Wash her well before she comes to me. I feel revitalized! We shall celebrate most vigorously."

IX

"What do you mean, he disappeared?" Brad asked the shaken Val.

"They took him away. I don't know where."

"Show me."

Val projected his ¡see into the secured Intimeet.

Brad peered at the screen. "This is really shaky. Where was your ¡see?"

"On my head in a big cloth cap!"

"Oh god. Really? You haven't shown this to ANYONE else, right?"

"No one."

Brad watched the crowd waiting around Val and Skid. Generally, they were stronger-looking people than many he had seen, but there was a heaviness to their gait and a lights-have-gone-out-for-good look in many of their eyes that chilled him. Before he had time to speculate on the reason for this, it arrived on a two-man rickshaw pulled by two powerful henchmen.

"What am I looking at here?"

"This is Bagwipe the quarrymaster. We dubbed over all the Azhuurse as usual, so you can hear."

"Wait, she's not dubbed," interrupted Brad the first time Alva spoke.

"No. And she spoke to us in Yute from the get-go. I didn't realize we looked so *not* Azhuurse. That coulda been real dangerous."

"Probably not as dangerous as the risk she took speaking Yute."

Val sped through the long trek down the ramp and into the pit. "You get the picture. Huge open-cast mine being dug out by hand by thousands of peasants. Scene from the Dark Ages . . ."

Brad watched the scene unfold in front of him. He saw the henchmen punch Skid in the stomach and shove a rag into his mouth.

"He never got to say who he was?"

"No," said Val. "I had to work the rest of the day to not blow my cover and get out safe. I'm sure Bagwipe would have killed me if he had discovered me. You have no clue how dangerous this shitty stunt was." The footage showed Skid being frog-marched up the ramp and out of sight before going completely dark. "That's where Bagwipe hit me for staring and broke my ¡see."

X

The Utterminster and the Archixprest sat back in their respective thrones.

"Clarion, turn on that vile contraption and let us be done with this irksome gathering."

"Yes, Your Utterness." The Clarion addressed the ¡box: "Intimeet *So You Wanna* 383."

The ¡box purred and sprang to life, revealing Brad, Flower, and Vincent ranged expectantly around their conference table.

"Hello, Bradley, you called?" said the Utterminster. "Clarion, you may leave us."

"I don't see Nikolian," responded Brad. "He was supposed to join us."

"I am here," Nikolian said, after joining in a subscreen. He appeared to be sitting on some windswept heath.

"Nikolian, why don't you join us here in the Utterminster's chambers?" said the Archixprest. "You would be much more comfortable."

"I thank you for your solicitude, Archixprest, but I am perfectly comfortable here. The air out here is clean, fresh, and vivifying."

The Utterminster's face briefly darkened. "Long may you benefit from it, Nikolian. Well, Bradley, we appear to have concluded the niceties and are quorate. You nudged us urgently. Do you have some inquiry or request you wish to share with us? We have already conveyed your suggestion to the Regent and Mistress Consort that they should marry. They are considering it."

Even the habitually poker-faced Flower could not help wincing at the Utterminster's oozing condescension.

Brad plowed right past it: "That is not why I called. If I may use the vernacular, WHAT THE FUCK ARE YOU TWO DOING? Where is Skid?"

"Ah, you heard?" The Utterminster smiled with infuriating indifference.

"Heard? I saw it! I have footage. What the fuck is going on? I need to know what's happening before I let something out in front of eight hundred million ¡balls."

The Utterminster seemed in no rush to answer. "Ah yes, your embedded ¡seer. At least his costume was better than usual. Now, when you say eight hundred million ¡balls, is that four hundred million people at two ¡balls each, or is it really eight hundred million people? I have long been curious on this point of your jargon, but reluctant to ask. Seeing as we are being so candid today, I thought this would be a good opportunity to unburden myself."

"Are you fucking kidding me?" Brad shot back.

"I think what Brad intends to say here," interjected Nikolian, "is that we have been caught off guard by these new developments, which hampers our ability to arc these new stories in the best way. We need to know where this is likely to go."

"Thank you for clarifying, Nikolian, the outdoor air does indeed engender concision in you. You should perhaps consider taking all our Intimeets remotely in the future. I am fully confident your scriptors are more than capable of *arcing* these new narrative developments, and if they are not equal to the task, the Archixprest and I would be happy to assist."

"That won't be necessary," replied Brad. "We can take some scriptors off this royal wedding scenario. But we need to know where this is going."

"Surely a little unpredictability enhances the appeal of your entertainment product?" said the Archixprest.

"I need to know where this Skid thing is going before I start to show the story. I don't like this kind of unpredictability."

The Utterminster grinned. "So timid, Bradley? Very disappointing. A little too much reality in your *creality* for your liking? I had taken you for a more swashbuckling producer. Ah well, if you must know, we will have a show trial and Skid will be rapped on the knuckles. We will convey the exact details to Nikolian in due course. Is there anything else?"

"We will show the footage," said Brad.

"Ah, splendid! I think we could make good use of it in the trial."

"On second thought, maybe we won't. Maybe this should come as a surprise to everyone."

"Suit yourself," said the Utterminster. "Is there anything else?"

"No, Utterminster, I don't believe so."

"Splendid! And ¡balls? Are they two per person or each one a whole person?"

"Each viewer is counted as one ¡ball," answered Vincent quickly, sensing that Brad was about to completely lose it. "I apologize if this terminology has caused you any confusion in the past."

"Thank you, Vincent. Most illuminating. Bradley, if you have any further frustrations you need to release, I suggest you direct your obscenity-laden diatribes at Flower or Vincent. I imagine that is what you pay them for. It has been real, has it not? Goodbye."

Without turning off the ¡box, the Utterminster stood up and left his chambers, treating the attendees to the spectacle of his back receding toward the door, his shoulders bouncing to his chuckles. The Archixprest did his best to look like this exit had not caught him completely off guard before he too left the room.

Brad removed the Utterminster's ¡box from the feed. "No one else is to know about this, Nikolian."

"No one?"

"Especially not Mooney or Wendy. I want their surprise to be real when we show the footage in the trial."

"Okay."

"Don't give me that look, Nikolian. They are ¡ball bait. They knew it when they got into this."

"I don't think anyone saw this coming."

"Nope, but we've got to make the best of it. Act surprised."

"I will. But as soon as they see the footage, they will know we knew."

"Not my laboratory; not my monkey. Brad out!"

∞

Nikolian stared at the dark window of his ¡think and unjacked. From the rock where he sat, he looked across the gaping maw of the pit at the encampment's distant lights. Somehow they made the darkness around him feel darker. He paced along the rim of the pit back to the encampment to rejoin the wondering and speculation about when Skid would return from his mysterious and impulsive "road trip."

XI

After twenty minutes of listening to the almost telepathic exchanges between the two Uilkitz sisters, Mooney was regretting his decision to accompany the Spinster to visit the Relict in her Quartel apartments. Out of courtesy, the two almost identical old sisters conversed in their stiff, tweedy Frockshow English, but Mooney still understood nothing. He would have been better off at another frustrating fencing lesson or bored out of his skull "supervising" the excavation.

"And how is the . . . ?"

"No worse, no better. And your . . . ?"

"Settling nicely . . ."

"Ha!"

"And that hole in the ground?"

"Still not quite big enough to accommodate the Utterminster's ego."

Here they chuckled softly together, the Relict Uilkitz stealing the occasional guilty glance at Mooney. The two sisters' combined ancientness treating him as the responsible grown-up in
the room was very disconcerting.

While their chatter continued, Mooney lost himself in the
clutter of the high-ceilinged room. The walls were covered in
postage stamps. The furniture was a dizzying mishmash of styles
and periods. The carpet consisted of interwoven dragons, uni-
corns, and griffins, all fornicating or devouring themselves or one
another on a bed of elaborately intertwined gold flowers all set on
a deep vermilion background. Mooney sat perched on the edge of
a zebra-skin chaise longue while the two sisters sat opposite each
other, each in her own time-worn red wingback armchair.

After a particularly long and enigmatic exchange of half sentences, the two sisters paused and sighed together, then sat back
as if in relief. From this, Mooney assumed the visit was nearing
its end.

The Relict tinkled a little glass bell on her side table. Within
seconds, a bright-eyed man who appeared to be in his sixties entered the drawing room. He steered an elaborate assemblage of
glass receptacles, tubes, retorts, and alembics the size of a small
donkey.

"Thank you, Cowan. Will you be joining us?"

"Uhm, no, mum. Not today, if you don't mind." He smiled
warmly at Mooney. "No offense, I'm in the middle of something."

"Will you join us, Master Regent?" asked the Relict sweetly.

"Join you . . . ?" stumbled Mooney.

"A little recreational herbalism. Sister and I are very partial
to it after our little chats. We find it most relaxing. Do join us.
I am certain you will enjoy it. This bong is of our own personal
design."

The Spinster Uilkitz nodded enthusiastically. "It is a pity my
nephew Cowan can't stay. Please do join us. We would enjoy the

company and, if I might make so bold, it may alleviate your general ennui and the impasse with your fencing progress you were telling me about."

Mooney shrugged. Cowan uncoiled and distributed three of the tubes connected to the apparatus. Mooney saw that the silver mouthpiece Cowan passed to him was unmistakably shaped like an erect penis.

"Ah, you appear to have *my* pipe," grinned the Relict. "My apologies. You must forgive an old woman her nostalgia."

Cowan swapped the Relict's and Mooney's pipes, then produced a cedar box from which he extracted a generous handful of small dried leaves. He rubbed the leaves between his palms and placed them on a mesh over the mouth of one of the retorts.

A small tesla coil hummed beside the mesh. The sisters watched the charge build. Their eyes widened with anticipation when the coil flashed and discharged and the leaves began to smolder and glow. Then they began sucking the pipes. Cowan bowed, twisted his nose, and left with a cheery "Enjoy yourselves!"

Mooney watched the smoke from the leaves fill the retort and make its way through the maze of glassware into the chamber where their individual pipes connected to the apparatus. When the smoke entered the final chamber, the sisters began to suck with renewed gusto. Mooney, not wanting to be outdone or seem rude, did the same. A rush of ice-cold, rum-tinted vapor filled his mouth. The sisters inhaled deeply and he did likewise. He had never tasted anything so smooth.

"Hold it in," the Relict told him, managing to speak without exhaling.

Mooney waited and exhaled only when the sisters did. The sisters put their pipes to their lips and began to draw again. Mooney tried to do the same but his lips suddenly felt like two very old car tires someone had glued to his face. He slumped back on the chaise longue and gripped the pipe in his fist, convinced it was vitally important to continued breathing.

He had a vague memory of what it felt like to fully jack in to an ¡think and this felt like a million ¡thinks simultaneously coming in-head, yet not the same harsh, invasive presence. He was aware of millions of voices in the ether. They were available to him, but they were not forcing themselves into his thinking.

"That's the rum," the Spinster's voice said. "You can trust it. It keeps them calm. You can go into and out of anything with ease. You won't get trapped."

"I am so glad you could join us," said the Relict from some-where very far away with appalling acoustics. "It will take a few moments for the herb to take full effect and then you will notice the timbre. That comes from the purity of the trepanium in the soil where the herb grows. We are not tawdry alleyway druggies shaving the innards of old ¡thinks into cheap herb."

Mooney looked at her and tried to smile. The effort of doing both things at the same time proved too much for him and his hand forgot completely about holding onto the pipe. It fell to the floor and seemed to take a couple of hours to reach the carpet with a soft plop. He stopped smiling and bent down to pick it up, being very careful to keep each one of these a distinct and inde-pendent action so as not to overtax what little was left of his mo-tor abilities. His hand reached the mouthpiece on the floor and decided to stay there. Mooney wanted to close his fingers around it, but his fingers were having none of it. He thought about sit-ting upright and immediately found himself sitting upright. He looked at the Relict. She smiled at him from two thousand miles away across the room.

"Well?" she said.

"Mrphgh splghb," he said. He closed his eyes, or rather his eyes closed themselves. When he tried to open them again, he realized he had no control over them. He thought *seeing* and was now floating near the ceiling. Near him floated the sisters, or at least the floatingnesses of them, for they, like him, were slumped in their chairs below, for all intents and purposes fast asleep.

"We are in here with you," said the Relict's thinking-seeingness. "As you can see, we are quite out of our carcasses. Isn't it thrilling?"

"At our age, it is so enjoyable to get out of one's carcass," said the Spinster.

"And away from the noxious Utterminster and that reptile Archixprest," added the Relict.

"Sister! You mustn't."

Mooney's mind was suddenly inside images of the Spinster's and Relict's lives. "Wait. What? You are D'Izmaïe's widow??"

"Yes, I am," replied the Relict calmly. "When he came to power, he chose our family to marry into to give him some re-spectability. I was the youngest of the three daughters and the unfortunate one he chose."

"So Cowan is—"

"No! God no! Cowan is really my nephew. We like to keep that quiet. The child of the Sistermost, our eldest sister. Merci-fully, mine was a purely political marriage. D'Izmaïe had his con-cubines and I had mine. He never bothered to consummate his marriage to me. And then, well, KA-BOOM. Bye-bye, D'Izmaïe." She threw her think-seeing arms wide in mime of an explosion and beamed delightedly at Mooney.

"We can talk of this another time," hushed the Spinster.

Mooney nodded and tried not to smile. He was about to speak but instead plummeted into a deep whorl of the ether and found himself declaiming in a cathedral-filling voice:

"*A damsel with a dulcimer*
In a vision once I saw:
It was an Abyssinian maid

And on her dulcimer she played,
Singing of Mount Abora.
Could I revive within me
Her symphony and song,
To such a deep delight 'twould win me,
That with music loud and long,
I would build that dome in air,
That sunny dome! those caves of ice!
And all who heard should see them there,
And all should cry, Beware! Beware!
His flashing eyes, his floating hair!
Weave a circle round him thrice,
And close your eyes with holy dread
For he on honey-dew hath fed,
And drunk the milk of Paradise."

Mooney's voice abruptly changed to a menacing growl: "ENOUGH! THERE WAS A DAMN GOOD REASON I WAS SENT FROM PORLOCK! STOP NOW! YOU HAVE SAID ENOUGH!"

Mooney jolted and felt his comatose body below reclaiming him, and try as he might, he could not sustain the floating. He drifted down and the room became dimmer until once again he felt the weight of his body around him. He sat inside his body for a long time, unconnected to it but reveling in its darkness and the soft voices of the ether. Eventually, his eyes reconnected to his will. The sisters were waiting for him when he opened his eyes.

"Delighted to see you again," chirped the Relict. "Sister, I think we have found an excellent traveling companion."

"I must compliment you on your recital of Coleridge," said the Spinster.

"What? Who?"

"The poem you recited for us. 'Kubla Khan.' Coleridge. You seemed to know more than—"

"Never heard of it."

"'A damsel with a dulcimer.'"

"Oh, THAT. There was lots more, but then it didn't want us to hear. Those are the words inside the light. There are lots of them. They are always there but you can only get to them from the inside. Sometimes with the Captain Dude statue, I could drift inside."

"Quite," smiled the Relict, and raised her eyebrows quizzically at her sister, who made a shake of her head indicating the subject should not be pursued.

"Sister, I think you must bring the Regent along with you on your next visit," the Relict quickly added.

"If my liege wishes," said the Spinster, directing herself to Mooney.

"I think I might like that. Wait. It's dark already?"

"Yes, it has a way of doing that with time," remarked the Relict. "Mind you, other times you can have weeks of flying in a matter of minutes. We have never quite got the knack of that time part. It's always a little surprise for us."

Mooney helped the Spinster into her cloak and then thanked the Relict for her hospitality.

"It was my utmost pleasure, Master Regent," she said, extending her hand, palm down, for him to kiss. He punched it gently. The Relict, having slightly overestimated Mooney's command of courtly behavior, took this gesture in the respectful spirit with which it was so obviously intended, and smiled warmly at him.

"Please do visit again, my liege. We so enjoyed your company. I hope next time my nephew Cowan can join us."

As they walked toward their carriage, Mooney was surprised by how light the Spinster Uilkitz's step had become. She sauntered along by his side like a woman of twenty. He too felt quite renewed and energized.

When they arrived back at the encampment, the Spinster bounced out of the carriage: "I must go now and attend to my duties. I suspect when next you return to your fencing, you will find a renewed clarity. The herb has a way of cementing things. I thank you for your company." She twisted her nose, lithely bowed from the waist, and hurried off.

Returning to his tent, Mooney noticed there was still no sign of Skid's motorbike.

XII

The only sound in the Hall of Conclave was the incessant gurgling of the Great Water Clock. Its glass body showed its inner mech-anism, symbolizing transparency, and its clear, handless, number-less clock face conveyed the timelessness of Azhuurse legal lore and how time was no object in the pursuit of justice. Under the clock at the High Bench sat the Utterminster, the Archixprest, and the Invigilator of Internality. High above them to their right was the Exalted Balcony where Mooney and Wendy sat. On the ground level below the High Bench, the Clarion stood to atten-tion in front of rows of empty pews.

The Utterminster glared down with distaste at the ticker feed that ran across the front of the High Bench. He and the Archixprest had protested bitterly that it ruined the majesty and solemnity of the proceedings, but ultimately had given in to Brad.

Brad had told them, "We need it for ¡balls. We need it to look like a real trial. It's what the ¡balls expect justice to look like. People on trial having lawarriors is quaint. What you need is a social mediator to sway the ¡ury. We need to do this or we will lose ¡balls. You want that? Then you can conduct your trial in the dark and no one will see it or care."

The Utterminster had wanted to send these arrogant Out-landers and their intrusive gadgets packing, but could not bear to have his remaking of Azhuur happen unseen.

Kevin Holohan

The Utterminster pulled a lever in the bench before him and the Great Water Clock fell silent.

"Justice out of time must be done," intoned the Clarion. "Duration is immaterial. Azhuur be served!"

"Let the charge sheet be publicly declaimed!" announced the Utterminster.

The Archixprest took the scroll from the Utterminster and passed it to the Invigilator, who stepped down from the High Bench and handed it to the Clarion, who broke the seal and began to read:

"On the 474,509th day of the Wake of Mög, in quarry 58 of Azhuur Kapital, the accused is charged with assaulting Quarrymaster Grade III Bagwipe as he attempted, as is his right, to take pleasure with one of his work crew. Subsequent complications from the groin injury sustained by the quarrymaster in this attack occasioned his sudden demise. Concurrent but seemingly unrelated events of an alimentary nature occasioned the demise of said quarrymaster's extended family, leaving him completely heirless, whereupon, in satisfaction of the Laws of Vengeance, the Powers of Azhuur bring the charges of the murder of Bagwipe, quarrymaster grade III, on their behalf against the accused."

The Clarion paused for breath and, despite all his efforts to maintain com-

¡amFrootfly: Woo hoo! Let's get this show on the road. Guilty! Guilty! So guilty! Can't we just move on to the sentencing and the hanging or whatever?

¡amAnybell: I love the water clock—classy

¡amMikey725: I am in love with the chick with the headscarf

¡amTomTom: there are real issues in the world—this is just polporn

¡amFrootfly: loving the whole scroll thing—so totally Spartacus

¡amShim: who is this Mög guy anyway? What's his deal?

posure, a look of alarm briefly clouded his features. This reminded him uncomfortably of the darkest days of the Generalitate when fit-ups, summary trials, and arbitrary punishments were commonplace.

"Let the accused be present," ordered the Utterminster.

From the ceiling came a clacking of gears as the cage was lowered from the holding room above. In the cage stood Skid, hands bound behind his back and his head covered in a black hood, but unmistakable in his sky-blue drape.

"Justice is blind. You come into its presence equally deprived of sight," announced the Clarion leadenly to the descending cage.

"Get this bag off me head before I split you, you dopey bastards!" shouted Skid.

"There will be silence!" commanded the Utterminster. "We have clearly established the identity of the accused. Let it be entered into the record that the Adjutant of Inner Azhuur stands before us. We may dispense with the hood."

The hood was drawn up into the roof of the cage to reveal a red-faced and frightened Skid.

"What the fuck is this?" shouted Wendy from the Exalted Balcony. "You can't treat him like this, he's one of us!"

¡amYadda: events of an alimentary nature? Whoa yeah! Shot while trying to escape here we come . . .

¡amShim: this is a set up if ever I saw one

¡amAnybell: Ooo that dude reading that thing looks GUILTY

¡amStoatmaster: black hood? Oh, we are going to see some real justice get done here, I can tell

¡amFashist: That is Skid!!! But seriously, who wears sky blue to a trial? #guilty-ofwhatever #fashionfail

¡amWalden4u: Skid is kinda cute when he's scared. I'd do him

"Oh, but we can," the Utterminster replied. "We will treat him exactly as we would treat one of the pubble. Do you hear yourself? *He's one of us.* There are no special privileges before the Law of Azhuur. I am sure that should please your egalitarian beliefs, does it not, Mistress Consort? Or are these *beliefs* simply virtue posturing?" He smiled coldly and blew into a pipe beside him. The back of the chamber suddenly filled with Utterforz armed with ridiculous ceremonial yet dangerous-looking studded clubs.

¡amAnybell: OMFG it's like the Shock Troopers from Mars Colony 5! This is awesome!

"Mooney! Wendy! Nikolian! Do something!" pleaded Skid.

"The Regent may not interfere in any proceedings of the Hall of Conclave," the Utterminster said. "So is it writ. So it must be. It guarantees fairness and impartiality. Azhuur be served!"

¡amStoatmaster: these guys wouldn't know fairness if it came up and pissed in their eyes

Wendy snorted. "You wouldn't know fairness if it bit you on the ass."

"There will be silence while His Thoroughness, the Invigilator of Internality, questions the accused on behalf of the Powers of Azhuur."

The Invigilator stood and put on his double-faced Abogate's mask before descending to the floor. "Sir, please identify yourself to the court."

¡amSoothSlayer14: A 2-faced mask like that promises great stuff

"I am Skid, you dope. You already know that."

"You understand the accusations before you?"

"No, I don't. All I did was knee him in the balls. He was fine when I was taken away."

"Yes. Let the assault be shown. Roll it there, Kolett!" called the Invigilator.

They watched as Val's footage was projected onto the wall behind the Utterminster.

"So, as we can see, you did injure Quarrymaster Bagwipe in the groin?"

"Well, yeah. But he was asking for it. He was—"

"Are you aware of the law of this land regarding workmasters' rights to take their underlings to pleasure?"

"Don't be stupid, I've never heard such crap in all my life."

"Ignorance, I am afraid, is no defense. You are subject to Azhuurse law. You interfered with Quarrymaster Bagwipe's legitimate right of pleasure, and in so doing, caused him fatal injury. But let us not be hasty. This, to all appearances, is a simple misunderstanding, an Outlander failing to grasp our time-honored practices and imposing his own morality on our culture. However, what is not captured here are the subsequent events that add dimensions to this transgression, consequences I am sure the Adjutant never intended and

¡amTremendo: ouch!!!

¡amSoothSlayer14: gotta say guilty as charged—no doubt. Probably jealous Bagwipe didn't want to fuck him

¡amWalden4u: SoothSlayer what is wrong with you?

¡amWalden4u: Atta boy! Knee in the balls!

could not possibly have foreseen, but sadly they are now inextricably linked to his impetuous and, some among you might say, chivalrous act.

"As mentioned in the formal charges, Quarrymaster Bagwipe died that evening from complications of his scrotal contusions. This made the matter now one of blood debt to be settled by duel. Regrettably, when messengers sought out the quarrymaster's kin, we found them all in the final throes of what appeared to be some kind of digestive collapse, occasioned perhaps by the rare mushrooms they had chosen to cook into their pottage. There being now no surviving kin to exact the blood debt owed, it now falls to the Powers of Azhuur to remedy this.

"I rest my case before the court. I have objectively prosecuted and defended as ordained. Let judgment be pronounced. Azhuur be served!" The Invigilator twisted both noses on the Abogate's mask and returned to the High Bench.

"Blood debt? What the fuck?" shouted Skid

"This is insane! Nikolian?" shouted Wendy.

Nikolian was already busily ¡ncrypting with Brad.

The Utterminster went on: "The Mistress Consort to the Regent will be

¡amAnybell: so wait? He is up 4 murder 4 kicking this rapey guy in the nuts? WTF?

¡amSoothSlayer14: Blood debt! Awesome!

¡amShoebalmer: that is their law anybell respect

¡amWalden4u: that is crazy no respect for batshit laws

¡amTomTom: are any of you surprised? Have you not been paying attention to this show?

¡amSoothSlayer14: trial by arms! trial by arms! trial by arms! trial by arms! trial by arms!

¡amShoebalmer: Uh oh this is going to get really interesting people. Someone's gonna die! Just watch!

silent. It is the ruling of this conclave that guilt in the matter be decided by trial by arms. There being no surviving members of Quarrymaster Bagwipe's family, a representative to take his part in the trial will be chosen by lot. This representative will face the Adjutant in a trial by arms to satisfy the blood debt at a date and time to be decided by the conclave in closed session. Until such time, out of deference to his high office, the Adjutant is to be kept in supervised liberty. This session is at an end. Azhuur be served!"

The Utterminster threw the lever in the bench and once more the Great Water Clock bubbled and gurgled back to life.

"Justice out of time has been done," announced the Clarion. "The waters of time run freely again until next stilled by perfidy. Azhuur be served!" Although this was a slight improvement over the justice system that had prevailed under General D'Izmaïe, where, if there was a trial at all, functionaries known as stoolsayers studied the accused's feces to decide guilt or innocence, the Clarion was still shocked by the blatantness of this show trial.

"Escort the Adjutant to his tent!" bellowed the Utterminster to his Utterforz, and left the chamber.

¡amTempl8: trial by arms! trial by arms! trial by arms! trial by arms! trial by arms!

¡amFrootfly: trial by arms! trial by arms! trial by arms! trial by arms! trial by arms!

¡amShook88: totally awesome!!!!

¡amTomTom: you people are depraved

¡amSoothSlayer14: what are you even doing in here TomTom? Go watch vintage washing machines. this is amazing stuff

¡amShook88: yeah TomTom why do you hate justice? you are not wanted here shut up

¡amSoothSlayer14: I can't wait to see where this goes! Fuckinawesome show!

¡amTomTom: SoothSlayer you are trying too hard here dude. Total propaganda plant!

THAT WAS NO RAP ON THE KNUCKLES!!! Nikolian hit *Send.* He was so engrossed in his messaging with Brad that he didn't notice the chamber emptying.

"This came as a surprise to you, Nikolian?" said the Clarion.

"Well, yeah, I have to say it did."

"But Skid didn't organize this little caper all by himself, did he?"

"Uhm, no, no, he didn't."

"You and Brad already knew the Utterminster had cause to harm Skid."

"You mean the motorbike . . ."

"Yes. The Utterminster's sexual proclivities are not unknown to us."

"We—well, Brad—thought if Skid were more visible in the show, it would protect him from the Udder." Nikolian suddenly dropped into a whisper and leaned closer to the Clarion: "Wait, *us*? Who is *us*? You are not fully on board with this new development either, are you?"

The Clarion shook his head sadly. "This is a very dark turn of events. The Utterminster is clearly feeling more powerful. That is not a good sign."

"Can you help Skid, Clarion?"

"Can you?"

"I don't know, but I will do what I can; I see now how stupid an idea this was."

"Let me think on this."

"And the *us*? Who is the *us*?"

"I think I have divulged quite enough for one day, don't you?" The Clarion smiled a sad little smile. "I will leave you to your communications with Brad. I hope you can convey to him the full gravity of this development and enlist his cooperation in whatever stratagems we might devise."

"I believe I can do that."

Then the Clarion casually said something in Azhuurse, an old proverb: "When you meet another good soul on a dark road, it becomes less dark." He watched Nikolian carefully, gauging his reaction.

After a long pause, Nikolian responded: "I'm sorry, was that Azhuurse?"

"Yes it was, Nikolian. Somehow I think you probably grasped its meaning." The two men locked eyes for what felt like an eternity to Nikolian before the Clarion bowed his head, twisted his nose, and walked out of the Hall of Conclave.

Nikolian stabbed at the screen of his ¡think. "Brad, we need a scrambled Intimeet, just you and me, ASAP."

XIII

Skid sat on a low stool in the living area of his tent. He rested his elbows on his knees, folded his arms, and dropped his head on them. He closed his eyes as tightly as he could and wished for night. He would never have to wake up from this night. It would be dark forever and everyone would leave him alone and eventually forget about him and everything around him would go away and never have been.

He pictured himself back in his ma's living room, sitting on the couch among her magazines and the generations of junk mail that never got thrown out. He opened his eyes and sadly acknowledged this was not the case: he was still in Azhuur. No amount of eye-scrunching was going to change any of this.

Wendy's voice was cracked with anger: "Fuck Brad! He fucking knew about it before the trial!"

Skid looked up and she was now pacing up and down in front of him. He closed his eyes and put his head back down.

Undeterred, Wendy continued: "He lied to us. He knew where you were and told us you were off on some motorbike trip. He knew the Utterminster had you but told us nothing. And then he gave them the footage to show at the trial. What a fucking reptile! How are we supposed to ever trust him again? Not that I ever trusted him. But Nikolian? I trusted *him*. He must have known too."

"They didn't need the footage, Wendy. They could have said I ripped his heart out with my teeth and it would have been accepted as evidence. Kangaroo court."

"But what the fuck were you thinking, Skid? What did you think you were doing smuggling yourself into the pit? Whose bright idea was that? Brad made it seem like it was yours. Was it?"

"No, it was his idea," said Skid without looking up.

"Why did you agree to such a stupid and dangerous stunt? You trying to upstage us? What's that about?"

"Brad said I'd be safer if I had a bigger part. If I was more visible. It's not like I really have much of a job here."

"Safer? Safer from what?"

"The Utterminster."

"What? Why did you need to be safer from him?"

"I kinda walked in on him wearing nothing but stilettos, getting spanked by a naked kitchen maid while he shagged a sheep. I don't think he appreciated the visit."

"Oh wow, oh wow, that is wild. Eeeeeew."

"Not a pretty sight."

"Well, if this stupid plan of Brad's was supposed to keep you safe from the Utterminster, it certainly backfired."

"No shit, Sherlock. He's framed me for murder, for fuck sake!"

"Well, Brad and Nikolian made this problem, they better help with it."

"Like fuck they will. This is great for them. This is loads of ¡balls. I have to have a fucking sword fight with some rando to prove my innocence? That's going to work out well, isn't it? And what the fuck do you think *you* can do about it? You're just another fucking puppet like me. And since when are you so interested in what happens to me anyway?"

"I just think it's wrong. I just . . . I just . . . Well, yeah, it's wrong . . ."

"And?"

"Honestly? What terrifies me is, if they can get to you, then they can get to me, and there are some very powerful people interested in getting to me, so . . . yeah . . . I'm scared. I want out of this."

"Yeah. Knut Ho must be really gunning for you. He's a mad fucker. You're right to be afraid of him. I want out of this too. I told Brad right after the trial."

"What did he say?"

"He said: 'No problem. Go right ahead. Good luck getting out of there. I'm sure Udder and Archie will be only too happy to help. See how long you last once you are no longer on the show.'"

"Oh shit, he's right. He has us completely fucking trapped!"

Before either of them had time to fully process this realization, they were distracted by a low murmur of voices outside the tent.

Stepping outside, Wendy found a dusty and harried group talking anxiously among themselves. They fell silent when they saw her and one of them, a slight young woman with intense eyes, stepped forward. She twisted her nose and bowed as respectfully as her tired, heavy limbs would allow.

"I'm Alva. We are outta the quarry, wanna see how Adjutant Skid is doing."

"You what? Who? How did you get in here?" said Wendy.

"We sold some stuff and shit and bribed the guards," replied Alva.

"It's okay, Wendy, I know her," said Skid from inside the tent. He then appeared and immediately the group went into fits of nose-twisting, bowing, and low, sad whooping. "Ehm, that's all very lovely now, but what can I do for you?"

"Long live Adjutant Skid!" a dry, cracked voice called from

the back of the group. The rest of them immediately took up the chant.

Skid held up his hands in an Adjutant-like gesture and the group fell silent. "Listen, that was all very nice. My name is just Skid, okay? Skid. Thank you all for coming to see me. Alva, I'm glad to see you. I hope you're okay. As you can see, I am standing on my own two legs, so that is good. Really appreciate you visiting. So cool you stopped by, but I am not really up for a big hero-worship deal right now. We cool?"

The group looked to Alva, who translated for them, and then one by one each came forward, bowed solemnly to Skid and then to Wendy, and walked silently away. They did this in such a dignified way that Skid, for the first time since he arrived in Azhuur, detected a deep genuineness in this show of respect, so unlike all the other rote ceremonial showiness. It made the hair stand up on the back of his neck.

When the small crowd cleared, it revealed Nikolian, who had been standing at the back watching. He looked sheepish and uncharacteristically hesitant.

"Well, check out who's here to fix everything," mocked Wendy.

Nikolian stepped toward them. "Look, I came to—"

"Say you're sorry? Well, that's fuck all use to me now!" interrupted Skid.

Wendy strode up to Nikolian and started poking him in the chest. "How could you let this happen? Your job is to keep us safe. Including from any of Brad's stupid fucking ideas."

"Brad cooked this up without telling me. He went straight to Skid with it. I didn't know about it until after Skid had been arrested."

"How could either of you give Udder and Archie the chance to get at any of us? They are like the fucking collective id of Azhuur and you give them a golden opportunity to fuck with one of us? . . . Why are you looking at me like that?"

"Did you just say 'Wizard of Oz'?"

"No, I fucking did not, I said 'id of Azhuur'! Anyway, what does that have to do with anything?"

"Uhm, nothing."

"So?" said Skid quietly, moving closer.

"It was a really stupid idea," conceded Nikolian.

"No shit. And? You came to say sorry? That's it? You got anything more to offer? Listen, man, your *sorry* is not really much use to me right now."

"Maybe I can help," said Nikolian.

"Yeah? How?"

"Maybe there is a legal way out of this. I studied law for a while. The Spinster Uilkitz already said I can use the Quartel library."

"Then you're going to need this." Wendy took a small cloth parcel from her pocket and handed it to Nikolian.

"What's this?"

"Marzipan from the Sisterhood. *Special* marzipan. Made me able to read Azhuurse. Unless you have other plans for some intensive language course?"

"Uhm, no, right. Yes, that's very helpful. Thanks." Nikolian put the marzipan in his inside pocket.

The three of them stood together in the awkward silence of spent anger before Nikolian self-consciously moved to go. "Well, I suppose I should get to the library then."

"Yes, I suppose you should," said Skid flatly.

Nikolian walked slowly away.

"Great," muttered Skid. "Nikolian out of his head on trepanium marzipan playing amateur lawyer. That's all I need!" He stomped back into his tent.

"I'll, uhm, see you later?" Wendy called after him, intuiting that her company was not being asked for.

XIV

"You have to sense the air telling you where it is not," intoned the Blade Master as Mooney picked himself up for the far-too-manyeth time.

Mooney blindly smacked the floor around him, searching for his staff.

"Feel with your ears," said the Blade Master.

Mooney rolled his blindfolded eyes to heaven and continued hunting for his staff. He felt a sharp blow to his shoulder.

"A warrior without urgency is a bow with no bowstring!" shouted the Blade Master, whacking Mooney with another blow to the knee for good measure.

"A blindfolded man with no stick being hit by one with no blindfold and a stick is a fool!" snarled Mooney. He searched more urgently while the Blade Master continued to hit him. After a few more blows, he finally found his staff and flailed in the direction the last shot had come from.

"The bird will not sing from the same branch twice. You must see with the eyes of your enemy," said the Blade Master from somewhere behind Mooney.

Mooney sighed and heavily raised himself to his feet. He felt a swish of air to his left and just managed to ward off what would have been a stinging blow to the head. Maybe the Relict's herb had helped a little after all.

"Good! In the garden of pain grow the flowers of caution."

"What?" shouted Mooney over the hellish sound that now enveloped them.

The Blade Master repeated his nugget of wisdom, which was this time completely drowned out by the propeller sounds of an airship passing fifty feet above the Tower of Thrones. The Blade Master stood at the tier's edge and watched the underside of the ship pass overhead and was barely able to react in time to parry Mooney's huge swinging attack. He pivoted and used his two staffs to wrench Mooney's from his hands before pinning Mooney to the floor, scissoring his staffs at Mooney's neck. "The fruit of opportunity must be plucked in its ripeness. You did well, my liege. Our training is at an end for today."

He helped Mooney up and then, as he had done after every lesson, offered his razor-sharp dagger to Mooney, hilt first: "For any hurt caused you, I am yours to do justice to. Azhuur be served!"

Mooney took the dagger and reversed it, handing the hilt back to the Blade Master as usual. "You are absolved. Justice is done. Azhuur is served."

XV

Nikolian banged his head slowly on the heavy table in the Quartel library. He had been reading the annals and the codices of law for fifteen hours. He had eaten the marzipan Wendy had given him; it helped keep him awake, even though he did not really need it to read Azhuurse.

Still, after hours of research, he could find nothing in Azhuurse law to weaken the case the Utterminster had so deviously assembled against Skid. He knew Skid's side of the story, but legally that didn't actually help. He felt numb, tired, and very fragile.

For the first time since he had left Newer York, Nikolian was unable to shut out Eduard. He had grieved when Eduard died but now realized that, since he had sold the house, he had not been brave enough to allow himself to really think of him. The newness of Azhuur was beginning to pall, and into the space left by worn-out novelty poured the appalling absence of his beloved husband.

Nikolian had stroked Eduard's face as he lay in the bed apologizing for being a burden. He watched Eduard morphine-sleep fitfully through the pain of his bones decaying from the inside out. Nikolian felt him squeeze his hand with the full force of what little strength he could still summon, right before he closed his eyes for the last time.

He could feel again the disbelief and hopelessness of that moment when Eduard slipped from being into not, and left him for good. He felt the tears sting his eyes as they ran down his face and gathered in the lines at the corners of his mouth. He did not notice the Clarion come in until he felt his hand on his shoulder.

"Is everything all right?" asked the Clarion softly.

"Oh, Clarion, you gave me a fright. I'm fine. Overtired. It's nothing. Wait, no, sorry? What did you say? Was that Azhuurse?"

The Clarion smiled and took a seat beside Nikolian. They sat together at the table in silence, watching the motes of dust in the sunlight that now flooded the library.

"You understood what I said. You are a Watcher, no?"

Nikolian froze.

The Clarion rapped the table lightly. "I thought so. When you warned us that the rider statue was on the move, your job was done. Why did you come here with it?"

As if a great tension had just abandoned him, Nikolian sat back and stretched wide. "Yes, I am a Watcher. I don't know why I came here. I just set it all in motion and then did nothing to stop it happening. And now I'm here. In this. Whatever all of this is."

"But to throw up your whole life? Because of that statue?"

"There was nothing to stay for. My husband died two years ago. Bone cancer. I got rid of the house, got rid of our things, and started living in a motel. I was broken, empty, alone. I felt drawn here. I told Brad I was ex–Secret Service and could speak a little Azhuurse. He hired me."

"Please accept my profound condolences. You were born in the Outlands, were you not?"

"Yes. My father was born here. He was one of the original Watchers sent abroad. I was born in Boston."

"I knew him. I was sorry to hear of his death. We were friends before the . . . before D'Izmaïe."

"Thank you."

"I thought I saw the resemblance when I spoke with you after the trial. Hence the proverb. I must say, you did a poor job of feigning incomprehension."

"Yes, yes, I did. You caught me off guard."

"And your mother?"

"She moved back to Canada. She is well, thank you."

Nikolian listened to the Clarion's slow breaths, and before he knew what was happening, he was reminiscing about Eduard. Nikolian spilled out over the sides to the Clarion: from the silliest details of the first time they met to the battle he had with Eduard's family about the cremation and scattering of his ashes on the lake in Mexico where they had spent their honeymoon; to the emptiness that had seeped into him from Eduard's absence in every tiny corner of their home. He paused and smiled ruefully at the Clarion. "I'm sorry. You got more of an earful than you bargained for."

"Grief is not tidy. I too have experienced such a loss," said the Clarion. "You have confided in me, so it seems only right that I reciprocate in some way. It is twenty years now since I lost my daughter. It took me ten of those to find the strength to open myself again to the life that I inhabit. I found myself on a type of journey, but inward. I became enselfed to the point of virtually disappearing from my own existence. I participated in the world around me in only two dimensions, if you understand me: I pretended to be. We each take a journey with our grief, but the return is far more difficult than the getting lost. But there is a return. There are moments when that is hard to believe, but there is a way back.

"My office is greatly important to me. It was my father's before me, and his father's before him, and in some ways provided me with the strength to carry on. It was for some time an analgesic, a physical koan to give shape to my lostness. Only recently am I fully part of it again, despite the distasteful trajectory D'Izmaïe and the Utterminster have decided for this land. Being Clarion is no longer something I wrap around myself for concealment. To come back takes time and perseverance. There is, unfortunately, no other solution."

"I did not know you had lost a daughter. I am so sorry."

"Inexplicable heart failure. A woman in her prime. She was one of twins. The Relict Uilkitz raised them pretending they were orphans of her household. Her brother is now a man and is a great source of consolation to me. He is a quiet scholarly soul with no interest in the doings of state."

"Won't he become Clarion after you?"

"It is hard to envision."

"And your wife?"

"Not wife, per se. A member of the Sisterhood. The Relict and Spinster's eldest sister. We are sundered by law. We can consort in private, but never share a life."

A slightly embarrassed silence followed, both men suddenly aware of how much they had shared and how quickly. The Clarion stood up and walked to the window. He blew into the mouthpiece set into the wall and muttered something.

Moments later, the dumbwaiter pinged and the Clarion retrieved a beautiful tray bearing two slim stemmed glasses and a chilled bottle.

"You will join me in a sherry to toast our new, dare I say, friendship? In a world like this, such closenings, however small or brief, should be marked, treasured, and acknowledged."

"Gladly," replied Nikolian.

The Clarion poured.

Nikolian inhaled the crisp clean odors of Jerez: "Your health."

"To dear memories and making them part of a new path."

The Clarion tilted his head, took a sip of the cool, pale wine, and sighed in satisfaction.

"Oh, for a beaker full of the warm south," said Nikolian dreamily.

"Full of the true, the blushful Hippocrene," smiled the Clarion. He refilled their glasses.

After a few minutes of silence, Nikolian blurted: "I came to see if there's a way to fight this trumped-up case against Skid."

"I suspected as much. If I may be candid, it was a foolhardy stunt to send him into the excavation. I regret to tell you this, but you will find no legal way to contest the charges, and any trace of malfeasance in the demise of Bagwipe and his next of kin will have been thoroughly erased. I trust you understand what I mean."

Nikolian nodded. They sipped again in silence.

"You know why I'm here?" asked the Clarion.

"To spy on me?" Nikolian smiled.

"I have been sent to search the annals for the procedures to choose the Adjutant's adversary."

"Everything must be done by the book, eh?" sneered Nikolian. "Well, if there's anything I can do to help . . ."

The Clarion shook his head. "I understand your skepticism. Thank you for the offer of help, but this has fallen to me and I can neither shirk nor share this odious responsibility. And please believe me, it is odious to me."

"I can see that. I should get back to the encampment, if there is nothing to be found in these books."

The Clarion refilled their glasses. "One for the road? To new friends!"

"To new friends!"

XVI

"I don't think that is any of your concern, Clarion. We set you a task and it is your duty to carry it out," snapped the Utterminster. "So, if you will please dispense with the tedious moralizing preamble and pointless bellyaching, tell us what you have compiled. You have already taken far more time over this than was necessary, which is why we have had to come here to remind you of your obligations to Azhuur."

"Utterminster, can we dispense with this tiresome pretense? You know as well as I do what is in the annals of Mög. You two and D'Izmaïe wrote them and concocted this Mögian faction. You were part of the cabal that invented Old High Azhuurse. You were the one who pushed for inventing the ridiculous old script. You were the engineer of the Reedification Fields, the rewriting of our history into Right Remembering, and the elimination of all copies of real history and anyone caught keeping it intact. You oversaw the cruelty of the Vale of Victory. So please, spare me the indignity of having to regurgitate this fatuous twaddle as if it were sacred history."

"Clarion, I have always suspected you are not a true believer, but I am sure you realize that you still have too much to lose to dare cross me. You think I do not know who the Relict Uilkitz's ward is? I will not be thwarted. WE will not be thwarted. So? You have found the protocols for choosing the state's combatant?"

"I have. I have transcribed them. They are on the table in front of you. I have already added my seal."

"Good. Then you will communicate what is necessary to the Bradleys and other disgusting Outlanders who need telling. The Archixprest will coordinate the work teams. We will all continue to believe in Mög and his annals and you will temper your insolence, if you know what is good for you."

"Very well. Azhuur be served!" answered the Clarion.

"You may go. Convey my regards to your, ahem, *son*. Long may he continue to enjoy safety and good health. Azhuur be served!"

The library door closed behind the Clarion.

The Utterminster picked up the document the Clarion had left. He gave it a cursory glance and slid it across the table to the Archixprest. "See to this. Has the Clarion always had that impertinent streak or has he been corrupted by the Outlanders? Is their noxious presence inciting chaff like the Clarion to talk back to me, to denigrate the annals of Mög? This insolence is intolerable. It is all that disrespectful Brad's fault. His time will come."

"It is insufferable, Your Utterness, but we will, for the moment, forbear it. We still need the insolent Brad. The show is a success. It is achieving our aims. Azhuur is beheld by millions. Soon they will see the full glory."

"Well, we shall soon put an end to the bad influence of the Outlanders. I have a particularly appealing plan for Brad. Do you remember D'Izmaïe's Diet? Castor oil, wood alcohol, bread crumbs, and sawdust? How the general force-fed that insurrectionist scum leader Ivac and then watched him shit and vomit himself to death? I cannot wait! We will get a glass barrel and make Brad's own ¡sees broadcast every moment of his torment and humiliating death. But for now, we cannot afford any distractions or disturbances. We are so near the time and no interference can be tolerated. We have waited so long for this moment. Azhuur will no longer cower in the shadows. We shall be restored to the great glory of the reign of General D'Izmaïe and all will prostrate themselves before the steely greatness of Azhuur. Ensure the proper combatant is selected. The Adjutant will be dispatched. There is to be no possibility of failure. Is that understood?"

"It will be so, Your Utterness. And Kanker? Should I make arrangements?"

The Utterminster smiled. "No. I have already seen to our pliant friend. He is fully repaid for his services to us. He is now an honored and permanent part of a retaining wall in the pit alongside our *mysteriously disappeared* Invigilator of Internality.

There are no loose ends. It is time to return to the encampment and make preparations. I want the work rate of the excavation increased. We must be ready in one month. I feel our hold over the pubble slipping. I smell the Outlander cartels plotting to take our trepanium."

"And the reenactment of the Vale of Victory?"

"I have not decided yet. But I am tending toward the idea— start with a nice clean sheet, instill some deep fear. I want the plans for it perfected and the troops in place on the day. I will decide then. Understood? Azhuur be served!"

"As you command, Your Utterness. Azhuur be served!"

From his hiding place in the dumbwaiter shaft, the Clarion heard the door open and the Utterminster and the Archixprest leave the Reading Room. Their receding footsteps left behind them a silence of dark alarm. The Clarion let out a long breath and waited until he was certain the Utterminster and Archixprest were clear of the Quartel before he made his way through its dark and empty streets to retrieve his horse for the trip back to the encampment.

XVII

"Good morning, Clarion," said Wendy. "This is a pleasant surprise. I didn't know you liked riding."

"I have not ridden for pleasure in a long while and felt it was perhaps time to dust off my skills."

"Well, this comes as a welcome distraction. Where shall we go?"

"I thought we might take an excursion into the hills. I have brought a picnic lunch and plenty of water."

"Uhm, I hadn't planned being away for so long. I thought I should be around for Skid, you know, to help out, show support, be present, in evidence, solidarity . . . whatever . . ." Wendy's voice trailed away as the pitiful vapidity of her sentence ground on her ears.

"I believe this excursion may be of some help to you and perhaps young Skid."

"Now you're being all mysterious!"

"Come. Let us ride. We can speak more freely once we are clear of the pit and the encampment."

They rode along the side of the paved main road until they got past the old refinery. Then the Clarion directed them toward the hills to the northeast.

"Where are you taking me?"

"I have something to show you, then I can tell you some more."

"You're being really shady. You're making me nervous."

"Can I trust you, Mistress?"

"Not if you keep calling me Mistress."

"I am sorry. Wendy it is then. The Utterminster and the Archixprest came to visit me in the library. After they dismissed me, I hid in a dumbwaiter shaft and listened in on them. I heard some of their plans for the launch. I have to admit I am fearful of what they intend."

They rode on in silence until Wendy couldn't take it anymore. "That's it? That's all you're giving me? And now I'm supposed to ride into the hills with you alone?" She drew her horse to a halt.

The Clarion rode back and drew up beside her. "You want details?" In a superlatively good impression of the Utterminster he continued: "*I have a particularly appealing plan for Brad. Do you remember D'Izmaïe's Diet? Castor oil, wood alcohol, bread crumbs, and sawdust? . . . I cannot wait! We will get a glass barrel and make Brad's own ¡sees broadcast every moment of his torment and humiliating death.*" He took a deep breath: "That is but a part of it."

"That is so fucked up. But how does he think he'll be able to do something like that? Does he think there will be some *So You Wanna* prize for hurling that stupid statue into space? You get to murder the producer?"

"I honestly don't know, but he did seem very confident about having the capability to carry out this act of vengeance on Brad. There is more, but first you must see where we are going."

The Clarion made to move off but Wendy stayed put. "Why are you telling me this?"

"I think it is only fair that you have as clear a picture as possible of what you are surrounded by. Initially, I thought this would all be a superficial publicity stunt and you would all come, make some silly public appearances, play some silly games, and leave, but it is not looking like that anymore, is it? I want you to take the threat to Skid very, very seriously."

"I do! I do!"

"Then I want you to understand the deep reasons why you should, and why it constitutes a threat to all of you now."

"How do you get away with it? Shouldn't you be dead in a ditch by now? Why do Udder and Archie tolerate you, if you are not fully in lockstep with them?"

"They need the Sisterhood. And for that they need the Clarion. I am son, grandson, great-grandson of a long line of Clarions and I am the sole channel of communication between the Sisterhood and the Utterminster and Archixprest. I am the only way. The Sisterhood would burn the Outlying Hermitage to the ground with themselves in it rather than communicate directly with either of them. It goes back a long way and is very raw and real to this day."

"Would that place even burn?"

"I doubt it. I was speaking figuratively."

"Why doesn't the Sisterhood stop Udder and Archie and this D'Izmaïe statue crap?"

"At the first sign of interference, the Utterminster would take horrible vengeance as he and his ilk did at the beginning of D'Izmaïe's rule. They threatened to flay a captive outside the Hermitage for every day the Sisterhood resisted forging the statue. There was no doubt they would have done it, so the Sisterhood relented. Normally, trepanium in that kind of concentration would react against itself and decay into dust. The Sisterhood somehow managed to cast it. The process almost destroyed the Hermitage. All trace of how it was done was lost. The current standoff or stalemate is the most cordial and stable this fractious relationship is ever likely to be."

The Clarion urged his horse forward. From the set of his shoulders, Wendy could tell he was done talking for the moment. She clicked her tongue and her horse moved on to follow him toward the hills.

𐅍

The horses picked their way reluctantly over the ridge and then down the side of the valley. Below them, Wendy and the Clarion saw the unnatural gray hulk of the dam wall fall sickeningly to the valley floor some thousand feet farther down, and massed behind it, stretching back into the valley, the deep, dark, unmoving waters. There was not an opticon in sight.

"Here we are: Aquifer 1, Reservoir 1," announced the Clarion. "Aka the Vale of Victory; aka, unofficially, the Valley of the Disappeared." He glanced around warily, even though they were completely alone.

"Creepy! And what the fuck are those?" Wendy pointed to the flotilla anchored in the middle of the waters.

"Hostage barges."

"What?"

"The Utterminster keeps hostages related to anyone who serves him. Also, some ambitious families among the lower gentry send their children into the Utterforz. They too must give a hostage as collateral against any insubordination. If a soldier or a servant displeases, the hostage is drowned in the lake."

"And the fires?"

"To ensure the local Utterforz or the populace never turn on the Utterminster, he has a standing order that if anything untoward should ever happen to him, these barges and all the hostages aboard are to be burned immediately. The braziers burn day and night in readiness."

"But there must be hundreds of people out there!"

"Seventeen barges, eight hundred and eleven hostages, last tally."

"But how would they know if anything happened to the Utterminster?"

"Each barge has a small opticon that can receive whispers."

Wendy did not know the detail of how General D'Izmaïe had rounded up thousands of political prisoners and dissidents and brought them to this huge valley to build the dam and then dig deep caves into the hillsides behind it. She did not know that D'Izmaïe then had them gated and locked in the same caves they had dug out, to drown "like the parasitic rats in the granary of the Fatherland they are."

She did not know he had arranged for the executioners themselves to be garroted in their sleep by his elite troops and then deposited in the caves with their erstwhile prisoners. She never heard his speech when all the caves were filled with prisoners and they readied to close off the dam and flood the whole valley, how he declaimed that henceforth he could forever "drink deep of the taste of victory from this river's waters." She did not know he had joked that these malefactors had been digging their own graves from the very moment they opposed him and he was merely bringing the cycle to its logical conclusion.

Wendy knew none of that, but she did sense its effects, and she could not fail to notice how there were no animals in the nearby woods and how birds would not cross the air above the water, nor sing anywhere in earshot of it. The wrongness of the place buckled and thickened the air and dirtied the light.

They dismounted and their horses backed away from the water to the top of the ridge. Both animals shook their heads and raised their noses to the wind as if searching for cleaner air.

Wendy approached the balustrade that adorned the top of the dam wall.

"Keep out of sight of the barges."

"I've seen shit like this on shows, on old stuff like stone circles, and on megaliths. Look at these wild carvings all over it. Crazy old."

"But touch it," murmured the Clarion.

Wendy ran her hands over the stonework. "Ugh, it feels like warm plastic."

"It is a sand compound devised by the Sisterhood, similar to concrete but much more versatile and easier to work with. The Archixprest designed the runes, and I have to admit they are quite convincing."

"So, this is recent?"

"Oh yes. General D'Izmaïe commissioned it."

"And everyone knows this ancientness is bullshit?"

"Most people. For younger people, it is the only story they have ever known. But there is knowing, Mistress—apologies, Wendy—and then there is believing. The people of Azhuur, who wished to survive D'Izmaïe's Reedification Fields, learned to believe that this dam was built a thousand years ago by our heroic, broadsword-wielding, Old High Azhuurse–speaking forebears using ancient magical techniques long since lost to our fallen times. It was certainly a strain. Yet the genius for staying alive allows people to believe something they know to be patently untrue, if their lives depend on it. Like a reluctant convert. It becomes second nature, an internalized and veracified untruth.

"The annals, Mög, Old High Azhuurse—it's all fabrication, invented to paper over the memory of what D'Izmaïe did to this country. Hundreds of indentured linguists worked day and night to contrive and codify Old High Azhuurse and then they were set

the task of *recreating* the lost archives. All of the linguists mysteriously disappeared the night the archives were declared finished.
We suspected the worst. The pubble learned to recognize some
key words and phrases in Old High Azhuurse, and the nobles who
sought advancement engaged in grammar contests and spelling
bees to display their proficiency in the ancient tongue. In recent
years, some of this enthusiasm has faded, but the willful belief is
still there, and I have seen the beginnings of a resurgence among
the gentry since the return of D'Izmaïe's statue."

"So, what is with the really weird energy here?"

"Come, let us move away from the water. It is most uncomfortable to be near it."

They climbed back up to the ridge and Wendy stared down
at the grotesque dam while the Clarion sat on the grass beside
her and talked in a low and frightened monotone. By the time
he was finished, they were both in tears and Wendy was painfully
familiar with all the vile ingredients that comprised the powerful
wrongness that emanated from the Vale of Victory and the toxic
legacy of General D'Izmaïe.

After a long silence, the Clarion quietly added: "From my
hiding place in the library, I heard the Utterminster consider
deploying soldiers to reenact the Vale of Victory on launch
day."

"You mean he plans to drown people in the pit as a show of
power?"

"I fear he might."

"Does the Sisterhood know anything about this?"

"They know everything that I know."

"Are they going to do something to stop him?"

"They have to tread carefully. It is a precarious balance."

"What? Are they afraid of hurting the Utterminster's feelings?"

"I already told you what was done to force them to make the
statue. It left its mark on the sisters."

"It sounds like there will be more than just a mark if they don't try to stop him. I want to meet them."

"You know that is impossible."

"We are kind of through the looking glass here, Clarion. Even I can smell the dirtiest kind of knife fight coming on, and you're worrying about the etiquette of who stands where? You know how bad it is. Otherwise you would never have brought me here."

Wendy mounted her horse and started back down the ridge away from the valley.

XVIII

SANDRA

Welcome to this special live stream of *So You Wanna Run a Country? The Id of Azhuur*. New *Id of Azhuur* merch is available on your app! Right now, we are waiting for the selection of a combatant to fight the Adjutant Skid in a battle to the death. (Backtracks, in case you missed why this is happening, appear at the bottom of your screen.) This huge crowd stretches from the edge of the pit as far as the pubble's shanties. Even with all these opticons to watch, some have climbed on top of the shanties to get a better view of the real thing. The courtiers have lined up by tonsure for hours to be winched up to their corresponding tiers. The Tower of Thrones is full to capacity. It is quite an astonishing sight.

TOM
It is indeed astonishing, Sandra. The pomp, the pageantry, the solemnity of these ancient rituals is so inspiring! The willingness of the gentry to sit on the Tower of Thrones, where most of them, except for the ones sitting around the edges of the tiers, can see nothing, not even an opticon; this is impressive.

SANDRA
That is one *red* sunset. It is such a weird sound: thousands of people gradually falling silent. Look, Tom, there's something coming out of the glare of the setting sun. I think it is . . . yes, it is, it's an airship!

TOM
An airship, a dirigible, a zeppelin, whatever you want to call it—I think we have to admit that this is yet another Azhuurse triumph of style over efficiency. Let's face it, Sandra, it may be a slow way to get around, but it looks fantastic in this light.

SANDRA
Yes, Tom, spectacular.

TOM

I see the airship's image all around
us in the giant opticons dotted among
this huge crowd.

SANDRA

I'm told our technical people are
still mystified by those opticons.

TOM

They certainly are, Sandra. The logistics of the last couple of days
have been astonishing. Three thousand scribes working around the clock
to get thousands of names onto individual fortune cookie-sized slips of
paper; each slip of paper then placed
in a hand-blown gelatin bubble and
placed in the drawing drum in front
of the Tower.

SANDRA

That is absolutely amazing, Tom. And
you mentioned the drum itself has a
most unusual history?

TOM

Yes, Sandra, it does. The drum is,
in fact, General D'Izmaïe's former
bath. Forty feet in diameter. A hundred carpenters worked all night to
dismantle it, move it from the Quar-

```
tel, and reassemble it here. An as-
tounding undertaking.
```

```
          SANDRA
Absolutely astounding, Tom.
```

The airship positioned itself over the drum. When it settled level with the antepenultimate tier, the Utterminster rapped on the floor with his Staff of Office in signal.

Mooney walked to the lectern at the edge of his tier and cut the outbreak of reverential whooping with an unusually impatient gesture. He draped a scroll over his right hand and the Clarion joined him. The Clarion took Mooney's left hand in his right and spoke into the tiny glass carp on behalf of He Who Is Too Mighty to Sully Himself with Public Speech. As he spoke, the last of the sun's light faded from the sky.

```
            TOM
Our producers tell me that what
the Clarion just said in Old High
Azhuurse is: "If Mög isn't too busy
doing anything else, wherever he is,
it would be nice if he would give the
selection his blessing." Look! One of
the shanties just collapsed.
```

```
          SANDRA
Did you see that? That sudden flash
of light?
```

A floodlit figure fell out of the opened doors in the underside of the airship. Everyone stared at the plummeting shape. About three quarters of the way down, the shape began to slow and a bungee cord could be discerned in the light from the airship. The figure plunged into the drum and then the bungee whipped it back up toward the airship. About a hundred feet below the airship, the figure caught onto a rope ladder and was winched back into the airship. The door snapped shut and the airship glided toward the Tower of Thrones.

                    SANDRA
        Oh my, that was the most terrifying
        ten seconds of my life.

                    TOM
        Actually, Sandra, I clocked it at
        just over eighteen seconds all told.

The airship stopped above the antepenultimate throne. The doors in the bottom of it opened again, bathing the Tower below in intense white light. A rope ladder dropped out of the light and onto the Tower.

                    SANDRA
        Oh my god, someone is climbing down.
        Look at that cloak! Those are the
        whitest feathers I have ever seen.
        Amazing. We can't see the face be-
        cause of the blindfold.

The figure bowed, twisted its nose, and stood motionless. The Clarion waited for the airship to leave, then approached the figure and removed the blindfold.

                    SANDRA
        This is amazing—it's the Archixprest.

> And he has a slip of paper between
> his teeth.

The Clarion took the slip of paper from the Archixprest's mouth with small silver tongs and presented it to the Utterminster, who nodded solemnly before handing the paper back to the Clarion, who then read the name aloud.

> TOM
> What did he just say?

> SANDRA
> Did he say "Anthrax Kitchen"? There
> is cheering of sorts in the crowd.

> TOM
> Or was it "Mandrake Itching"? The cer-
> emony is over. Again, that Azhuurse
> avoidance of finality—things don't
> formally end, they just stop. The op-
> ticons have all gone dark. I guess
> that's it from us for this episode.
> We will certainly find out what we
> can about this mysterious opponent.
> Don't forget, highlights from all
> episodes in the weekly roundup of
> *So You Wanna Run a Country? The Id
> of Azhuur* are available this Friday
> wherever you get your ether.

☸

"So what the fuck was that all about?" shouted Skid from his place on the Tower of Thrones.

The Utterminster nodded and smiled his most infuriatingly

condescending smile. "Your opponent has been chosen. A chap called Mandrak Kitxchenn, I believe. Azhuur be served!" He passed on toward the elevator, followed by the Archixprest.

Skid tried to go after them but felt a restraining hand tight on his arm. He wheeled around to see Nikolian's tired and worried face.

"Don't, Skid. Don't give him the satisfaction."

⚙

"Okay, crew, what's with the secret Intimeet?" asked Brad.

"You stupid fucking eejit. You got me into this. Who the fuck is this Mandrak Kitxchenn?" demanded Skid as he smoked yet another cigarette that he really did not want.

"Yeah, man, sorry, Skid," answered Brad. "Listen, I don't know. It's not our doing, but I bet he's a ringer."

"But how? I mean, there were a million names in the drum," said Mooney.

"I think it's probably quite simple," said Nikolian. "We were all so dazzled by the preparation and the trappings that it never struck us that it was all a hoax. The simplest thing in the world: some Archixprest stunt double bungee jumps out of the airship, bursts a few thousand bubbles, springs back up, the doors close, Archie steps onto the Tower with a piece of paper in his mouth, and we all assume it came from the drum and not his pocket."

"Excellent hypothesis, Nikolian. Now what?" said Brad.

"Yeah, now what? Exactly. YOU have anymore bright ideas, Brad?" hissed Skid.

"Can you at least delay it somehow, Brad?" asked Wendy.

Brad hesitated. "It would need to be a convincing reason for the Udder and Archie and my people too. It needs to have increased ¡balls written all over it in BIG LETTERS. Listen, we are seeing huge pretraction out there in the S¡milireality gaming for some royal wedding thing between Mooney and Wendy. Not saying you have to go through with it, but if you want to distract from this trial thing, you might want to think about it.

That's strictly between us, okay? That's my gift to you. Thinking hats on, y'all. Oh, you might have noticed the rebranding: *So You Wanna Run a Country? The Id of Azhuur.* Thanks for that, Wendy!" Brad waved somewhat less cheerily than usual, and the Intimeet on Nikolian's ¡think went dark.

Wendy glared at Nikolian. "You told him about my 'id of Azhuur' comment?"

"Sorry, Wendy, but I still have a job to do. It's a good title. He heard 'Wizard of Oz' at first too. Weird. That's the only thing I told him from that conversation. Anyway, don't we have more pressing things to deal with?"

XIX

"Intimeet runacountry 397," the Clarion told the ¡box on the wall early the following morning.

The ¡box lit up and Brad's face loomed at them from the wall of the Chamber of Councils. "Archie! Udder! Clarion, old boy! What's up? Mooney, Wendy, nice to see you again. I see we are missing Skid. Not surprising. Must be important for you to wake me up in what is the middle of my night, so let's have it. It's just me on my end. I gave the suits the night off. So. Go!"

"Well, as you requested, Regent, here we have the Extraordinary High Council," said the Utterminster. "Brad, the producer is Intimeeting with us. May I ask what we have to discuss?"

Mooney stood up sheepishly. He held out his hand to Wendy, who got up as well. Nikolian could not believe how well Mooney had taken his midnight coaching session.

"We have an announcement to make. We have decided we would like to formalize our relationship in the eyes of our people. We would like to be married by the rites of Azhuur."

"I am liking what I am hearing here, people!" cheered Brad. "This has ¡balls galore writ large on it! I could almost forgive you for waking me up at this uncivilized hour."

The Utterminster beamed as widely as his stony face could manage. "This is splendid news. We shall have to make arrangements."

"We already thought about that."

"Oh yes?" said the Utterminster.

"We thought it would be nice to have the wedding be part of the launch-day festivities."

The Utterminster frowned and leaned toward the Archixprest. The Archixprest whispered something in his ear.

"Perhaps it would be better to put it off until another day. We don't want to take any importance away from either of these events by putting them together."

"I disagree, Utterminster," countered Mooney. "It would make it a truly glorious day for Azhuur. To link these momentous events together would provide an unparalleled opportunity for celebration. Has there ever been such a day in all the history of Azhuur? Should we not make it a day of days in Azhuurse history? Imagine the spectacle! I am sure no Utterminster ever presided over such a wonderful day-long ceremony."

Brad eagerly chimed in from the ¡box: "Regent dude's got a point there, Udder."

That did it. The Utterminster's vanity was aroused. He leaned once more into conference with the Archixprest. Mooney felt Wendy's grip on his hand tighten. It was time to press home.

Mooney cleared his throat. "It has further occurred to us that to complete the day, we could include the trial by combat. That would make a truly uplifting spectacle for the people of Azhuur and the ¡balls to witness. Mixing the terror and the joy and the glory all in one day would be an unforgettable reminder of Azhuur's greatness. Picture it: General D'Izmaïe launched into the skies to preside over the trial and then our wedding. Unprecedented! It would keep the pubble well in their place."

The Utterminster's face clouded as he considered this.

The Clarion exploded from his seat: "This is barbaric! You

cannot seriously be proposing this. I thought I was here for a happy announcement of an engagement. How can you sit there and consider trifling with a man's life as a warm-up show for a wedding? This is beyond repugnant!"

Mooney fixed the Clarion with a steely glare which, even though they had rehearsed it, struck the old man like a blow to the chest. "I think, Clarion, you are overstepping the mark. Remember your place here. You are perhaps losing sight of the greater purpose of these celebrations for the good of Azhuur. Once General D'Izmaïe has ascended, the trial as a preliminary to our wedding would provide a truly, how should we say it, cathartic and awe-inspiring moment for the edification of the pubble. I believe we all understand how important it is to keep them edified, stupefied, and firmly in their place."

The Utterminster cleared his throat and stood up. He adjusted his robes like some basso Shakespearean preparing to deliver The Big Speech. He made eye contact with everyone in the room and then with Brad. "I believe the Regent has grasped something that to many of us has remained obscured by mere logistics and planning. Instead of concentrating on the spiritual and inspirational nature of these ceremonies, we have merely focused on the grim matters of organization. I think he has brought all these events together into one compelling, uplifting, and unforgettable celebration of what beats at the core of Azhuurse identity. We shall postpone the trial and follow the Regent's suggestion. Clarion, you will see to the planning of this. Let there be this Day of Days. Azhuur be served!"

"Sing it loud, Udder, it's party time!" beamed Brad from the ¡box on the wall.

The Utterminster twisted his nose to everyone and exited the Chamber of Councils, followed closely by an Archixprest too stunned by this development to even manage an "Azhuur be served!"

၆

"Nikolian, can I have a word?" said Wendy quietly as the others were leaving. "So? Did you find anything at all when you went to the library?"

"No, there is nothing. They have stitched Skid up nice and tight. It is all according to their law and they have eradicated every trace of what really happened to Bagwipe. But I did find this." Nikolian sat down and took out his ¡think. "I searched for the real person behind Mandrak Kitxchenn and was astonished to find it was not an alias. There was no attempt to conceal his identity, and a few well-directed queries around the Dark Services constellation of the ether gave me this: Mandrak Kitxchenn's own contracting node."

Wendy sat beside him and watched. The visuals were sparse and dark. The text intro scrolled *Star Wars*–style up the frame over a Stockhausen-meets–death metal soundscape:

> *With over thirty years of experience in the bespoke termination industry, with a client list as impressive and extensive as it is top secret, Mandrak Kitxchenn is, without doubt, one of the most dangerous and efficient operators in the profession today.*

> *An excellent marksman with both bow and bullet, a PhD in applied toxicology from the Pluriversity of Damm, a Carnage Institute certified explosives expert, an accomplished swordsman, master of many martial arts including the highly secretive and now outlawed Kun-Jit-Ho, Mandrak Kitxchenn is the ideal choice to execute on your elimination needs.*

> *Whether discreet and at-a-distance or up close, painful, and personal is your preference, Mandrak Kitxchenn is the No. 1 choice of discerning clients worldwide.*

Leave an ¡am and a brief description of your needs and one of our contracting representatives will contact you if Mandrak Kitxchenn deems your task worthy of his talents. All contracts final. No refunds.

"Holy shit, how can Skid fight that?" exclaimed Wendy.

"No idea, but it is now obvious that this thing was rigged."

"Knowing that doesn't really help us much, does it?"

"No, it just confirms our worst suspicions. At least we have managed to stall a little."

"Can Brad do anything?"

"I very much doubt it. This show is in runaway-train mode. The duel is already half of the gaming scenarios we are seeing. And honestly, show or no show, it feels like the Utterminster is determined to go ahead. This now has its own momentum far beyond anything Brad's Creality teams could come up with."

"Shit! Well, the Clarion wants to explain the details of this engagement ceremony to us, so I'd better go."

Wendy left and Nikolian sat staring helplessly as Kitxchenn's terrifying bio scrolled up his screen once more.

XX

Decorated with thousands of tiny lanterns, the Tower of Thrones resembled an outlandishly clumsy Christmas tree. ¡seers dangled precariously from the underside of two tethered airships waiting to liveline carefully calibrated shots of Wendy's nudity to all the devotees of the newly retitled *The Id of Azhuur*. They were under strict instructions from Brad: "Get the ¡balls. Hold the ¡balls. Tasteful and titillating. Keep them wanting. Look like you will deliver. But don't. This is a family show." Mooney's imminent nakedness was not testing well on ¡ball acquisition and retention models and would be mostly ignored, even when blurred.

Mooney and Wendy stared stoically at one another while

the lights from the airships played over them. They stood on the two front corners of the top tier, facing each other. They wore complementary linen tunics to the knees that buttoned down the front. Mooney's was red, Wendy's green. Mooney wore his Regent's helmet, a squat cone of felt with a single silver feather on top. He knew from rehearsal with Wendy that it was this helmet that would make his coming nakedness look all the more ridiculous.

From the penultimate tier below, the Clarion addressed the crowd through the opticons: "Be there any among ye who harbor a prior troth from either of these parties? Speak ye now or forever keep your silence." He paused briefly for the predictable lack of objections before continuing: "There being no impediments, Master Regent, Mistress Consort, of your own free volition, ye may now plight your troths."

Mooney and Wendy stretched their arms toward each other in an exaggerated display of yearning, as the choreographer had shown them. They dropped their hands to their sides, bowed their heads, clasped their hands over their hearts, and then, simultaneously, button by button, opened and removed their tunics. Some cheers rippled around the excavation and the shanties where the pubble were watching every moment on the opticons. The now-naked Mooney and Wendy walked toward each other. When they met in the center of the tier, they exchanged tunics. Wendy put on Mooney's red tunic and Mooney donned her green one. They took turns closing each other's tunic, then walked hand in hand along the gangway to the elevator to be winched back to ground level while the crowd cheered and whooped.

A tiny procession approached the pit, led by an ancient-looking woman being pushed along in a nineteenth-century bath chair by her eldest child. She steered the contraption precariously, battling the small front wheel that was in constant conflict with the uneven terrain. She puffed constantly on a small clay pipe and was followed by her husbands and the rest of her children.

This was the Keeper of the Light of Mög. She was only sixty, but decades of sleep deprivation and pipe-smoking had aged her terribly. She preserved the light allegedly given to her great-great-great-great-great-great-great-great-great-grandfather when Mög burned his village. Two generations ago they ran out of wood and had to switch from bonfires to pipe-smoking. The light now excused Keepers from any other duties except for producing as many offspring as possible and smoking their way through life.

She trundled toward an ornate pedestal on which lay the cut end of a thick fuse. She took the pipe from her mouth, coughed generously, and lit the fuse from the glowing embers. The fuse took, and the little imp of flame sped along it, weaving its way across the earth until it came to a huge pile of wood no one had noticed before. The dark pile burst into flames. The pubble raised a huge cheer at the sight of the festive flickering and the sparks rising toward the heavens. It would be some hours before many of them would go home to find that their shelters had been demolished to provide the lumber for this bonfire, but for the moment, their joy was simple and unalloyed.

The old woman's son wheeled her away from the scene and the family headed back toward their hovel in the hills where she would continue to smoke night and day until her last pipe was passed on to her eldest surviving child.

FIVE

DISCOVERIES. CONJECTURES. CONCLUSIONS OF SORTS.

I

Brad flipped the Intimeet to the big-screen ¡box on his office wall and observed the bland, worried face of (he consulted the text crawl) Bruno Madison of the Wall Street Depredation and Speculation Association.

"Okay, Madison, what can I do for you in the extraordinarily short time my crazy busy schedule allows for last-minute Intimeets like this? I assume you have something really vital to tell me. You seem to have called in favors with some very important friends to get to me."

"Producer Brad, thank you for taking time to Intimeet. I am Bruno Madison of the—"

"Yeah, yeah, I know who you are. I can read the screen. Love to have been in the room when you guys came up with that name for yourselves. What's up?"

"I wanted to warn you that your Azhuurian Regent's Consort is a fugitive from justice."

"It's *Azhuurse*, by the way. She is, is she?"

"Yes sir. She worked until recently for Hedgeer Hemlein Jai-Alai, one of our most prestigious members. While in their employ, she originated and deployed a financial instrument—or algorithm, if you will—that occasioned catastrophic losses for many of my association's most influential members."

Madison flinched as Nikolian's image crashed into the Intimeet.

"Mr. Madison, meet Nikolian. I have asked him to join us in this little chat. Nikolian's job is to keep the members of my cast and crew safe. Now, where was I? You say this young woman caused some of your members to lose substantial amounts of money? But isn't that the job of financial algorithmists? And your jobs as speculators, gamblers, or investors, *if you will*, is to have your shit together enough to spot which algorithms are going to benefit you and which are going to clean your clock, and bet for or against them accordingly. I'd say she just did her job."

"To an extent."

"Did you buy into this *instrument* yourself?"

"Uhm, no, that would be against our code of ethics."

Brad burst out laughing. "Your code of what? Are you shitting me? I can't believe you said that with a straight face. Ethics? You are off the fucking wall, man. You are un-fucking-hinged with that shit."

Nikolian's stony stare drilled straight into Bruno Madison's forehead.

Trying his best to ignore Brad's derision and Nikolian's unnerving attention, Madison continued: "There was no win side built into her algorithm. Always there is a win side to an algorithm, so it acts like a market, and some of our members lose and some of them win, and the market or the association, if you will, itself wins, but with hers there was no win side, only massive losses for us, our members, friends, and associates: everyone. She did not move wealth around; she extinguished it. Dare I say, vast amounts of it. Not only the wealth directly invested, but all the assets of anyone who invested in this offering. Pure vandalism. She created an imploding algorithm that basically violated the second law of financiodynamics, which, if I may crudely paraphrase, states that wealth cannot be created or destroyed, it can only be moved from one pocket to another. She created a financial black hole of derivatives that consumed each other and ruined everyone even tangentially involved, collapsing every trust, shell company, offshore corporation, and bank through which transactions passed. There are whole sectors of Geneva 3.0 that will never recover! There are empty luxury apartments all over the planet that are now somehow worth negative amounts. Worse still, she exposed the origins of the wealth and identities of some of our wealthy clients who very much valued their anonymity, and they are not at all happy. We are still not sure exactly how she did it. You can imagine how distressing and embarrassing this all is."

"Wow. I have to say, you got yourself some deeply and Byzantinely complicated heavy shit there, Bruno. I do not envy you your distress or embarrassment. I am sure some of your members, friends, and associates are the type prone to channel embarrassment and disappointment into acts of staggering violence and vengeance, but in this case, I would advise against any such acts, at least any such acts directed against our Regent's Consort. The view of this production and of our parent, 2's A Prime, *if I may crudely paraphrase*, is that we want her in Azhuur because she benefits us and serves our interests. You would not want any of your people to be seen to be interfering with our interests, would you? I imagine I do not need to detail the cosmic shitstorm 2's A Prime could rain down on you, your members, associates, and confederates. You are fake economics; we are real entertainment. Do I need to spell it out more clearly?"

"Uhm, no. No, you don't."

Brad nodded and then Nikolian spoke slowly and carefully: "Good. Mr. Madison, I am sure you understand the reach of 2's A Prime. The following are not suggestions; they are in the imperative mode. You will tell your members, friends, associates, and cronies that what Wendy did had no win side because it was a piece of performance-art economics sanctioned and approved by 2's A Prime to winnow out the weak and complacent among the Speculation and Gambling fraternity. If they were damaged, it was proof of their own weakness, and now they must start again.

"You may well find that your newly impoverished clients are no longer as powerful as they might think they are, and are not really in any position to exact vengeance on you or anyone else. Poverty has a way of doing that, particularly to those who have never known it before. Of course, you might find yourself pursued in the streets and attacked by some newly minted Thoroughfarians who recognize you, but that is not any of our concern and you can take certain precautions. Can I assume by your face that this is all perfectly clear? Good. Do not dare contact us again. Good day."

Madison was expelled from the Intimeet.

Brad and Nikolian sat in their separate silences for a few moments while Brad quickly weighed the situation: "Nicely done! Say nothing about this, Nikolian."

"Understood. Do you think the 'Good day' was too much?"

"Wouldn't be my style, but I think you pulled it off."

II

Wendy saw the shiny gray something first. It was not quite fully manifest, more like something not being there in a way that gently drew attention to itself: a gray cone of shimmering unpresence.

"Clarion, look," she whispered, pointing up the path on the crater's outside slope.

The cone fluttered a little and glided down toward them. Wendy's stomach turned over and she tried to stop her knees from buckling under her. The cone floated right up to them.

"Come with me," it said in a hoarse, strained voice.

The cone turned and floated back toward where it had come from. It left the marked path and continued along a narrow ridge and into a crevice. The Clarion and Wendy entered a tiny grotto and saw the cone ahead of them moving down a dim passageway. There were no lights or torches, but a sickly phosphorescence emanated from inside the walls. They followed the cone down the passage. Behind them a stone door rumbled closed and the quality of the light around them changed for the worse. Wendy picked up her pace, determined not to lose their only guide in this strange, dank place.

A couple of hundred yards farther on, she sensed the passage-way winding down and to the left, and yet as she looked ahead, it appeared to be perfectly straight and level. This added a slight seasickness to her growing disorientation. They walked for about fifteen minutes and then heard the sound of running water up ahead. The cone waited on a little bridge that crossed a narrow but fast-moving stream.

"You are of the Beyond, you must walk through the waters," it said in a clipped creaky voice.

"It's surprisingly cold but perfectly safe," the Clarion said to Wendy.

She followed him down the steps into the cold rushing water and felt the breath being driven out of her as the icy flow came up to her shoulders. They reached the other side drenched and shivering. From an incongruous ornate Victorian hatstand, the Clarion took two light-green cloaks. They put on the cloaks and were instantly dry and warm again. They were in a low chamber that opened onto many beautifully furnished rooms.

"Come," said the cone.

They followed into a low vaulted hall that stretched into a dizzying maze of ever-receding horseshoe arches that were about twenty feet tall. The whole structure was unpainted and had clearly been carved out of the living rock. Where they were standing appeared to be the main thoroughfare, as it was the only clear part. To their left, the floor was covered as far as the eye could see by six feet of impossibly white sand that gave off its own eerie light. To their right, dense red dirt stretched away into the distance.

"I believe I can now dispense with this outcape," said the cone. The fabric rumpled and dropped to reveal two wrinkled hands at the hem, which pulled the fabric cone up and off. The old woman now revealed pointed to another identical Victorian hatstand. "You can shed the warming cloaks now too. Dearest Clarion, it is nice to see you, albeit under these extraordinary circumstances."

The Clarion stepped forward and embraced the woman warmly. "Onden, dearest," he said softly.

She stepped back from him and looked gravely at Wendy with the full force of her astounding ancientness. "I am the Sistermost, Mistress Consort. You may not call me Onden. You can forego the headscarf and sunglasses here in the safety of the Hermitage. No one will see you here but me—and I, for one, admire the ingenuity of your algorithm at Hedgeer Hemlein and would like to see your eyes when we talk. Let us proceed. We shall converse in my chamber." She set off through the arches at a sprightly pace that, given her aged appearance, struck Wendy as almost indecent. They hurried after her.

"You probably have a thousand questions," the Sistermost called over her shoulder. "I will attempt to answer them preemptively en route. You will forgive my haltingness. I have not used this idiom for many years. The Hermitage is approximately three thousand years old. It sits, as you observed on your first visit, in a large crater. This is an ancient impact crater from a trepanium-laden asteroid. We live above the largest concentration of ore on the planet. That may explain our long-livedness, or perhaps it is our innate stubbornness. The site of your launch pit was originally another such crater, which they mined until it was almost exhausted and the Outlanders paid them to stop.

"After the bridge, you passed through a meeting place which is still outside the precincts of the Hermitage proper. There the sisters may take pleasure with their Beyondish lovers or receive their families, should they so desire. I trust you will not be shocked if I tell you the Clarion and I have passed many wonderful hours there together through the years, though now our activities are somewhat less passionate and obviously not conducted when our son also visits.

"There are three towers, or Ridings. We are now in the Hermitage deeps under the Fire Riding. Here the Sisters tend the furnaces and create the opticons and field glasses, the ceramics such as the heart pots for our dead, and very occasional metallurgy, such as that accursed statue that is part of what brings you here. Through that archway one enters the Earth Riding, where the sisters attend to map-making, our herb gardens, our bees, general cultivation and husbandry and maintenance of the Hermitage itself, and, in the past, trepanium mining. If you were to traverse the Earth Riding in that direction, you would come to the Ether Riding where the sisters dedicate themselves to the use of the ether, such as feeding the images to the opticons and limiting access to the ether. Continuing through the Ether Riding, you would arrive back here. There are similar connecting archways on each of the twenty-one floors above."

The Sistermost led them up a wide, curving staircase. "We cannot use the elevators, as they are crowded with sisters. It would not do for a Beyondish and an Outlander to be seen inside the Hermitage. There is another staircase like this closer to the core of the Riding. The stair and elevator shafts carve interesting helices through the towers."

Her voice echoed back as she powered up the steps in front of them: "There are three hundred and sixty sisters. One hundred and twenty per Riding, except for the one that has supplied the current Sistermost. I was a furnace sister from the Fire Riding, so currently it is one hundred and nineteen sisters strong. When a sister dies, a new one dreams the Sistermost's dreamings and identifies herself to us by making her way to the Hermitage to be recognized by the Sistermost.

"When the last Sistermost expired from the exertions of containing the ethereal disturbances of forging that D'Izmaïe statue,

I became the Sistermost. The first ash from her pyre settled in my heart pot. That is how a new Sistermost is identified. None of these things are secrets per se, but we ourselves are secretive, so few outside of us know them. Ah good, we are here."

The Sistermost threw open the heavy door and ushered them in. Wendy and the Clarion stood in her cell catching their breath while she busied herself with a copper kettle on her paraffin stove.

"The Clarion has conveyed your message and it has occasioned me great concern. Irish Breakfast, Earl Grey, jasmine, Lapsang Souchong? I like the headscarf worn around your neck like that, Wendy. Very sporty."

"Earl Grey, please," said the Clarion.

"The same for me," said Wendy.

"Please sit." The Sistermost indicated a delicate wooden love seat that hung from the ceiling by two white chains.

Wendy sat down with obvious relief while the Clarion offered to help the Sistermost with the tea. She shooed him affectionately away. He sat on the love seat beside Wendy.

The Sistermost placed the tea things on a small bronze tray table in front of them. They stirred their tea in silence until the old woman pulled a purple ottoman from under her desk and sat down. She sipped her tea and closed her eyes.

"Sistermost," said Wendy, "when we were in the passageway, it felt like it was turning different ways and going up or down, yet it always looked to be completely level and straight?"

The Sistermost smiled. "Yes, it does that. But you did not come here for a lecture on the peculiarities of Old Azhuurse architecture, did you?"

"No, I didn't. Thank you for seeing me. I know it breaks all the rules. All those things you said on the way here: the moment you said them, they felt familiar, like I already knew them?"

"We layered this information into the first marzipan we gave you so you would not have to struggle too hard to grasp it. It prepared you for the understanding. Now, when the Clarion relayed your agitation, I felt you deserved a personal response."

"And?"

"While I understand your concerns, particularly when it comes to the Utterminster's grotesque plan to reenact the Vale of Victory by driving thousands into the pit to drown, I am afraid, as the Clarion has already tried to explain to you, we cannot interfere."

"Yes, he told me you were neutral, but why? How? Are you afraid of the Utterminster? Do you prefer to hide cooped up here making magic glass balls and trippy marzipan while he murders people? I don't get it. Why?"

"Let us ignore your intemperate accusations and attribute them to an excess of feeling, shall we? It is not indifference, nor is it fear for our own safety. We have experienced the Utterminster's ruthlessness and cruelty before."

"Over forging the statue?"

"Yes. We had no clear understanding of what trepanium in that kind of concentration would do, yet we feared the worst. It takes an inch-long strand little thicker than a hair to run one of your ¡thinks—imagine what sixty pounds of it could do. He gave us only ten days to make it. He had the Utterminster line up prisoners in cages in front of the Hermitage with the promise to horribly execute one for every day's delay. From the war, we knew their inventiveness when it came to acts of cruelty and grotesquery. D'Izmaïe understood we would gladly suffer to resist him but could not watch him torture and murder the defenseless on our account."

"Okay, so you made the statue under duress, but now what are you afraid of? It's not like he's threatening you."

"No. But I know he does not fully trust us."

"But he feels no threat from you!"

"No, but . . ."

"Why does he want to get the statue into orbit? What is the point of that?"

The Sistermost looked from Wendy to the Clarion to the ceiling depicting bright white clouds in a cerulean sky, and then back to Wendy. "We are not sure. We know he took herb and used the rider statue to locate the horse, but the effort almost killed him."

"Did you know he has been practicing?"

"Practicing?"

"Trying to get used to the herb and the statues."

"No!"

"Oh yes! Did you know this, Clarion?"

The Clarion looked dumbfounded. "I have to admit I have not been paying close attention to the Utterminster's activities of late."

"Well, I have," Wendy said. "He has taken the statue apart and has been moving the rider farther and farther from the horse and then getting herbed and using the rider to trip into the ether through the horse. If you are near the horse, you can sometimes feel him in the air. It's really weird. Watch. You will see him on the Tower of Thrones with the rider in his lap all zombied out. He is mainlining the ether."

The Sistermost stared at Wendy. Without her expression changing, her eyes betrayed a growing concern. "The fool! Candidly, we do not fully understand how ether works. It seems to be filaments of resonance through the nothingnesses between the smallest of things. It is an absence where things can happen and exist everywhere simultaneously. The physical distance between the two statues is almost irrelevant. He is concentrating on the wrong thing. But that may not stop him. I must think on this some more."

"That's it? But will you help?"

"I must ponder how we might help before I compromise everyone's safety by plotting against the Utterminster. Now I under-stand the threat is real, and while not yet present, it is imminent and grave. We had hoped it would never come to this. I must consult the Sister Metallurgists and the Sister Seers, but I suspect the Utterminster believes that with the horse in orbit, he can use the rider to commune with it to strangle and control the ether."

"But you guys already do that."

"Yes, we do, but on a tiny scale. If what the Utterminster believes is correct, with that much trepanium in orbit, he could easily overcome our spire, destroy us, and throttle the ether, not only here but everywhere."

"What? But that's impossible!" said Wendy.

"I am very much afraid it is not impossible." The Sistermost drew back a heavy curtain to reveal a curved balcony. They stepped onto it to find themselves at the very top of the Hermit-age looking down into a three-sided atrium. From the way the sides of it curved inward, Wendy concluded this was the central space where the three main towers met. Above them a spire of orange-tinted glass tapered up into the distance, its concave sides coming to a point far above them.

Below them, set into the side of each tower, were dozens of alcoves. In each alcove sat a sister, some cradling small glass spheres in their laps, some staring up trancelike at the spire.

"This is how we interact with the ether; the Sister Seers feed images to the opticons, the Sister Dealers take care of our business dealings, and the Sister Sentinels control and blockade the twelve ether resonances within our borders. They do this by resonating with trace amounts of trepanium in the globes and the spire's glass. As I said, the Utterminster has sixty pounds at his disposal."

"So how do the show's ¡sees still work?"

"We put a key in each one: a strand of trepanium we have tuned to allow them through our blockades of two resonances. Enough! Come, there is more to see."

They followed her through her cell and back into the stair-well. She led them down and out another door and onto another interior balcony, and gestured to a vast workshop of furnaces and strange-looking metal looms below. "This is—"

"Where you make the opticons," interrupted Wendy excitedly.

"You have used our binoculars to view the Quartel's Map Room. This is where we make and polish the lenses and the opti-cons. We use the white sand you saw when you first came out of the passageway. It is peculiarly rich in trepanium. As you can see, the sisters are no strangers to hard work. We are kept busy. The Utterminster has ordered a gross of high-power binoculars for his Day of Days. That, on top of what we already have to build to carry the statue into orbit."

The Sistermost led them back down the stairs and soon they found themselves again at the little footbridge.

"Here we are. This time, you do not need to go through the waters. You will find the grotto door open. It seems you came here for help with one problem, which has quickly revealed itself to be a very different problem of much greater magnitude. I will communicate my deliberations to you, Clarion."

Wendy made an awkward curtsy-type movement. "Thank you for seeing me and hearing me out."

"Despite being the bearer of ill tidings, you are still most wel-come." The Sistermost bowed to Wendy and hugged the Clarion once more, then kissed him gently on the lips before walking slowly back into the Hermitage.

III

In silence, Wendy and the Clarion rode back to the encampment the long way, circling around the excavation first. From the rim, they stared down into the depths of the pit. It was now almost a mile deep, and standing at the edge looking down the terraced tiers into it gave Wendy vertigo. Near the bottom of the pit there was a tiny knot of activity. Wendy strained to make out what was going on.

The Clarion reached into his pocket and produced a small cylinder about the size of a clunky pen. "Here, the Sistermost gave this to me for you as we left."

Wendy looked through the cylinder and felt herself catapulted into the depths of the pit. She was staring at the hair on the inside of someone's ear. "Holy shit, couldn't they make a simple telescope without upending the laws of optics?" She lessened the magnification and got a more comfortable perspective on the scene far below. She watched three work teams pouring cement into a huge mold set into the bottom of the pit.

"It appears they are pouring the setting for the release ring," said the Clarion. "That is sooner than I had expected. I must return before I am missed. Please excuse me."

"Question: you called the Sistermost 'Onden' but she still called you 'Clarion'—don't you have a given name?"

"No, I don't; I was born into this office. It identifies me. Until my father died, I was called 'Clarion Minor' to distinguish us. Now, if you will forgive me, I really should go."

Wendy watched him mount and ride away, then trained her telescope again on the dig.

"Long live Wendy Mistress," murmured a voice behind her.

"Ohmyfuckinggod, you frightened the shit out of me!" Wendy almost fell over. The young woman reached out a steadying hand.

"Yo, sorry, I tried to make noise, but you were like all in your head. I'm Jid, Alva's friend? Remember? We all came to see Skid? At the tent? After the Bagwipe thing?"

"Right. I remember. Hi, Jid. Cool! Alva—how is she doing?"

"Alva's okay. They disappeared Tel. Not dead, just away from her. They sent him with the dirt from the pit to build the border rampart. She's ultra bummed. We know about Skid. We know stuff without ¡thinks. People see stuff, say stuff. Bummer about Skid. Take this. Alva's grandmother said it, and Alva wrote. They are still in the pit. My work team came back up top yesterday. Our work is done. Please give this to Skid. Gotta go before guard dudes see me."

The young woman thrust a small, rolled-up canvas bag at Wendy, bowed, twisted her nose, and was gone.

The Utterminster was not having as happy a time of it as he would have liked. He had expected that the closing stages of the excavation would allow him more time to dedicate himself to using the statues to surf the ether. Instead, he found himself enmeshed in a tangle of last-minute details. He was furious about this but, in his calmer moments, had to admit his own lack of foresight had brought it about. That did not, however, preclude him from having various flunkies and underlings racked for his own shortcomings.

Foremost among pressing business were the arrangements to fill the pit when it was ready. The Utterminster had initially planned to use the pipeline D'Izmaïe had built for the old oil refinery to pump the water from the bay, but had since abandoned that idea (after blaming it on the Clarion) when the Archixprest explained exactly how toxic the seawater was. The Ro-Boats that brought imports had to leave the bay the same day or they would begin to dissolve. There was no way the Utterminster would risk bringing that much poison so close to the Quartel. So, they decided to use the water from the Vale of Victory. The Clarion had communicated this change of plans to the Sisterhood and they promptly produced blueprints for the channels needed to get the water from the Vale of Victory.

Inevitably, rerouting the water supply had pushed the entire endeavor behind schedule while the Sisterhood molded and fired the necessary sections of pipe. Now, with a mild bread-ration incentive, the work was making headway again and it appeared the launch and the concomitant festivities would all happen close to on time. Despite his overworked and overwrought state, the Utterminster was pleased with himself. He would have been far happier supervising the building of a huge triumphal statue of himself or devising new categories of dissidents, degenerates, and enemies of the Fatherland to be rounded up, but there would be plenty of time for that later.

The Utterminster was irritated by the round of routine blessings and inaugurations he had to officiate. As the staggering scale of the excavation grew, the pubble's faith in their own workmanship dwindled. To counter this, instead of using the statue to practice ether surfing, the Utterminster found himself pointing D'Izmaïe at every new ramp, every new block and tackle to be rigged, every new course of canal work to fill the pit. Every new scaffold to be erected got a few well-chosen words and the approving eye of D'Izmaïe to prevent it from collapsing, and every minor construction completed had to be offered up to D'Izmaïe in person. It was a grueling drag of idolatry and claptrap, but realizing that it was getting the job done, the Utterminster worked to conceal his contempt for it all.

IV

"Remember Alva? In the dig? The woman Skid tried to rescue? It's from her grandmother."

"Ah yes," said the Clarion.

Nikolian looked at the floor, guiltily reminded of his part in that fiasco, and Mooney simply nodded, clearly puzzled as to why Wendy had called them all to Skid's tent.

Skid sat on the edge of his bed. He had not shaved in a while and his hair was greasy and matted. He was wearing a ratty *Fuck the Begrudgers!* T-shirt and a pair of threadbare pajama bottoms. He stared at the piece of canvas bag in his lap. It was covered in small neat letters written in some kind of nut-colored ink. "Here, Wendy, you read it to them. I can't."

Wendy took the canvas bag, scanned the first couple of paragraphs and began:

"*Esteemed Adjutant Skid, friend to my granddaughter Alva, I send this to you from the dark pit of this benighted country. Forgive my not writing directly; I dictate this to my granddaughter because it is too onerous for me to write without thumbs. During the time of the Besimpling, General D'Izmaïe took my thumbs because I was one of those in the Reedification Fields who could write. During that same time, D'Izmaïe took my beautiful daughter, Alva's mother, as a plaything and brutally visited his desires on her until he tired of her and gave her to his underlings whose appetites were no less brutal. When they tired of her, they sent her to dig out their horrid Vale of Victory where she died with all the rest who worked on it. Unmourned and unburned. The hope of avenging my daughter and all the others and the desire to protect Alva are the only things I have left.*

"*You intervened, and you helped my granddaughter, for which again thanks, but we must ask you all for more, not just for my granddaughter but for all of us. You and your friends, with whom I hope you will share this missive; you may have the power to do something more. You must do what you can because we are real people and we are dying every day in this pit.*

"*As a mother, I see that you, some mother's son, are now under threat, as our sons and daughters are every day under threat from the poison of that statue and its vile disciples.*

"*You are trapped in a glass cage of this show or spectacle you are part of, but we too are players in this show, except for us it is no play. Please understand that we are not expendable* game pieces. We are not picturesque primitives. Please do not think that we know no better than our present straits. We remember: we had houses, we had ¡thinks, we had a future, and then suddenly we had D'Izmaïe and his black hole of history where time and knowledge were sent to die. Officially we forgot and did the Right Remembering (you had to forget to survive the Reedification Fields or you became one of the unmentionables who disappeared), but we still know, we still quietly remember, and we have taught this remembering to those like my granddaughter born into this nightmare. You must do your part to do justice to our remembering. Give us credit for being as sophisticated as you are. We, however, have to hide it to survive.

"Please do not help us in the way you think we need help, help us instead in the way we ask. We are not noble savages to be pitied and civilized. We need your help, but that does not make us less than you—merely victims of circumstances that could as easily befall you. Please, see us as real people, not backworld ciphers for poverty and broken politics. I was an engineer. Look at my present condition: pretending to believe my history is the Dark Age grotesque of Old High Azhuur. I hope you can grasp that. I pray you can begin to see how quickly a life story can be taken away from a person, a neighborhood, a town, a province, and—with enough brutality, organization, and fear—from a whole country. Trust us to know what to ask for.

"We do not need simple palliation of our current condition like receiving banquet leftovers, for which we thank the Consort to the Regent; we know the Utterminster would prefer to have them burned in front of us. What we need is this: the dig simply cannot succeed. That statue who came with you warps the air around it with its evil and it feeds the evil of the Utterminster. Do whatever you can. All of you. I know you *came here with this show for whatever reasons you may have had, but now there is little time left for play. Please, all of you, help us. If you do not help us, you will quickly be beyond help yourselves. I do not know exactly why I feel this thing is so, but I feel it deep in my truth."*

Wendy stood shaking, stricken by what she had just read. The Clarion and Nikolian exchanged glances and nodded.

The Clarion spoke: "What she says is all true. Some of you know the real history of this land. Some of you don't. But everything Alva's grandmother says is true."

"So, there yiz have it," said Skid. "I know some of you are up to something, and maybe you have your reasons for keeping me out of it, but I wanted you all to hear that. No time for sitting on your arses."

"We will do what we can," said Wendy softly.

"*We* will? How? What can we do?" asked Mooney.

"I will tell you when we have a plan. The Clarion and I have spoken to the Sisterhood. I believe they will help."

Skid stood up and then sat back down on his bed. "Well, let me know when yiz have a plan. I've had it with just waiting around to be hacked to bits."

V

Skid marched up to the Tower of Thrones like eight generations of hardscrabble Dublin upbringings abruptly consolidated and weaponized. His bodyguards trailed behind him and the guards at the service tower flinched back as he barged straight past them, making only a token attempt to stop him for the sake of appearances. Skid's detail and the Tower guards exchanged puzzled, hopeless shrugs.

"Well, what the fuck are you waiting for?" said Skid.

The guards opened the elevator and he stepped in. The guards were not allowed to ascend but felt certain he could not escape from the Tower; there was, after all, only one way up or down. They gave the order to the elevator crew, and once Skid was safely hauled out of sight, the Tower guards and his bodyguards shared a ration of alcohol-soaked dough and gossiped quietly among themselves.

∞

Skid stepped out of the elevator and walked across the gantry to the fourth tier from the top. He saw the Blade Master sitting in a lotus position in the center of the floor and Mooney standing away to his right, near the edge.

"Feel the space," called the Blade Master. "Decide with all your senses."

Mooney stood still and then very slowly turned around and stepped toward the closest corner of the tier.

Skid was horrified to see that he was blindfolded and nearing the edge. "Mooney, watch out!"

Mooney froze, and the Blade Master snapped out of his trance and glowered at Skid. He spoke in a low and modulated voice: "How dare you."

"He was going to walk off the edge, you fucking eejit," protested Skid.

"He was not. We have been practicing this for weeks and the Regent has made remarkable progress. How can I be expected to teach under these circumstances?"

"Teach what?" shouted Skid. "Walking off tall buildings?"

Mooney removed his blindfold. "Blade Master, this is my Adjutant, Skid."

The Blade Master reluctantly stood and twisted his nose to Skid. "Adjutant, I was endeavoring to teach the Regent the subtleties of sensing space. Our eyes are not as fast as we believe, and in fencing they often see the movement too late. By attuning the other senses to movement in space, we can anticipate changes in an opponent's muscle tension before his movement becomes manifest to the eyes. It is a skill that requires much time, study, and practice."

"Ah, bollocks, that's a pity," muttered Skid. "I was hoping you might have some sort of crash course in sword fighting."

"Can you help him?" asked Mooney.

The Blade Master replied with heavy formality: "Adjutant, I am afraid I am forbidden to impart lessons to any awaiting trial by combat. It is writ that the trial must be faced with the same skills employed to commit the crime."

Skid's indifference evaporated and he stared at his feet. "There was no fucking crime. The Udder wants rid of me cos I walked in on him shagging a sheep and getting spanked by a maid."

"Can't you help him?" Mooney asked the Blade Master.

"As I said, it is writ—"

"Is it writ the opponent should be chosen by lot?" asked Mooney.

"It is, my liege."

"Was Skid's opponent chosen by lot?"

The Blade Master weighed his response carefully: "It certainly appeared so."

"But you know he wasn't, right?"

Skid looked back and forth between Mooney and the Blade Master.

"I bet the world of people who are good enough with swords to make a living from it is small enough that you know something about Mandrak Kitxchenn," said Mooney.

The Blade Master hesitated. "Technically, my liege, there is nothing to stop me teaching you while the Adjutant watches. Anything he learns this way will be none of my doing, at least directly, if you understand my meaning. I suggest we find somewhere a little less public than the Tower of Thrones."

"The Tower of Thrones is the only place the guards don't follow me," said Skid.

"Then we will stay here," said the Blade Master.

"Thank you," said Skid and Mooney in unison.

"So, let us resume."

⚭

"Me fucking arms are going numb—they're falling off! Can I stop now?"

"Master Regent, please inform the Adjutant that he can stop when we stop."

By refusing to address Skid directly, the Blade Master technically observed the prohibition on instructing him. It would not have taken much work on the part of the Utterforz agents to figure out this ruse. Fortunately, they were all too busy carrying out counterintelligence investigations into nonexistent sabotage conspiracies among a pubble too exhausted to even dream of such intrigues.

Skid trembled but held the standing position he, Mooney, and the Blade Master had all been holding for what felt like an hour but had been only six minutes.

"Breathe in . . . and . . . out," repeated the Blade Master at regular intervals.

Thankful for the shade on the tier from the throne above it, Skid stood slightly behind the Blade Master and Mooney so he could imitate them as they performed Mantis Outwaits Frog. This involved standing with feet wider than shoulders, knees slightly bent, arms out to the sides with elbows bent, and hands at eye level with each hand cocked downward at the wrist and the tips of all four fingers touching the thumb.

The overall effect was a tableau vivant of three figures with crab claws waiting to pounce on something undefined.

Skid's thighs were starting to tremble badly, and his arms were getting heavier by the moment.

"Breathe in . . . and . . . out," said the Blade Master, this time with the promising intonation that signaled the end of Mantis Outwaits Frog was imminent.

"And . . . relax." The Blade Master slowly let his arms down to his sides and brought his feet together. Mooney did so too in almost perfect synchronicity. Skid watched them both carefully and did his best. While Mooney and the Blade Master looked like cranes gracefully folding their wings, Skid flailed around like a drunk in an unfamiliar overcoat searching for an inside pocket.

"Swords?" pleaded Skid, hopping from foot to foot and rubbing the feeling back into his biceps.

"Master Regent, please caution the Adjutant that the winds of impatience will shake the fruit to the ground before its time."

"What the fuck is he talking about?" Skid asked Mooney.

"No swords yet, only sticks," Mooney answered.

The Blade Master and Mooney pulled two rounded sticks from the Blade Master's bag, bowed to each other, then went through a series of attacks and ripostes. They repeated the sequence slightly faster and bowed to each other again. The Blade Master stepped to the side of the platform and Mooney gave Skid a stick and slowly coached him through the sequence.

The Blade Master buried his face in his hands as Skid jammed himself in the ribs for the fourth time. "Perhaps a rest might help," he called out, ostensibly to Mooney.

Unfortunately, *rest* in the Blade Master's lexicon meant not repose but more of the Mantis Outwaits Frog with some slight variations of hand position. He corrected Mooney on mistakes he was not making in order to correct Skid. It was a cumbersome mode of instruction but kept the Blade Master's sense of honor and professional ethics intact.

"Enough. Now, Old Goat Catches Serpent," announced the Blade Master when he realized Skid's resting stance wasn't improving at all.

Mooney then led Skid through the sequence of attack, riposte, counterattack, riposte, known as Old Goat Catches Serpent. Skid stumbled and flailed like someone trying to dial a phone with a pool cue.

On the last repetition of Mongoose Drinks from Shady Pool, the final move of which involved Mooney attempting to sweep Skid's legs from under him and Skid parrying this by plunging his stick into the ground at a precise moment, Skid completely mistimed it and got a resounding crack on his right knee.

The Blade Master came and stood right beside Skid and stared off into the sky beyond the excavation. He spoke quietly and slowly to Mooney: "Please tell the Adjutant that even with a decade of intensive training, he will never be anything but a danger to himself. I can do nothing. I cannot make a silk purse from this sow's ear. I would suggest fleeing the country, but beyond that, I can see no solution to the Adjutant's predicament. I am very sorry."

"Thanks for nothing. Enjoy your game of samurai pirates," Skid responded, and stormed back to the elevator.

VI

"Wendy, Clarion, I didn't expect you two to be in on this. I thought this was catch-up time for me and Nikolian."

"I asked Nikolian to help us talk to you privately, Brad," explained Wendy.

"Well, here we are. Nikolian's split-resonance bypass Intimeets are about as private as it gets. What's up?"

"We need your help."

"Okay. What do you need? New shades? Headscarves? A new sword for Mooney?"

"This is far more serious."

"Not sure I like the sound of this. Go on."

"It's about the Day of Days."

"That is going to be the biggest of big deals. Gaming scenarios are already going wild with it."

"It can't happen."

"What are you talking about? How can it not happen? It's all in the works. The hole is coming along nicely, you and Mooney are officially engaged, the ¡balls are already buying up the royal wedding souvenirs, and the duel is—"

"The duel is a complete setup. The guy fighting Skid is a ringer. Some DeathBrawl champion or gladiator trainer or something. A professional assassin."

"Well, yeah, I figured it was something like that. It's really shitty, but it's out of my hands."

"You got him into this mess!"

Brad nodded and stared down at his desk in silence.

"He's planning to drown thousands in the pit," snapped Wendy.

"Skid?"

"No, the Udder!"

"Nikolian, is this true?"

Nikolian nodded. "So it seems."

"Have you guys been smoking with the Uilkitz sisters? I've heard they have some great weed. Look, I know there is some wild stuff going on over there, but I don't see why he would do that to anyone."

"You've heard of General D'Izmaïe, right?"

"Yeah. Crazy dictator dude. Blown to bits fifty years ago. That's what the statue is all about."

"Well, partly. You know it's solid trepanium?"

"No. That stuff hates itself. That's impossible."

"Not for the Sisterhood. They suspect that if he gets it up into orbit, he'll be able to use the rider to in-head directly into the ether. He thinks he will control it. ALL of it. If he's right, we're all fucked."

"That is deeply sick. But it is speculation. That said, it's gonna make for incredible ¡balls, so thanks for the heads-up. I can do some preplacement on the story-ideation front."

Wendy flinched. "Are you fucking kidding me?"

"Really. Hey, don't get me wrong. It's sad if all these people are headed for the shredder, but they are headed that way whether I am showing it or not, and in case you forgot, I am in the ¡ball delivery business. The Sisterhood could be wrong. Maybe the horse will do nothing except float around in space."

"Then you deserve everything you have coming to you."

"How do you mean?"

"You're so full of yourself, Brad; you have no fucking clue. You really think you can outwit and outmaneuver the Utterminster and the Archixprest? They put up with your shit only because it serves their ultimate purpose. If the Udder does get his chance, you are so utterly fucked. We have no idea how powerful that statue might get, but boy does the Udder have plans for you! He has a strong taste for war crimes and atrocities."

Brad's facial expression made it clear that Wendy had his undivided attention.

"Do you want to hear what the Utterminster has in mind for you?" said Wendy.

"No, but I think you're going to tell me, and I think I'm probably going to listen."

"I believe you should, sir," said Nikolian before Wendy continued.

"D'Izmaïe's Diet, they call it. They are going to force-feed you a mix of castor oil, industrial alcohol, bread crumbs, and sawdust, and then put you in a glass barrel and have the whole world watch you puke and shit yourself to death. They plan to ¡cast the whole thing. That should deliver some ¡balls, eh? What do you think of that, Brad? You still only interested in the ¡ball delivery business? You can stay there in Newer York, but they will probably still get you. If that statue goes into orbit, they will probably get everything they want. You won't be safe. We won't be safe. No one will.

"In case you haven't noticed, you have made an implacable enemy of the Utterminster, and he is one cruel, relentless, vengeful motherfucker. You need all the help you can get, and we need your help if you or any of us are going to stand any chance. Are you in?"

Brad slumped, sat back up, suddenly looking far too old for his skate-park-casual clothes. He nodded solemnly. "I'm in. What do you want?"

"We are not sure yet," said Wendy.

"You don't HAVE a plan, do you?"

"Not as such, no," said Nikolian. "We are working on one. With the Sisterhood."

"The kooky glass-blowers? Oh well, that's reassuring. Go team!" Brad punched the air. "You have some hunch about the statue taking over the ether. You have no plan so you decided to spread the despair—is that it? Nikolian already explained to you, Wendy: This thing is almost out of our hands. We are not driving the story anymore. It has a life of its own. I couldn't stop the Day of Days even if I wanted to. What the fuck do you want from me?"

"I don't know," said Wendy. "I don't KNOW anything. It all just feels really wrong."

"I don't see how we get this genie back in its bottle. Nikolian?"

"Knowing what I know," said Nikolian, "I can't see anything we can do. Wendy, do you honestly think the Sisterhood can help?"

"I don't fucking know. I thought you guys could help. I don't know what to do. Oh shit, I want out."

"We've talked about this before, Wendy. You are free to leave the show, but we are in no position to extract you safely from there. You would be on your own. By the way, while we are in this sharing mode, I had a talk with a very agitated Bruno Madison dude from the Wall Street Depredation and Speculation Association. They know who you are and where you are, and they would very much like to hurt you, but they won't bother you while the show is on. After that, I can't say. So, I guess we are all square on the dire warnings now, okay? Are we done? I need to take a walk, a long walk."

"We're done," whispered Wendy.

VII

From his station at the tent entrance, the Clarion cupped his hands to his mouth and voiced the D suspended fourth chord mandated for a prenuptial banquet. The buzz in the tent suppressed itself into an uneasy blend of impatient excitement and dread. This was the first-ever Regent/Mistress Consort prenuptial banquet, and few had any idea what protocol dictated and how long it might all take. The presence of D'Izmaïe's statue on a low altar in front of the High Table promised some kind of ceremonial business.

The Spinster Uilkitz and the Archixprest stepped into the tent. On her head the Spinster wore a moonstone vulva sculpture, and on his head the Archixprest wore an aventurine phallus. Then a group of pages spreading lotus petals on the floor led Mooney and Wendy into the tent. Both wore simple red wraps cinched at the waist with gold chains of interlocking carps. It was not a good look for either of them. Wild whooping greeted their entrance and there was much toasting and drinking to their health as they made their way to the High Table.

Mooney and Wendy took their places at the center of the High Table. The Archixprest sat beside the Utterminster and the Spinster Uilkitz sat beside Skid.

"Great, ehm, matriarchy hat there," slurred Skid to the Spinster. "I don't think I'd wear it myself, but fair play to you. It's bold. It's out there."

"My headgear is not of my choosing, but I take your compliment in the spirit offered." The Spinster Uilkitz pursed her lips and then smiled, and Skid felt he had been gently scolded then forgiven and adopted for life.

"This is unlike your bachelorette or stag night where you come from, I imagine?" shouted the Utterminster, quite obviously drunk.

Wendy smiled painfully. "I have little experience of such events, but yes, I imagine it is."

"So long as you don't end up bollock naked, painted metallic blue on a car ferry headed to Roscoff, you are ahead of the game!" announced Skid, and poured himself another huge glass of wine.

Halfway through the meal, the speechifying began. Out of politeness, the din of eating quieted down but the pace of stealthy drinking perceptibly increased throughout the tent.

"Well, if we are all doing party pieces, I'd like to do mine before I fall over," Skid announced after several long toasts had been given. He burst into song at the top of his lungs to the tune of "Tie Me Kangaroo Down, Sport":

"Bestiality's best, boys,
Bestiality's best!
Fuck a wallaby!
Bestiality's best, boys
Bestiality's best!
Shoot yer load in a toad, boys,
Shoot yer load in a toad!
Shoot yer load in a toad, boys!
Shoot yer load in a toad!
Bestiality's best, boys,
Bestiality's best!
Fuck a wallaby!
Bestiality's best, boys!
Bestiality's best! . . ."

Skid shrugged off several attempts to usher him back to his seat and everyone waited with differing degrees of horror, fascination, or impatience as the song ground through the tortured rhyming synonyms for copulating with stags, horses, shrews, moles, ducks, horses again but called steeds for the purposes of rhyme, goats, baboons, badgers, foxes, frogs, geese, mules, seals, squids, voles, yaks, ants, cod, skunks, crocodiles, swine, cows, and nits.

The last verse Skid sang with extra vehemence and directly to the Utterminster:

"Get bollock deep in a sheep, boys,
Bollock deep in a sheep!
Fuck a wallaby!
Get bollock deep in a sheep, boys,
Bollock deep in a sheeeeeeeeeeeeeeeeeeeep!"

When it became clear that Skid had finished, there were a few moments of uncomfortable hesitation before a tentative ripple of polite applause tiptoed through the tent. Skid staggered back to his seat under the Utterminster's burning glare.

"I don't think the Utterfucker liked your song, Skid," whispered Wendy.

"Not really surprising, is it? Sheep shaggers are very touchy that way."

Wendy exploded into nervous laughter, which drew curious stares from all except the Utterminster, who knew or suspected exactly what she was laughing at.

After dessert, the Archixprest and the Spinster Uilkitz stood up and reenacted the conflict with Outer Azhuur. In a gaudy fake proscenium, they did their grotesque Punch and Judy show and beat one another with scaled-down cloth versions of the Stave of Conciliation and the Cudgel of Compromise for about fifteen minutes, until the Archixprest collapsed to his knees in a showy mockery of Outer Azhuurse weakness. The Spinster Uilkitz leaned over him and triumphantly ground her vulva headpiece on his phallic one. Wendy had never seen the Quartel flunkies laugh so hard.

The laughter died suddenly when a procession of black-cloaked attendants carrying midnight-blue candles burst into the tent. This entourage hurried up the main aisle and stopped in front of the High Table. Then, at a nod from the Utterminster, the Clarion began to hawk his lungs out through his nose as he delivered himself of some peroration in Old High Azhuurse.

Ten agonizing minutes later, the Clarion had officially in-formed the guests that, it being Mooney's official farewell to bachelorhood and D'Izmaïe's departure was imminent, it was fit-ting that these two longtime companions should retire together into seclusion for the night and make their farewells.

The Utterminster removed the figure of D'Izmaïe from its horse and passed it to the reluctant Mooney. Then, in absolute silence, a black-feathered escort, now followed by Wendy and a pale and sweating Mooney carrying the unhorsed D'Izmaïe, filed twice around the perimeter of the banquet tent and then marched out into the night.

"Wow, that's your idea of a stag party?" shouted Skid, and stood up to leave. "I didn't expect much but that was totally shite; it looked more like a fucking kidnapping!"

"No, no, you must stay!" yelled the Utterminster. "We are about to begin the entertainments! The wrestling girls should be here shortly, and as a special treat we have an all-naked five-a-side scuffle of hungry proles, winners get the leftover food from tonight."

"Thanks, but I think I've had enough of your entertainment for one day."

Skid stood outside and watched Wendy, Mooney, and the line of black-clad figures march off into the dark. The fresh air suddenly drove all the wine to his knees. He reeled to his right, checked himself, wobbled unsteadily, and lurched in the direction of his tent.

"Here, let me help you." Nikolian put his big arm around Skid's shoulders and steered him down the path.

"Jaysus, I'm wrecked!" shouted Skid.

"You are that, but fuck it, eh?" said Nikolian.

"Yeah, fuck it! Fuck 'em all!"

They both flinched as the first screams of the Utterminster's *entertainments* came to them across the wind.

The procession wound its way out of the encampment and up to a cave in the hills above the excavation. Mooney's head was buzzing a little from the marzipan Wendy had given him. She had warned him that it might be a little odd, but it would ensure the Utterminster could not use the statue to get inside his head. Now that they suspected how he had suggested the *So You Wanna* audition to Mooney in Newer York, they were very wary of what the Utterminster might try.

They arrived at the cave and the escort formed two ranks on either side of its entrance. As Mooney and Wendy passed by, the escorts blew out their candles. When they reached the mouth of the cave, the last two escorts handed Wendy the Two-Legged Stool of Mög's Vigil and then extinguished their candles.

Mooney stared into the clammy interior of the cave. The sweat prickled and itched on the back of his neck. A ribbon of panic grew and twisted in his belly, but then the marzipan revved up and kicked in harder. His inner ear was suddenly alive with a chorus of songbirds and he became fascinated by the little lanterns he could see inside the cave and all the different colors they contained. This was obviously not intended to be a night for sleep. This was to be a night of wakeful and reflective meditation. The impractical and uncomfortable Two-Legged Stool of Mög's Vigil was further evidence of this: its legs were close together on the same side. It might have been symbolic of the twin pillars of Azhuurse society—Mögfulness and Right Remembering—but was totally useless as something to sit on.

Mooney took the stool from Wendy, nodded reassuringly, and stepped into the cave. Immediately, the escorts rolled the sealing rock across the entrance.

Out of nowhere, the Spinster Uilkitz, now relieved of her headdress, appeared at Wendy's shoulder. "I shall accompany you to your tent. It is traditional that you be taken to your sleeping place on this night by an unwed woman of the elite."

"That's handy, cos between you and me, you are the only one of the *ladies* I can stand."

"Between you and me, the feeling is mutual, my good sister excepted."

"Understood."

Inside the cave, Mooney was now alone with his Captain Dude, more nakedly alone with him than he could ever remember. Only the soft hissing and crackling of the lanterns provided any relief from the dense silence. Mooney called out, "Hello?" The harsh, pointy echoes that rushed back like a riot made it clear he was not going to be able to pass the night by singing or talking to himself.

He put Captain Dude down on the ground and sat awkwardly on the stool. He poked at the stones at his feet. He waited. He felt nothing. He got up and sat right beside the statue. Still nothing. He concentrated as hard as he could. Was there a flutter of Utterminster or was he imagining it? It was hard to tell with all the protective clamor of cures for hangnails, the melting point of silver, pi expressed as a hexadecimal number that, thanks to the

Sisterhood's marzipan, streamed from the Hermitage spire into his head.

Mooney hurled the two-legged stool away and moved to a nice flat rock. He checked his neck. The joint of "recreational herbs" and the tiny tesla coil lighter that the Relict Uilkitz had slipped him as he entered the banquet tent were still there on their string. He lit the joint and took a hefty toke.

∞

Watching the naked wrestling and the death match for the leftovers had greatly aroused the Utterminster. He wanted to in-head and *feel* the porn eddies of the ether. Too drunk to manage the tesla coil on the herb engine, he used a candle flame to light it. He smoked two bowls of the trepanium herb and lay back naked with the statue of D'Izmaïe's horse beside him. He tightly gripped the pommel that protruded from the saddle. He briefly remembered something about never using a naked flame to light the herb, which at that moment kicked in with unusual force to demonstrate why. When the two statues connected, the Utterminster was slung into the ether in an unfamiliar and frightening way.

Before he could orient himself and start looking for the porn eddies, he was sucked into the whirlpool of Mooney's beherbed and marzipanned mind. This was not at all like the time when he had visited Mooney's mind in Newer York. He had been in control then, able to lurk on the periphery of Mooney's consciousness and insinuate his ideas among Mooney's own. This time he was powerless, battered and drowning in the roiling maelstrom of Mooney's accelerated thoughts and chaotic unstitched memories.

Mooney had just decided that the light from the lanterns in the cave was made up of particles and not waves and had split himself into an almost infinite number of parts to fly along with each individual particle. It took every last shred of the Utterminster's will to pull himself out of the ether before Mooney irrevocably scattered his essence with the light. He pried his hand off the horse and rolled away from it, his cock now shriveled between his trembling fingers. He curled into a shivering, stricken knot of exhausted, terrified half dreams.

VIII

At dawn, Wendy and the Spinster Uilkitz stepped forward from the crowd gathered outside the cave. Wendy carried a hazel branch in her hand. When she reached the sealing rock, she stifled yet another yawn and tapped the branch three times on the rock. There was a pause and then the black-cloaked escorts rolled back the rock. Wendy half expected to see Mooney's charred cadaver beside a grinning Captain Dude. She was relieved when the daylight spilled into the cave to reveal a beaming Mooney carelessly holding the D'Izmaïe figure under one arm.

Mooney stepped out into the sunlight and hugged Wendy with his free arm. The crowd broke into whooping and cheering. Pages came forward, took D'Izmaïe, and handed him to the dazed Utterminster, who placed him back on the horse that stood on its processional altar.

Mooney and Wendy walked behind the altar, followed by the rest of the dignitaries. Mooney was still a little bit stoned and Wendy was exhausted from the night she had spent arguing with the Clarion.

"You okay?" asked Wendy as they boarded the airship.

"Better than okay. That cave is wild. I feel great, different, lighter. I'm not afraid of tunnels anymore. Everything looks crisper, less . . . occluded."

"Amazing. *Occluded?* Wow, bonus points for vocab there."

"Strange. It's like suddenly finding a whole new set of rooms you never knew existed. I feel like there's more of me than before."

"You're still stoned."

"Yes, a little, but this is not just the herb, this is not fading, it's getting stronger. Thanks for being concerned."

"Hey, we're engaged, aren't we? Of course I'm concerned. Don't want to be widowed before I get wed, do I?"

"Seriously, thanks."

"Hey, not a problem. We're on the same side of whatever this is, right?"

"Yep." Mooney reached for her hand and squeezed it.

Wendy could feel the difference. Something had shifted inside him.

∾

Something had also changed in the Utterminster. He was on almost total shutdown. He sat trembling beside the Archixprest and a cold sweat sheened his forehead. His vision flickered like a faulty television and sometimes flashed scenes from total elsewheres. The flame-lit herb, Mooney's mind, and the erratic resonances of the huge reserves of raw trepanium ore from the dig stockpiled in the far recesses of the cave had partly shattered his senses. Had he been less frazzled, he would have understood how very close he'd come to frying his mind completely.

IX

As the airship wound down into the pit, Wendy looked out the window to see the lines of pubble making their way up the ramps. On the opposite lip of the chasm another airship hovered low, moored at the ready for something or other. The giant globe sat below them on the bottom of the pit. As they got closer, it became clear that, unlike most things in Azhuur, this globe was no triumph of form over function. The Chariot of D'Izmaïe was no ornamental piece of hardware; this was a utilitarian metal globe designed to withstand intense physical strain. It resembled an ugly, oversized, bathysphere, all bolts and rivets, devoid of any aesthetic appeal. It was all business and stood fifteen feet tall.

Once they disembarked from the airship, the Utterminster took the D'Izmaïe figure off the horse and handed it to a technician, who carefully carried it to the Chariot of D'Izmaïe and passed it to another technician inside. There followed some clanking and squealing of heavy metal parts. After a final bolt-tightening, the technician clambered out of the porthole.

The Utterminster stepped forward and peered inside. "You have inspected it thoroughly? The general is properly secured?"

"It—I mean *he*—is. We have triple-checked the Sisterhood's work, Your Utterness. It is all as it should be. Azhuur be served!" The technician twisted his nose at the Utterminster and then at the globe, and walked to where a team was waiting with the circular door to seal the porthole.

"Let the leave-taking begin!" announced the Clarion.

One by one, beginning first with Mooney and Wendy and ending with the Archixprest and the Utterminster, the dignitaries stepped forward and stood by the porthole twisting their noses and bowing their heads before backing away from the globe.

"Mög's speed. We wish you swift ascent and eagerly await your triumphant return. Azhuur be served!" The Utterminster stuck the statue of the horse inside the globe, made it bow, and then backed away with it in his arms.

At a signal from the Archixprest, the technicians trundled the heavy door forward, hoisted it up, and bolted it into place. A separate crew wheeled another contraption alongside the Chariot. This was the Hydrogenator, one more device of the Sisterhood's making that somehow used light to split water into hydrogen and oxygen. It resembled an old horse-drawn fire engine except for the large glass orb on top to gather and concentrate the light. The technicians took a hose from its innards and connected it to a coupling in the side of the Chariot.

The Archixprest mumbled some prayerful-sounding Azhuurse and then turned the elaborate brass switch on the Hydrogenator's side. The water in the tanks began to gurgle, the bellows started up, and the dials and counters on the front panel flickered and rolled.

"Throw a match at that fucking thing and let's be done," muttered Wendy to Mooney.

"I think if that was a workable possibility, the Sisterhood would have recommended it," whispered Mooney.

"Like fuck they would. Useless fucks," spat Wendy.

The noise of the bellows intensified and a piercing steam whistle indicated that the Chariot was now at full pressure. The Archixprest threw the brass switch again and the Hydrogenator slowed. As soon as its noise died down, everyone became aware of the approaching airship revving its engines at them across the gawping expanse of the pit.

Wendy scowled at the airship as it slowly rose. The array of sails suspended from it looked like a giant upside-down Christmas tree built out of dark-blue glass. As it got closer, Wendy could see the sunlight glinting off the thousands of fjord-like cuts into the edge of each triangular sheet of glass that hung from the central spine. She recalled how calmly the Clarion had relayed the Sistermost's explanation of how the sails worked when he and the Spinster Uilkitz came to her tent after the banquet, as if that would help her accept the situation.

"I don't give a shit about the cuts adding more edges to ionize the oncoming particles to draw it up through the atmosphere," Wendy had responded. "What I don't understand is why is the Sisterhood helping the Utterminster succeed. Weren't they coming up with a plan to stop the fucking statue from getting into orbit? Wasn't that what we talked about?"

"There was a change of plan," the Clarion had said.

"Yeah? What exactly is the new plan? Hope the Utterminster is so pleased and excited with his success that he dies of a heart attack?"

"Wendy, it pains me to tell you this, but there is no plan; the Sisterhood have decided."

"Decided what? To do nothing and just let this happen?"

"Yes. There is nothing they can do. They have endured much. They will either endure what comes or they will perish."

"That's where they got to after all their so-called deliberations?"

"Yes. It is what they have decided."

"But he will eat them alive!"

"They are fully aware of that. They have made their peace. An entire world dominated by the Utterminster is not one they wish to struggle against."

"But they could stop him!"

"They cannot. This is beyond them. They are united in this; they will endure or they will be extinguished. They cannot and will not attempt to stop this. It will be whatever it is meant to be."

"What kind of fucked-up fatalistic shit is that?"

"It is where their deliberations have led them. I have no way to change that. This is what they have concluded."

"So this shit is going to roll all over us and that's it? We all go zen with the Sisterhood and accept it as our fate? That is bullshit! You have to talk to them."

"Wendy, I have known and loved the Sistermost for decades. There is no renegotiation, there is no turning this back. It grieves and frightens me too, but I must surrender to this higher wisdom."

"Are you fucking kidding me? You call this wisdom? This is capitulation. This is defeatism. This is rolling over and dying."

"Dying is not a thing they fear. It is something that comes in its own anointed time. It is as it was always supposed to be— implacable, unavoidable, the underpinning of all life. They are decided."

"So we are all fucked?"

"Wendy, I cannot tell you how to take this; it is simply so. What you choose to do with this knowledge is entirely up to you.

I must now make my own peace. I am afraid I have no way to help you in that journey."

"That's it?"

"That is it."

"We could poison his herb," the Spinster Uilkitz cut in.

"What?"

"We could gradually increase the trepanium residue in his herb until it paralyzes him."

"Oh yeah? And how long will that take?" Wendy said.

"Once he has used up his current supply, perhaps a week."

"We don't have that kind of time. You know that. As soon as that thing gets up, the Utterminster will have the entire fucking ether in a choke hold. What a shit plan."

"That is what we have."

Wendy could not remember exactly what she said at that point. All she could recall was storming out of her tent and furiously walking the entire perimeter of the excavation with the Spinster Uilkitz scurrying to keep up in her duties as chaperone, and then falling exhausted onto her bed and into a shallow sleep while the Spinster kept vigil in her armchair.

She now watched despairingly as the airship hovered overhead and the sails were winched down onto the Chariot where the technicians secured them into the coupling.

X

"I can't, Alva! I can't."

"Yes you can. Three more steps."

Alva pulled her grandmother to where the ramp doubled back on itself so they could rest against the side, out of the steady foot traffic. Her grandmother fell on top of her and for a minute neither of them could summon the energy to move.

"We can rest now, Grandmother. We will be safe here for a while. The crowds are small." This close to the top, where the hole was so wide, it was hard to detect the curvature of the sides and it was quite disorienting. They sat with their backs against the wall and took what residual warmth they could from a large embedded stone; they had been climbing in darkness through the night and were chilled and stiff.

Alva looked up and could see only the grim, contourless cliff stretching up to the washed-out blue of the sky. It was hard to be sure how close to the top they were. "We are almost out, Grandmother." A steady line of tired bodies continued to trudge past them.

For the last two days they had been climbing, and for the ten days before that they had been living in the bottom of the pit where sunlight barely reached. As the dig edged toward its bottom, there were fewer workers, yet Alva and her grandmother had been unlucky enough to be part of the dwindling workforce that could fit into the narrowing base of the conical hole. An airship dumped water on them twice a day and they drank what they could from the ground and their clothes. Those lucky enough not to be killed by the food rations dropped down on them got to eat.

Once the Chariot of D'Izmaïe had been set in place, they had been told they had four days to get out. They would do well to be as far from the floor as possible when the water was turned on. Mercifully, the surviving workers were too exhausted to rush for the ramps. The last ten thousand had begun their long climb back to the surface, pausing to watch the cluster of gentry around the ugly iron ball and the peculiar glass fins being attached to it. That was apparently what this mad hole in the ground was all for.

Alva's grandmother, lulled to sleep by the warmth of the rock, snored and snorted softly beside her. Alva must have somehow dozed off too: she woke with a start. Her grandmother was now screaming. On the far side of the pit near the top, a gaping hole had opened, and a huge stream of water was gushing out into the air and plunging into the huge emptiness below. The distant roar and crush of the water echoed around the pit. Her grandmother rushed to get up.

Alva put her arm around her. "We are safe, Grandmother. We still have time; it will take days to reach up here."

∛

From the rim, the Utterminster and Archixprest also watched the first waters fall into the pit.

"So, you see, Your Utterness, the physics of the situation did not justify a ceremony," said the Archixprest. "The vision of a massive geyser shooting out to the center of the abyss before cascading down like a waterfall of great artifice simply does not work. There is no way we could create such pressure. There is most certainly pressure and an outflow, but it does not manage to get a hundred yards before it begins to fall, and as you can see, there is no crashing onto the bottom, it merely hits the side and flows down." Careful not to gloat, he added: "Of course, this way we avoid any risk of damaging the capsule."

"So, with the minimal splashing, are you saying we could have used the water from the bay after all?"

"Good heavens, no. That toxic brew would dissolve the capsule. Remember, Utterminster, when the Day of Days comes, the roar of the water crashing into the near-full pit will be astonishing. That will indeed be worthy of us."

"It had damn well better. Now I must go lie down. I am in need of rest. Make sure I am not disturbed."

"As you wish, Your Utterness. Azhuur be served!"

XI

The Sistermost took the scroll from the Sister Apprentice Apiarist. She looked through it, making marks beside each of the 201 lines of text. She moved with the easy speed of practice and familiarity until she was close to the end. Then she stopped and peered quizzically at the scroll and circled one whole line in the text and wrote some notes in the margin.

"Please take this back to the Sister Apiarist. Ask her to repeat the divining. What I see here is most unusual and must be verified."

⚭

In the garden on the Earth Riding's roof, the Sister Apiarist watched her apprentice return. She had been expecting this to happen after she transcribed the divining and recognized the oddity in it.

"Mistress, the Sistermost—"

"Wants me to repeat the divining?"

"Yes, Mistress."

"Tell her it will be several hours before the bees return and I have ample time to arrange the divining plane anew. Then return here to help me."

The Sister Apiarist began resetting the divining plane that sat on top of the hive. She lit the small paraffin stove and set the pot of wax to warm on it. Then she walked toward the first of the tall slender poles that surrounded the hive in a perfect circle. She rapped the pole and the beautiful variegated glass globe it held popped out of its holding cup and fell softly into her outstretched palm. She noted with satisfaction that the nearby almond trees were coming into flower.

The globe was about the size of a ping-pong ball, and inside it swirled a galaxy of colored glass globules, filaments, and flecks arranged in patterns whose beauty was readily apparent to the untrained eye although their meaning was discernible only to the bees and the Sister Apiarist. She popped the globe into the velvet bag she wore around her neck and tapped the next pole five feet to her left. Another globe fell into her palm. It was identical in size to the first but completely distinct in color and pattern, as were all 201 globes, including the two new ones the Fire Sisters had recently made for the Sistermost.

She was almost finished gathering the globes when her apprentice returned. She popped the last globe off its pole and handed them all to her. "The wax should be ready. Recoat the divining plane and then set the globes back on the poles."

They had not done a full reset of the globes for at least a year. The Sister Apiarist often felt it should be done more routinely and not only when the readings predicted a big shift somewhere in the market. That said, in the last year of unchanged globes, the Sisterhood's secret investments had been unfailingly and inordinately successful.

It was all quite simple, once you freed your mind from the crude planks of cause and effect and let the ceremonial purity of the exercise pour through. The bees, on their return from foraging, would circle the hive by flying a full circuit of the glass globes before approaching the platform on top of the hive. Then they would dance on the minutely sensitive and impressionable wax and orient themselves toward the globes of which they appeared to have news. Each globe represented a financial instrument or derivative that the Sisterhood had an interest in, and when the bees had all returned inside the hive, the Sister Apiarist would read the tracks in the wax, refer to the beads the tracks were pointing to, and, based on the number, depth, spacing, and direction of the tracks, make predictions about the future value of particular investments.

The Sister Apprentice replaced the globes on new poles and the Sister Apiarist reviewed them. Then they waited for the bees to return an hour later. The Sister Apiarist repeated the full divining, her apprentice attentive to every observation, notation, and calculation. Satisfied the results were accurate and consistent, she compiled the news onto a new scroll.

"The results are exactly the same. We will both bring this to the Sistermost."

"The bees are never wrong," intoned the Sister Apprentice Apiarist solemnly.

"No, they are not. It is we who can err in the reading, and for this we must be ever watchful." The Sister Apiarist had dedicated her life to this office, and although she knew how to read the dance and commission new globes as needed, she had no idea how the bees did what they did. The Sistermost had once confided that she too had scant idea how the bees knew anything but suspected it had something to do with the trepanium in the glass-making process and the trepanium-rich soil where the flowers the bees took nectar from grew.

⚭

The Sistermost scrutinized the new scroll, checked the original one, and nodded her head. "It is incontrovertibly right, odd and surprising though it may be. Take this to the Sister Dealers and have them prepare the necessary adjustments to our portfolio."

"I will take this to them myself," said the Sister Apiarist. She knew her apprentice was still quite afraid of the Sister Dealers, who performed their duties by connecting directly to the ether without any mediation, tuning their minds directly into the resonances of the spire.

The Sistermost raised an eyebrow. "Very well, but you, Sister Apprentice, must overcome your squeamishness about our sisters who commune directly with the ether. There is no shame in this gift. It is disconcerting to witness, but they too are part of the we."

"I will accompany the Sister Apiarist and endeavor to overcome this fear," said the apprentice.

The Sistermost waved them out of her chamber: "Very well, off with you two then. There is no time to lose. We must take full advantage of this foreknowledge and make the necessary adjustments now so we may act decisively when the time comes."

XII

"Hey, Nikolian, welcome. How's it going? Come to pay your respects?"

"This arrived for you in the production supplies last night." Nikolian held up a garment bag.

Skid opened the note that was pinned to it:

Greetings from Glasgow. We all got tired of seeing you on the telly in the same tatty old drape. Costumier Sally ran this off for you. Try to come back in one piece. xxx, Kate

Skid opened the garment bag and removed a beautiful jet-black drape with crimson silk lining and burgundy velvet trim on the collar, cuffs, and pockets, along with immaculately tailored black pants and a gold silk vest. He lifted the jacket and examined it. He set it on a chair and put on a white shirt, pulled on the pants and vest, and then slipped into the jacket. It all fit perfectly. He slipped on the pair of burgundy suede crepe-soled shoes that were tucked into the bottom of the bag.

"Cool! Deadly!"

Skid did a little twirl when Wendy and Mooney came into his tent.

"Very handsome. Here, I got you this." Wendy held out a shoestring tie cinched with a silver and turquoise eye.

"Thanks, Wendy. Brilliant. People, I think we have an outfit!" shouted Skid, a little too loud.

"I think you will make what you would call a proper fuck-you entrance, Skid," said Mooney.

The thin mist of gaiety suddenly evaporated from the room. Skid took off his drape and sat on the bed.

"Skid, remember what we talked about," said Nikolian, "the big entrance, the bike, the whole lot. You know that vain Kitxchenn will be putting on a show. So you do too. Right? I brought you a cigar."

Wendy glowered at Nikolian. "How the fuck is that supposed to help?"

Nikolian shrugged.

"Here, I got it from the fencing master." Mooney offered Skid a bright, slightly curved sword in an elaborate sheath.

"Thanks, I'll try not to cut myself with it," said Skid with a forced smile.

Wendy shook her head sadly. "Okay, Mooney, we gotta go. Apparently, we're getting married today. Let's get our pantomime costumes on. Good luck, Skid."

"Yeah, right," said Skid.

Nikolian stepped forward and shook his hand. "I am sorry, Skid. If I could take your place, I would."

"If you could take my place, I have to say I'd let you. Thanks for the loan of your ¡think. Could you all just leave and give me some space? I'm going to call my ma."

"I had the Sisterhood retune it and set up the Olde Time Landline app. You should be all set. I'll be back for you in a couple of hours," said Nikolian, and followed the others out.

XIII

SANDRA

Welcome, everyone, to *So You Wanna Run a Country? The Id of Azhuur's* much-anticipated Day of Days.

TOM

Hi, Sandra! It's great to be here. This is without doubt the biggest day we have ever seen in the history of the *So You Wanna* franchise. This easily beats the finale of *So You Wanna Run a Country? Krablikistainia,* when Edgore Paache filled the ducal palace with every available piece of paper currency and torched the whole thing.

SANDRA

Yes! Amazing! There is so much to look forward to today. While we wait for the arrival of the elite dignitaries, Tom, you said you had invited a special guest to join us?

TOM

Yes, I did. Joining us we have Stavnik Respigni, CEO and founder of DEATH CAGE—NO QUARTER.

CUT TO CLOSE-UP: Mussolini-like bulbous head of Respigni.
LONG SHOT: Respigni in high-backed Louis XIII-style gilt armchair in front of a portrait of himself.
CLOSE-UP ON PORTRAIT: Respigni on a wind-swept hill brandishing a broadsword at a lightning bolt while flanked by two bounteously oiled, naked women who admire his long flowing locks and hungrily caress his statuesque, rippling musculature.
PULL BACK TO: The bald, unattractive, poorly proportioned, bad-tempered Respigni, who sits in his gaudy chair in front of his fantasy portrait.

TOM

Thank you for making the time, Stavnik.

RESPIGNI
You will call me Mr. Respigni!

TOM
Uhm, Okay. Welcome, Mr. Respigni. What can you tell us about the combat part of today's program, the duel between the Adjutant and Mandrak Kitxchenn?

RESPIGNI
Bullshit! Not a duel. Not even a warm-up. Mandrak Kitxchenn could dispose of this decadent weakling with one bare hand. The only question is how much he will toy with this pitiful opponent and hurt, maim, and break him before he finally ends his pitiful life.

TOM
I see. So, what you are saying—

RESPIGNI
You will not interrupt. You will not paraphrase or speculate. I will tell you exactly what I am saying, and when I have said what I wish, this interview will be at an end. Is that understood?

Tom
Yes, Mr. Respigni. Quite clear. Please, continue.

RESPIGNI

I would first make a deep cut at the
left elbow to reduce defensive capability. A good deep cut. Much bleed-
ing. Public will go wild. Then some
face wounds. Always lots of blood,
and good ¡balls with face wounds.
Then perhaps the ligaments at the
back of the knees. But maybe this
will make it too easy. Maybe Kitxchenn will allow one free blow. Maybe
not. It depends on his mood. I have
seen him decapitate opponents on the
first stroke. Maybe not today. Maybe
today a little more foreplay, a little more entertainment.

SANDRA

Mr Respigni, is there any way the
Adjutant could survive this ordeal?

RESPIGNI

Ha ha ha. This, Mr. Tom, is why you
have a woman here? To ask the truly
stupid questions? Please tell her
there is no chance.

TOM

Thank you, Mr. Respigni. I am being
told we have no more time. We thank
you for your time.

RESPIGNI
I am not done. I will tell you when
this interview is—

SANDRA
Over! And that's all the time we have
for Mr. Respigni. Goodbye! Now, Tom,
what comes to mind first when you
look back on that interview with Mr.
Respigni? Toad? Cockroach? Dog turd
caught in the treads of a running
shoe?

TOM
Uhm, uhm, well . . .

SANDRA
Right, it is so hard to choose, isn't
it? So many repugnant analogies to
choose from. Isn't nature amazing?

TOM
Uhm, yes, I guess.

SANDRA
Tom, when we watched the selection of
Skid's opponent, you mentioned the
sightlines from the Tower of Thrones.
Tell us more about that.

TOM
Uh, yes, Sandra. On most of the tiers,
only the very front rows of seats can

see anything directly. People around
the edges can see opticons, but the
ones in the center of the tiers can't.
It's like geometry.

SANDRA

Oh my god, that's amazing! Do go on.

TOM

Well, it just doesn't work for looking down at things.

SANDRA

Ha ha ha. I have to say, that is
crazy ironic for a throne. Get it? No
good for looking down on things? So,
amazingly, there may be dignitaries
on the Tower of Thrones who will see
nothing at all? Worse than the pubble
on the ground? Not even be able to
see an opticon?

TOM

Yep.

SANDRA

Amazing. And yet since three o'clock
this morning when the elevator tower
opened, dignitaries have been lining
up behind their banners to get their
tonsures checked and be winched up to
their terrible seats.

TOM

Yes. But don't forget the prestige of
being on the Tower of Thrones. That,
for the Azhuurse gentry, counts for
much more than being able to actually
see anything. The Tower is almost
full now. I am being told we can expect the Regent and Mistress Consort
very soon.

SANDRA

That is a whole lot of prestige! What
a day of spectacular contrasts this
is going to be.

XIV

The crowds were already massing around the edge of the pit and
jostling for vantage points. Most of them would see nothing directly and only catch the events on the opticons, but the important thing was to be there, to be present at the Day of Days, to be
able, in years to come, to point at a patch of dirt and say to some
acquaintance or descendant: "I stood *there* on the Day of Days."

On the antepenultimate tier sat the Clarion, the Spinster,
and the Relict. They moved their thrones a little in from the
edge to take advantage of the shade from the Utterminster and
Archixprest's tier above.

In keeping with tradition, Mooney and Wendy were the last
to ascend the Tower of Thrones. No one on the Tower was permitted to see them ascend. According to something the Archixprest
read on the walls of the Quartel, tradition dictated that on this,
their wedding day, they must arrive on foot. For the purposes
of decorum, they wore identical gray ankle-length smocks over
their wedding raiment and were flanked by a phalanx of Utterforz

in their dull metal battle masks. A fresh hauling team winched them to the top.

&

In the cordoned-off area at the pit's edge, the hoisting teams made final adjustments to the trial barge. They tied down the nearest mooring ropes while crews carried the heavy coils of rope to the side moorings needed to keep it in position on the water.

The wedding barge sat on its stanchions and looked almost ashamed of its festive gold canopy and garlands, so frivolous compared to the dismal black trial barge with its bare deck and high, spiked deck rail, which made it look like what it essentially was: a floating death cage.

The Utterminster stood up dramatically and a breathless silence, broken only by the continual crashing of water into the pit, radiated out from the Tower of Thrones across the crowd. From his cowl, the Utterminster took a small porcelain carp. He coughed into it gently. All around the pit, the hundreds of opticons started to vibrate and hum and they echoed the Utterminster's cough around the countryside.

"Honorable Regent, Mistress Consort, peers, dignitaries, citizens of Azhuur, interloping Outlanders, let us prepare to make our temporary farewell to General D'Izmaïe, who will be lost to our sight for a short time when he ascends on high, the better to shine his goodness down upon us. The waters near their full point. Azhuur be served!" The Utterminster replaced the carp in his cowl and twisted his nose toward the bottom of the pit, where D'Izmaïe's statue, he hoped and prayed, was safely in the capsule under all that water. He shouted to the Clarion below.

The Clarion walked to the edge of the antepenultimate tier and shouted up: "Yes, Your Utterness?"

"This is too slow. Signal the dam. Tell them to use the old diesel pumps; we need more water and faster."

The Clarion hesitated.

"Don't stand there gawping at me like some frightened reptile! Get them to start the pumps!"

"Very well, Your Utterness."

"Then do it. Send a whisper and get those damn pumps working."

The Clarion spent what was to the Utterminster an agonizing ten minutes shouting into the communication pipe and the end of the gantry. When he returned, he climbed the ladder connecting the top three tiers at the rear and announced: "Your Utterness, I have received confirmation from the Hall of Whispers that all the diesel pumps have been engaged and are operating at full capacity. Your Utterness should see the effects and the increased flow in some fifteen minutes. Azhuur be served!"

"Good. We will never speak of this aberrant use of diesel again. Understood?"

"Understood, Your Utterness. Azhuur be served!"

The Utterminster glowered across the pit at the roaring flood of water that cascaded down. He grabbed his field glasses and looked again. It was still below the line in the side indicating the minimum needed to get the globe going. The noise was tremendous and the spray from the water rose high in the air and the breeze brought its welcome freshness to the Tower, but the Utterminster continued to simmer and seethe with impatience.

XV

The hoisting crew were securing the side ropes to keep the duel barge in place when Mandrak Kitxchenn, Skid's opponent, burst through the crowds, standing astride two black stallions at full gallop. Several dozen were trampled underfoot but most survived to cheer him on. Most had only the vaguest idea who he was, though anyone with gold-encrusted armor and two huge swords strapped to their back, straddling two galloping horses while twirling long flashing daggers in each hand, was good for a cheer and a whoop.

Kitxchenn spun and sheathed his daggers, then dismounted with a spectacular double somersault. He whipped his two swords from behind his back and strutted and posed beside the pit, slashing at the air. A thousand Mandrak Kitxchenns filled the opticons and were greeted by a mix of cheering and hissing. Kitxchenn put away his swords and stood with his arms crossed, peering straight ahead at the Tower of Thrones.

"*Kit-chen! Kit-chen! Kit-chen! Kit-chen!*" chanted some paid impostors in the crowd. Others took up their cry.

On the swell of this adulation, instead of waiting to be lowered into the small skiff and rowed out to the barge after the launch, as was the plan, in an ostentatious show of bravado, Kitxchenn turned his back on the Tower of Thrones, did some quick stretching and lunging, then dashed to the water's edge and along the taut mooring ropes to make a spectacular leap onto the barge and balance precariously on the top of the rails before doing a double backflip onto the deck, planting the landing perfectly and finishing with mortal combat's equivalent of jazz hands. The pubble cheered wildly at this reckless swashbuckling display on the opticons.

⚭

The Utterminster watched the water level approach the line the Sisterhood had added to indicate when the underwater pressure would release the sphere. From that point, it was estimated it would take ten minutes for the sphere to rise through the water, charge its sails, and reach the surface.

The airship Nikolian was using as his command center to direct the ¡seers and ¡flys descended close to the rim above the sluice gate. A ramp flashed from the underside of the gondola. The ¡sees were all trained on it and the Sister Seers allowed the footage into the feed and onto the opticons. An engine revved, and then down the ramp sped Skid on his motorcycle. A huge cheer burst from the crowd when they saw his image on the opticons.

With a big cigar clenched between his teeth, he wore his jet-black drape and pants, neon-green socks, burgundy suede shoes, mirrored sunglasses, his sword strapped across his back, and a striking silver helmet the Clarion had given him at the last minute. Skid pulled a wheelie and the crowd cheered louder, drowning out the roar of the water that had now almost filled the pit. The crowd drew back as he began his ride around the edge of the pit.

When Skid reached the trial barge, Kitxchenn went into a paroxysm of strutting and posing, only to have Skid give him the finger and continue his ride around the pit. Kitxchenn swore and pounded on the rails with the hilts of his swords.

↮

Wendy noticed how the crowd pulling back from the water to get out of Skid's way caused the ring of Utterforz encircling them to buckle and break. She turned to Mooney and whispered in his ear. Mooney called the Clarion to his side. They conferred and the Clarion nodded gravely.

↮

After his additional circuit around the pit, Skid stopped in front of the trial barge and sat on his bike revving the engine and puffing on his cigar. He watched Kitxchenn's antics with studied disinterest. He heaved his bike onto its kickstand, dismounted, and leaned against it. He took off his helmet, cocked his head to one side, made sure he was on the opticons, and took the cigar from his mouth and theatrically mouthed, *Asshole*, for the benefit of every *Id of Azhuur* fan who was following the ¡cast. When he mouthed it again in Azhuurse, the crowd exploded in laughter.

Mooney rose from his throne and held up his arms for silence. The opticons all showed him, and the crowd fell quiet.

He took out his scroll and held it out in front of him in his right hand.

The Clarion, as mouthpiece for He Who Is Too Mighty to Sully Himself with Public Speech, stood beside him, held Mooney's left hand in his own right hand, and spoke into the porcelain carp's open mouth: "Mistress Consort, dignitaries, citizens of Azhuur, interloping Outlanders . . ." began the Clarion.

Mooney was freshly shocked by the ridiculously clear reproduction of the Clarion's voice from all the opticons.

"Today is a momentous day. Today is the DAY OF DAYS!! Today we will see Azhuur in all its splendor: the great ascent of the General D'Izmaïe to his rightful place in the firmament and Azhuur's return to greatness; the intractability of its justice as combat decides the guilt or innocence of the Adjutant; and finally, the timelessness of its power as shown in the marriage of my dear Consort and I before all the world to preside over the Fatherland's new glory.

"But first, I command you all to contemplate the nature of what is about to unfold before you. As a show of the esteem in which we hold General D'Izmaïe, on the count of three, let all of you standing take one pace back from the waters."

On "three," the crowd rippled back from the pit's edge. The Utterforz who had positioned themselves in a massive ring twenty-five yards from the edge expanded ever so slightly to accommodate the push, as they had when Skid's motorbike had passed.

The Clarion continued: "Let us redouble this gesture and take five paces back from the scene of glory."

The crowd bobbed back a little more, this time calling out as they did: "Moo-nee! Ooo-en-dee!"

"And redouble again to ten steps."

The crowd rippled back further: "Moo-nee! Ooo-en-dee! Moo-nee! Ooo-en-dee!"

The rings of Utterforz buckled and broke under the pressure of the receding crowd.

"Bloody preposterous idolatry!" roared the Utterminster. "Let them get on with the launch and then have that Skid disemboweled, they can do their stupid wedding, and then we can get on with our real work." He noted that the water had almost reached the launch line, then pulled the statue of D'Izmaïe's horse against his chest.

"And redouble again and retreat thirty more paces from the scene of awe."

"Moo-nee! Ooo-en-dee! Moo-nee! Ooo-en-dee! Moo-nee! Ooo-en-dee! Moo-nee! Ooo-en-dee! Moo-nee! Ooo-en-dee! Moo-nee! Ooo-en-dee!"

The ring of Utterforz was now so distended that it dissolved into many individual troopers lost among the crowd. They were no longer in position to herd anyone into the pit or anywhere else. Mooney squeezed the Clarion's hand in signal.

"The time is near," intoned the Clarion. "When the waters are full, the launch will begin. Azhuur be served!" He bowed, backed away, and Mooney sat again on his throne.

The opticons cut from the crowd to the Tower of Thrones, to Mandrak Kitxchenn, to Skid, and back to the gates where the water continued to gush into the pit and crept ever closer to the launch line. It was during this cross-cutting of points of view that the first dark shapes were spotted in the geyser pouring into the pit. After the first few, there were none for a minute, and then suddenly the water appeared to change color with the quantity of shapes it now carried into the pit.

The Clarion noticed this strangeness on the opticon nearest him

The "Moo-nee! Ooo-en-dee!" chant was beginning to lose force when the dark shapes from the geyser emerged from the foaming churn and started drifting out across the water.

Most people had already stepped too far back from the pit to recognize what these shapes were until the opticons abruptly stopped their cross-cutting and settled on the pit to reveal thousands of perfectly preserved bodies floating in the pit. The chanting died. Every opticon showed the same slow pan across the pit. Isolated howls of recognition sprang from the crowd as the remains of family members were spotted. More voices joined and gradually coalesced into one sustained lament of awful, long-repressed, communal trauma.

The production Intimeet was afire: "Nikolian, where are you? What the fuck is this? This was not on the schedule. You should hear the inane shit the commentators are coming out with trying to make sense of all this."

Nikolian's ¡think split between Brad's terrified face and the current ¡cast feed, which was still locked on the bodies in the water. From the gondola of his director's airship, he looked down on the water below. ·

Brad screamed through the crew channel: "Cut away from this! Field crew, get the ¡sees on the barge, on the crowd, anywhere but the water! Nikolian, find out what the fuck is going on! Research, get something plausible to the talkover idiots stat!"

SANDRA

Well, Tom, I can't see clearly, but it
looks like there are objects in the
water. Big objects. People, maybe?

TOM

It's hard to say, but one thing is
certain: they just started appearing in the last few minutes. Wait,

```
I'm getting an update from our ground
crew. It appears these are some of
the Azhuurse elite who are so devoted
to General D'Izmaïe that they have
acquired scuba gear and . . .
```

Brad exploded into the production Intimeet: "Are you fucking kidding me with this shit? See? They make us all look stupid. THAT is the best they could come up with? Nikolian, what the fuck is going on? This was not what we Crealitied. Get the ¡sees off the water and onto the barge, the crowd, the Tower, anything. Just stop showing the dead bodies in the fucking water! This is grievously depressing shit."

"I am afraid I can do nothing," said Nikolian. "The technicians can do nothing. We can shoot what we want, but those opticons decide what makes it into the feed."

"But what the fuck is this?"

"You really want to know?"

"Yes?"

"Brad, these are Azhuur's disappeared, the bodies of D'Izmaïe's enemies who were the forced labor to build the dam, and others who were apparently buried alive with them when the Vale of Victory was finished and flooded. Water from the Vale was directed to the pit to fill it and brought with it these unfortunate exhumations."

"Okay, but that was all ages ago. These look fresh."

"I suspect the trepanium ore found in the valley has some preservative power."

"Thanks for the science lesson, but let's face it, they are a downer. Can we make them disappear from the ¡cast?"

"How are the ¡balls?"

"Steadily growing, but something else needs to start happening soon."

"You could tell them what I just told you, but I doubt you're going to do that. I must go. Stand by."

Nikolian pocketed his ¡think and looked down on the water and the throng of people who were still standing and staring at the opticons and crying and keening from the roots of their collective soul.

∞

The Sister Seers sat in their high alcoves facing into the atrium below the spire. Each one had her small opticon in her lap, into which she poured the think-seeing vision she had of the Day of Days. The Sister Herbalists were in attendance to make sure each Sister Seer had the optimal balance of the trepanium-tinted herb fumes in her alcove to keep the visions going.

The Sistermost stood behind the Sister OverSeer's alcove. The Sister OverSeer had on her lap a wooden tray containing a replica of each Sister Seer's small opticon in which she could see what each one currently saw. By touching one or another of the opticons in the tray, she determined the images that appeared on the giant opticons around the pit and, by extension, the live feed of *The Id of Azhuur*.

"Move off the bodies in the water," said the Sistermost. "For the moment, we must avoid an escalating panic."

The Sister OverSeer laid her hand on an aerial view of the Tower of Thrones.

"Good. Keep it moving but leave the bodies out of sight for now. I must consult with the Sister Dealers."

The Sistermost ran up two flights of stairs to the topmost row of alcoves occupied by the twelve Sister Dealers. They too were attended by Sister Herbalists to help them maintain their unmediated connection to the ether. The Sister Superior Dealer stared fixedly into the empty space of the atrium.

"Our positions are intact?" asked the Sistermost.

"Our positions are consolidating toward optimal," answered

the Sister Superior Dealer in a clipped, toneless delivery that indicated most of her was still in direct contact with the ether.
"The shares we quietly sold over the last two weeks are still at 87
percent of the price we sold them for. We're waiting for the drop
to 40 percent that the bees predicted."

"Good. You know exactly when to begin purchasing?"

"We do."

"You must be fast, and you must get to 55 percent of total
shares before the rally is detected."

"We will. Each Sister Dealer has identified a target sector of
the market. We estimate we will garner 62 percent before the
panicked algorithms will be able to react and recalibrate."

"Excellent work."

The Sistermost ran back downstairs to continue her observation of the Sister Seers.

⚭

Tom

> . . . It appears these are some of
> the Azhuurse elite who are so devoted
> to General D'Izmaïe that they have
> acquired scuba gear and are deter-
> mined to be as close to him as pos-
> sible during these momentous, uhm,
> moments . . .

XVI

"Did I tell anyone to turn off the pumps? Find who turned them
off without my orders and have them flayed."

"No, you did not, Your Utterness. But as you can see," said
the Clarion, "the water has now reached the appropriate level."

"Then extend my clemency to all involved!"

"As you wish, Your Utterness," said the Clarion, and walked
back toward the elevator.

Despite the bright sunshine, the flash from the water's depths was visible to everyone. Those who had started walking back toward the pit, drawn by the macabre spectacle of their dead loved ones, hesitated.

The Archixprest stepped to the front of the tier. When the opticons showed his image, he spoke into the porcelain carp. His voice echoed from the opticons: "Be not concerned! This is as was foretold. The Chariot of D'Izmaïe is released and now ascends toward the surface."

The pit grew unnaturally still and then throbbed once more from its depths. At its center, the water started to vibrate as if being stirred from below. A faint blue-white luminescence from within tinged its quarry-dark depths. Another throb pulsed through the earth and the vibrations at the center intensified, sending out expanding ripples toward the sides.

"Is that supposed to happen?" asked the Archixprest.

"Why do you ask?" snapped the Utterminster, whose knuckles were white with strain from his grip on the statue of D'Izmaïe's horse. He had smoked two small hits of herb on the way up in the elevator. He was very jittery and uncomfortable in the four-dimensional world and anxious to get back into the ether as soon as possible.

⚭

"Where's Skid, Mag? Is he all right?" called Clare, her best friend, from the kitchen where she was busy making sandwiches. "They haven't shown him in ages." Clare had basically been living in the house with Skid's ma, Mag, since Skid's trial.

"Don't know. They haven't shown him since he called yer man with the scimitars an asshole. I have to say, it wasn't very bright of Skid to provoke him like that, but . . . JESUS CHRIST!"

"What is it?" Clare ran back into the living room and stood in the doorway watching. "Ah, that doesn't look right. That's not natural at all."

They both watched the center of the water pulse pale blue in a foaming circle now fifty feet across. The circle got wider and brighter with each pulse and increasingly large waves rippled outward toward the shore.

"Look, there's Skid!

"Get away from that water, Skid, it's not right!" yelled Mag at the ¡box.

⁂

SANDRA
Tom, I don't think Mandrak Kitxchenn is too happy about being aboard that barge right now.

TOM
Well, I certainly wouldn't be. The way it's bouncing around in that freaky water would not make me comfortable. I bet Skid is relieved he's still on dry land.

⁂

With far more care than when he boarded, Mandrak Kitxchenn climbed up the railings and, waiting for the calmest moment between the ever larger waves coming from the foaming center of the water, dropped carefully onto the gunwale and then onto the shortest mooring rope. The rope was considerably slacker than it had been when he'd made his entrance. He was about to step onto it when another surge from the center hit the barge and the rope slackened further. Feeling the molten heartburn of humiliation boil up inside him, he clambered down and sat astride the swaying rope. He reached forward with his hands, clasped the thick rope between them, and pulled himself forward.

"Ha, rope burn on the bollix! How's that working out for ye?" shouted Skid, right before it dawned on him that Kitxchenn wasn't just coming ashore, he was coming for HIM. He turned toward his bike to find a phalanx of club-wielding Utterforz standing in front of it. "Fuck!" He watched Kitxchenn painfully but steadily inch down the swaying rope. It would take awhile, but he was coming ashore. Skid backed away, transfixed by Kitxchenn clinging on for dear life at the rope's lowest point, where it swayed wildly.

"I will pull your heart out through your asshole, you puny shit!" yelled Kitxchenn.

⅋

"Skid, for fuck sake, stop staring at him like an eejit!" screamed Mag at the ¡box. "Wobble that rope! Knock the fucker off!"

"Yeah, Skid, are you stupid or what?" Clare gestured fiercely at the ¡box with her sandwich. "That evil little fucker is coming to get you!"

⅋

The few who were still walking back toward the pit thought the better of it when they felt the throbbing coming from the water and saw the glow in the center intensify. An unnatural bubble of blue-white air broke through the surface and rose above the water. It quickly stretched a hundred feet upward like an upside-down teardrop of molten, seething air.

⅋

"Now, cut to the center but show some bodies," said the Sistermost.

The Sister OverSeer placed her hand on the corresponding small sphere in her lap and the ¡sees and opticons all around the pit showed the cadavers being pushed toward the sides by the waves emanating from the pillar of light now in the center.

"That is good. We need a little more panic to shake out the last few stubborn holdouts."

An exhausted Sister Dealer appeared in the doorway. "It's almost done!"

⅋

It should have made a sound, but it didn't. The teardrop of shimmering air had extended two hundred feet above the water when the first sails broke the surface. It was impossible to tell what color they were now. All trace of blue was bleached out by the intense light splintering off every tiny edge and cut in the glass. There was a sudden rushing sound like a backward thunderclap, a plosion that could not be described as ex- or im-. When the globe broke the surface, the water heaved and shuddered and sent out one massive wave before closing back on itself. The globe continued its rise, drawn upward by the balloon of hyper-fluxed particles above it. It still gave no sound, which made the astonished shrieks of the crowd all the more terrifying.

SANDRA

Tom, what exactly are we looking at
here? Aeronautically-wise?

TOM

Basically, Sandra, the sails keep
charging the air above to the opposite of themselves, creating forces
of attraction that continually draw
the globe upward. How that happens,
we have no clue. What we are witness-
ing here is the birth of propulsion.

SANDRA

ProPULLsion! I see what you did there.
Very good.

The opticons returned to Skid. Kitxchenn was only fifteen feet from shore. The sweat streamed down Kitxchenn's face as he hauled himself up the last steep stretch of rope. Skid watched him edge closer and became conscious of the powerful glow rising up from the water. Another wave hit the barge and it juddered closer to the shore, further slackening the rope, and hampering Kitxchenn's climb. It was all he could do to not slide back down the rope, and yet he kept coming. With the shifting of the barge, most of the rope behind him was now in the water.

"Fuck it," said Skid, and flung his sword at Kitxchenn. It flipped and fluttered through the air like a broken-winged bird, hit the rope, and fell harmlessly into the water.

Kitxchenn grinned viciously at him and scooched a foot closer on the rope. He was almost ashore.

Skid glanced back and noticed that the Utterforz who had been hemming him in were staring horrified at the pit and backing away. Beyond the barge, he watched the weird glow rise into the air and the swell of water moving toward him. In the second that Skid decided to make a run back to his bike, Kitxchenn drew one of his daggers and launched it at him. It made a direct hit on the left side of Skid's chest. Skid looked down, but instead of the blade being buried in his chest, the dagger was lying at his feet. He felt the breast pocket of his drape where the dagger had struck. He put his forefinger and thumb into the pocket and drew out the heavy, sharpened steel comb that had just saved his life. "Nice one, Kate," he whispered. He flicked the comb at Kitxchenn, who had just hauled himself ashore.

The comb caught Kitxchenn off guard and nicked the corner of his left eye and sliced off the top of his ear. It was just enough to make him lose balance. As he fell back into the pit, he managed to throw one arm around the unwieldy rope. Skid watched horrified as the huge man hung for a moment, then swung his legs up and locked his ankles around the rope and resumed his inexorable climb.

Skid ran to his bike and peeled away from the pit behind the hastily retreating Utterforz and fleeing crowd.

The final shock wave hit and washed out of the pit. It crushed the barge, and Kitxchenn with it, against the side wall. In the afterswell, Kitxchenn's broken body washed ashore with all the others, an ironic end for one who made his living from death and whose family had taken so prominent and enthusiastic a part in D'Izmaïe's butchery of their fellow countrymen at the Vale of Victory. The sound that came from the pubble who watched this on the opticons defied description, a tiny bass note of relief in a chord otherwise made up of the horror of seeing the bodies of long-lost family washed onto the shores of the pit.

∞

The Utterminster watched the globe's steady ascent, pulled upward by its blue-white plume. Its image now filled every opticon. He pulled the horse to his chest. He closed his eyes and concentrated. He felt the statue hum slightly in his arms.

He fixed his stare on the rising Chariot. He felt a sudden panic as he realized that with each second it was getting farther and farther from him. He tried to feel the resonance of the horse in his mind. He pushed his agitated thoughts outward and upward, desperately searching for an echo from D'Izmaïe's statue.

There was nothing. Could he have been deceived? Had the Sisterhood somehow tricked him? Panic, anger, and herb roiled in his head, and for a moment he forgot about trying to reach out to D'Izmaïe. In that instant the ether insinuated itself into his mind. He was suddenly aware of extra space for his self. He was looking down on the pit as if from the rising globe, though as soon as he tried to direct his sight in a particular direction, he lost his hold and was back seeing through his own eyes. He tried desperately to relax and let the connection find him. As the globe rose farther into the sky, he sensed the ether for him to occupy expand, yet if felt thinner. He caught sight of himself as if viewed from one of the nearby opticons. He felt the horse start to connect to the rider. He had a momentary glimpse of the

Hermitage, with a feeling that he could almost see inside it, if only he could . . .

"Damn it all to hell!" he hissed. He was back in his own head again.

"Can I help in any way, Your Utterness?" asked the Archixprest.

Before the Utterminster could answer, he again slid into the ether. He sensed the distance from the orb growing, yet also felt more closely tethered to it. It was not the satisfying, robust *click* of full connection he had been expecting, but there was a new intensity to the way the ether held him each time. He somehow just knew now that he could see out of any opticon around the pit. He could see from the globe. He could look out from the top of the Hermitage tower. He was in! He was lifting out of himself. His mind surged and splintered and flickered and was in the horse and in D'Izmaïe and in every point of the nothingnesses between them.

XVII

"Mistress Consort! Regent!" exclaimed the Clarion. "What are you doing down here? You should be on your thrones!"

"Yeah, like that kind of etiquette matters anymore," said Wendy. "Look at that fucking thing. Sailing up into the sky. Why? Why couldn't the Sisterhood help?"

"Because it has to be this way," both Uilkitz sisters responded solemnly.

"Well, this way is going to be a fucking catastrophe," said Wendy.

Mooney pointed at the sky: "Wait, look, it's turning off course."

From the edge of the antepenultimate tier they all watched the intense point of light in the sky begin to veer to the left.

"It's going to crash!" cheered Mooney.

"I am very much afraid it is not," said the Clarion. "It is simply turning into its first low orbit. It will begin to circle the earth now and will gradually climb until it reaches its full orbit."

"So, we're fucked?" said Wendy.

The Clarion and the Uilkitz sisters exchanged glances, but none of them could meet Wendy's eyes.

"So we *are* fucked," said Wendy softly, and stared at the dot of intense light now moving across the sky.

∞

The Archixprest stood on the edge of the penultimate tier with his arms held aloft as if his powers were bringing all of these events about. The Utterminster was peripherally (if his current state of mind could be said to have anything as dimensionally confining as a periphery) aware of the Archixprest saying something, but it was too close to focus on and too far away to hear. It was irrelevant. The Utterminster was present everywhere but his body. He was one with the ether flux between the two statues. His mind melted into the horse and surged through the interstitial nothingnesses to D'Izmaïe. All he could feel was speed and the infinite ether flashing past, through, and around him. It was everything. It was everywhere. *He* was everything. *He* was everywhere. Kitxchenn's death was of no consequence. Soon he would be in a position to turn the ether on Skid and anyone else he chose. Destroying Skid's mind first and then his body would prove more satisfying than having Kitxchenn carve him up.

The Utterminster had never before been so out of, yet effervescently present to, himself. While his body slumped on his throne clutching D'Izmaïe's horse, his mind could see everything, including himself from outside. He noted the Archixprest's self-aggrandizing posturing with disdain. His point of view was anywhere he wanted it to be. He saw every detail of the launch pit at once. He discovered that he could not only see inside the Hermitage itself but he could get inside the Sister Seers's points of view; he could feed himself into the ¡sees and the opticons

The Utterminster's voice now boomed from every opticon and ¡see: "The events you see before you—the sinking of the trial barge, the escape of the murderous Adjutant, the reappearance of the traitors from the Vale of Victory—these are nothing compared to the glory of this launch. The ether will be mine! The Adjutant will be found and punished, most cruelly and spectacularly. I will see to it personally. But that too pales beside *this* achievement!"

The Utterminster's avatar threw his arms wide and then every opticon and screen was filled with a long shot of the globe and its glowing plume high above the earth. Anyone in-heading *The Id of Azhuur* had the terrifying experience of the Utterminster suddenly intruding directly into the fabric of their thoughts.

Soon the globe would cross the horizon and be out of sight of the horse. Bracing for this, the Utterminster pulled the last vestiges of himself from the horse and into the statue of D'Izmaïe.

∞

The Sister OverSeer stared in horror at the image of the Utterminster that filled the spheres in her tray. She felt the Sistermost's hand rest gently on her shoulder.

"Don't fight him. Let him. He has all the power now. If you push back, he will destroy you and the Sister Seers, break your minds—or worse, absorb them."

"So he has won?" the Sister OverSeer asked.

"So it seems. I must go. Keep the Sister Seers safe: do not attempt to take back the seeing."

∞

SANDRA

```
Well, as if proPULLsion wasn't weird
enough. That was a most extraordinary
and, frankly, frightening speech.
```

TOM

Totally. Our researchers are working hard to verify if what the Utterminster claimed is even remotely
possible.

NIKOLIAN

You idiots, no one can hear you! It
is all Utterminster, all the time,
on every device there is. You are
talking to yourselves!

∞

Wendy slumped into the Relict Uilkitz's throne. "He's done it. The fucker has it now. Poison his weed over the next week? Bullshit. That was never going to work. Look at what he can already do. In a week he will be in-heading himself everywhere. That fucker *owns* the ether. I hope the Sisters are proud of themselves. We are so utterly fucked."

XVIII

"What are you doing? Don't touch it, he'll take you with him."

The Clarion spun around to see a shimmering there-but-not-thereness of the Sistermost that frightened even him. "I came up to see if there was anything I could do. I thought if I took the statue from him—"

"He would eat your mind. I see, however, that you have taken care of the Archixprest." The Sistermost pointed to the unconscious heap on the floor, her rarified voice seeming to come from everywhere but nowhere.

"Nothing left to lose. I could not think of anything else to do. I have waited years for the opportunity to strike him. He was so busy pretending to control all of this, he didn't even notice me approach."

The spectral Sistermost watched the dot of light which now

appeared to be setting behind the hills. "He is approaching the horizon. This falls to me." She placed herself in front of the Utterminster, who was now hunched over in his throne like an abandoned sock puppet. She braced herself and seemed to solidify a little. She grasped the Utterminster's wrists and pried his hands from the horse. She took the statue out of his lap. She buckled and fell to her knees as if under a huge and sudden weight.

"No!" she shouted as the Clarion stepped forward to help. "You mustn't!" She felt the chill rush of the Utterminster in her mind. He sensed her. His long-festering hatred reached back through the ether to crush her.

With a massive effort, the Sistermost disentangled her mind from his and dropped the horse onto the floor.

"Leave it there! Do not touch it!" she scream-whispered at the Clarion, and then, as suddenly as it had appeared, her there-but-not-thereness was gone.

The Clarion edged away from the horse and swallowed back the metallic taste of fear and disgust that clawed its way up his throat. "Stay back!" he shouted to Mooney, Wendy, and the Uilkitz sisters, who had come up to see what the commotion was.

The Archixprest, who had regained consciousness, got to his knees and took hold of the statue. He stood up shakily and moved toward the Utterminster. Then he crumpled to his knees and fell on his side, his essence shattered and sucked out of him into the maelstrom of the Utterminster's mind. The inert shell of him twitched once and went deathly still.

"That is why no one is to touch the statue," said the Clarion.

"What's going on?" asked Wendy.

"I really do not know," said the Clarion. "Go back to your tiers. I will stay here and watch over this."

"No way," said Wendy. "There is safety in numbers. It's not like anyone is paying attention to us right now anyway."

The Uilkitz sisters and Mooney nodded in agreement.

XIX

"With this launch, I, the Utterminster of Azhuur, through the power bequeathed me by the great General D'Izmaïe (revered be his name), now rule the ether. Yes! Rule! The entire ether! Azhuur be served!"

To emphasize his point, the Utterminster forced the image of his avatar holding the D'Izmaïe figure above his head to every opticon and screen. Every opticon, every ¡see, and every ¡think, ¡box, and ¡gantic in the entire world (whether tuned to *The Id of Azhuur* or not) was then filled with a fantasy avatar likeness of a youthful, slim, attractive Utterminster wearing General D'Izmaïe's gala uniform, making his triumphal speech from atop the globe as it hurtled through the stratosphere. Two million Onan Net subscribers had their masturbation sessions traumatically and irrevocably disfigured by the intrusion of this image.

Brad almost fainted when he saw the image of his future self being force-fed D'Izmaïe's Diet and puking and shitting himself to death in a bloodied glass barrel while the Utterminster laughed and applauded. He, like so many others, had been watching in horror as the Utterminster invaded every screen and device.

⚇

Skid rode around the left side of the Tower of Thrones. Behind it, the crowd was less dense as there seemed to be an instinct among the pubble to get as far from the Tower as possible, and Skid was able to pick up a little speed. The Utterminster's voice echoed off the opticons around him and Skid thought he heard his own name, but had too much to do to navigate through the pubble to focus on it.

Once clear of the crowds, Skid cut to his right over the flat stony ground and soon came to the paved main road. He passed the Quartel and then the road narrowed. He had to stop and walk the bike over the poorly covered pipe laid to fill the pit. He continued north, the bike going as fast as Skid had ever pushed it. The opticons flashed by him. They now showed a triumphant fantasy avatar of the Utterminster in procession down Newer York's Fifth Avenue, hauling a naked Brad in a glass barrel behind. Skid focused on the road in front of him, struggling to suppress the voice that kept asking: *Where the fuck to you think you're going? You know you'll hit the border eventually. What then? Hold your breath and ride across the poisoned dirt? Then what? The great, big, Outer Azhuurse Welcome Back Skid party?*

Ahead of him he spotted a small group of pubble emerging out of a dip in the road. He slowed down. It was clear they had seen him. One of them was waving vigorously at him. He approached them slowly. Now with the engine quieter, he could hear the Utterminster's fantasy self announce from the top of Mount Everest that the sun would never set on the New Greater Azhuur.

XX

For over an hour, Mooney, Wendy, the Clarion, and the Uilkitz sisters had sat, paced, crouched, and cowered together on the antepenultimate tier, watching the Utterminster's unending triumphal address to the world, wishing it really was just a glorified TV show and not what was now their actual lives being broadcast in real time. They paid little attention to the various vying displays of panic, excitement, despair, exultation, fear, and joy that bubbled up on and around the Tower of Thrones. The pubble milled around, many frantically searching among the bodies that had washed ashore, others running to their shanties to grab their meager possessions and flee to the hills.

"There it is!" shouted Mooney, pointing at the scintillating dot of blue that glided into their sky again. It was definitely higher, its progress across the sky now a little slower.

As it drew almost directly overhead, the dot abruptly disappeared.

"What was that?" cried Wendy, desperately hoping some catastrophic accident had befallen the globe.

"Don't get your hopes up. I believe that simply means it has achieved its stable orbit," said the Clarion.

As if to confirm this, the images from the Utterminster's mind in the opticons showed the plume abruptly contracting and the sails returning to their blue color and the Chariot of D'Izmaïe progressing placidly through the sky.

"Wait, what was that flash?" called Mooney.

The Sistermost stumbled and caught herself on the Sister Over-Seer's seat back. She watched, with grim satisfaction, a new plume appear in the sky. The cuts in the glass sails that had taken the globe up into the stratosphere now reversed their resonance to generate a repellent force that drove the globe down into the atmosphere at many times the rate of normal falling acceleration. The small spheres in the Sister OverSeer's lap flickered wildly.

"Do nothing," whispered the Sistermost. "Let the Utterminster's terrified mind spew into every device. Let them all see him for what he is and always has been." With a sharp intake of breath, she then buckled at the knees and folded into an exhausted heap on the floor.

"I've prepared all my life for this moment and you will not destroy it with your meddling!" shrieked the Utterminster. His voice reverberated off every opticon. "You will not stand in the way of General D'Izmaïe's triumphant return. There will be an end to this Möglessness and the pubble will know real discipline again."

Panic is a very physical experience: the prickling sweat, the thickening blood in the hammering heart, the rapid swallowing of the dry mouth, the urge to flee the self with nowhere to go. The Utterminster was suddenly trapped in the suffocating knowing of his panic without anyplace to put its physical symptoms.

He seethed and flailed, looking for somewhere to put the fear, to give it expression. His search for a way back to himself focused his perception and he saw, to his horror, the mighty Utterminster of Azhuur in his moment of triumph, slumped in his throne in his glittering gala robes, a husk of absence. The statue of D'Izmaïe's horse was not in his hands where it should be, but on the floor between his own useless feet and the inert heap of the Archixprest. This, too, the Utterminster broadcast to every opticon and device.

Desperately trying to find a locus for his self, he continued to bleed out into the ether, every flicker and flash of him, every memory, fear, and hope, ricocheting into every opticon and every device on the ether. He think-saw the globe and now understood it was leaving orbit; it was reversing course and descending.

❀

A dreadful silence fell over the crowd when the opticons showed the Utterminster's plan for the ring of Utterforz to push thousands into the pit while he gave one of his big-hand-gesture speeches from the Tower of Thrones—until that image was replaced with the young officer Utterminster beside his commander D'Izmaïe watching the prisoners in the Vale of Victory as the valley flooded. A slow roar of recognition and hatred surged through the crowd.

The Utterminster tried desperately to change the image. When he did, it became him as a young boy being spanked by a maid, while his mother looked on and sipped champagne. The harder the Utterminster tried to suppress images, the more impossible it became to keep them out of every opticon, ¡think, ¡gantic: a young Utterminster being pummeled in the schoolyard and later paying a young Mandrak Kitxchenn to stab his assailant; the globe now plunging down through the atmosphere and the bottom of it beginning to glow white hot; the Utterminster sending Kanker to kill Bagwipe and his extended family and then Kanker being garroted by Kitxchenn and his body being buried

in the side of the pit; Skid crashing into the pantry tent and finding the Utterminster in mid sheep-shagging; the Utterminster
playing with his vast army of model soldiers; the Utterminster pa-
thetically trying to repair D'Izmaïe's broken sword; the Utterminster being the first to seize Alva's mother when D'Izmaïe gave her
to his troops after he had tired of her; the Utterminster betraying
his own father to D'Izmaïe's secret police; the Archixprest, the
Clarion, and the Uilkitz sisters all crucified onto the walls of the
Quartel; the ruined and smoking shell of the Outlying Hermitage
and then the globe again with its white-hot sails now engulfed in
a ball of flame and plummeting through the atmosphere.

∞

"Mag, come quick! That Utterfucker is in a coma and that stupid shuttlecock with the statue is going to burn to bits!" Clare
danced around the living room pointing her beer at the ¡box.

The Utterminster's transmission froze on the plummeting
globe. The hull was now so hot that it became transparent, and
for a split second the figure of D'Izmaïe was visible, before it too
heated into transparency. The globe and the sails disintegrated in
one blinding flash and the statue continued to plunge through the
afterglow. It quickly ceased to have any resemblance to D'Izmaïe
and became a ball of green-white light. The crowds backed away
from the intense light coming from the opticons, and the display
settings of tens of millions of devices went into shock.

"But where is Skid?" Mag asked the ¡box. "Where'd he go?"

∞

The Utterminster sensed his self shatter and disperse. Existence
closed in about him as the statue began to melt and vaporize,
trapping him on an ever thinner thread of ether until abruptly
there was only his fearful self and it too was slipping away from
him like a hyper-accelerated dementia, the words to think for
himself abandoning him in droves, until all that was left was this
single, eternal impression of self in total darkness forever, un-

thinking, impotent, aware only of struggling to grab a breath that would never be there.

$$\infty$$

The tiny falling point of intense light in the sky pulsed twice and burst into a plume of white-green gas and was gone. The opticons, ¡thinks, ¡gantics, and ¡boxes all went dark and the statue of D'Izmaïe's horse on the floor beside the Archixprest emitted a screeching sound and then crumbled to gray dust, finally freed to oxidize itself into uselessness, as large concentrations of trepanium should.

"He's gone?" asked Mooney.

"Yes. His mind is scattered across the infinite ether and extinguished. That is what is left." The Clarion gestured to the Utterminster's lifeless remains.

"You absolute fucker!" shouted Wendy. "You could have told me there was a plan! I thought we were all dead!"

"I did too. I knew nothing of this until I saw the Sistermost shimmer onto the Tower and take the statue from the Utterminster. Even then I had no idea what she was doing."

"They didn't tell you anything?"

"No. The slightest flicker of knowing and the Utterminster might have heard it. The trepanium can do that sometimes. I suppose they dared not take the risk."

$$\infty$$

The opticons and the *Id of Azhuur* feed came back to life and the Clarion took the porcelain carp from the Utterminster's pocket and spoke into the stunned silence around the pit: "You have seen and heard these last moments of the Utterminster. Some of you are too young to remember the Generalitate. Some of you, because of the Reedification Fields, are still too afraid to remember it correctly, but you heard the Utterminster say it: D'Izmaïe was coming back, or at least the Utterminster was intent on bringing back the Generalitate. The statue was the vehicle to take him into orbit and make him one with the ether. That would have made him more powerful than anyone can imagine. We have been saved from that. The Utterminster's Outer Azhuurse mercenaries are dropping their arms and fleeing north as I speak. Let them go. Let them take their chances crossing the poisoned border. If they make it across alive, the burden of what evil they have done here will haunt them.

"These events have, as you can see, returned to us the remains of those disappeared in the Vale of . . . what used to be called the Vale of Victory, but most of you have quietly and rightly called for years the Valley of the Disappeared."

Here he faltered, as if the very name of the place had stuck in his throat. He struggled to continue: "It falls to us now to honor our long-lost dead. This is not the Day of Days anyone expected, but it is here now, and we will seize it. I ask the Sister Seers to help us and, beginning here opposite the Tower of Thrones, circle slowly and show us as many faces as they can of our lost brothers and sisters so their families can claim them. Any family that does not have a heart pot will be provided one."

Instantly, the opticons started showing the bodies on the shore closest to the Tower of Thrones, splitting into multiple images, ten at a time. At first a few people, then more, began to move with slow dignity toward the pit, some to claim a loved one but many simply to help position the dead so they might be recognized. Those who had no family to search for moved away from the opticons to let those who did get a view. The first bodies to be retrieved were those lying near the remains of Mandrak Kitxchenn, who was left to the crows.

The *So You Wanna Run a Country? Id of Azhuur* audience, for the most part, was too stunned and exhausted to look away.

XXI

Mooney and Wendy, accompanied by the Clarion, Skid, Alva,

her grandmother, and Tel, stood at the front of the crowd that had drawn well back from the Tower of Thrones. The opticons cut away from the long shot of the Tower and showed the wattles piled around the throne leg nearest them. Beside Kitxchenn's abandoned body, a delegation of workers from the pit threw the stiffening forms of the Utterminster and the Archixprest.

"That will be the end of it," said the Clarion quietly. "There will be no other vengeance. They will lie there unmourned and unburned and the crows and rats will feast on them. The Sisterhood has instructed it must be so. It needs to be done. It is done."

"It's not like they don't deserve it; it's just kinda shocking," conceded Wendy.

"It is the way of these things sometimes," added the Clarion. "Forgetting cannot always be enough, and sometimes there needs to be a brutal settling of accounts to close an old wound."

They were all exhausted. The last twenty-four hours had been a grueling process of identifying and moving the remains to the Tower of Thrones. Each corpse was carefully placed on the Tower, the heart pot placed over the heart and the lid with the deceased's family rune positioned under the body. When it was all done, each family would receive the pot with the ashes it had settled over and its lid. Bodies were placed on the tiers in the order in which they arrived at the two service elevators; there was no rank or hierarchy and absolutely no attempt made to establish one.

"Tell me, Clarion, I never thought to ask before, but is the Tower of Thrones *made-up* ancient like the dam or *real* ancient?" said Wendy.

"It is genuinely ancient, but it is something we can do without, and this is the most fitting use for it we can think of."

Tel had been among the group Skid had met on the road. He had implored Skid for a ride back to the encampment to search for Alva. Skid, having no real plan and seeing the Utterminster begin to fall apart on the opticons, had embraced this new purpose. When they found Alva and her grandmother, they were carrying between them the perfectly preserved body of a young woman who appeared to be in her thirties. You could see the resemblance in the three women's faces. This was clearly Alva's mother.

Alva's grandmother also carried with her a heart pot and lid already etched with the family's rune. "This I have kept safe all these years. Finally, we will get to make some kind of peace with her murder."

Since then, Skid and Tel had been like two spinning tops careening through the crowds, looking for anywhere they could be of help. Now they all stood and watched the first stars appear behind the looming hulk of the Tower of Thrones.

"Is that singing?" asked Alva. She strained to catch the sound. "Yes, it's coming from over there. Many voices singing very softly." She pointed in the direction of the encampment. The voices grew louder and a crowd of people emerged from the encampment and moved slowly toward the Tower.

"They walked from the hostage barges in the valley," said Nikolian, just as the opticons flickered and began to show the returning hostages. "When the order was sent to burn the barges, the Utterforz saw that the Utterminster was finished and they fled."

Cries of relief dotted the crowd and nearby family members ran to look for their loved ones among the escapees of the Valley of the Disappeared.

∞

A phalanx of Sister Archers, joined by a delegation of pubble archers and deserted conscripts from the Utterminster's troops, placed themselves in front of the crowd. They loosed a flight of flaming arrows at each leg of the Tower of Thrones. The wattle piles around each gigantic leg took fire and the flames swept up the structure.

It was at that point that the opticons around the Tower went dark. The Sister Seers sent only one middle-distance shot of the Tower of Thrones to the *Id of Azhuur* viewers and the opticons in the rest of Azhuur. Everyone watched the Tower of Thrones transform into an enormous funeral pyre.

♋

From his window, Brad watched the ¡gantic in the park below his office. Ever since D'Izmaïe's destruction, ¡balls had skyrocketed. All through the recovery of the dead, ¡balls had remained steady. Now, the single static shot of the burning Tower of Thrones was hypnotic and a record viewership watched in fascinated silence as the flames flickered and leaped upward from tier to tier. Sandra and Tom, the commentators, had been retired through exhaustion and inanity overload minutes after the first bodies washed up onto the shores of the pit. If anything, according to the metrics, their absence increased ¡ball counts.

As each tier caught fire, the rising heat intensified, so by the time the flames reached the top tier, it was consumed in under ten minutes and softly pancaked down onto the penultimate tier, and ten minutes later, that collapsed onto the antepenultimate tier, and so on, until the lowest tier and the legs finally settled with a massive crackling thump. Brad heard the crowd around the ¡gantic below make a strange sound: a brief, strangled, awkward keening cheer that erupted out of nowhere and just as suddenly fell silent.

XXII

It was close to dawn when the first families began to approach the ashes to retrieve the heart pots of their dead. The Tower of Thrones had so thoroughly and so vigorously burned that what few ashes were left were easily watered so they could be walked on, and the heart pots were already cool to the touch. The first families to go in carried as many other pots out of the ashes as they could, and gradually lines of pots arranged by rune clan surrounded the ashes of the Tower of Thrones.

When every heart pot had been retrieved, a strange, bereft inaction settled over everyone around the pit.

"Launch the wedding barge," said Mooney.

"What?" snapped Wendy.

"It's okay. Calm down. It's not for us."

⽤

"But the show is done," Brad explained. "We are moving on. *So You Wanna Run a Religion?* premieres in two hours."

Wendy walked right up to the ¡box in the late Utterminster's former office. "You understand how close you came to shitting yourself to death in a glass barrel in front of the whole planet, right? You get what has been going on here? You need to show this!"

"Wendy, I'd love to help out, but really, the decision is above my pay grade."

The Clarion leaned forward and whispered in Wendy's ear. She nodded and turned to Brad again: "If that's what you're worried about, then you can expect to hear from on high very soon. In the panicked sell-off of 2's A Prime during the bodies in the water and the burning globe, the Sisterhood acquired a controlling interest before the algorithms could stop panic-selling. You will be hearing from your superiors very soon. Then you will see if you are still showing *So You Wanna Run a Religion?* or the extra bonus episode of *The Id of Azhuur*."

"Nikolian, is she serious? Is this true?"

"She is. And it is."

"Uh, okay? That makes sense. I'll be in touch. I guess," managed Brad.

⽤

Mooney, Wendy, Skid, the Clarion, and the Spinster and the Relict Uilkitz waited by the pit's edge.

The crowd gathered around them grew silent, then parted

as Alva's grandmother walked out of the throng flanked by Alva and Tel. She cradled her daughter's heart pot in her arms. The crowd around the pit hummed a quiet processional as every opticon glowed with this image. Skid surreptitiously glanced at his ¡think to make sure Brad was showing it all.

Wendy greeted the new arrivals. She bowed to Alva's grandmother. The Spinster made to twist her nose and the old woman stopped her.

"No, we do not make that stupid invented gesture anymore. This is the start of the righting." She kissed Wendy gently on the forehead, the Sister Seers sending her words through every opticon. The crowd cheered briefly.

The Clarion's voice echoed from the opticons: "My fellow Azhuurse, you were promised three events on the Day of Days: a duel that was really a glorified execution attempt, the ascension of the Chariot of D'Izmaïe, and a wedding. The duel never happened and Skid is still here to tell the tale. The idol of D'Izmaïe burned to frightened smoke and was scattered to the winds and the Utterminster's essence with it. The remains of the Utterminster and the Archixprest are cast out for the crows, unburned and unmourned. It is over. The Mögness D'Izmaïe invented is gone too. We have been through so much and endured so long, but we cannot dwell in this sadness. Even though our hearts are heavy with grief for ourselves and our land, we can still celebrate a wedding. We must begin the recovery of our selves today, even though we are exhausted, even though we would rather weep than smile."

The crowd applauded respectfully and fell silent.

Wendy now spoke: "The wedding barge is ready. But not for Mooney and me. We do not matter in this picture and our wedding was only a dumb plan to delay things." She beckoned Nikolian out of the crowd. His image and voice filled the opticons.

He spoke carefully in Azhuurse as if he had rehearsed it before repeating himself in English: "This will be my last day on *The Id of Azhuur*. I am of a family of Watchers, sent abroad to track the statue. I am home now. My real work is done. We have all seen enough horror. We need to celebrate a new union to clean this lake of all the evil intent that was in it. Let us make a gesture to the future to honor the friends and family taken from us by the ugliness of the past. Let's celebrate their stories that were hidden in the toxic fog of fake history. Now you can tell their stories and remember them right. There is much to regret and much to repair, but let us step positively onto the new road ahead of us."

"Shall we?" The Clarion indicated the gangplank to the wedding barge.

Once aboard, Alva and Tel stood side by side under the canopy on the central platform in front of the Spinster Uilkitz. Mooney, Wendy, Skid, Alva's grandmother, the Clarion, Nikolian, and the Relict Uilkitz all joined hands and encircled the platform.

"We are assembled on this day to mark a new beginning for Azhuur," announced the Spinster Uilkitz through the opticons. "You out there in the wide world who have watched these events unfold, mistaking our reality for some staged entertainment, you have now seen enough to know what we have lived through.

"We are here to witness the bonding of these two young people in marriage. They, like so many of you, are too young to have known the Generalitate, but have survived the bitter times of the Utterage and, most recently, the darkness and cruelty of the pit. They now look to the future. This is the old bonding rite, outlawed and ordered forgotten by D'Izmaïe. Alva? Tel? Are you willing?"

Tel and Alva looked at one another and then answered: "We are willing."

"Within this two-spouted wedding cup is the simple water without which we could not survive. Drink ye of the water from this cup."

She handed them the cup and they each drank from the spouts. They returned the cup to her.

"This is a symbol of your oneness and the sharing of the good, the elemental."

She then dropped the cup on the deck, where it shattered. She took two sizable shards and gave one each to Alva and Tel, then threw the remainder into the water.

"These fragments are symbols of your independence within your oneness and the sharing of the joys, the sadness, the pleasures, the bitternesses of life. Keep them safe. Are ye wed?"

"We are wed," answered Alva and Tel in unison.

"Then so be it. Here are your new family heart pots with your runes entwined. Be ye wed," announced the Spinster Uilkitz.

There was a brief, hesitant silence as everyone reflexively waited for the customary "Azhuur be served!" but none came. The circle raised their joined hands above their heads and the crowd made a strange sound, the sound of utterly exhausted and shell-shocked people trying to believe they are free and safe enough to express any joy or relief.

"And now, to close the ceremony, the Clarion of Azhuur will sing Teram's wedding song, not heard in this land in living memory."

Wendy could not help herself and winced at the prospect of a musical outing in Old High Azhuurse.

"Don't worry," whispered the Spinster, "it is a genuine old folk song, not one of those wretched, contrived Mögian inventions."

The Clarion began softly and his voice grew into a flow of the most beautiful series of tones, notes, and shadings. A rapt silence drew everyone into its breathless spell. Tel and Alva held each other close. The Uilkitz sisters flanked Alva's grandmother, all holding hands. The tears rolled down Mooney's face. Wendy squeezed his hand. With her other hand, she reached for Skid's. He gripped her hand tight to stop from shaking. Nikolian stood alone, comfortable in his private grief and remembrance, and wept quietly.

When the Clarion was finished, the crowd continued singing snatches of the tune. Wendy ran to him and hugged him. "So lovely," she said. She then whispered in his ear. He called for silence.

"At the Mistress Consort's . . ." Wendy glowered at him and he started anew: "At the Mistress Wendy's request, you will all remain where you are and generous celebratory provisions in honor of Tel and Alva's nuptials will be distributed to all."

A cheer rose from the crowd and then they resumed the Clarion's melody.

The Clarion spoke over the music: "These are but small beginnings. Today we mourn and commemorate. Tomorrow we begin the long task of clearing the ruination of the Utterage and building back what has been destroyed over decades."

The crowd's singing intensified and the Clarion led the wedding party down the gangplank back to shore.

XXIII

Instead of walking toward the grotto as Wendy had expected, the Clarion and Cowan continued up the switchback path. The Uilkitz sisters followed, and right behind them walked Mooney and Wendy.

Coming down the other side of the crater wall they could see three carriages waiting for them in the shade.

When they got closer, it became clear the carriages were driven by members of the Sisterhood.

"What is this? Sisters outside the Hermitage?" whispered Wendy to the Spinster.

"Most unusual. I suspect it is not the end of surprises for today."

The Clarion and Cowan's carriage in front, the little convoy rode toward the Hermitage. When they arrived, instead of turning right where Wendy had done to reach the spindle window, they turned left and curved into the space between the two towers.

"Why am I even here? Skid isn't," Mooney said to Wendy.

"I don't know. Maybe cos they're still treating you as Regent?"

"Feels weird."

"I get it. Just go with it. Don't you want to see the Hermitage?"

Mooney shrugged. His head was still spinning from everything that had happened. One more piece of crazy was unlikely to make much of an impression.

The canyon between the towers narrowed and the carriages drew to a halt. At first it seemed like a trick of light and shadows, but then the grinding of huge mechanisms deep in the stonework corroborated that a small embrasure was opening at the juncture of the two towers. The masonry screeched and squealed and a large section of each tower swung slowly inward to reveal the tall atrium beneath the Hermitage's glass spire.

They all stepped down from their carriages and stood gaping at the opening.

"Have you ever seen this before?" Wendy asked the Spinster Uilkitz.

"I had no idea this gate even existed."

A sister stepped forward from the entrance to greet them: "I am your Sisterguide. All is ready. The sisters are assembled. The heart pots of each Riding are in place." She gestured to the arrayed sisters in their bright-blue tunics and the three triangles of heart pots that radiated out from the pyre in the center of the atrium like clay petals. "The Sistermost Who Was expired from the effort of projecting herself to the launch pit and resisting the Utterminster's attempt to drown her in the ether. Mooney, Wendy, thank you for joining us. Clarion, Spinster, Relict, Master Cowan, you have our condolences. She knew the risk. She was happy to do it. I see the people of Azhuur made their own decisions regarding the Utterminster and the Archixprest. It is brutal. It is done. It is now the past."

The Uilkitz sisters took the Sisterguide's hands in theirs and spoke in perfect unison: "We shed these no-man, dead-man titles. We reclaim our names. Spinster no more, now Bina, Relict no more, now Tryna."

Cowan stepped forward and handed the Sisterguide a heart pot.

The Clarion put his arm around his son's shoulders and spoke haltingly: "Please place this on the pyre. It has both of our runes. She had it made a long time ago, Sistermost Who Was, Onden my wife who could not be, and ever-absent, ever-loving mother to our son here whom I have tried to hide from the Utterminster and his ilk all these years. We both understood the Sisterhood needed to be closed for its own protection. We endured our sep-arateness and relished the times we could be together."

The Sisterguide bowed. "Of course. We all knew of your love. It is an honor to finally meet you, Cowan. Your mother loved you very, very much. The gift she has given us means we no longer have to administer the Hermitage like a fortress. The atrium gate has been opened for the first time in over a hundred years. We hope not to have to close it again."

Cowan bowed and blushed and choked back a sob.

Once the new heart pot was in place, the Sisterguide took a burning torch from an attendant sister and handed it to Wendy.

"Me? Why? Because I am to blame for all of this?"

"No, no, not at all. What happened had to happen," said Bina and Tryna, their words falling over each other. "She knew that long before you even came here. She was our sister. We would be honored if you would do this. Please do."

Wendy put the torch to the wattles under the platform and they immediately took fire. Everyone stepped back and watched the sparks and the rippling heat haze rise into the spire, whose sides had opened back like a gigantic glass lily. There was a burst of flame and everyone followed the glowing mote that rose into the spire and then circled the atrium, slowly burning out before fluttering down, a tiny petal of ash, into a heart pot near the back of the Earth Riding section.

There was a slight commotion and then a woman made her way out of the crowd and walked toward the Beyondishers and the Sisterguide. The woman stood before them, her back to the pyre, and bowed deeply: "It appears I am the new Sistermost." She stood in silence beside them while the pyre burned. The heat was intense and the crowd gradually edged back from it and then closer again as the fire died and the ashes began to cool. The new Sistermost retrieved the heart pot from the ashes where it had settled over its lid. The miraculous clay was already cool to the touch. She held it in front of her and bowed to the Clarion. "I would be honored if, instead of me as tradition dictates, you would return in one week to make the dough and mix in some of the ashes of the Sistermost Who Was to nourish the birds of the air."

"This is an unprecedented honor, Sistermost. I will await your summons."

The Sistermost handed the heart pot to a nearby sister. "It falls to me now to dream the next new sister. I will escort you all back to your carriages."

They walked in silence through the ranks of sisters. Only when they reached the carriages did the Sistermost speak: "We are much relieved to see that the glass sails did their work."

"They did, and we thank you for that," said the Clarion. "It has been a long, dark journey. I imagine we will have much to discuss in the coming times."

"Feel free to visit us anytime you wish. And by the way, Wendy, on the former Sistermost's instructions, the Sister Dealers also acquired Hedgeer Hemlein—so you have nothing more to fear from the now-penniless Knut Ho." The Sistermost bowed once more and then waved them into their carriages, something in her manner eerily reminiscent of the Sistermost Who Was.

∰

For a short time, the six of them stood in silence on the ridge of the crater and looked back at the Outlying Hermitage. The last wisps of smoke rose out of the open spire and slowly the three sides closed back up. The bittersweet sounds of the crowd around the pit drifted through the air toward them.

"None of this would be happening if it wasn't for her," said Wendy.

"Indeed, she did a great service," said the Clarion. "I will miss my dear Onden."

Cowan bowed his head.

"Ever in our thoughts," lilted the Uilkitz sisters.

"We have together been part of banishing the last, rotten vestiges of General D'Izmaïe," murmured the Clarion, "so there is some consolation in that. That is a legacy one can be proud of."

"Cursed be D'Izmaïe! I am no longer his Relict!" Tryna spat on the ground.

Wendy linked the Clarion's arm in hers and squeezed it tightly. "I am so sorry."

"It is life. It was the way we had to live our love."

"Is this the end of the Sisterhood?" asked Mooney.

Bina Uilkitz smiled. "No, no, there will always be a need for the Sisterhood. There will always be people who do not fit the Big Square World, as you would call it, and need a quiet place to make their lives work. It is a life that is offered, never imposed on anyone. And, of course, there are all the other things they do, managing the ether and our money, keeping all of it out there at bay. We need to heal and rebuild this broken land, and they will be the engine of that. But now, they no longer need to hide away."

"And you, Clarion?" said Mooney. "Is this the end? I mean, are you the end of Clarions? Will your son take over?"

"If there is a need for such, perhaps he will, but I am happy to be the last of my line. I do not see a need to continue with these ostentatious hereditary offices anymore. Some, like mine, are genuine, but most were invented along with Mög and Old High Azhuurse and all that toxic hokum. We will find our way. I imagine I will find a use for me. My son, he will make his own way. He does not need to be a glorified announcer of the obvious."

Cowan smiled but said nothing.

As they approached the crowd around the pit, the Clarion stopped and turned to Mooney and Wendy. "I suppose you will be leaving us soon. You know, you two could always stay and help us rebuild."

Mooney burst out laughing. "Clarion, that's all very nice, but seriously, look at us. Me and Wendy, we're two people who met in a pipe. We don't know the first thing about running a country. That's precisely why they picked us for the show: we have no clue. You have more than enough brains and goodwill to make a go of this place."

Wendy shrugged and added: "I don't know much about the world and I am not in a position to offer advice about many things, but I do know how money works; that's how I ended up here in the first place. You know how much trepanium you are sitting on here. Even what's sitting in the back of that cave where Mooney spent the night is enough to destabilize prices. Remind the market from time to time. They know you could decimate trepanium prices if you mined even a tiny fraction of what you have, so they will leave you alone. You know they can never invade you or try some ether attack, cos they are scared shitless of the Sisterhood and so they should be. Take the money they give you not to mine it and keep them all away. Use the control of 2's A Prime carefully and quietly. As long as no one gets too greedy or stupid, I think you should all be okay. I think you know what is needed. And whenever you are in doubt about what to do, ask yourselves what Archie or Udder would do, and do the opposite."

"People here have seen and done much that is awful. I do not know how we rebuild," sighed the Clarion.

"I don't know either, but of all the fucked-up places that have ever had a chance, you have the best chance. Take your time and I am sure you will figure it out. You have so many examples to look at where it was done wrong, so at least there is plenty you know to avoid."

The Clarion nodded a little sadly. "Well, stay as long as you would like, and when you want to leave, leave, but please know that you are welcome back at any time—and that obviously goes for Skid too."

"And Nikolian?"

"Oh, Nikolian is of us. He already knows this is his home."

EPILOGUE

FRACTALS, UNIONS, DIVERGENCES

"What will you do, Skid?"

"Fuck, Wendy, I dunno. Go back to Glasgow? Cash in on my celebrity for the few months it lasts? Open a pub? Yeah, I'll open a pub! Call it the Mandrak Kitchen."

Wendy laughed. "You know you could stay here."

"And do what? I wasn't any good at being here when it was just play-acting. I almost got myself killed. Remember? I can't be of any use. Anyway, I need to see Kate. I owe her."

"Wait, you're going too?" said Wendy when she noticed Mooney's bag.

"Yep," said Mooney.

"To Glasgow?"

"Yep. I think I'll try it for a while. New statue, new skateboard. Skid tells me you can make a decent living there doing stuff like that."

"I'll miss you," said Wendy.

"No you won't. And that's okay."

"Thank you."

"For what?"

"Saving me from Knut Ho back in Newer York."

"Finders keepers, as they say. I found you, so it was my duty to help you. I'm glad I did."

Skid kicked his bike into life. He revved it loudly and Mooney got on the back. They waved to the small group who had come to see them off before riding away toward the airfield and the small 2's A Prime courtesy plane that waited for them there.

∞

"Just round them all up and throw them into the Valley of the Disappeared," snapped Tryna Uilkitz.

"Sister, I understand your anger," said Bina softly, "but we need a solution that doesn't just push the hunger for vengeance down onto a new generation. Most of the gentry are now so frightened of the Sisterhood that they are quite amenable to change."

"We could have proper trials with proper courts and humane but fair punishments for crimes committed?" ventured the Clarion.

"Ha! Fair punishment for the Utterforz?" said Tryna. "And humane at the same time? Contradiction in terms there. Burn them at the stake, I say!"

"Maybe we force them to live with the victims of their acts?" suggested Nikolian.

"Yes, perhaps you have something there, Nikolian," said Tryna.

"What about Outer Azhuur?" asked Bina.

"What about it?" answered Tryna. "If you're talking about the reunification of Azhuur, we do not want that land. Let the wind scour it of all traces of the violence and cruelty done. We have enough of our own legacy to contend with here. No one need live there; they can come here if they are of good heart, but that land has much healing to do before decency can ever hope to take root there."

"Aaaaah, there is so much to do! D'Izmaïe set us back hundreds of years," said the Clarion. "We need to repair the reservoir, start restoring dwellings, farms, schools, hospitals, all the fundamentals need to be rebuilt from scratch. The cruelties of the Generalitate and the Utterage have to be acknowledged and answered for. We need to restore all the archives and the history D'Izmaïe and the Utterminster burned and replaced with their Mögian nonsense. We cannot let lies and unfounded hearsay be the story we tell ourselves. It will get twisted in each telling."

Tryna nodded and spoke softly: "It will probably get twisted in some way regardless, but you are right, we do need some honest, shared repository of our past that is as neutral and as complete as can be. I am told that the people have been leaving their stories on the Quartel bridge: handwritten on sacks and scraps of rough paper or carved into pieces of wood or stone—poems, plays, drawings, some are even standing on the bridge reciting their family history. Cowan will have my household see to the transcription and preservation of all of this."

The Uilkitz sisters simultaneously released an exhausted sigh.

"I know I'm on my way out the door here," said Wendy, "but remember, you don't need to do this all by yourselves. You have the wealth. I'm sure you can find people, honest people, who know how this should be done."

"Outlanders?" said the Clarion.

"Why not?" answered Nikolian.

"I don't know why not," said the Clarion. "I'm not sure why I even asked that."

↪

The night before she was due to leave, Wendy woke into herself walking across the moonlit crater toward the Hermitage.

The new Sistermost stood in the open gateway waiting for her. "Wendy, I could not be happier that yours was the dream that met mine tonight. The Sistermost Who Was thought very highly of you. You are most welcome."

"I wasn't sure what was going on. I was dreaming about being in a dream you were having about me walking here, and then I just woke up and I was on the way here."

"Yes, it can be a little disconcerting, but I am glad you did not reject it. You are invited to be of the *us* now."

"You mean a Sister?"

"Yes. Do you wish that?"

"I never thought about it, but yes, yes I do."

"Excellent! Come, first thing we must do is commission a heart pot. You don't have a rune, do you?"

"Uhm, no, I don't."

The Sistermost bent over some sand on the ground. "When I dreamed our dream, I saw this. Does that seem right?" She drew with her finger in the sand, ⦿

Wendy looked at the symbol. "Yeah, that seems right. It was in my dream too and it felt familiar."

"Excellent. I believe you are destined for the Earth Riding. I am told the bees have been expecting you."

⽆

Nikolian read his note one last time before he placed it and the small urn on the spindle window and pulled the bell cord. The note read:

> I know this is an unusual request, but could you please take all of these ashes and add them to the dough for the birds?

Just as he was about to grab it all back and flee, the spindle window turned. The urn and note disappeared into the Hermitage. There was a brief wait and then the window turned again to reveal a heart pot and another note:

> Dearest Nikolian, you know you could have gone to the open gate, but we understand your desire for discretion. We will make dough with some of the ashes. The rest we think you will want to keep. There may be pain in remembrance, but it is foundational. We lose part of ourselves and diminish in the forgetting. We took the liberty of making a family rune for you and Eduard. We hope it is correct. Please know that your

father's home in the hills survived the worst of the ravages.
You may find it restorative to take time there when your duties
allow.

Nikolian smiled at the rune on the heart pot: so unexpected, so strange, and yet suddenly so perfect and right. He whispered a hoarse "Thank you" into the window. He couldn't be certain, but he could have sworn he heard a familiar voice on the other side whisper back, "You're welcome."

⁝

The Clarion took a small scoop of ashes and added it to the dough he and the Sistermost had made in the kitchens. He looked around him. The view from the roof of the Hermitage, unchanged for centuries, was entirely new to him. Not so long ago, it would have been unthinkable for a Beyondish such as he to stand on the roof of the Hermitage. Now, with Wendy's dream-calling, there was even an Outlander member of the Sisterhood. Things were indeed changing.

"Your new recruit is doing well?"

"Yes, Wendy has taken to things very nicely. She seems preternaturally in tune with the bees. That Bruno Madison and his Depredation and Speculation Association have been nosing around trying to take 2's A Prime back. She has dealt with them. It made what she did to Hedgeer Hemlein in Newer York look like child's play."

The Clarion handed the dough back to the Sistermost and she placed it on the small table set in the branches of one of the almond trees. The first birds approached as soon as they walked away.

When they returned to the atrium, the Sistermost took the heart pot from the Clarion and placed it in the nook that had been carved out for the Sistermost Who Was among her predecessors.

Beside it there was a small brass plate engraved in plain lettering:

It is a far, far better thing that I do, than I have ever done; it is a far, far better rest that I go to than I have ever known.

THE END

Acknowledgments

I am hugely indebted to Johnny Temple at Akashic Books: friend, publisher, editor, who can always see where I am getting in my own way, and whose patience and collaboration have made this a much better book; and also to Aaron Petrovich and Johanna Ingalls at Akashic, whose careful reading reined in some of my overzealous rewrites.

Thanks also to Kara Gilmour for the hospitality of the bucolic seaside escape, where much of the rewriting of this book got done.

My profound gratitude to Patrick Burke, Brenda Copeland, Lyn Corewyn, Brian Dolan, Theo Dorgan, Jason Fogelson, Kathleen Hill, Tim Ledwith, Jenifer Levin, Honor Molloy, Paul Power, and Ben Tyner, who so kindly read various formative shards and versions of this novel along the way.

Many thanks to my long-suffering friends, confidants, correspondents, and coconspirators: Brian Brady, Chris Fabricant, Ruth Gallagher, Joseph Goodrich, Johanna Lane, Paul McDermott, Peter McDermott, Lucy McDiarmid, Kieran McEvoy, Belinda McKeon, Joseph O'Connor, Éanna Ó Lochlainn, Vishal Seecharran, and Feargal Whelan, who have given their support and encouragement over the years while listening so patiently to the anxious self-scrutiny, doubting, and second-guessing that accompanied the making of this book. It takes a village.

And most of all, immeasurable thanks to my wife Lisa and

my son Leo, whose belief, patience, support, and unconditional understanding of what I am up to when I am scribbling in notebooks, murmuring with the trees, or staring into space make it all possible.